The Energy Caper

or

Nixon in the Sky with Diamonds

The Energy Caper

or

Nixon in the Sky with Diamonds

William Scott Morrison

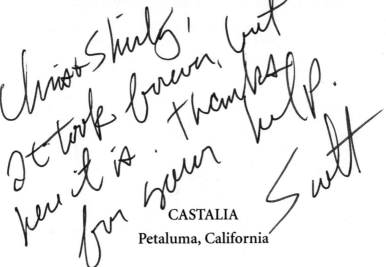

CASTALIA

Petaluma, California

CASTALIA

Copyright © 2008 by William Scott Morrison

Published in the United States by
Castalia Publishing, Inc.,
Petaluma, California 94953

ISBN 978-0-929150-26-0

www.energycaper.com

Library of Congress Cataloging-in-Publication Data

Morrison, William Scott.
The Energy Caper, or, Nixon in the sky with diamonds / William Scott Morrison.
p. cm.
ISBN-13: 978-0-929150-25-3
1. Nixon, Richard M. (Richard Milhous), 1913-1994--Fiction. 2.
Leary, Timothy Francis, 1920---Fiction. 3. Energy development--
Fiction. 4. Drug control--Fiction. 5. Marijuana--Fiction. I. Title. II.
Title: Energy caper. III. Title: Nixon in the sky with diamonds.

PS3613.O7779E54 2007
813'.6--dc22

2006012473

Cover design: W.S. Morrison
Cover illustrations: Kelli Bullock, John Garvey
Cover background: adapted from "Hemp Field in Old Kentucky,"
a postcard postmarked 1923, artist unknown.

Acknowledgments

I am lucky to have had the help of many "volunteers" at various stages of the numerous drafts and revisions of this novel. I am also fortunate to be a member of two unique writing communities—the Veterans Writing Group, founded by Maxine Hong Kingston, and Novelpro.com, an on-line critique group founded by J. R. Lankford. I would like to thank those who have assisted in everything from critiques of content and style to fact-checking, graphic design, and typing my illegible handwriting. Among those who deserve thanks are: Keith Allen, Wil Atkinson, Don Berman, Pat Brown, Joylene Butler, Dad & Mom, John Dvorak, Jo Edgerly, Nadine Ferguson, Jack Herer, Chris Hoare, Rob Hopke, Alan Jackson, John Kreuzer, Jack Nau, Brad Smith, Petra Sperling-Nordqvist, Garth Stein, Rebecca Sutherland, Anastasia Terris, Justin Tiret, Kathryn Toyer, Tom Volk, Dave West, Tanya Wilkinson, Annie Whiteman, Don Wirtshafter and others too numerous to mention. I am also deeply grateful to my wife, Padma Catell, for her insights and for her tolerance of my obsession.

Author's Note

It's been fun being in charge of history, with the power to rewrite the America of my youth and leaving out the part about Vietnam. In imagining what might have been, I have taken liberties with the characters and a few minor details. At the same time, I strove to be accurate with both the science and the historical record, and throughout the novel to employ the language of the times to evoke the social conventions, the cultural conditions, and the common knowledge which prevailed in America in that era.

For the victims of

the War on Drugs

Prologue

BACK IN THE NINETEEN-FIFTIES, EVERY KID ON THE PLAYGROUND KNEW WHEN a bad nickname got started that the only way to get out of it was to fight back, fast and hard, punching out anybody who used it each and every time until they stopped. If that didn't work, and the nickname stuck, then the only way out was to get down on your knees and pray that your parents moved to another town—or better yet, to another state—where nobody knew who you were, so you could start all over again.

Sometimes politicians got stuck with bad nicknames, but by then they were usually much too famous to just move away and start over. That's how it was for an ambitious second-term Republican Congressman named Richard Milhous Nixon, who got stuck with his during what many historians still call the sleaziest Senatorial campaign in American history—the 1950 California Senate race between Nixon and his opponent, Democratic Congresswoman Helen Gahagan Douglas.

Nixon made political hay as a "red baiter," whipping up the Red Scare and trying to hang the nickname "The Pink Lady" on his opponent because of her support for Franklin Roosevelt and the policies of the New Deal during the Great Depression and World War II. Her brand of patriotism did not sit well with Nixon, who employed what would one day come to be known as political "dirty tricks" to make the nickname stick.

One trick was mailing voters "Pink Sheets," printed on pink paper, accusing her of being "pro-communist" and a "pinko" for supporting New Deal programs such as Social Security, a forty-hour week, the right to unionize, health and safety standards in the workplace, and an estate tax on inherited wealth. But Nixon's favorite trick was personal, a punchline he delivered up and down the campaign trail, winding up every stump speech with a flourish. "She's pink!" he would shout, raising his hand high in the air and shaking his fist at the crowd, "right down to her underwear!"

The line always got him a big laugh, and some even say it won him the election. But The Pink Lady enjoyed the sweet taste of cold revenge and had the lifelong satisfaction of knowing she'd stuck Nixon with a nickname that captured the essence of his character, and which he came to despise more than anything—"Tricky Dick."

———————

Honesty may not be the best policy,
but it's worth trying once in a while.
— Richard M. Nixon

Chapter 1

V's for Victory

Earth One, January 20, 1973

THE SKY WAS AS GRAY AS AN OLD SCHOOLHOUSE BLACKBOARD, WITH A FEW scattered snow flurries in the air, but the throngs lining Pennsylvania Avenue didn't seem to care. They cheered wildly as President-elect Richard Milhous Nixon and his wife, Pat, passed by in the back seat of the open-air limousine.

The driver, U.S. Navy Lt. jg Michael Mulligan, could see Nixon in the rear-view mirror, grinning, waving, thrusting his hands high in the air and flashing his famous two-fisted V-for-Victory signs to the crowds. Mulligan held himself ramrod straight and kept the speedometer at a steady five MPH as the motorcade proceeded toward the Capitol Dome. He glanced in the side mirror to check the limo carrying Vice President-elect Spiro Agnew and his wife. Everything was A-OK.

Coming up at tree-top level was a TV camera in the basket of a cherry-picker. He imagined his dad and Uncle Danny and the guys down at the United Steelworkers Union hall cussing up a blue streak as they watched him chauffeur their arch political foe to his inauguration. He quickly put them out of his mind. His concern today was for his men, the Search-And-Rescue squad from the frigate *Fitzhugh*, who only yesterday had completed the two-week processional driving school run by the Secret Service. They knew what an honor it was to drive in a presidential inaugural, but would they keep a proper military bearing—no winking, no grinning, no waving to mom? They'd better.

Mulligan was startled to feel a tap on his shoulder. It was Nixon, leaning forward and trying to speak to him. A conversation with the President-elect was not part of the meticulously-drilled procedure. He stretched back as far as he could and said, "The crowd's too loud, Mr. President. You'll have to speak up, sir."

Nixon yelled, "Save the Mr. President crap for later, Lieutenant. Until they swear me in, I'm just plain old Nixon, and Nixon wants to enjoy being a private citizen for as long as he can. Less than an hour now. Ha!"

Mulligan knew Nixon was famous for slipping into the third-person when talking about himself—Nixon this and Nixon that—as if he were an observer, hovering outside his own existence.

Nixon inched further forward. "My girls want to personally thank you for saving them, Lieutenant. We will be seeing you and your men on the party circuit tonight, won't we?"

"Aye, sir. Mrs. Nixon sent invitations to the ball at the Watergate Hotel and even fixed up some of the men with dates. They're very excited."

"Good, good. The girls told me to be sure to tell you to keep your dance card open. You know how women are about these things."

"I, uh—"

"You know this morning at breakfast I was asking Pat and the girls to guess what the best thing about this whole day was going to be for me, but they couldn't do it. Weren't even close. How about you? Care to guess what the best thing about today is for Nixon?"

"I wouldn't presume to, sir."

"Then I'll tell you," Nixon said, and he cupped his hands to his mouth like a megaphone, projecting his voice while shielding his lips from the cameras and his salty vocabulary from his wife. "For the first time in twelve years, I won't have to see a single Kennedy face all day fucking long. Ha!"

Going against the modern tradition that a defeated incumbent should attend the inauguration of the victor, the Kennedys had reverted to the bare-knuckles tradition of the Founding Fathers. Historians pointed to the similarities between Nixon's inaugural and Thomas Jefferson's, in 1801, when John Adams refused to attend and left town on the early-morning stage. Just as Jefferson sent Adams packing off to Boston, so Nixon was packing the Kennedys off to Cape Cod. He considered it an auspicious beginning to his presidency.

For the first time since 1956, Nixon would relish the sweet taste of victory, savor its essence. He knew too well the rancid taste of defeat that stuck in your craw like a rotting fish bone. He had tasted it in 1960, when Chicago's Mayor Daly cheated him out of the Presidency. He tasted it again in 1962, when he lost the California gubernatorial race to a nobody and made the worst mistake of his political life, drinking too many vodka martinis as he watched the returns come in and snarling at the press in his concession speech, "You won't have Nixon to kick around any more."

He sat out the primaries in 1964, let Goldwater take it. Nobody could have beaten Jack Kennedy, not the way the country was rooting for his recovery after the botched assassination attempt. The press covered Kennedy's every twitch and quiver as he went from a hospital bed, to a wheelchair, to crutches and then to the damned silver-knobbed cane the son-of-a-bitch took to twirling like he was dancer Fred Astair himself.

In 1968, a "new Nixon" won the Republican nomination, and the Democrats nominated Jack's brother, Bobby. Unfortunately for Nixon, Jack had ended the war in Vietnam in 1966, and the economy was booming. A majority of voters saw no need for a change, and once again the Kennedys stuffed the fishbone of defeat down Nixon's gullet.

His political fortunes took a turn for the better when the youngest Kennedy brother, Teddy, drove a car off a bridge on Chappaquidick Island and swam away, leaving a young woman in the front seat to drown. Then movie star Marilyn Monroe held a tearful press conference, giving intimate details of her long affair with Jack and her weekend flings with Bobby. Wiping back tears, Marilyn told the world, "Jack promised he'd get a divorce and marry me as soon as he was out of the White House. And now…now he won't even *call*."

Marilyn's confession prompted a raunchy men's magazine to offer $5,000 to anyone who could document an illicit affair with a politician. The offer brought forth a bevy of starlets and secretaries with kinky tales of initiations into *Air Force One's* Mile High Club by various combinations of Kennedys. The press dubbed them "the Mile-High Bimbos," and the public ate it up. The bimbos were the final straw for the former First Lady, Jacqueline "Jackie" Kennedy. She fled with her and Jack's kids, Caroline and John-John, shacked up on a Greek island with a billionaire shipping tycoon named Onassis who was old enough to be her father, and filed for divorce.

But the scandal that foretold Bobby's defeat in 1972 came in the summer of 1969, when Bobby took the presidential helicopter to the last night of the Woodstock music festival. He choppered in at dusk, said hello to the crowd with a brief, "Let's get down," and went backstage. Soon, rumors swept the audience that the President had dropped a tab of the high-powered LSD known as "orange sunshine." At dawn, when guitarist Jimi Hendrix began playing a psychedelic version of the "Star Spangled

Banner," Bobby dashed out on stage, stood at attention, and put his hand over his heart. He seemed kind of wobbly, and when Jimi ripped off a high-energy riff at "the rockets red glare," the President snickered, choked down a giggle, and doubled over in a fit of belly laughs.

If it wasn't one Kennedy for this, it was another Kennedy for that. After twelve years in power, the Kennedys' image as knights-in-shining-armor was peeling up at the corners, like cheap chrome in a public restroom.

Nixon won the 1972 Republican nomination by attacking the Kennedys with a vengeance. Neither of his opponents for the nomination, not the B-movie actor who was Californian's governor, Ronald Reagan, nor New York's silver-spoon rich boy governor, Nelson Rockefeller, could match Nixon in calling Jack "a sex-crazed degenerate," labeling Teddy "a drunk and a coward," or accusing Bobby of being "a drugged-out hippie with a *Haawvard* accent."

The election was close. Bobby had ended the draft in 1970, and polls showed that the generation of "war babies" thought Bobby was "cool." But no one under twenty-one could vote, and Nixon's "Dump the Dynasty" slogan and relentless attack ads, especially the one showing Bobby belly laughing during the blasphemous version of "The Star Spangled Banner," convinced voters there would be no drugs in a Nixon White House. And no bimbos. The public could rest assured that no one, not even the President and the First Lady themselves, would be joining the Mile High Club on Richard Nixon's *Air Force One*.

It had been a rocky climb, and soon Nixon would swear a solemn oath on his mother's Quaker Bible to protect and defend the Constitution of the United States. Today was his day, and by God, he would enjoy it.

He surprised Pat with a playful kiss on her cheek, then stood up in the back of the limousine, flashed the two-fisted V's-for-Victory signs his followers loved so much, took off his top-hat, and tipped it to the crowd. He would think no more today of Kennedys. Old scores could wait. Revenge, Nixon knew, was a dish best enjoyed cold, with dignity, grace, a fine wine, and plenty of ketchup.

Art McGill was in his bathrobe sautéing onions and bell peppers for his tastiest Spanish omelet. His new partner for the moot court trial, Deborah something-or-other, was in the shower of his one-bedroom Berkeley bungalow warbling an off-key "Both Sides Now." What a night it had been.

The guitar had done it again.

McGill was surprised when the phone rang. None of his law-school pals would be calling this early on a Saturday morning.

He picked up the receiver. "Hello."

"Arthur, are you watching the inauguration?"

"Oh, hi, Dad. Is it on already?"

"Of course it's on. Why aren't you watching?"

"It's only a quarter after eight out here. I'll catch the speech."

"No, go turn it on, right away, and pay close attention to Nixon's limousine. You're in for a big surprise."

"His limo? But...why?"

"Don't ask questions, Arthur, just do it. Calls across the country cost out the ass. They charge by the goddamned mile, you know. Did you send your application to that address I sent you?"

The address had come from the chairman of the Pennsylvania Republican Party, so his application would, in his grandfather's words, "bypass the usual rigamarole" and go right to the top. McGill had demonstrated his loyalty to Nixon and the Grand Old Party. He came from a Republican family, had volunteered for Nixon's campaign in '68, cutting two weeks of classes to hand out leaflets door-to-door, and again as a precinct coordinator in Nixon's victory last fall. He hoped that his work for the party, along with his upcoming Juris Doctor degree from the University of California's prestigious law school, Boalt Hall, would assure him a position in the new administration. There would be thousands of jobs—fine plums of patronage—to be filled by loyal Nixonites like himself.

"Yes, Dad, I sent it off as soon as my grades came in. I even put in a copy of that old *Milltowne Gazette* photo."

"Photo? What photo?"

"You know the one, from the '56 election, when I was in second grade. I'm up on your shoulders at the train station holding an 'I LIKE IKE' sign and Nixon's leaning over from the caboose and mussing up my hair."

"Yes, of course...I'd forgotten all about it. That was good thinking, Arthur. A personal touch goes a long way, in business or in politics."

It was a rare compliment from his father. "But Dad, I don't graduate until December. Then I've got to pass the bar exam. I may be too late."

"Don't worry, Arthur. A new administration needs time to get its feet wet, and you've got the credentials. With a rock-ribbed Republican like Nixon in the White House, your timing couldn't be better. Now turn on your TV and pay attention to Nixon's limo. You're in for a big surprise."

"But Dad—"

"Don't argue with me, Arthur—do it."

"But why can't you just tell me?"

"Because then it wouldn't be a surprise, would it? And write to your mother. A stamp is cheaper than a phone call. Thrift is something you have to practice every day if you ever hope to get rich. Good-bye."

Click. Nobody but nobody squeezed a nickel tighter than his father.

He went back to stirring the onions and peppers, added the chopped mushrooms, then hurried into the living room, unplugged his portable black-and-white TV, and moved it to the coffee table so he could watch from the kitchen while he cooked.

Deborah came in and took a deep breath, savoring the aromas. "Mmmm...smells *wonderful*, Art. Who was on the phone?"

"My dad. He wants me to check out Nixon's limo."

"His limo? But...why?"

"He's a car dealer, so there must be something special about it."

"A car dealer?"

"Yeah, Chevys and Cadillacs. My grandfather started it in the Twenties. There's a bumper sticker on the fridge."

She read the small silver-and-black sticker on the refrigerator door:

McGILL MOTORS
WHEN IT COMES TO CARS,
MILLTOWNE IS McGILLTOWN.

He propped the TV up with a thick law book and turned the switch. The tube blinked and went dark, crackling with static electricity as it warmed up. He went back to the stove and was flipping bacon when a picture finally appeared.

"Turn it up, will you, Deb. I can't hear it in here with the fan going."

Deborah adjusted the rabbit ears, and when she turned the knob, Walter Cronkite's soothing voice filled the room: "...a presidency Nixon has vowed will be characterized by law and order, and an unrelenting war on drugs."

McGill saw nothing special about the limo. It wasn't even a Caddy, but a Lincoln. Then the camera zoomed in on the driver, a military officer in a white uniform. "Holy shit!" he yelled, waving the spatula at the TV. "The Mulligan Man's driving Nixon's car!"

Deborah perched on the arm of the couch, peering closely at the TV on the coffee table. "Isn't that your Navy friend who saved the Nixon girls?"

"That's the Mulligan Man all right. Can you believe it?" Imitating the nasally voice of the Culligan lady in the water-softener commercials, McGill cheered like in the old days when Mulligan would make a big play and the Milltowne stands erupted in chants of, "Hey, Mulligan Man! Hey, Mulligan Man!"

Deborah picked up the five-week-old copy of *Time Magazine* off the couch and turned to a dog-eared page with a photo of Nixon's daughters—Tricia, the pretty blonde, and Julie, the perky brunette—both up on their tiptoes, simultaneously smooching the freckled cheeks of a tall and very embarrassed redheaded Navy officer.

Cronkite's voice said, "Tell us about the sailors doing the driving. That's normally a Secret Service job, isn't it, Dan?"

A young reporter named Dan Rather said, "That's right, Walter, but Nixon wanted to surprise Tricia and Julie by having the Navy crew that rescued them from that burning yacht in the Bermuda Triangle do the driving. The Secret Service wasn't happy, but Nixon got his way. Behind the wheel of Nixon's car is the rescue boat's commander, Lt. Michael P. Mulligan of Milltowne, Pennsylvania...."

Deborah leaned closer to the tube. "Your friend's a dreamboat, Art."

McGill twinged with the same old jealous pang he used to get in junior high when the girls looked through him like he was Mr. Invisible and swarmed to Mulligan like bees to clover. Girls loved jocks, and when it came to girls, The Mulligan Man always scored.

Just then Nixon leaned forward, cupped his hands over his mouth, and said something in Mulligan's ear. "Look at that! Nixon's bullshitting with Mulligan like they're at a baseball game. His dad and his Uncle Danny must be shitting bricks."

"I can see why they'd be proud," Deborah said.

"No, it's not like that at all. Mulligan's dad's a shop steward in the steelworkers union. And back in the Fifties, his uncle was playing guitar and touring with Pete Seeger and the Weavers. He was hitting it big when the Red Scare came along, and Nixon's committee put him on the blacklist so he couldn't get gigs, and now he's a truck driver. The Mulligans have hated Nixon forever."

McGill dished up breakfast as Nixon stepped to the podium to take the oath of office. He and Deborah sat on the couch, plates in their laps, and ate as they watched Nixon's inaugural address in which the new President vowed to "keep America safe from communism," "clean up the moral stench in the White House," and wage "an unrelenting war on drugs."

When Nixon finished and the applause began, McGill said, "Let's celebrate. Why don't you roll one while I clean up?"

"Sure. Where is it?"

"In the dresser. Top drawer. There's Zig-Zags and matches too."

She went to find the stash as McGill cleared the table, rinsing dishes as he watched his best friend drive the President and First Lady to 1600 Pennsylvania Avenue. He shook his head in amazement and wondered out loud, "How am I ever gonna top the Mulligan Man on this one?"

Jenny Abruzzi left Yale University's law library and trudged home through the deepening snow to Mrs. Hall's rooming house. She took off her boots in the foyer and opened the inner door to a noisy, smoke-filled room with three dozen coffee-drinking female graduate students in jeans and bathrobes, many with their hair in curlers, most of them hissing and booing as they watched Nixon flashing V-for-Victory signs like he was Winston Churchill himself.

She shut the door with an angry slam. "Who put that on?"

"May as well watch," somebody said. "The driver's a real cutie."

"Besides, it's history," somebody said.

"No! *Herstory!*" somebody shouted.

Mrs. Hall's was the closest thing to an institution women had at Yale, which had no undergraduate female students. Known affectionately by its residents as Lib House, to those who did not approve of women's liberation it was Bitch House, or worse. Much worse. The building was a converted four-story Victorian mansion, and each of its thirty residents had a tiny studio with a private kitchenette and shower, and they shared a communal first floor with a fireplace and a color TV. The us-against-the-world camaraderie bonded them into a kind of sisterhood and helped them through the rugged academic grind toward their Masters, Juris Doctor, and Ph.D degrees at Yale's male-dominated graduate schools.

Prior to the election, the women of Lib House often sat around the fireplace discussing how they would work for equality and justice in a second Bobby Kennedy administration. Nixon had snatched their eggs from the hen house just as they were about to hatch, and now the high-powered jobs that should have been theirs—at Justice, State, Treasury, even the White House itself—would go to troglodytes. Like a carton of milk gone sour, Nixon was stinking up the whole refrigerator.

"Anybody else see that article in the *New Republic* about how state government is where to fight for change under Nixon?" somebody asked.

"No grass roots for me. I'd rather die than live in Trenton."

A debate erupted over whose state capital was the worst—Harrisburg, Lansing, Sacramento, Austin, Albany, Springfield, Trenton, Little Rock, Tallahassee, Columbus. Nobody won. Compared to Washington, they were all third-rate.

A guest suggested, "Why don't you go to work for civil rights with Martin Luther King?"

"Because King can't keep his pecker in his pants," somebody said. "I say we go to work to pass the Equal Rights Amendment. Once women are equal, we can do anything."

As always, Jenny tried to be practical. "I don't know about you, but I can't afford it. I have loans to pay back."

"Oh come on, Jennifer," somebody said. "All you have to do is call up Hugh Heffner and tell him you've changed your mind."

"It wasn't an open offer," Jenny said, hoping to kill the topic.

A guest asked, "Is it really true they wanted you to be a centerfold and you turned it down?"

Jenny hated talking about it. Last Fall scouts from *Playboy Magazine* had secretly come around, scouring the campus for a woman to represent Yale in a "Girls of the Ivy League" feature. She had no idea they used a telephoto lens to take photos of her working out on the high dive, and she was dumbfounded when she got a call from Hugh Heffner offering her $10,000 to come to Los Angeles for a photo shoot at the Playboy Mansion and be Miss June, the graduation centerfold, despite her modest B-cup. Half of Lib House was aghast she would even consider exploiting her body to satisfy primal male urges; the other half turned green as grass with envy.

It wasn't an easy decision. Picturing her brothers' faces when they saw her jiggling out at them as they opened their centerfolds was almost funny, but she cringed at the thought of her mom's diatribe. And her paternal grandmother, Mama Antonia, would invoke the saints, wag her finger in her face and shout, "Puttana! Puttana!" And her poor father would never live it down if the men at the fire station knew the centerfold on their locker doors was Captain Abruzzi's daughter.

She knew she had what some called a "guilt trip" about her beauty. Not even her best friends at Yale knew that her nose once looked like a dill pickle, or that her sixth-grade nickname had been "Honker." In the summer of 1960, before starting junior high, her mother got her a rhinoplasty—a nose job—and everything changed. Her new nose made its public debut the first day of seventh grade, and it was as if God had flicked her popularity switch from OFF to ON. The same boys who once honked at her under their breath in the hallways turned into puppy dogs, showing off, opening doors. But the biggest shock was how girls she thought were her friends talked behind her back, trying to convince the boys her new face didn't count because it wasn't natural. But the boys didn't seem to care, and as she grew older, males of all ages seemed compelled to compare her to movie stars. Some said she was sultry, like Natalie Wood, while others thought her sweet, like Audrey Hepburn. After the TV show *The Avengers* became a hit, they began comparing her to Mrs. Peel, the sexy spy in the black leotard. And every so often some guy would go bonkers, proclaiming undying, eternal love and making her wish she could stick a pickle on her nose and go back to being Honker.

"So why did you turn *Playboy* down?" somebody asked.

Jenny tried to be diplomatic. "I wasn't about to sell out for a few thousand. Now maybe for a few million—"

"Speaking of millions," somebody said, "what are you going to do with yours, Catherine? How much are you coming into? Five million? Is that right?"

All eyes turned to her best friend, Catherine DeWolfe, who was sitting quietly in the corner of a couch. No matter how hard Catherine tried, she could not get away from the fact that her family had money...serious money. *Forbes Magazine* estimated that the DeWolfes, with three billion to their collective names, were the seventh richest family in America. Catherine's father alone was worth an estimated $300 million. In addition, *Forbes* revealed that on their twenty-fifth birthdays all of timber-baron J.C. DeWolfe's "legitimate" descendants came into an equal share of a trust fund. Currently worth $135 million, or about five million for each of the twenty-seven eligible heirs, the trust provided a lifetime monthly stipend to its beneficiaries regardless of other circumstances. For J.C. DeWolfe's luckier descendants, like Catherine, who as an only child would one day come into her father's estate if he didn't disown her first, the trust was inconsequential. For many of her cousins, the trust was all there was.

While most Americans would consider a guaranteed income from a five-million dollar trust to be a fairly nice start in life, in the rarified circles in which the DeWolfes traveled it was a pittance of an inheritance. While no one could say for sure, *Forbes* estimated the trust was less than half what heirs of the twelfth richest family, the Kennedys, automatically came into, and peanuts compared to what heirs of fortunes founded by names like Vanderbilt, Rockefeller, DuPont, Mars, Mellon, Hearst, Whitney, Ford and Getty would have to struggle to get by on.

"Look," Catherine said, "it's not like I'm getting fifty million like the Mellon kids who bankrolled Timothy Leary. I'll have a small income, but I can't touch the principal."

"A *small* income?" somebody said. "Let's see…a yield on five million of, oh, let's be conservative, say…two percent, is what?"

"A hundred thousand a year!" somebody yelled.

Catherine's eyes narrowed into angry slits. Despite her gilded pedigree, she had a corn-fed, farmer's-daughter look about her. No one would ever mistake Catherine for a poor little rich girl. She was what men called "attractive," like actress Vanessa Redgrave. Standing six feet tall in her stocking feet, she was almost always the tallest woman in the room, so high heels were completely out of the question. She also had a quick temper, and only her very closest friends knew she had a black belt in judo.

Catherine did all she could to live down the rich-girl stereotype. She let her auburn hair drape to her waist like a silken shawl, and wore long, flowing "Earth Mother" dresses that disguised her athletic swimmer's build. She used only the slightest hint of make-up, and no razor had violated a single hair of Catherine's body since 1967, the Summer of Love. In many ways, she was the most ardent feminist Jenny knew. At Pass-the-ERA rallies she would take to the podium and exhort her sisters to free themselves from "The tyranny of the razor" and recite a fiery poem she had written herself: "Women Under Arms!" She would proudly display her unshaven legs and armpits, explaining to all who would listen how reading *The Feminine Mystique* and seeing how the liberated women of Europe lived had opened her eyes to how American women had been brainwashed by the mass-market advertising of Gillette and Schick for the last fifty years.

While Jenny thought Catherine made good points about how the missionary position sustained male dominance, she found Catherine overly dogmatic on the subject of shaving, and she wasn't about to let anybody, not even her best friend, shame her into quitting. Not with her Mediterranean complexion. No way! If she ever showed up back in Pittsburgh looking like she'd just gotten off the boat from the old country, her brothers would pin her down and shave her themselves. Shaving did not make her a traitor to the feminist cause, no matter what anybody said, even Catherine.

"So what are you going to do after you graduate, Catherine?" somebody asked. "It's not as if you need a job like the rest of us."

"I don't know what I'll do, but—"

"What's wrong with you!" cackled a shrill voice from above. "Why aren't you getting ready? It starts in an hour."

Glowering down from the top of the staircase was Cornelia Kibbitts, tall and gaunt in a lime-green terrycloth bathrobe, her hair up in a matching towel. Cornelia had earned a law degree and was pressing on in academia for a Ph.D. in Feminist Anthropology. Just last week she received an advance from a major New York publisher who was betting that her dissertation, *Chivalry: How to Finally Kill It*, was a sure-fire best-seller.

"Please, Cornelia, tell us it's not another bra-burning," somebody pleaded. "I only have a couple left."

"Yeah, Corny, it's easy for you, but some of us actually need them."

The room crackled with laughter, and somebody asked, "So what's this thing called again, Corny?"

Cornelia called down, "Sisters After Yale Law!"

"S-A-Y-L," somebody said, pronouncing each letter. "So how do you say it? Like Yale, but with an S...*sale?*"

"*Exactly!*" Cornelia said, like a teacher proud of a pupil.

Somebody started chanting a variation of the catcall used by generations of non-Yalies to mock Yalie pomposity. "Saylies in their tailies. Saylies in their tailies. Saylies in—"

Cornelia pounded the banister with her hairbrush, like an angry judge gaveling for silence—BANG-BANG-BANG. "Idiots! Your right to control your own bodies can be snatched back in an instant by the male chauvinist pigs Nixon's going to put on the court. Don't you understand? Tricky Dick is in the White House...*Tricky Dick is in the White House!*"

On the first Monday morning in his new job, Nixon was gazing out the Oval Office window, sipping coffee from a monogrammed mug with

RMN in gold letters on one side and the Presidential Seal on the other. Two Negro gardeners were pushing wheelbarrows across the barren winter grounds toward the Rose Garden. His gut said to fire the gardeners and tear out the damned roses, but the tree-hugging environmentalists would rip him to pieces if he did. He could see the headlines now: "Nixon Kills Jackie's Roses." It wasn't worth it.

The Rose Garden could stay, but the gardeners were another matter. He knew they were protected by Civil Service, like so many other Kennedy bastards. He picked up his yellow legal pad and wrote a memo to Bob Haldeman, his chief-of-staff: "Get new gardeners!" Haldeman wouldn't bother him with details. He'd fire them or give them a promotion, but he'd move their asses the hell out of there one way or the other.

It would take years, perhaps his entire first term, to ferret out the thousands of Kennedy toadies who had wormed their ways into every rat hole in Washington. All of them, Nixon knew, would be lying in wait, eager to sabotage his policies. Twelve years of patronage could not be rooted out overnight, but root it out he would. He needed his own people at every level, from the Joint Chiefs of Staff right down to the White House gardeners. As Nixon often told his aides, "Just because you're paranoid doesn't mean they're not out to get you."

Two weeks after the inauguration, E. Grayson Gridley was sitting outside the door to the Oval Office, chain-smoking as he waited for his meeting with Nixon. Soon he would know whether he got the appointment to head up the new Drug Enforcement Agency he had talked Nixon into creating.

He picked up a magazine, riffled through, and put it down without reading a word. He checked his watch, crossed his legs, smoothed his bushy mustache, and ran his palm across the top of his rapidly-balding cranium. What was taking so long? He was lighting another cigarette when the door swung open, and Haldeman said, "Come in, Grayson."

Gridley took a drag and stuffed the butt out in the ashtray's sand. His heart was pounding as he strode across the thick blue carpet with the Presidential Seal woven into it and extended his hand across Nixon's desk. "Congratulations, Mr. President."

Nixon stood up and gave him a firm handshake. "Thank you, Grayson. You had a big role in the victory, no doubt about it. That 'war on drugs' slogan you came up with was worth a hell of a lot of votes. I might not be here today if it hadn't been for you."

Gridley swelled with satisfaction. "Thank you, Mr. President. It's gratifying hearing it from you."

"Yes, of course it is," Nixon said. "Now Grayson, let's cut the crap. I want to move ahead on all fronts in the war on drugs, give it to the goddamned hippies with both barrels."

"So do I, Mr. President, so do I."

"We know you do, Grayson, and we have something for you that fits your talents. I came up with the name myself—Office of Narcotics Operations. The O.N.O. It has a ring to it, don't you think? The hippies will scream 'Oh no!' when they see you coming. Ha."

This was not what he wanted. He wanted the new Drug Enforcement Agency, with thousands of agents under him. "But sir, the D.E.A.—"

"Now Grayson," Nixon said, "we'll be shuffling people in from the old Narcotics Bureau and those other agencies. A new bureaucracy needs a firm hand on the tiller to oil the gears. And you have to admit, Grayson, you're not an administrator. You're an idea man. An action man."

"It's true I like action, Mr. President, but—"

"I'm glad you agree, because I want you coming up with ideas to nail the druggies. No boring day-to-day operations for you, Grayson. I want you strategizing for all the agencies in the war on drugs—this new D.E.A., Customs, A.T.F., F.B.I., Coast Guard—all of them. Think of yourself as a kind of drug czar, watching over all the little kingdoms."

"Drug czar? Hmmm…so they'd all report to me?"

"Not day-to-day," Nixon said, "but you'll have my approval to kick them in the ass, put their feet to the fire, and nail their balls to walls. Paper-pushers don't think big-picture like you and me, Grayson."

Shit. There was no talking Nixon out of it. This meant he would have a puny little office with a secretary, two if he were lucky. He had to get what he could out of Nixon, and get it right now, something that crossed all jurisdictions so nobody could freeze him out. He played his last card.

"Mr. President, you know I'll do anything for you, but I want to be the one to go after Timothy Leary."

———

Nixon liked Gridley, recognized his talents, but his close advisors all agreed Gridley had a screw loose, and it would be unwise to give him too big a horse to ride. Gridley never would have come to Nixon's attention if the Pied Piper of LSD, Dr. Timothy Leary, hadn't dropped into Gridley's lap like an overripe apple. When some hippie heirs of the fabulously rich Mellon family gave Leary the run of a fifty-five room mansion on a 2,500 acre estate in Millbrook, New York, it was the break of a lifetime for an unknown assistant District Attorney in the backwater jurisdiction of Poughkeepsie. Gridley recognized his good fortune and made the most of it. He tapped Leary's phones, harassed his guests, raided his parties, and hammed it up for the cameras every chance he got.

Nixon had liked what he'd seen of Gridley on TV, arresting Leary while, in the background, police hauled bags of marijuana from Leary's barn. Gridley used the publicity to run for Congress, but it had blown up in his face when laboratory analysis proved the bags contained not pot, but peat moss, and Republican voters declined to nominate a candidate for Congress who couldn't tell pot from peat moss.

Gridley didn't nail Leary, but he did drive him out of Millbrook. Not long afterward, Leary was arrested on the Mexican border, taking the rap for a pinch of pot in his teenage daughter's suitcase and becoming the first American to ever be convicted for smuggling drugs *into* Mexico. Leary appealed and, to everyone's surprise, won, convincing the Supreme Court that the Marijuana Tax Act was unconstitutional.

Leary's victory had been short-lived, for he was soon arrested again, this time under California law when a cop with a history of planting evidence "found" two half-smoked roaches in the back seat of Leary's rented car. Leary was sentenced to thirty years in prison, but a year later he broke out in a daring escape and skipped the country with the help of a radical underground group called the Weathermen.

It didn't matter to Nixon that Gridley couldn't tell pot from peat moss. He was tough, loyal, and knew how to work the media. He could keep the pressure on the hippies, and if anyone could bring in Leary, it was Gridley.

Nixon walked around his desk and put his arm on Gridley's shoulder. "Grayson, I want Leary behind bars as much as you do. Running around loose out there, flaunting justice and telling this pussy-assed generation coming up to turn on, tune in, and drop out, why, he's the most dangerous man in the world and a threat to national security worse than Mao and Castro put together. You have my full authority to do whatever it takes to bring him in. Get him, Grayson, get him!"

Chapter 2

The Real World

Spring 1973

JENNY WAS CHATTING WITH CATHERINE AND SEVERAL OTHERS OVER COFFEE at the Lib House dining-room table when the doorbell rang.

"Mail call!" somebody yelled, and women from throughout the house flocked to the big table. As they sorted and handed out letters, a thin envelope came up addressed to Ms. Jennifer Marie Abruzzi from the Supreme Court of the United States, and the room went silent. They knew what it was. They passed it along, averting their eyes.

Jenny slit it open and read aloud, "Dear Applicant—"

Catherine put a comforting arm on her shoulder. "Don't, Jen."

Jenny fought back tears. "It's not fair! I had better grades than Newbury or Tegal or Thompkins. I wrote for the law review. I beat them all in moot court, but they get the clerkships."

"I hate to say I told you so, Jennifer," somebody said, "but I did."

Jenny ripped the letter in two and would have torn it into a zillion pieces but somebody yelled, "*No!* It's evidence for the class-action lawsuit."

Their dreams of working for Bobby Kennedy to finally bring justice and equality to America were deader than old batteries. In a few weeks, they would leave Yale's ivory-towered halls and ivy-covered walls for the real world, a world in which Nixon called the shots. Bobby's defeat had changed everything. Suddenly, it was every woman for herself. They had about a minute to figure out their own, very personal, plan B's.

Out of Jenny's post-election gloom, a childhood fantasy had bubbled to the surface—Paris. At Bryn Mawr, she carried a double-major—Psychology and Romance Languages. Perhaps her best Plan B for the near future would be to combine her language skills and her Juris Doctor degree with a post-graduate degree from the Sorbonne?

Catherine wasn't convinced. "Jen, we've been in school forever. We need a break."

"But this will be more like a vacation. It's France, so the tuition is free, and the bank will lend me five thousand to live on."

"But you're always talking about having to pay your loans back."

As wise as Catherine could be in some matters, when it came to the compromises ordinary people made over money, her blue-blooded friend was out to lunch, which in Catherine's case meant champagne and caviar at the Waldorf-Astoria. "It's different for you, Cate. You don't know what it's like to have a mountain of debt blocking your way."

"But Jen, you're the one who's always telling everybody to be practical."

"But that's the point…I *am* being practical. What's another five thousand on top of the eighty I already owe? Payments are deferred as long as I'm in school, and I'm not ready to sell my soul to a law mill just to pay it back. Not yet, anyway. If Nixon won't let us change the world, why not see the world?"

All graduating Yale Law students were invited to a private session with a Yale alumnus famous for placing graduates in America's top law firms—the Honorable Josiah Q. Higgins, Chief Justice of the Connecticut Supreme Court. Appointments were alphabetical, and Jenny was the first of the her class to meet with him.

She was not sure what to expect, and as she walked in he arose from his chair, as gentlemen for centuries had been trained to do when a lady entered the room. He gave her a welcoming smile. "Aahh, so this is the lovely Miss Abruzzi I've heard so much about."

There were some things about the old school of courtly manners she would miss in the coming New Age. She extended her hand and said, "The pleasure is all mine, Mr. Chief Justice."

Warmly and softly he reached out and took her hand in his. "The alumni are very proud of you and our other ladies, Miss Abruzzi."

"Thank you, sir, but with all due respect, we're not ladies, we're women, and we do not wish to be defined by our relationships to men. Most of us prefer Ms. to Miss or Mrs."

He snatched his hand back like he'd burned it on a hot stove. "As you wish, Ms. Abruzzi, as you wish. Please, have a seat."

He looked through her file, praised her articles in the law review, and was pleased she had been accepted at the Sorbonne. "So what do you plan to do when you're finished there?" he asked.

"I'm not sure, sir. I had been planning to work in government. Now I think I might be most effective at the United Nations."

"I had the same idealism when I was your age. I wanted to right the world's wrongs, free the innocent, defeat the forces of superstition and ignorance, and be the next Clarence Darrow. But life has a way of altering one's perspectives. Let me make some calls on your behalf. You know your own home town is America's third biggest corporate headquarters city, after New York and Chicago."

The last thing she wanted was a corporate job back in Pittsburgh. "But I'm leaving for Paris in a few weeks."

"Introducing yourself now will position you for when you return. Corporate America's demand for lady lawyers—sorry, I mean female attorneys—has never been greater."

She knew a line when she heard one. "What you mean is they're worried the Equal Rights Amendment will pass and they need a few token women so they can't be accused sexual discrimination."

He sat back, pursing his lips. "I suppose there's some truth to that. But you have the honor of being the vanguard, the point of the spear."

"But corporate law just doesn't interest me."

"We all make compromises, Ms. Abruzzi. And what's wrong with testing the waters? A smart lawyer keeps his options open."

She chided him good-naturedly, "Or her options, Mr. Chief Justice."

His eyes narrowed, burrowing into her like a dental drill. "I am not your enemy, Ms. Abruzzi. I am doing my best to place you in a position commensurate with your talents. But I cannot abide a student correcting my grammar—*mine!*—in the name of...of...what? Political correctness? Do you think the English language is a patriarchal plot to keep females barefoot and pregnant? Is that it, Ms. Abruzzi?"

She was startled by his vehemence. "I meant no offense, sir, I—"

"Ms. Abruzzi, I suggest you drop such nonsense. Leave it in my wastebasket on your way out the door. Sophomoric debates are fine for college dormitories, but they have no place in the legal profession."

She hated to be patronized. "I'm sorry, sir, but if we don't do it, who will? Like you said, we're the point of the spear."

She was surprised as his mouth curled up in a smile. "Turn my words around on me, will you? Well, bully for you. A good litigator thinks on his feet—or hers—and you've got the instincts. But if you want to get ahead in the legal profession, fights like this will not serve you well. By the way...is it true you ladies have formed an all-girl Yale club?"

She wanted to say all-women, sir, all-women, but held her tongue. "Yes sir, we have. It's called Sisters After Yale Law."

"Saylies," he muttered, sighing and rubbing his chin as he shook his head in dismay. "A word of advice, Ms. Abruzzi. A good attorney picks his battles carefully. His, not hers...*his*. If you want to abolish the language of Shakespeare, Chaucer, and Shaw you should be writing novels or singing in some infernal music group, but do not try to do it through the practice of law. Do I make myself clear?"

"I understand your point of view, sir, and I'm sorry if I offended you. But what did I say that was inaccurate?"

"Won't give an inch, will you? Well, young lady, I like your spirit. Apology accepted. Now, about your future...."

She agreed a few interviews couldn't hurt, so he arranged a whirlwind of appointments with Pittsburgh's top law firms and the legal departments of its giant corporations: Alcoa Aluminum, Gulf Oil, Heinz Foods, Mesta Machine, Pittsburgh Plate Glass, Rockwell International, U.S. Steel, Westinghouse Electric, and Mellon Bank.

Graduation from law school was as scary as it was exciting: the thrill of change coupled with the weepy good-byes marking the definitive end of youth, with an Ivy League kick out the door. Jenny enrolled in a post-grad course in International Legal Procedures at the University of Paris, and Catherine put off a decision in order to spend the summer at Timber Crest, her family's thirty-room summer "cottage" on Lake Charlevoix, where she spent so many summers as a girl. Her plan was to study for the bar exam, swim herself back into shape, and set up a dark room for her photography. Perhaps the lakes of northern Michigan's "Hemingway country" would help her think more clearly?

The arguments began the first morning. She was toweling off after a workout in the pool when her mother began nagging about her refusal to shave for the past seven years.

"Just look at yourself, Catherine. No wonder you're not married. No respectable man would consider a woman who presented herself like...like...*that*! We used to be so proud of you, and now we can't take you anywhere. Can you imagine what the DuPonts would say if you showed up in Palm Beach looking like a washerwoman?"

"Mother, why do you care what the DuPonts say?"

"Because there are dozens of DuPont boys who would be very pleased with a DeWolfe as a wife. And you're almost twenty-five. You're not getting any younger, Catherine. Quite frankly, we're worried."

"Mother, you're not marrying me off to some snively DuPont so you can move up in the Social Register."

She put on her robe and sat at the poolside table. Her father joined them, and as the maid poured coffee he took his turn at the hectoring. "Catherine, you're finished with law school now, and you'll be coming into your share of the trust next month. You won't have to ask me for money any more. You're in the real world now."

"Yes Daddy, I know."

"Well, it's high time you grew up, young lady. You're smarter than any of your fool cousins. You could run the whole show some day if you put your mind to it. Forty-seven thousand people on five continents work for us. You'll have to prove yourself, it won't be handed to you, but being a lawyer will put you in the thick of things and give you a leg up on your cousins. We're in court every day fighting the damned tree-huggers and bureaucrats."

"Or each other," she said, thinking of the notorious family feuds.

"Yes, there's that too. But you'll be good at it, even if you are a woman. It's your destiny. It's time for you to accept it."

She wanted no part of the family in-fighting, and could not imagine going into court to defend DeWolfe Forest Products practices of clear-cutting, polluting, and union-busting. "I just don't think it's me, Daddy," was all she could say without reigniting their great-great-granddaddy-was-a-greedy-ol'-Robber-Baron argument all over again.

It started when she was in fifth grade, after a field trip to the Hartwick Pines State Park, near Grayling, to see what Michigan had been like a century before. A park ranger led the walk, explaining that they were under the canopy of the last virgin stand of the immense White Pine forest which had once blanketed lower Michigan, now reduced to a single lonely patch of arboreal grandeur, a scant fifty acres out of millions. In the museum they saw before-and-after photos of pristine forest landscapes next to the stump-ravaged moonscapes after Michigan had been stripped of its "green gold," which had been worth more than all the yellow gold mined in California. Photos of lumber mills with "DeWolfe" on the belching smokestacks started her classmates hissing and booing at her as if she had wiped out the forests all by herself.

"You should be proud of your heritage, Catherine," her father told her when she came home in tears that day. "DeWolfe timber rebuilt Chicago after the fire. Besides, the damn forests will grow back."

She smiled to herself at the recollection of that long-ago day as her father droned on with his interminable lecture. "…and I promise you, Catherine, if you don't show a change in attitude I'm cutting you out of my will, and the trust will be all you ever get. I can't change that, only a four-fifths vote of the Heirs Committee can do that. But I will not leave three hundred million dollars to an unshaven hippie who's going to turn around and give it to the goddamned Sierra Club. Do you hear me, young lady? You have your legacy to consider!"

"Daddy, if you want a legacy so much, why don't you found a university, or a medical institute?"

"Damn it, Catherine, it's not about money, or about getting my name on some damned building. It's about *capital,* and passing it on from generation to generation. That's how families like ours make the world go round—with *capital.* Do you know how hard it is to keep capital growing from one generation to the next with the damn Democrats in Washington trying to tax it all away?"

She knew he was lying to himself. He had always wanted a son, and her mother couldn't have any more children. That was why he pushed her so hard. Both she and her former therapist were sure of it.

She avoided arguments, studied for the exam, and set up a dark room. She swam laps every morning until she was as in shape as in high school, when she'd won the state butterfly championship, and then starred on Vassar's swim team. Three times a week she drove her convertible Corvette up to Petosky and worked out at the judo dojo. But her greatest joy came from refitting the *Athena,* the thirty-five-foot Hunter sloop her grandfather had given her for her twelfth birthday. For the last eight years, all through college and law school, the *Athena* had been up on blocks in the Timber Crest boathouse.

She hired workers from the marina to refinish the hull, install the latest communications system, and fit her out with new sails and lines rigged for a solo sailor. She repainted the name on the stern herself:

ATHENA
CHARLEVOIX, MI

At sunrise on the day before her twenty-fifth birthday, which by pure chance coincided with the annual meeting of the Heirs Committee, she motored behind the Beaver Island ferry under the Lake Charlevoix drawbridge and into the blue waters of Lake Michigan itself. She turned off the engine, unfurled the *Athena's* sails, and set course for historic Mackinac

Island, "The Crown Jewel of the Great Lakes."

The Heirs Committee always met on the verandah at *Beau Lilas*, the clan's ancestral summer home, with its magnificent view of the lake. Built in 1873 by timber baron Jean Claude "J.C." DeWolfe, it perched on the bluffs overlooking Lake Huron and was the most magnificent of all the cottages of the midwestern Robber Barons who had made fortunes in railroad-speculation, meat-packing, timber, and mining during the heyday of the Gilded Age.

Twenty-three of the twenty-seven eligible heirs showed up. They sang her "Happy Birthday," and her great-aunt Audrice, a spry ninety-seven years young, welcomed her as a voting member and gave her a copy of the family by-laws, which stipulated that only "legitimate" biological heirs of "good moral character" could share in the family trust.

The trust's executive director, a balding Detroit banker in a plum-colored, pin-striped suit, distributed the annual report and the monthly checks—this month for $9,501.63. A cousin she had never met complained returns were down, and the infamous DeWolfe infighting began. At every vote, she followed her father's lead.

The summer season in the North Country traditionally ended on Labor Day, when tens of thousands of tourists and summer residents headed south for the suburbs of Detroit, Chicago, Flint, Gary, Indianapolis, and St. Louis. The servants departed for the estate in Grosse Pointe in a caravan of Buick station wagons, followed by her parents in the Fleetwood limousine. She stayed on, just her and old Jonas, the groundskeeper. She welcomed the autumn colors and the solitude.

———

On October 6, 1973, Yom Kippur, the holiest day of the Jewish year, the armies of Egypt and Syria had launched a surprise attack against Israel. The Israelis had rallied and stopped the advance but had run low on ammunition and supplies, leading to the possibility of a dangerous military stalemate.

"God fucking dammit!" Nixon screamed into the phone at his Secretary of Defense, Melvin Laird. "I don't give a shit what the assholes in the State Department say about pissing off the Arabs. *I'm* the goddamn President, and I say give the Israelis everything we've got. *Everything!*"

The Pentagon cranked into gear, filling the skies with an "air bridge" of giant C-5A cargo planes brimming with weapons, spare parts, and ammunition. Resupplied, the Israelis counter-attacked, routing the Syrians and destroying the Egyptian army.

The Arab oil countries, blaming the United States for yet another humiliating military debacle, used the defeat as an excuse to nationalize the assets of American companies and impose an embargo on sales of oil to America. The disruption in supply fueled the fires of inflation and created an "oil shock" that threatened to plunge the world into a global recession, or even another Great Depression.

Nixon could only brood as the lines to buy gasoline grew, day after day, week after week, longer and longer. In some places, it was rationed by license plates, with cars with plates ending in even numbers allowed to buy only on even-numbered days, and odd only on odd-numbered days. It wasn't Nixon's fault, but it was his watch, and voters would not give him a second term if he didn't fix it.

Like all Presidents, Nixon brought his own style to the Oval Office. He preferred to work alone, often late into the night, reading reports and writing memos on a yellow legal pad. People who knew him well agreed his personality could be quirky, even prickly. A reporter once asked one of his cousins what Nixon had been like as a child, and the cousin said, "Dick was not the kind of boy you wanted to pick up and hug."

Only a small inner circle of advisors saw Nixon on a regular basis. He had two loyal aides who acted as gate-keepers to the Oval Office: Bob Haldeman, his chief-of-staff, had a flat-top haircut, the demeanor of a drill sergeant, and liked to brag he was, "Nixon's son-of-a-bitch"; John Ehrlichman, Nixon's legal counsel, looked like a grumpy Humpty Dumpty. The press quickly dubbed them the "Berlin Wall" because of their Germanic names and ruthless methods of walling off the President.

Those whose advice Nixon did seek included Henry Kissinger, his national security advisor, whose realpolitik views mirrored Nixon's own. Other confidants included his pipe-smoking Attorney General, John Mitchell, his press secretary, Ron Zeigler, and Bart Bullcannon, his fiery speechwriter. They were together in the Oval Office one day as Nixon, his late-afternoon vodka martini in hand, was pacing in front of his desk, venting at the lack of options. He suddenly stopped, put the glass down, unskewered the olive from the toothpick, sucked out the tangy red pimento with quick *thwurp*, and growled, "Fighting this god-damned embargo is like swatting flies with a fucking shovel."

Kissinger was the first to agree. "Dat's exactly right, Mr. President."

Mitchell puffed his pipe and said in his gruff voice, "It's a sorry-assed state of affairs, Mr. President."

Unlike the others, Bullcannon was almost chipper. "Mr. President, you need to look at it as an opportunity. Play this right, and it will be Richard Nixon who gets the last spot on Mount Rushmore."

Nixon sighed, wondering if it might be possible. He sipped his drink and stroked his thick five-o'clock-shadow. With his ski-jump nose, a scowl like a vulture, and sandpaper jowls, Richard Nixon was an easy target for political cartoonists.

He walked across the Presidential Seal woven into the carpet and stopped in front of a magnificent, five-foot tall globe on a mahogany stand—a gift from Queen Victoria to President William McKinley. The globe depicted America's new empire after the Spanish-American War, and was Nixon's favorite historical artifact in the entire White House collection. Despite being decades out-of-date, he used it all the time. Sometimes, just for the hell of it, he would flip it upside down, putting Antarctica at the North Pole, give it a twirl, and speculate how history might have been different if the North Star had been the South Star.

He turned it to the Middle East, glared at the Persian Gulf, mumbled, "Damn shit asses," and gave the globe a spin. When it began to slow down, he spun it again, a bit harder, more of a push than a spin, then again, harder still, and suddenly he went into a fury—push-push-push—getting madder and madder as he spun the globe faster and faster until he filled the Oval Office with a high-pitched, metal-on-metal whistle. The old globe could have used a drop or two of oil.

"What the hell am I supposed to do!" Nixon shouted. "Start a fucking war and send in a million GI's?" Push. "I can hear that little bastard Bobby now—Nixon's trading blood for oil!" Push-push-push.

The always-dour Ehrlichman agreed. "They'd be all over you, sir."

"Damn straight they would," Nixon said—push. "And how could I save the oil before the rag-heads blew it up? Nuke the bastards? Then nobody's got it. I'm damned if I do and I'm damned if I don't, and no matter what I do the fucking Kennedys will be on me like stink on shit. Like stink on fucking *shit!*"

Kissinger pushed his glasses higher up on his nose. "You vill think of something, Mr. President. You alvays do."

Nixon gave the globe a final, angry shove, rocking the stand back on its legs and nearly toppling it over. He slugged down his martini, and everyone watched in silence as the globe spun slower and slower, until it creaked to a heavy stop. Silence. Short of starting a war, there seemed to be little a President could do, even one as bold and daring as Nixon.

The day after Halloween, workers came around to take down the summer dock before the lake froze over. Catherine took the *Athena* out one last time, then she and old Jonas put her up on blocks in the boathouse. It was time to get on with her life.

She had resolved to move to Washington, Nixon or no Nixon. She would pass the bar exam, fight for women's liberation, and find a way to atone for her family's Robber Baron crimes. She left Timber Crest in her Corvette, stopping for a night to visit her parents in Grosse Point. Then it was on to the nation's capital, where her father's secretary booked her a suite at the posh new Watergate Hotel until she found a place of her own.

She loved the Watergate's panoramic views of the Potomac river, the Washington monument, and the Capitol Dome. She even considered purchasing one of the Watergate's condos, but her heart was set on Georgetown, something quaint, with a yard and a garden. The recession had walloped the market, and many fine properties were available for a song. It only took a few days to find a two-story, red-brick townhouse with white shutters on a shady side-street. Built in 1832, it came with a Supreme Court Justice up the street, a U.S. Senator around the corner, and the Secretary of Commerce down the block. But what convinced her were the huge lilac bushes inside the wrought-iron gate that the owner said bloomed like crazy every spring. Moving in was easy; one call to a decorator did it all.

She had never held a paying job, so filling out the work-history sections of the applications was embarrassing. She soon learned that with Nixon sweeping liberals out of town with a push-broom there was no place in government for a liberated woman in an Earth Mother dress, even one with a famous name and a Yale Law degree. Her best hope lay with non-profits like the Sierra Club, the Red Cross, and the Humane Society, but they were swamped with applications from out-of-work Democrats with long résumés who were desperate to stay in Washington.

She enjoyed seeing musicians like Neil Young and Joni Mitchell in the small, intimate settings of the Georgetown clubs, but the meat-market of the bar-scene turned her off. The horror stories of being single in

Washington were true: there were indeed five women to every decent guy.

The Sexual Revolution was going strong, but free love wasn't what it was cracked up to be. Penicillin had conquered the clap, The Pill had conquered pregnancy, and Roe v. Wade had legalized abortion. But it wasn't women who were set free by the new technologies and legalities, it was men. Since women were taking care of everything, men didn't even bother carrying rubbers in their wallets any more. She was astonished the first time she used the ladies' room of Georgetown's hippest club and saw a vending machine marked "Ladies' Choice" purveying French ticklers in exciting day-glo colors right next to the tampon dispensers. Now it was women who had to carry rubbers if they expected men to use them.

Catherine thought of herself as a feminist, but she knew she was a romantic. She couldn't help it. She was a Cancer, a mothering sign. She wanted children. Every astrology book she ever read said she was supposed to love children, so her yearnings made perfect sense, even for a feminist. Yet here she was, twenty-five, in the prime of life, and hopelessly single.

In early January she took a train to New York for a fund-raiser for the Pass-the-ERA campaign and a slumber party at a Greenwich Village loft with some friends from Yale. The others told depressing tales of the ass-pinching, male-chauvinist-pig work environment, and were bubbling over with plans to put the Equal Rights Amendment over the top, and critical of her for doing nothing to advance the cause.

On the train back to Washington she found herself staring out the window at the bleak winter landscape, thinking they were right. How could anyone starting life with a five-million-dollar trust fund and the prospect of hundreds of millions more ever begin to understand the real world? She was aristocracy, a leech, sucking on the breasts of society, giving nothing back. All DeWolfes were. If she didn't atone for the wealth she had done nothing to deserve, she would be as guilty as any of her Robber Baron ancestors. Maybe worse.

But how? She knew her law degree, combined with her trust-fund, could empower her like no other feminist she knew. And as a DeWolfe, she had automatic entrée to the most exclusive Republican circles whenever she chose—but she would have to play the game.

And so she resolved to be a spy, an agent provocateur. Instead of running from her famous name, she would embrace it, use it as a weapon to give herself a secret identity—like Batgirl, or Wonder Woman. She would infiltrate the political establishment by taking the quickest route to the heart of power: she would become a White House intern.

All her life she had hated buttering up her father, but if her mission were to succeed, it had to be done. So she flew home for a surprise visit.

"Daddy, can you help me get in?"

As usual, her father was skeptical. "I remember one of the DuPont boys did that when Ike was in the White House, but he was just an undergraduate. Being an intern is beneath your dignity, Catherine. You're an attorney. And a DeWolfe."

"Things are different for women, Daddy."

"Yes, you have a point there."

"And I'll make contacts and learn my way around. What better place to start a career than in the White House?"

"Hmmm…maybe. If you promise me you're finally growing up."

"Oh I am, Daddy. Really, I am. I promise."

"You'll have to shave, you know. That will make your mother happy."

"Yes Daddy, I know."

"And you'll have to cut your hair to a decent length and start acting like a proper young lady and not the wild-eyed women's libber you've turned into ever since you went to those drug orgies with that bastard Timothy Leary. Do you know how much it cost to keep your name out of the papers? And how hard it's been to keep it from your mother?"

Her freshman year at Vassar she and some friends had snuck out of the dorms to go to a "happening" at Millbrook, a nearby estate on loan to the League for Spiritual Discovery, Timothy Leary's foundation, from heirs of one of the few families in America even richer than the DeWolfes—the Mellons. Millbrook was the counter-culture's ultimate utopian retreat, and it was just bad luck she was there the night that dozens of police swooped out of the woods and hauled her, Leary, and fifty others off to the Dutchess County jail. An abominable district attorney named Gridley told the press they raided that night to save the girls from being deflowered because "the panties were dropping as fast as the acid." Her father's lawyers had been able to keep her name out of the papers with a hefty contribution to the Gridley-for-Congress Committee.

"Daddy, I'm not ashamed. I'm proud. It was a spiritual exploration of consciousness. I've told you I'll tell Mother all about it if you want."

"Don't you dare upset your mother! You should be ashamed of yourself for even considering it."

"But why, Daddy? Dr. Leary wasn't dealing drugs. He was expanding consciousness. He's a psychologist."

"I saw it on TV. The police hauled bags of drugs away."

"It was only peat moss, Daddy. That's how stupid the cops were. Besides, I was only nineteen. I'm twenty-five now. I'm past that stage."

"Well, you'd better be. Are you sure this is what you want?"

"Oh yes, Daddy. It's a good career move. Really."

He agreed to help. She returned to Georgetown, and the night before her interview she filled her tub with her favorite bath oil, Eau De Lilas, and put on a stack of albums—Joan Baez, Laura Nyro, Judy Collins, Janis Joplin, and Joni Mitchell. She dug out her razor from the bottom of her make-up kit and changed the rusty, seven-year old blade. She knew from reading Toqueville's *Democracy in America* that "the tyranny of the majority" demanded one thing: To get along, she must go along. To be an effective spy who could bring Nixon down, a Mata Hari for feminism and environmentalism, she must pretend to conform. She slipped into the tub and lathered up, chanting, "I am not conforming, I am not selling out, I am infiltrating. I am not conforming, I am not selling out, I am infiltrating. I am not conforming...."

She had never shaved a thick, seven-year growth. She nicked herself a few times, little owwies, nothing bad, though when she finished, her legs looked like she'd run through a blackberry patch, and her underarms were speckled with tiny red pricks that would itch for days.

The interview went well, and thanks to her Bachelor of Arts in Social Psychology from Vassar, her Juris Doctor from Yale Law School, and especially thanks to her father's phone call to the chairman of the Republican National Committee, she was offered a position as an unpaid volunteer in Richard Nixon's White House Intern Corps.

Chapter 3

Can-Can au Go-Go

Winter, 1974

JENNY HAD KEPT HER INTERVIEWS WITH PITTSBURGH'S TOP LAW FIRMS AND corporations, and was gratified to discover her newly certified legal skills to be in great demand. The offers were financially intriguing, but she had no intention of being the token woman in a corporate law firm in Pittsburgh or anywhere else.

Before flying to Paris in August she had looked up old girlfriends, but they were either married or divorced, and they all had children. She had her nephews, though, and spoiled them with trips to Kennywood Park to ride the Thunderbolt, the world's tallest roller coaster, to Dinosaur Hall at the Carnegie Museum, and to Pirate games at the new Three Rivers Stadium.

She thought she had things figured out. On the first of every month, Mellon Bank promised to send her a student-loan check in care of the Paris office of American Express. If she stuck to budget, she would have enough when classes ended in the spring to spend time in Italy. If nothing turned up to keep her in Europe, like a job at U.N.E.S.C.O., she would return to Pittsburgh and live at home until she passed the bar. Then, with degrees from Bryn Mawr, Yale Law, and the Sorbonne, and fluency in French and Italian, she could write her own ticket. Either way, her mountain of student-loan debt would be manageable.

Her heart sank when the university assigned her to a room on the fourth floor of a shabby student hotel with no elevator. Her window opened to a narrow alley and a classic Parisian view of a grimy brick wall. To see if the sky was blue or gray, even at noon, she had to stick her torso out the window, hold tight to the frame, and look straight up. The room had a stiff-backed chair, a lumpy bed, a splintery dresser, a one-drawer writing table, a lamp with a horrid mint-green shade, a sink, a toilet, a bidet, and peeling wallpaper that had to date to the Franco-Prussian war. There was no refrigerator, and no hotplates were permitted. Everyone on the floor shared a tub and shower at the end of a dingy hall. After a few days she bought earplugs to shut out the din of the nightly howling from the cat fights among the trashcans in the alley.

As always she had no lack of male admirers, but except for a brief fling with an Irish medical student who lived up to the hard-drinking stereotype, she had been celibate. And lonely. Mr. Right did not seem to be wintering in Paris this year. In November her twenty-fifth birthday had come and gone with only a birthday card from her parents. She was halfway to fifty, a quarter of a century old. Life was slipping by.

With its large Arab population and its dependence on foreign oil, France had not cheered as enthusiastically for Israel in the Yom Kippur war as had America. Tens of thousands of demonstrators in Paris burned the Stars-and-Stripes and hung Nixon in effigy, and the State Department warned Yanks overseas not to advertise their nationality.

As oil prices soared down and down went the dollar, from four francs to three, leaving little for amenities like a cappuccino. She would have taken a job as a translator or a waitress, but it was impossible to obtain working papers on a student visa in socialist France. Being broke may have been a romantic adventure for expatriate Americans in the 1920's, but in the winter of 1974, poverty in Paris was totally depressing.

One dreary January day, she was down to fifteen francs, less than five dollars. Her check from Mellon Bank was over two weeks late. Was it lost? Stolen? The university was on break, so the student cafeteria was closed, and her sour-mouthed concierge, with Fifi the yapping poodle always cradled in his arms, kept hounding her for the rent.

Every day for two weeks she had taken the Metro to American Express, praying for her check to arrive. Today, rather than spend a franc on the Metro, she walked. A clerk looked in the mail slots, shrugged and said, "N'y a rien, Mademoiselle. Perhaps in the afternoon post. It comes at four."

She would wait. She went across the street to a café, planning to nurse a café-au-lâit all afternoon. On the next table was a copy of America's overseas newspaper, the *International Herald Tribune*. On the front page was a story about Nixon's sixty-first birthday party at his seaside house in San Clemente, California with a photo of him walking on the beach in a suit and tie...and wing-tip shoes. Ha! She couldn't help snickering.

A voice next to her said, "Bon jour, Mademoiselle."

She looked up to see a burly man in a natty camelhair overcoat and a white silk scarf. He removed a black beret, revealing a shiny baldpate fringed with curly, salt-and-pepper hair, and said in halting English, "Mademoiselle look down, like dollar."

What kind of a come-on was that? He was in his fifties, much too old to be Mr. Right. She was in no mood for small talk, and looked down at her newspaper.

"Hard to be student, no working paper, no way make money...oui?"

How did he know she was a student? His English had an eastern European accent, Polish maybe, or Russian—not French at all. She continued to ignore him, hoping he would take the hint.

"Mademoiselle, how you Americans say...broke, need money, oui?"

How could he know that?

"Maybe Oskar can help." He lay a business card down right in front of her, with a graphic of a woman dancing in a go-go cage. It read:

Olympique Au-Go-Go
Oskar Prokrazny, Propriétaire
Place Pigalle, Paris

The infamous Place Pigalle, known to American GI's in two World Wars as "Pig Alley," was the bawdiest anything-goes district in all of Paris. This was not the usual come-on. She asked, "Are you offering me a job?"

"Maybe," he said as he looked her over, slowly, head to toe, like he was buying a horse. "Good face, good legs. Small tits okay, long you not too flat. You dance, zay like, you make one, two, three hundred francs, every night. Clean. No tax, no working paper."

Not too flat? She was tempted to scream *They aren't that small!* But three hundred francs was over a hundred American dollars. She picked up the card. "What kind of dancing?"

"Go-go disco. You want to try, you come to ze club, show ze card, say Oskar send. Au revoir." He bowed congenially, put on his beret, and left. She couldn't help thinking about the *Playboy* offer she turned down. Was go-go dancing any different than being a centerfold?

Two hours later she watched the postman leave American Express. She gave them a few minutes to box up the mail, and with her stomach churning with hunger and hope, she crossed the street and approached the clerk. He shrugged, shook his head, and turned up his palms.

The glamour of Gay Paree was chipping off like cheap nail polish. Her stomach was growling at her, angry at having just a small yogurt for breakfast and only coffee since. If she hurried, she might make it to the little boulangerie that sold bread for half-price at closing time. As she came out, a gust of wind bit her on the neck. She buttoned up for the long walk, stuck her hands in her pockets, felt something and pulled it out—the card.

She stared at the graphic logo of the go-go dancer, thinking *Three hundred francs a night.* She weighed the condemnation she was sure to get if her family and friends ever found out against her angry stomach, said, "Screw it," and marched like a trooper to the Place Pigalle.

It was still the Place Pigalle of Toulouse-Lautrec and the Pig Alley of two World Wars, but updated for the Seventies with bikers, hippies, and go-go discos. Throughout the decades the Place Pigalle was never quite, yet always exactly, the same. Most of the wild stories about it were true.

OLYMPIQUE AU-GO-GO flashed in ruby-red neon above the entrance to the largest club. She showed the card to the doorman, who summoned a bouncer who escorted her to a corner table with a RÉSERVÉ sign. A waiter brought a glass of red wine, compliments of Oskar.

The night was very young, and the boisterous, smoky discotheque, its strobe lights flashing in synch to the deafening music, was filling with the hip, the cool, the fashionably decadent.

A go-go cage trimmed with tiny blinking lights descended from above with a woman in a leopard-skin outfit gyrating inside. The dancer worked up a glistening sweat that streamed down her torso in crystal rivulets, and at the end of every song the dancer removed an article of clothing. When she was down to a two-piece bikini, she responded to the hoots and howls of the crowd and slipped off her top, revealing glittery pasties with fringed tassels covering her nipples. Jenny felt a surge of embarrassment as the dancer went into a frenzy, spinning the tassels like airplane propellers, first to the right, then—boom, to the left, then—boom, in opposite directions at once! How does she do that? Men under the cage urged her on in half a dozen languages and tossed coins and wadded-up bills into the cage.

Suddenly Oskar appeared at the table, husky in a tuxedo, looking like he had stepped out of a Humphrey Bogart movie. With him, wearing a dark suit and a skinny black tie, was a pig-faced man with a head like an upside-down water bucket. She guessed he was a bodyguard. He hovered a few feet away, keeping a discrete eye out for God-knows-what.

Oskar smiled and said in English as he went to kiss her hand, "Ah, you have come." He snapped his fingers and a waiter appeared with a champagne bucket and presented the bottle; Oskar nodded his approval.

As the waiter popped the cork she wondered how many women Oskar had lured into his lair. When the waiter left she asked in her best French, "Monsieur Prokrazny, why have you asked me here?"

He smiled and spoke, now in French, but with an accent just as odd as it was in English. "You need money, oui?"

"Let's say I do. What do I have to do for it?"

He pointed to the dancer in the cage. "Dance, like Collette."

"I'm not going to be a stripper."

He thumped the table with a meaty fist. "No streep. Dance! Discotheque, boy meet girl, make true love. Olympique is, how Americans say, class act." He pointed at the cage. "Voila...ze pasties, zay stay!"

She glanced up at the dancer, who still had pasties on; there had to be something he wasn't telling her. "You mean all I'd have to do is dance?"

He reached in his pocket for a blue pack of Gauloises cigarettes. "Some girls have...sideline. Not my business. My business dance, make happy."

Could she be a dancer? What would everybody say? With pasties, she would be legally dressed, even under blue-nosed Pennsylvania statutes.

He glanced at his watch. "Oskar busy. You want to try?"

It was dancing, she told herself, not stripping. Dancing. But nobody must ever know. Her mother would be mortified, and her friends would accuse her of exploiting her body to titillate male chauvinist pigs. She took a deep breath and said, "Oui."

"Where you from?"

"Chicago," she lied.

"Ah, like ze gangster, Al Capone. What you name?"

"Susan," she lied, giving him the name of the stuck-up queen bee at Camp Tioshango that everybody hated, "Susan Coldbridge."

"Susan," Oskar said, turning up his nose at the name like it was a bad piece of meat. "No...too anglaise." He stubbed out his cigarette, lit another, and blew a procession of perfect smoke rings. She couldn't begin to guess what was going through his mind. A smile brightened his face. "Ah, not Susan—*Susannah*, like ze cowboy song. Mais oui, I like. *Come.*"

He led her upstairs to a door with a faded gold star, knocked three times, very loudly, grabbed her by the wrist, and barged in. The smoky room was filled with dancers in various stages of undress, primping and sipping tall glasses of a greenish-yellow drink she assumed was Pernod— or could it be the dreaded absinthe—*The Green Fairy*—outlawed for rotting minds since the turn-of-the-century?

The dancer in the leopard-skin costume was fixing her makeup at a dressing table. A young girl, maybe nine or ten, was kneeling next to her on the floor, counting money into two piles. The girl looked up and said in French, "Mama did good, didn't she, Uncle Oskar?"

"Oui, magnifique." He picked up a pile of money and counted it for himself.

The girl looked at her and asked in French, "What's your name?"

"Jen...uh...Susan."

Oskar wagged his finger at her. "No Susan...*Susannah*."

"Susannah," she repeated to the girl. She wasn't used to lying, except to her parents and her brothers, though once she began practicing law she knew she would have to be able to lie as casually as brushing her hair.

Oskar took her into a walk-in wardrobe closet and rummaged around. He handed her a robe, a white cowboy hat, black cowboy boots, a Lone Ranger mask, a set of silver spurs, a black halter top with western fringe and a matching mini-skirt, red bikini panties and a pair of shiny, star-shaped silver pasties that, except for the red tassels, looked like sheriff's badges. "When you ready," he said, "come to my office."

The dancers helped her, giggling when they realized she didn't even know how to stick on pasties. They showed her how to apply the yucky white glue, like runny cold cream, spreading it evenly by rotating the little cups over her nipples to force out the air pockets. Once in place, they made her jiggle her breasts, really shake them, to make sure the pasties were on tight. She asked, "How do you make the tassels spin?"

They were delighted to demonstrate the technique they called *les moulins*—the windmills. They took turns, arguing who had the best moves. They spun their tassels in a blur, first to the left, then—boom—back to the right. The hardest move was spinning them simultaneously in opposite directions—*les moulins fous*—the crazy windmills.

As she watched them try to outdo each other she thought of all the diving meets she'd been in, imagining judges holding up score cards and rating tassel-twirling like swan dives and back flips—8.9, 9.1, 9.7. She tried to emulate them, but her breasts just jiggled around every which way, and the tassels wouldn't spin at all. The others giggled, then assured her it just took practice.

When she was ready as she'd ever be, she pulled on the ill-fitting boots, tied the sash of her robe tight, put on the cowgirl hat, and to shouts of "Bonne chance" headed down the hall to Oskar's office. The bucket-headed bouncer saw her coming, rapped on the door, and let her in.

Oskar was on the phone. An elaborate stereo system dominated the room, with an upright piano in a corner. She waited, shivering more from embarrassment than from the chilly room or the skimpy outfit. He hung up, smiled and said, "Oskar no bite." He lit a cigarette. "Ready?"

"I think so."

"Take off ze robe."

She removed the robe and draped it over a chair.

He made a circular motion with his hand. "Turn, slow, like ballerina."

She turned slowly, like in ballet class, three-hundred-sixty degrees.

"Put on ze mask," he said. He swiveled in his chair, put a record on the turntable, and Aretha Franklin's "Respect" boomed out.

"Dance," he said, then sat stone-faced as she tried to bump and grind like Natalie Wood in the movie *Gypsy*. When it ended he put on some horrible disco thing and yelled, "Ze mask...*off!*"

She took off the mask, and a few seconds later he yelled, "Ze hat...*off!*" and a few seconds later, "Ze gun...*off!*"

When she was down to a halter-top and bikini briefs he yelled, "Ze top...*off*," she hesitated, then yanked it off with a flourish and kept on dancing, but did not attempt *les moulins,* much less *les moulins fous.*

Oskar shook his head, obviously disappointed. "You go, practice, come tomorrow, at eight. Ze men zay like, you work. Zay no like," and he gave a Gallic shrug that said *C'est la vie.*

He stood up and handed her an album from the shelf—*The Rolling Stones Greatest Hits.* "Oskar tell you secret. You practice in ze mirror. Make you hot for you. Zat ze secret. Make you hot for you, zen zay like."

She changed, put the costume in a paper sack, and went out into the bleak January streets of not-so Gay Paree for the long walk back. She was excited at the prospect of a job, scared she might fail, and terrified anybody would ever find out. She was ashamed of herself for having tried out, and furious with herself for nearly flunking the audition. The champagne must have slowed her down. It wouldn't happen again.

In the morning she put on the red bikini bottom and the black fringed skirt, applied the yucky white glue, and stuck the pasties on her nipples. She put on the cowgirl hat and stood before the mirror, laughing at the memory of Dale Evans singing "Happy Trails" with Roy Rogers. What would her friends say if they could see her now? She put on the halter top and pushed her breasts together to increase her modest cleavage while wondering what life would have been like without a nose job. *Playboy* would never have offered Honker a centerfold, but could Honker have been a go-go dancer? Would the hungry-eyed men under the cage care about a dill-pickle nose if her breasts twirled tassels like crazy windmills?

She borrowed a record player, and remembering Oskar's advice—*Make you hot for you*—practiced in front of the mirror being sultry, fetching, and sexually provocative. After a while she could get her tassels going, but more like lazy windmills than crazy windmills.

Before leaving for her big debut she went to freshen up with a shower. She put on a robe and was halfway down the hall when the concierge, with Fifi the barking poodle cradled in his arms, came around the corner and flipped out. "You no pay ze rent, and you steal ze hot water!"

She hurried to the bathroom and shut the door. He stood outside, making sure everyone on the floor knew she had not paid rent and had showered yesterday and the day before that as well. A whole month's worth of hot water! When she came out he was waiting, and started yelling all over again. She walked quickly down the hall in her bathrobe with him hard on her heels harping-harping-harping and Fifi barking-barking-barking. When she reached her room she spun around, shouted, "*Fungu!*" in her grandfather's best Italian, gave him the finger an inch from his nose, and slammed the door in his face.

She went into the American Express office an hour later, the cowgirl costume in her daypack. If her check was there, she would mail the costume to Oskar with an apology. The clerk shook his head. "N'y a rien, Mademoiselle. Perhaps tomorrow."

The *Olympique Au-Go-Go* was once a vaudeville theater, and the banks of curtains, scaffolding and lights had been adapted to the needs of a go-go disco. To get to the cages, which dangled on cables high above the dance floor, dancers had to skitter along a narrow wooden walkway with thin metal railings. A grizzled attendant with a gap-tooth smile opened the cage door for her. She gave him her robe, and he held her hand as she stepped in. The cage rocked a bit as he shut the door.

The spotlights came up and the deejay announced, "Susannah, La Cowgirl Américaine."

As the cage started down, the baritone saxophone intro to the Rolling Stones' monster hit "Satisfaction" came blasting out like a gust of wind in a thunderstorm. She tried to focus on what her dance teachers called *the trance,* and her college diving coach called *the zone.* Her nostrils were assaulted by the sickly-sweet, clammy miasma that wafted up and engulfed her like a steamy blanket, a mixture of smoke, liquor, perspiration and heavy French perfumes.

The dance floor was filled with a sea of people—factory workers, truck drivers, clerks, civil servants, secretaries, college students. A clump of desperate men congregated under her cage. Collette and the other dancers had told her that catering to the clump was the key to good tips. The trick was to tease them on, make them throw their coins without ever making eye contact. She would know she was doing well when she felt coins tapping on her body, like raindrops. It took a while to feel the first coin and hear it clink on the cage's metal-plate floor. Then came another…and another. Not hard, little taps.

With each song another piece of clothing came off until, halfway through the last song in her set, the long version of the Doors' "Light My Fire," she whipped off her halter-top, and danced as if her life depended on it. She tried *les moulins*, and for the first time really got the tassels going, and then, *les moulins fous*. It was working! She was doing it! Coins pelted in, faster and faster. When the cage went up she was drenched, exhausted, panting for breath. The attendant opened the door and steadied the swaying cage. How had she done? He gave her a gap-toothed smile, pointed to the money on the floor of the cage, and said, "Très bien, très bien." She had expected to feel guilty, humiliated, degraded, but to her amazement she felt excited, exhilarated, exultant. They loved her!

The attendant handed her a towel, a bottle of Perrier, and a black velvet sack with a drawstring. She dried off and gulped down the water. He handed her the pieces of her costume to put in the sack, then he used a whiskbroom to sweep the crumpled bills and coins into a dustpan. He had her hold the sack open as he dumped in the money.

Soon she was sprawled on the dressing room couch, savoring the anise flavor of a tall Pernod, and giggling with the other dancers like schoolgirls at a slumber party. She was astonished at how wonderful she felt.

Nicole, who everybody agreed would grow up to be either a banker or a madame, emptied the bag and counted the money into two piles, half for the staff—the bartenders, waiters, and bouncers—and half for her. As Nicole neared the end she kept saying, "She might do it, she might do it."

The room was hushed as she counted out the last coins, confirmed the exchange rates on the business page of *Le Monde*, made some calculations on her pad, and called out, "One hundred and eight!"

The dancers cheered—a new record for an Olympique debut! She had earned fifty-four francs for herself—almost seventeen dollars! And the night was young, with three sets yet to go.

Her debut went so well that the next day Oskar had a tailor measure her for a costume, bought her a pair of red-leather boots in her size, and came up with other Old West props, including a toy bullwhip and what was to become the crowd's favorite—a broomstick pony with red plastic reins, a polka dot head, and a shaggy yellow rag-mop mane she rode suggestively between her legs. Giddy-up, giddy-up. Hi-yo Silver...*away*!

A few days later the other dancers turned green with envy when Oskar paid a band to record a rousing, rocked-out version of "Oh! Susannah" for her entrances and exits. It wasn't fair she had a theme song and they didn't. Jenny had no words, in French, English, or Italian to describe what it was like having her own theme song, like *The Lone Ranger* or *Bonanza*. She felt like she was in an episode of *I Love Lucy*, where Lucy gets into a crazy predicament twirling tassels to earn extra money to buy Ricky, her hot-tempered Latin husband, some new golf clubs while worrying Ricky would kill her if he found out.

The Olympique's top floor was a kind of dormitory for dancers who needed a place to sleep after a long night—*quarters* they called it, no men allowed. Some lived there all year round. It was very safe, guarded by Oskar's bouncers, who were rumored to be in an underground network that smuggled refugees from behind the Iron Curtain. Each dancer had a small private room, barely big enough for a bed and a dresser, with a light-bulb hanging from the ceiling. They shared a small kitchen and a sitting room that opened onto a balcony overlooking the bustling Place Pigalle. In many ways it reminded Jenny of Lib House. Compared to the student hotel, quarters at the Olympique was like a penthouse at the Ritz.

The best thing about it was the elegant, claw-foot iron bathtub, and the fact that there was no concierge to complain about wasting hot water, though the other dancers thought it very strange that she took a bath every day. She told them over and over most Americans took a bath or shower every day, but nobody believed her. Once Nicole even asked with childish concern, "Does your skin disease hurt bad?"

She was dumbfounded. "What makes you think I have a skin disease?"

"Everybody says it's why you have to take a bath every day."

By the time classes started she had earned almost two thousand francs, over six hundred dollars. Her money worries were over. She settled into a routine: sleeping and studying in her student room and attending classes during the week, and dancing and sleeping at the Olympique

Friday, Saturday, and sometimes Sunday nights.

She didn't tell any of her classmates at the Sorbonne about her job, and told no one at the Olympique anything. To them she was Susannah from Chicago. Like a character in a spy novel, she lead a double life. By day she was Ms. Jennifer Abruzzi, Esquire, alumnus of Bryn Mawr and Yale Law School, graduate fellow at the Sorbonne, feminist and future champion of justice and equality. By night she was Susannah, La Cowgirl Américaine, the star attraction at the *Olympique Au-Go-Go*, and the toast of the Place Pigalle.

Chapter 4

The American Dream

MCGILL RECEIVED HIS JURIS DOCTOR DEGREE IN DECEMBER, GRADUATING near the top of his class. He could now add *esquire* to his signature: Arthur Bolton McGill III, Esq. It had a dignified, Republican ring to it.

He had sent in his application to join the Nixon administration a year earlier, but no call or letter ever came. His father accused him of sending it to the wrong address, but he was convinced it was because his law degree was from Berkeley. Nixon's people must have assumed he was a radical; it was the only possible answer.

Unlike most new recipients of a prestigious JD degree, he did not consider a clerkship or working for a law mill or a large corporation. He wanted to be in politics. He put his eggs in Nixon's basket, but nothing hatched. His student loans were gone, and he would soon have to begin paying them back. He could make beer and pizza money singing in bars and coffeehouses, but not enough to pay off the loans. Passing the bar exam must be his priority. After that, he would move to Washington and pound on Republican doors until somebody let him in.

To pay the rent while he studied for the bar exam, he took a job on a construction crew, cash under the table, no taxes, no deductions. His first day they rode in the back of the foreman's pickup truck across the San Rafael Bridge to a hillside condominium in touristy Sausalito.

They were building a redwood deck and installing one of the new hot tubs that were all the rage in fad-crazy Marin County. At the ten-o'clock break he sat with his back against a wall, drinking coffee and eating a jelly twister from Donut Delight. Other guys lit cigarettes. He must not. It had been two months, and he was sticking to his New Year's resolution and finally quitting his two-pack-a-day habit. God, how he wanted one.

The sun was warm on his face, the hills were a deep green. Californians had no idea how good they had it. They actually called this winter. It was a pleasant sixty-five degrees, while back in Pennsylvania, at almost the exact same latitude, a foot of new snow was on the ground.

He sipped coffee and took in the salty breeze. Dozens of sailboats bobbed in the harbor. A double-decker ferry, crowded with tourists, was docking at a pier. A couple of miles across the Bay, the San Francisco skyline glittered in the sunlight like the Emerald City of Oz. A container ship passed in front of Alcatraz Island, The Rock, once home to gangster Al Capone, and for the millionth time McGill asked himself which area of the law he should pursue if he couldn't work for Nixon. Corporate law sounded excruciatingly boring, and while criminal law was exciting for a TV lawyer like Perry Mason who never had a guilty client, he did not want to spend his life helping to free the guilty.

When the foreman left one of the guys in the crew wearing an olive-drab U.S. Army fatigue shirt with three stripes on the sleeve asked him, "What's your name, man?"

The guy was a couple of years younger, maybe twenty-two or twenty-three. With his sun-bleached, surfer's hair he could have stepped off the cover of a Beach Boys' album.

"Art. You?"

"Vince. You smoke?"

"No, I'm trying to quit. New Year's resolution."

"No, I mean you want to smoke a doobie?"

McGill perked right up. "That's different."

It was different. The Surgeon General's report left no doubt that tobacco was a killer. On the other hand, Nixon's blue-ribbon Shafer Commission, charged by Congress to investigate the truth about marijuana, had concluded that it was not addictive, had never killed anyone, did not lead to harder drugs, and should be decriminalized. As much as McGill admired Nixon, he could not understand why the President was ignoring the unanimous advice of his own, hand-picked commission.

"It's Panama Red," Vince said as he lit the joint, took a toke and passed it. "Hard to find with Nixon's bullshit war on drugs."

McGill took the joint. "Thanks." It did not seem like a good time to mention he had worked on the NIXON NOW election campaign. He took a hit, held it in and said in a pinched voice as he passed the joint on, "One thing about Nixon, he's out to lunch on pot."

On that point the guys in the crew were in total agreement.

"Yeah, man."

"Right on.

"No shit."

"Fuckin' A."

McGill exhaled the smoke in a billowing huff. "Wow, nice stuff. Thanks."

When the joint came back it had burned down to a stubby roach.

"Time for the bird," Vince said. He opened his lunch box and took out a metal object that looked like a cross between the flying pterodactyl in toy dinosaur sets and a long-legged, wading bird—a heron, or an egret.

Vince clipped the roach in and passed it. McGill noted how easy it was to handle the clip. He toked and passed it along. When the roach was gone McGill asked, "Can I see your clip?"

Vince tossed it to him. "Guess what it's made out of."

McGill turned it over every which-way. The head was a spring-loaded electrical connector used by electronic hobbyists, and the clip's thin legs were soldered to a round steel slug two inches in diameter. "Lets' see. The head's an alligator clip, the base is a slug, and the legs and wings…hey…it's a fork, right?"

Vince grinned. "Took you long enough."

McGill was impressed. "I like it. It's a really cool clip."

"It's way better than cool," Vince said. "It's the world's best roach clip. It stands up on its own, and it's super-easy to pass. Thing's great."

McGill's newly-minted legal mind cranked into gear, checking the statuette for copyright and trademark symbols, a patent number, country of origin, company name, anything to identify it. Nothing. "You make it?"

"Found it. Some hippies split on the rent and left a bunch of crap in an apartment we were painting. Finders keepers."

The four-tined dinner fork had been cut into two pieces. The handle was soldered to the back side of the base of the tines, and bent into a swooping tail. The two outer tines were twisted into spirals, like a bird's furled wings, and the middle tines were stork-like legs soldered to the slug. It almost looked alive.

McGill grabbed a tape measure. It was five-and-a-half inches long, from the end of the tail to the tip of the beak, and four-and-a-quarter inches high, from the base to the peak of the alligator clip, which looked like a bird's feathery tuft.

"I gotta come up with a name," Vince said as McGill checked it out. "Which do you like better—the Grassbird, or the Roachrunner?"

"Hmmm…when you told me about it, you just called it 'the bird.'"

"Yeah. So?"

"So when in doubt, use the KISS principle."

"The what?"

"The KISS principle. It means 'Keep It Simple, Stupid.' I'd just call it

'The Bird.' What are you gonna do with it?"

"Sell a million of 'em. Hardest part's finding the right forks."

One of the guys said in a mocking tone, "Vince thinks he's gonna get rich making roach clips."

The others roared in laughter, but not McGill. He had seen a lot of roach clips in his time, but never one so cute, almost cuddly, as this groovy statuette. It stood upright on its own, it was easy to pick up, and easy to pass. And it was made out of a fork. People would love it for that alone. This was a work of folk art which served a real need, a bonafide better mousetrap, with Get Rich Quick written *BIG* all over it. His heart was pounding with excitement, like suddenly finding himself on a lonely tropical beach with a horny *Playboy* centerfold.

He tried to disguise his enthusiasm while pumping for information. "Have you researched the patent and copyright aspects yet?"

Vince turned sullen. "I ain't gonna worry about that shit."

"Not worry about it? Are you crazy? You make any money on this and somebody's gonna sue your ass, guaranteed. This is America, sue me, sue you. Know what I'm saying?"

"Yeah, it's America all right," Vince said, "and I can do anything I want."

McGill tried a different approach. "So what kind of structure have you set up? Proprietorship? Partnership? Corporation?"

Vince stared down, saying nothing, apparently mesmerized by the sawdust and wood chips on the deck. Just then the foreman's truck horn blew and they heard a shout. "Break's over. Get to it."

For the rest of the day McGill pounded nails and learned to plumb a hot tub while planning how to convince Vince he needed a partner. The market for roach clips was enormous. "Head shops" were sprouting like dandelions in April as millions of "war babies" came of age and joined the counter-culture. Except for the Mulligan Man, all his friends smoked pot, every last one, and they all needed a Bird. It was the epitome of the better mousetrap. People would beat a path to the door of whoever made the Bird. It would sell millions, even tens of millions. Easy. And it was completely legal. If he played his cards right, the Bird could be the key to opening the door to the get-rich-quick American Dream.

Chapter 5

The War Effort

NIXON CLENCHED HIS FIST AND POUNDED ON THE BIG TABLE IN THE WHITE House cabinet room—WHAM! "Dammit, national security is at stake here. *National fucking security!*"

The room turned whisper quiet. Somebody muffled a cough.

Nixon knew he got himself in trouble when he became too emotional. He used an anger-management technique his psychiatrist had taught him after he blew up the night he lost the California gubernatorial race and snarled at the press on his way out the door, "You won't have Nixon to kick around any more!" Three deep breaths, in and out, in and out, in and out. Count to ten. He steepled his fingers and said in a calm voice, "To guarantee national security America must become self-sufficient in energy. As of today, energy independence is this administration's highest priority."

The all-white, all-male faces around the table looked even paler than usual. They just didn't get it. It was time to rattle their cages.

Protocol demanded that no one be seated when the President is standing, so Nixon put his hands on the edge of the table, and without warning he pushed his chair away and stood up as fast as he could, chuckling to himself as they scrambled out of their chairs to get to their feet. Sometimes being President could be a lot of fun.

"Now that I've got your attention, sit your asses down and listen up." He began circling the room, behind their chairs, speaking as he walked. "The United States is the most powerful country that ever existed. We can put a man on the moon, so why in the hell are we sucking up to rag-headed camel jockeys? Tell me—*why?*"

Nixon stopped and waited, but nobody had the balls to speak his mind. He snorted in disgust and said, "There's an old saying that luck is what happens when preparation meets opportunity. Well, there's a silver lining here somewhere, and we've got to find it. We can't pass the ball to the sorry-assed generation coming up behind us. Thanks to the damned Kennedys, there's no war to test their courage and no draft to teach them discipline. Boys with hair down to their assholes, girls screwing everything in sight. Free love my ass! And that crap they call music. The whole damned generation is nothing but a wild orgasm of anarchists sweeping across the country like a prairie fire! They need a purpose, a goal, something higher than getting laid. What do we want them to want? Energy independence! Project Independence will be Nixon's manifesto!"

It sounded good, even profound, but no one was quite sure what Nixon meant. Later, when he read what he had said, even he wasn't sure.

A few days later a transcript of his diatribe leaked. Haldeman, Ehrlichman, Bullcannon and Zeigler were in the Oval Office as Nixon read the *The Washington Post*'s editorial: "Pie-in-the-sky hyperbole."

Nixon crumpled the newspaper, hurled it at the wastebasket, and watched it bounce off the rim and onto the carpet. "Hyperbole my ass! What kind of bullshit Harvard talk is that? What the hell do they expect me to do? Pull another Saudi Arabia out of my asshole? Those liberal sons of bitches have hated me since I nailed Alger Hiss. They want to see me eat crow. But Nixon does not eat crow. Not Nixon! I want the bastard who leaked it. Those were my people in there."

His speechwriter, Bart Bullcannon, was almost jovial. "Mr. President, whoever it was, I think you should be glad they leaked it. If you ask me, the Nixon Manifesto has a ring to it, like the peal of a church bell. It was you at your best."

Nixon drummed his fingers on the arm of his leather chair. "Hmmm…you might be on to something here, Bart. Monroe and Truman have doctrines, but nobody has a manifesto. Hmmm…."

Bullcannon's cherubic cheeks glowed like pink Easter hams. "I say we run with it, Mr. President. Making America independent in energy is something voters can understand. Start by calling a conference of experts you can trust. And get ordinary people involved. Ask the public to send in ideas, so it seems like we're doing something."

Nixon would have preferred kicking commie ass in Vietnam, or sending in the Marines to blow Castro out of the water, but he had to play the cards he was dealt. The game was poker, and all he could do was bluff. "Okay, let's try it. It could be good PR, even if it is smoke and mirrors. Invite the public to send in ideas. John, organize a conference, a small one, a trial balloon to test the waters. We'll hold it at Camp David, away from the cameras, and see how it plays in Peoria."

At the next press briefing Zeigler announced, "The President has faith in the ingenuity of the American people, and wants anyone with ideas on how to solve the energy crisis to write directly to the White House. Address the letters to Project Independence."

Ehrlichman convened a two-day conference of experts from the energy sector: nuclear, solar, wind, oil, gas, coal, hydro. They met around the big table in the rustic conference room at Camp David, and Nixon personally attended the sessions. He learned from geologists that the huge shale-oil deposits in Colorado and Wyoming and the tar sands in Canada contained enough oil to last the whole world for hundreds of years, so America was not about to "run out" of oil. The problem was that turning shale and tar sand into fuel was many times the cost of refining liquid petroleum. It came down to money. It always did.

After the experts left, Nixon and the inner circle were sitting around the fireplace in the President's lodge, evaluating the ideas over drinks. Several experts had advocated opening the Naval Petroleum Reserves to commercial drilling, but Kissinger was opposed. "Mr. President, it vill diminish national security. The Soviets vill see it as a sign of veakness."

It was an easy call for Nixon. "I will not jeopardize national security."

One idea that everyone agreed would save energy—keeping daylight savings time all year long—had been proposed two centuries earlier by none other than Benjamin Franklin. Nixon signed an Executive Order, and it was done.

Another idea was to lower the speed limit to fifty-five to increase fuel efficiency. Attorney General John Mitchell piped up in support. "I like it, Mr. President. It will let ordinary people feel like they're fighting back."

Bullcannon strongly disagreed. "Mr. President, with all due respect to John, he's spent too much time in Manhattan. Slowing America down is a terrible idea. Truckers already call fifty-five the 'double-nickel' in states that have it. They hate it. You can tell people it's patriotic and they'll go along...for about a month. Then they'll start to resent it and before you can say Jack the Ripper, they'll be calling it 'Nixon's double-nickel' and you'll have the most flouted law in American history on your hands."

Nixon calculated the political algebra. The only big union to ever endorse him was the Teamsters. He didn't want to piss them off if he didn't have to. "Nixon's double-nickel?" he said with a strong shake of his head. "I don't like the sound of that, don't like the sound of that at all. And I won't encourage disrespect for the law. We'll keep that arrow in the quiver."

When the Gallup Poll came out, Nixon's approval rating bumped up three points. It was the first good news in weeks. "Let's keep the momentum going," Nixon told his inner circle. "Another conference, but make it more visible. People want to see their President out there on the court swinging for the goalposts."

Ehrlichman called a bigger meeting, and included representatives from other fields: economists, demographers, biologists, psychologists, sociologists, even the clergy. They gathered in the war room of the White House, forty all-white, all-male delegates at the big circular table.

Nixon listened to each presentation. When his turn came, a rumpled professor of agronomy with a shock of white hair that sprouted from his head like a haystack said, "Mr. President, if the goal of energy independence is to succeed, we must convert from a hydrocarbon economy to a carbohydrate economy that runs on alcohol. Mr. President, for America to become independent in energy, we must grow our own fuel."

Nixon knew a good slogan when he heard one and jotted *Grow Our Own* on his pad. "Are you talking about carbohydrates, like in potatoes?"

"Yes sir," said the professor. "Henry Ford used to say alcohol is the fuel of the future, and that there's enough alcohol in one acre of potatoes to run the machinery to harvest that acre for a hundred years. His early Model T's had dual fuel tanks so you could switch between alcohol and gasoline."

A representative from the American Petroleum Council laughed and said, "Mr. President, what Ford should have said was 'Alcohol is the fuel of the future, and it always will be.'"

Everyone chuckled except the professor, who flushed red and pointed his finger at the oil man. "For a hundred years your industry has used every trick in the book to keep the American farmer from growing his own fuel. There would have never been a farm crisis or a Great Depression and we would have no energy crisis today if your industry had not stood in the way of American farmers growing their own fuel."

The oil man gave a derisive snort and said, "Oh, bullshit."

"Whoa!" said Nixon. "We're not here to fight amongst ourselves. Go ahead, professor, please finish."

"Thank you, Mr. President. Ethyl alcohol, or ethanol, is known as 'grain alcohol' because it is made from fruits and grains. But another alcohol, methyl alcohol, or methanol, often called 'wood alcohol,' can be made much more cheaply from any source of biomass, such as wood chips, sawdust, corn stalks, cow manure, natural gas, coal—even garbage."

Nixon raised an eyebrow. "Garbage?"

"Yes, Mr. President. Every landfill creates large amounts of methane gas which can be used as a fuel for generators or converted to methanol for liquid fuel. You could power the world with leftovers if you had a big enough refrigerator."

The professor held up an old newspaper clipping. "I'd like to read what Henry Ford had to say about using farm products for industrial purposes:

> *Why use up the forests which were centuries in the making,*
> *and the mines which required ages to lay down, if we can*
> *get the equivalent of forest and mineral products in the*
> *annual growth of the fields?*

Next the professor held up a book. "Ford sponsored annual conferences on what was called 'farm chemurgy' all through the 1920's and Thirties. This was the bible of the chemurgy movement, *The Farm Chemurgic*, by a scientist at Dow Chemical. Their slogan was: 'Anything that can be made from oil can be made from a carbohydrate.'"

"No wonder it never went anywhere," Nixon said with a laugh. "A slogan has to trip off your tongue, not trip you up."

"Mr. President," said the professor, "with all due respect, the farm chemurgy movement only ended because of the war."

Somebody asked, "Professor, isn't grain alcohol the same thing as moonshine?"

"Yes, that has been a big problem," said the professor. "The oil industry's support of the federal tax on alcohol is directly responsible for our energy problem today."

Nixon knew about hillbilly "moonshiners" making "white lightning" by the light of the moon, but didn't know much about the tax. He took notes as the professor related the history of alcohol taxation in America.

"In the 1700's," the professor said, "farmers along the Allegheny frontier could not get their corn and rye to market before it rotted, so they distilled it into whiskey before hauling it over the mountains. In 1794, Treasury Secretary Alexander Hamilton convinced Congress to pass a tax on 'spirits' to pay off debts from the Revolution. The tax fell hardest on farmers in Western Pennsylvania, and when tax collectors came around, angry mobs of 'whiskey boys' tarred-and-feathered them in what was known as the Whiskey Rebellion.

"To end the challenge to federal authority, George Washington put on his old Revolutionary War uniform and led an army of twelve-thousand militia toward Pittsburgh. Newspapers of the day called it 'The Watermelon Army.' It was the only time in American history that a Commander-in-Chief personally commanded an army in the field. The whiskey boys melted into the woods without a fight, and the tax remained in effect. In the election of 1800, Thomas Jefferson defeated John Adams partly on a promise to repeal 'the infernal tax,' which he quickly did. Except for a brief period during the War of 1812, there was no federal tax on alcohol until Congress imposed a 'temporary' tax of $2.08 per gallon to help finance the Civil War in 1862. But after the war, under pressure from the oil industry, Congress kept the tax in place."

Nixon interrupted, saying, "Whoa, hold your horses. The tax on booze is a sin tax, for crying out loud. Keeps people from overindulging."

"That's only partly true," replied the professor. "Congress did not differentiate between alcohol for drinking and alcohol for industry. Before the Civil War, America's farms produced ninety million gallons of alcohol every year for use as an illuminant in lamps. It was mixed with turpentine and camphor in what was called 'camphene' or 'burning fluid.'"

"But I thought everybody back then used whale oil?" Nixon said.

"No, sir, that's a myth promoted by the oil industry. They want people to think it was the discovery of oil in 1859 that kept America from going dark. It's propaganda, Mr. President. Far more people used alcohol and vegetable oils than used whale oil. The market for illuminants was very competitive until the tax. Thanks to the lobbying of the oil industry, Congress taxed alcohol at $2.08 but only taxed kerosene at ten cents a gallon, which amounted to an indirect subsidy to the oil industry of $1.98 per gallon. Overnight, alcohol was priced out of the market, forcing hundreds of distilleries to close. It was a disaster for farmers, who lost a major market for their crops, and precipitated a farm crisis that lasted for decades. It wasn't until 1906 that Teddy Roosevelt finally beat back Rockefeller and the oil industry and got Congress to pass the Free Alcohol Bill."

"The Free Alcohol Bill?" Nixon said. "What the hell's *that*?"

"It repealed the tax. Half the country still didn't have electricity, so the market for illuminants was still huge. The hope was that farmers would grow crops to make alcohol for illumination as well as for fuel for the new horseless carriages. But huge new oil discoveries in Texas and Oklahoma sent the price of oil so low alcohol still could not compete. When the country went dry in the 1920's, the oil industry had the Prohibition Bureau shut down research into using crops for fuel at universities like Minnesota and Iowa by claiming they were fronts for bootleggers. Mr. President, because of the tax, Prohibition, and the oil industry's efforts to kill the competition, our farmers have lost a hundred years of prosperity, and America has lost a century of research into our most reliable source of energy."

Nixon leaned back in his chair, unconsciously tapping his pen on the table. "Professor, are you saying moonshine can solve the energy crisis?"

"Only partly, sir. Ethanol has a place, but the long-term solution is methanol. You can't drink it, so there's no tax problem, and it can be made for half the cost of ethanol by a process called pyrolysis."

Nixon shook his head in confusion. "I don't get it. If it's cheaper and better and legal, why aren't farmers making it right now?"

"Making methanol requires sophisticated cracking plants, like those used to refine petroleum," the professor said. "Ethanol can be fermented and distilled with simple equipment made from junkyard parts."

"Like bathtub gin back in the Twenties?" Nixon asked.

"Yes, sir, and like in that TV show, M*A*S*H, where the Army doctors in Korea have a table-top still in their tent to make martinis. Any farmer can distill ethanol behind his barn, but he can't make his own methanol."

"How well does it work in cars?" Nixon asked. "That's what counts."

"In many ways it's better than gasoline. Indianapolis race cars use methanol, and...."

Nixon's mind trailed off as he jotted down ideas. The details were interesting, but good slogans were the key, and these were terrific. "Fuel From Farms!" and "America Grows Its Own!" He couldn't go wrong with those. With a rematch against that little bastard Bobby Kennedy coming up in '76, he needed a silver bullet and he needed it fast. Who could tell what crazy scheme might be the one that worked? Maybe if he watered the seeds, it could grow like Jack and the Beanstalk? "Thank you, professor. I'll have my people take a look."

At a cabinet meeting a month later his Secretary of Agriculture presented the conclusion. "Sorry to say, Mr. President, it's not feasible on a mass scale. Sawdust, garbage and cornstalks would work, but there is not enough of any single one, and each present different problems with collection, processing, and transportation. It just wouldn't be economical."

"Shit," Nixon said. "It seemed like such good idea."

At his next briefing, press secretary Zeigler read a terse statement: "After careful evaluation of the idea of using farm crops to make methanol for fuel, the Agriculture Department has concluded that there is no source of biomass which would make this an economically viable option."

Thousands of letters to Project Independence were flooding in. Rose Mary Woods passed a few along every day to give Nixon an idea of what people were thinking, and one day she handed him a letter, saying, "You might want to take a close look at this one, Mr. President. It's very unusual."

Nixon put on his glasses and read:

"Dear President Nixon:

My name is Lloyd Mosby. From 1928 until 1942, and again from 1946 until my retirement in 1968, I was employed by the Ford Motor Company. From 1933 until 1942, I was chief manager of Henry Ford's experimental farms at his secret research facility, Iron Mountain Station, here in the Upper Peninsula of Michigan.

Our primary goal was to find an efficient method of making methanol for fuel. I was excited after reading of your interest in methanol as an alternative to gasoline but was greatly disappointed when your spokesman later said there is no reliable source of supply. Mr. President, if this is what you have been told, you have been misinformed.

I suppose an examination of today's farm practices and crop yields would make your advisors believe this, but there is one crop which I am certain has not been included in the calculations. It was once the most widely-cultivated crop in America, and it is the fastest-growing crop known to man, yielding three times more raw material per acre than corn. I know, because I have worked with both.

The scientists at Iron Mountain called it a miracle plant. It grows from the tropics to the sub-polar regions, and doesn't need much fertilizer. Bugs don't like it, so you don't need pesticides, and it grows so fast it chokes out weeds, so you don't need herbicides either. And it does well in the Great Plains. Like Henry Ford said, if we're going to grow crops for fuel, we've got to do it where the land is.

When World War II came, Iron Mountain Station shut down and never started up again. I am in possession of the records of those experiments, and have equipment stored on my farm that was used in the government's World War II victory program to harvest this crop.

You would not be the first president to recognize the value of this crop. George Washington told his plantation manager at Mount Vernon to "sow it everywhere," and Thomas Jefferson called it, "America's most valuable crop."

I hope I may be of service.

Good luck, Mr. President, and God Bless America.

Sincerely,

Lloyd W. Mosby

Nixon's sixth sense was tingling. There was something to this, but what? "Why doesn't he just come out and say what it is?"

Rose Mary crinkled her forehead. "I don't know, Mr. President."

"I've got a funny feeling about this, Rose. Call this fellow up and tell him I'd like to have a chat. Who else have you shown this to? Bob? John?"

"Why, no one, Mr. President."

"Good. Don't bother anybody else with it. We don't want any leaks."

An invitation to the White House to brief the President is an honor few decline. Two days later, Nixon was at his desk when Rose Mary showed Mosby in. He was carrying blueprint tubes, a leather valise, and was followed by two Secret Service agents lugging a U.S. Army footlocker.

He sized Mosby up as they shook hands. He was in his seventies, and Nixon could tell his guest had been a working man by the way his Popeye forearms bulged out of his ill-fitting suitcoat.

"Looks like you brought some presents?" Nixon said with a smile, pointing to the footlocker as Rose Mary and the agents left.

"Yes, sir. The records of the research at Iron Mountain Station."

"So this was some kind of a laboratory?"

"Yes, sir. Ford wanted it to be to cars what Edison's lab in New Jersey was to electricity. There were scientists and engineers he brought over from Germany, a few farmers like me, and mechanics, plumbers, and such to keep things running."

"And what exactly was your job?"

"I worked my way up to chief farm manager. We tested everything, corn, wheat, flax, soybeans, wood chips, sawdust, you name it. But the best was hemp. Nothing else was close. That's why I wrote to you."

"Hemp?" Nixon said. "You mean what rope's made from?"

"It used to be, but not much since Congress abolished a tariff on Manila hemp in 1915. But that's a completely different plant, not nearly as good for rope as real hemp."

"And this real hemp is what you were talking about in your letter?"

"Yes, sir."

"So why beat around the bush? Why not come right out and say what the hell it is?"

"I was worried you might not listen if you knew what it was."

"Well, it seems to have worked," Nixon said as he walked to his desk and reached for his yellow pad. "Please go ahead, Mr. Mosby. You have my full attention."

Mosby opened a blueprint tube, took out a bundle of papers, removed a small poster from the center, and gingerly unrolled it on Nixon's desk.

Bright-yellow lettering jumped off the paper: "Grow HEMP for the WAR." A red sky framed the superstructure of a great battleship, its mighty gun turrets bristling a warning to the enemy, its bright searchlight beaming hope to a nation. A sailor in a blue uniform and a white navy cap stood on the bow, wearing a headset and talking into a microphone. Behind him was a braided yellow line stretched taut, tightly wrapped around a bollard, holding the great battleship steady.

Nixon felt a surge of nostalgia. "I was in the Navy, you know, and old posters like this from the war sure bring back the memories. I don't think I ever saw this one, though."

"This went up in post offices and grange halls all over the Midwest, Mr. President," Mosby said. "The idea was to show farmers who'd never seen an ocean that without hemp we wouldn't have a Navy. Farmers and their sons who signed up for the program were deferred from the military for the duration of the war—that's how important the Hemp for Victory program was to the war effort."

"And you were involved how?" Nixon asked.

"After the Japs took the Philippines, they cut off our supply of fiber, so the government set up a Hemp Production Board under the Agriculture Department. They asked me to run a program to teach farmers how to grow it."

"We had a Hemp Production Board?" Nixon asked.

"Oh yes, sir, Mr. President. Fiber was critical to the war effort. Everything from bootlaces to ships' lines to canvas for tents and backpacks was made from fiber. Without it, the war effort would have fallen apart like a pair of old shoes. The only crop we had that could do the job was hemp, but there were only a couple hundred farmers left, in Kentucky and Wisconsin, who even knew what it was."

Mosby bent over, opened the footlocker, took out a thick photo album and put it on Nixon's desk. He leafed through to a picture of a squad of soldiers with rifles standing guard in a big warehouse. The floor was filled with burlap bags piled five feet high. "Right after Pearl Harbor," Mosby said, "we went around Kentucky and commandeered all the seeds from the '41 crop for the war effort. What you see here is all there was in all of Kentucky, and if the Japs or the Jerrys had bombed this warehouse before we got it to the fields in the Spring, we could have lost the war."

Mosby took a pamphlet from the foot locker and handed it to him. It read: U.S.D.A. Bullet #1935: *Hemp*.

"They put this out in '43," Mosby said, "and reissued it in '52, during Korea. I even helped them make a movie on how to grow it."

"A movie?" Nixon said.

"Yes, sir. *Hemp For Victory*. Every farmer getting crop payments was required to watch it. They showed it at co-op and grange meetings and movie theaters all over the midwest. They promised me a copy after the war, but the Hemp Board was the first thing they closed down, and they told me all the copies disappeared."

Nixon felt his sixth sense tingling. "Disappeared?"

"Yes sir. I knew I was getting the run-around, but what could I do?"

"Mr. Mosby, did your project have anything to do with gasoline, or energy, or fuel in any way…any way at all?"

"No sir, the Hemp Board just wanted fiber. But at Iron Mountain, Ford wanted to make methanol—what he called 'wood gas.' We tried everything, and the scientists from Germany all said hemp was the way to go."

"Why?"

"They were way ahead of us. They'd have lost the First World War two years before they did if they hadn't been making fuel from coal and farm crops to run their tanks and trucks and airplanes. And they had a blend of hemp oil and methanol, 85-15 they called it, that made a diesel purr like a kitten. We ran all our diesels on it—trucks, tractors, you name it. Smelled like popcorn. And Ford wanted to grow crops near his factories to make his own electricity. One of the projects was making charcoal out of baled hemp that would have been cheaper than coal to run a generating plant. Another project was growing car bodies, and—"

"Did I hear you right?" Nixon said. "*Growing* car bodies?"

"Yes sir. Ford always talked about growing cars from the soil. We were perfecting a substitute for steel made out of compressed hemp fibers bound with a soybean resin when they shut us down. Let me show you some pictures."

Mosby flipped through the album. "This is me and Henry Ford, in 1939, right before harvest."

The photo showed a white-haired Henry Ford in a suit and tie next to a young Mosby in overalls. Towering over them was a field of spindly plants over twice their height. "How big are those things?" Nixon asked.

"Oh, anywhere from six to twenty feet. This field averaged about fourteen. You sow the seeds, give 'em some water, and up they come. Easiest things to grow you've ever seen. And they leave the fields in real good shape for the next crop. If you rotate a field with wheat, the soil gets stronger."

One photo showed Ford in front of a banner: *Chemurgy Council, 1939.* "Ford thought he could create millions of jobs, end the Depression, and beat the oil companies at their own game," Mosby said. Other photos showed white-smocked scientists with clipboards in the hemp field, and one showed a scientist at the top of a tall orchard ladder steadying a giant twenty-foot ruler balanced on the ground.

"Now here's a farm over in Wisconsin where they grew hemp for fiber to make things like fishing nets and fire hoses." Mosby showed Nixon a photo of a bucolic farm field, a barn in the distance, with scores of teepee-shaped stacks dotting the field. "We didn't harvest like that at Iron Mountain. We used the whole plant, cut it at the ground and baled it up for easy handling. But the engineers working on car bodies needed clean fiber, and it was easier for me to go down to Green Bay every fall and buy a boxcar from the mill than to try to do it ourselves."

He showed Nixon photos of several 1930's-era Fords. "These cars don't have any metal in the bodies, Mr. President."

"No metal?" Nixon said. "Is it like the fiberglass in a Corvette?"

"No, it was much stronger," Mosby said. "It had ten times the impact strength of steel, and it was a third lighter, too." He turned to a photo of Ford smashing a sledge hammer into a car fender. Next to it was a close-up of Ford pointing to where the hammer hit. "Hardly even scratched it. Do that to a Corvette, and you'd crush it. I'm telling you, Mr. President, if Iron Mountain had kept going, cars today would be lighter and stronger.

We'd be growing the bodies from the soil, and they'd be cheaper to drive because they'd be running on methanol we grew ourselves."

"Did anything ever come from all that research?" Nixon asked.

"No, sir. I was hoping Ford would start it up again after the war, but he told me he was too old to fight with the government. He did right by me, though. He made me the factory rep for farm equipment in the Upper Peninsula. After he died in '47, Iron Mountain Station just rusted away. In '52, the big-wigs down in Dearborn sold the land off. They didn't think anything worth saving, so they let me go in and take all my old reports and anything else I wanted. I have all the research records, and I bought most of the equipment for scrap value at the auction. I have it all stored in the barns on my farm."

"This is all very interesting, Mr. Mosby," Nixon said, "but what did you mean about Ford having a fight with the government?"

"They shut down my farms in the summer of '41. Confiscated every hemp seed we had and burned it."

"But...why?"

"After Ford showed the cars off at the Detroit car show, some agents from the Treasury Department came around and threatened to throw us all in jail. Ford too. He figured DuPont and General Motors pulled strings to stop us when they saw how far ahead we were on our car bodies. And they had the monopoly on lead in gasoline, and if we'd been able to make wood gas cheap out of hemp, they'd have been out hundreds of millions of dollars."

"I don't get it," Nixon said. "What were you doing that was illegal?"

"A couple years before, Congress had passed a law against it. The first time Ford heard about it was when the agents came around and said we were in violation. Ford said DuPont had snuck it through when nobody was looking."

Nixon's sixth sense flared like a rocket. "Snuck it through?"

"I don't know how it works in Washington Mr. President, but that's what he told us. He was getting ready to fight it, but the war came, and everything changed."

"I don't understand," Nixon said. "Why pass a law against a plant that makes rope?"

Mosby arched an eyebrow. "Are you putting me on, Mr. President?"

Nixon bristled. "The President of the United States does not put people on, Mr. Mosby."

"Well, if you don't know, you don't know. They told us we were violating the new tax act for marijuana."

Nixon shook his head, confused. "What in the hell does marijuana have to do with it?"

"The government claimed they were the same thing," Mosby said.

Nixon slumped back, drumming his fingers on the desk. Why was this a surprise? "But you said hemp is for rope. I don't understand."

"Hemp's like roses, Mr. President. You can breed roses for fragrance or for color. Or you can think of it like dogs. There's tiny poodles and big Great Danes, but they're both still dogs. Hemp's like that. There's all kinds of varieties. You can grow it for fiber or for seed, or you can grow it like we did, for the whole plant. The government knew ours was no good for drugs, but they wanted us shut down real bad, and used it as an excuse."

Nixon's sixth sense was ringing like a firehouse bell. How could he not have known that this hemp plant he was hearing about for the first time and marijuana were the same thing? Something stunk, and it wasn't roses. He recognized the faint, fishy odor of conspiracy, and if there was anyone in the history of the universe who could sniff out a conspiracy, it was Richard Milhous Nixon, the man who nailed Alger Hiss.

Mosby showed him more photos, documents, and blueprints. When he finished, Nixon said, "Can you leave these with me so I can have my people take a look?"

"That's why I brought them, Mr. President."

"Thank you. Is there anything you'd like to add?"

"Yes, sir, one thing. We were lucky we had enough seed to get the Hemp for Victory program started in World War II. But nobody's grown it in this country for twenty years, and even if you find seeds in a warehouse somewhere, they won't sprout for you. You got to grow hemp out every couple of years because the seeds don't keep. Now there's a lot from the old days growing wild, but it's turned to ditch-weed, good for nothing. And the stuff the hippies are smoking won't work either. If we had another Pearl Harbor today, I don't know where the hell you'd find the seed."

Nixon stood up, shook Mosby's hand, and bid him good-bye. "Thank you again, Mr. Mosby. And please, don't tell anyone what we have discussed here today. America's national security may depend on it. I have a sixth sense about these things, and something about this feels wrong, terribly, terribly wrong."

Chapter 6

Turn On. Tune In. Drop Out.

CATHERINE STARED AT THE WHITE HOUSE THROUGH THE IRON FENCE ALONG
Pennsylvania Avenue, wondering if the Nixons were home. Across
Seventeenth Street, the Old Executive Office Building loomed like a giant
granite wedding cake. She had read it had over two miles of corridors, five
hundred rooms, and nine hundred Doric columns. During the Civil War
it housed the War Department, but now everyone called it the E-O-B.

Her packet from the Intern Corps said to report to Room 4. She
showed her ID, picked up handouts at the sign-in table, and read over the
list of her fellow interns. Six were from Yale, all undergraduate men, and
two Vassar women, sophomores who started long after she graduated.
Good. She did not want to play who-do-you-know. She was glad to see
other famous Republican names on the list—Whitney, Taft, Branche,
Rockefeller. They would deflect attention from her own.

The new interns met for orientation in the ornate Indian Treaty
Room, a marbled chamber steeped in history. She felt out of place among
the lip-glossed girls and the fuzzy-faced boys, not a man among them. She
had never felt so...old. She had always stood out because of her name, and
for being so tall, but here she stood out because of her age. At least the
pimply boy interns wouldn't be hitting on her all day long.

She grew even more d0   epressed at the bubble-
headed girl-talk in the ladies' room. These women actually believed in
Nixon, were proud to serve him, and derided anything that smacked of
"libbers." She wanted to gag their mouths with Kotex and give them a good
talking-to about what Women's Liberation was all about, but she kept
silent.

As a "special circumstance" intern she had not been interviewed as to
her preferences. The supervisor took her aside. "You'll be a floater until
we can figure out where to use your talents, Miss DeWolfe. You're more
mature than most of our girls, and you have a law degree, which is very
unusual for an intern. How about something at Justice?"

The last thing she wanted was law enforcement. If she were to have
any chance of bringing Nixon down, she must be privy to policy decisions.
"No, I have an administrative personality. I'll take anything at the White

House itself, anything at all."

She spent a week as a courier, learning her way around the labyrinth of corridors. Then she floated, a different office every day, filing, copying, answering phones. She monitored the job announcements on the intern bulletin board. When a worker in the West Wing duplicating room came down with chicken pox and the doctors sent the whole department home, she volunteered. It was boring, tedious work, but she was now inside the White House proper, one of only three hundred secretaries, guards, kitchen workers, Secret Service agents, speechwriters, advisors and interns with dining privileges at the White House mess.

She kept a row of copy machines purring away in a corner of the West Wing basement, scanning everything she touched for something incriminating to bring Nixon down. The highlight of her days came in the late afternoons, when Rose Mary Woods came down to feed page after page of yellow legal paper filled with hand-written notes through the shredding machine. Nixon's writing? If only she could get her hands on those.

She made chitchat with Rose Mary, feigning awe at tales of her early days with Nixon. For her part, Rose Mary was fascinated by her stories of high society parties at Palm Beach. After a few chats Rose Mary surprised her with a proposal. "Catherine, how would you like to come to work for me?" Of course she would.

She was based in Rose Mary's side-office, two doors from the Oval Office itself, gofering, helping out when anybody needed an extra pair of hands. One day, while covering for Haldeman's receptionist, she felt a creepy chill. Out of nowhere a man had appeared at the counter and was staring at her. He was about five-ten, late thirties or early forties, with fierce, piercing eyes, a bushy mustache, and a head so totally bald it glistened like a polished apple. She felt an eerie déjà vu as he undressed her with his eyes.

Refusing to be intimidated, she walked to the counter and stared him in the face. "How may I help you?"

His eyes zeroed in on her name badge. "Why, Miss DeWolfe, it is you. Remember me?"

He did look familiar, but from where? "Have we met?"

"Twice. The first time was at the memorial for Secretary Morganthau."

Whoa, that took her all the way back to her freshman year at Vassar, when her father, uncles, grandfather, and six boring male cousins flew into Poughkeepsie on the DeWolfe corporate jet for a service honoring Henry Morganthau, who had been Secretary of the Treasury under Roosevelt. She tried to get out of it, but her grandfather insisted. "It will be good to have a woman along to represent the family, Catherine. And it's your chance to meet the most powerful families in America. You can tell how important a man was when even an enemy like me comes to his wake."

It had been a rare cross-generational gathering of the rich and powerful of both parties. She was introduced to the Kennedys—the President and Jackie, his mother, Rose, brothers Bobby and Teddy— former Presidents Truman and Eisenhower and their wives, Bess and Mamie, Governor Nelson Rockefeller, Eleanor Roosevelt, four Supreme Court justices, ten Senators...the list went on and on.

"We were at the same table for dinner," the bald man said. "I was next to Commissioner Anslinger of the Narcotics Bureau."

She would never forget being stuck at the same table with her father and some big-shots from law enforcement when the very personification of evil itself, J. Edgar Hoover, sat down at their table. She watched Hoover's every move, expecting him to fly out of his seat and shake a pitchfork in her face for being high on LSD, which of course she was. She had sat in silence as they obsessed over Timothy Leary, who was living high at the Mellon estate in nearby Millbrook, and remembered how furious they were over the #1 best-seller, *The Electric Kool-Aid Acid Test*, about novelist Ken Kesey and a band of acid-heads who called themselves the Merry Pranksters and went around in a psychedelic school bus handing out Kool-Aid spiked with LSD at "acid test" parties.

"I'm sorry," she said, "but that was a long time ago, and there were a lot of people there I didn't know."

"Then you might remember the second time more clearly," he said with a smile. "You and I and four of your friends had a little talk in the judge's chambers at the Dutchess County Superior Court. I did my best to give you girls a good scare."

She was suddenly cold, shivering. "Oh my god—that was *you*?"

"I only had them take you in that night to protect you from Leary's druggies." He held out his hand, beaming with pride, as if he expected her to thank him for throwing her in jail. "E. Grayson Gridley, Director of the Office of Narcotic Operations. I'm Nixon's drug czar."

She remembered him now, from the courthouse and from the Poughkeepsie TV news—his suit coat always flapping open to flash an oversize gun in a shoulder holster. Her skin grew clammy as he shook her hand. She hadn't mentioned the arrest on her White House application forms. Her father's lawyers had told her to forget it ever happened and assured her everything was fixed. Would he try to blackmail her?

She must be calm. "I remember now. But you look so...so different."

"It's the hair," he said as he arched his bushy eyebrows, rolled his eyes upward and pointed to his shiny, totally bald cranium. "When Nixon made me drug czar, I decided to set the best anti-hippie example I could. So I looked in the mirror and said to myself, Grayson, why do it half-assed? If you're going to be bald, by God, be *bald*! So I shaved it all off—beat Mother Nature to the punch. Mark my words, it's the beginning of a trend. So far there's me, the Dalai Lama, and Mr. Clean."

He smiled and rubbed his palm across his glistening cue-ball scalp. She wanted to tell him he was forgetting Curly, of the Three Stooges, and neo-Nazi skinhead gangs, but held back. How did he get it so shiny? Turtle Wax? Brasso? Lemon Pledge?

"What do you think? Like it?"

"It's, it's very distinctive, Mr. Gridley."

"Yes, my women tell me it gets their juices flowing." He leaned forward, proffering the top of his skull for her to touch. "Go ahead, feel it. It's smooth as a baby's ass."

Her stomach curdled at the notion. "Thank you, not today."

"Then you've got a raincheck. So, where's Bob?"

"I believe he and Mr. Kissinger are having lunch at the Willard."

Gridley handed her a large envelope. "Would you have him show this to the President? It's about your fugitive guru friend."

"You mean...Dr. Leary?"

Gridley smiled, giving her a wink, saying nothing. Was he trying to psyche her out?

"He's not my friend, Mr. Gridley. No matter what you think, I hardly even knew him, honest. And I've been over that stage for a long time now."

"We all have our youthful flings." He looked around, as if making sure they were alone, then leaned over the counter and whispered, "Between you and me, I know where he is, and I may be going after him, real soon."

"Oh?"

Gridley smoothed his mustache with his thumb and index finger. "It's up to the President now. Diplomatic considerations."

Like millions of others, she was dying for an answer to a question. "Was the evidence against Dr. Leary really planted by the police?"

Gridley gave her a knowing grin. "What does it matter if it was or it wasn't? He got what he deserved, didn't he? If you like, we can talk about it over dinner. There's a new Greek restaurant—circle dancing, smashing plates, the whole Greek magilla. Vice-President Agnew's cousin owns it, so it gets a very interesting clientele."

She couldn't believe it. He wasn't blackmailing her—he was hitting on her! "I don't think it's appropriate to date co-workers, Mr. Gridley."

"But we both work for Uncle Sam. There's millions of us."

She did not see anything wrong in dating anyone she pleased, but any excuse to turn down a vile creature who was at least ten years too old and gave her the willies would do just fine. "I'm sure it would be fun, but I don't think it would be wise."

"You don't know what you're missing, Miss DeWolfe. No woman ever said E. Grayson Gridley didn't show her a good time."

For a brief instant she considered the offer. She knew people with connections to the Weathermen who might be able to get a warning to Leary. Could she learn enough to save Leary by pumping Gridley for information? No, it was too much of a long-shot, and she was here to bring Nixon down. She was much too close to success to be distracted or diverted.

"Thank you anyway, Mr. Gridley. I'm very flattered."

"E. Grayson Gridley doesn't give up so easily, Miss DeWolfe. But I have to run. Make sure Bob gives that to the President."

"I'll give it to his secretary right away. Good-bye, Mr. Gridley."

"Not good-bye, Miss DeWolfe. Au revoir."

Chapter 7

Navy Men

A PRESIDENTIAL APPOINTMENT REQUIRED NIXON'S SIGNATURE, THE WINE FOR A state dinner needed to be approved…a dozen routine decisions required his attention. The last mixed law enforcement with diplomacy. Haldeman told him, "The C.I.A. has pinpointed Leary's hideout in Algiers. Gridley wants to go in there and snatch him."

Nixon read the update: Leary was lying low in Algeria, a major oil producer and land of one of America's oldest enemies, the Barbary Pirates. Snatching Leary would give the Arabs one more excuse to extend the embargo. "No, it's not worth pissing the rag-heads off any worse than they already are," Nixon said. "Tell Gridley it's just bad timing."

"He won't be happy about it, sir."

"Dammit, I'm not happy about it either, but he's a team player."

"He was hoping to use it for cover over that Shafer Commission report."

"That damn thing again? I told everybody to stonewall it."

"He's the drug czar, and it's all the press asks him about since it leaked. He thinks bringing in Leary will cool things down."

The study had been commissioned by Congress to determine the truth about marijuana once and for all, and Nixon had named all eleven members, stacking it with tough, anti-crime representatives. Chaired by a former governor of Pennsylvania named Shafer, who had a reputation as a law-and-order Republican and was angling for a federal judgeship, Nixon assumed they would rubber-stamp the war on drugs and be done with it. But to Nixon's great surprise, they took their job seriously and evaluated evidence impartially. Their report stated that marijuana had never killed anybody, did not lead to harder drugs, and was much less harmful than alcohol or tobacco. Given the facts, they concluded the laws against it were arbitrary, irrational, and downright un-American. All eleven members recommended it be decriminalized so resources would not be squandered on something which was not a real problem.

Nixon was not the kind to have his beliefs refuted by mere facts. When Haldeman gave him the report and told him what was in it, Nixon had stood up, kicked it across the Oval Office like a football, and screamed,

"Fucking bleeding hearts!"

"Bob, did that damned report say anything about energy?"

Haldeman seemed surprised. "Energy, Mr. President? No, sir, I don't think so."

Perhaps, Nixon thought, it was time to read it. "Get it for me, Bob, but keep it to yourself. If the press finds out I've even looked at it they'll say Nixon's going soft on drugs. They'd tear into me like piranha. Fucking piranha. It wouldn't be pretty."

"No, sir."

"Bob, play 'what if' with me on this energy thing."

"Of course, Mr. President."

"What if there is something that could replace oil, really kick its ass, and I decide we move on it? What opposition would it stir up?"

"The oil companies, for starters."

"Yes, the good ol' boys will throw a two-step shit fit. Tell me if I've got this right. The way those scientists explained it, if we would find enough of it this biomass crap could free us from oil if we used it to make cheap wood alcohol…right?"

"That's how I understood it."

"But the boys over at Agriculture came back and said it was impractical because no one crop could do the job…right?"

"Yes, sir."

Nixon went to his globe and gave it a spin. Twirling the sphere helped him think. Turf wars and leaks were inevitable on something this crazy. Best to keep everybody out of the loop. "Bob, don't tell Ehrlichman or Mitchell or Bullcannon about this. I don't want to get them riled up over nothing if it doesn't pan out. This is on a need-to-know basis, and not even you need to know. For now, everybody but me is out of the loop…understand?"

"Of course, Mr. President."

That night Nixon stayed up late, browsing the materials Mosby left. He was not trained in chemistry or engineering and he didn't read German. The only one on his staff who did was Kissinger, and he was the last person Nixon wanted in on this nutty scheme. If it went nowhere, he didn't want anyone to know he had even considered it. And if it leaked, what would the Kennedys say? Nixon wants to grow fuel to save the country? No. The bastards would say Nixon wants to grow dope.

He needed someone to evaluate it, someone with technical expertise, someone young and bright and green who could keep his mouth shut. No one came to mind, so he had Rose Mary bring him the files of young appointees who owed their jobs to him. Over the next few days, he spent hours in the Lincoln sitting room, leafing through the files of foreign service officers from State, economists from Treasury, MBA's from Commerce, lawyers from Justice, and military officers from Defense. He glanced at their photos, scanned their records, and reviewed job histories and academic transcripts. Nobody fit the bill until he opened a folder and recognized the tall, redheaded Navy lieutenant who had driven him in the inaugural, the one who'd rescued Tricia and Julie. The boy's name was Mulligan. He had been a star tight end at Annapolis, so he understood teamwork. He had straight A's in chemistry and mechanical engineering, rigorous subjects at the Academy. And three years of German. More A's. The boy had the qualifications, and it was Nixon who had promoted him. He might be trusted.

Rescuing Nixon's daughters put Mulligan on the Navy's fast track. After driving Nixon's limo in the inaugural, he was promoted to full lieutenant, months ahead of anybody else in his class, and transferred to the Pentagon and assinged to the ultra-secret Office of Strategic Influence, the O.S.I. Considered a plum assignment, the routine was deadly dull. He quickly came to despise his commander, the pompous Admiral Oarwell.

He got a small apartment in the historic Old Town section of Alexandria, and had a full social life, but no steady girl. He was looking forward to his tour at the O.S.I. being up, and had put in a request for sea duty on a destroyer in the Pacific or the Mediterranean.

One morning he was in his cubicle when the admiral came in. He leaped to attention. "Good morning, Admiral Oarwell, sir."

The admiral snarled, "Report to the White House, on the double."

"Aye, sir. What is it? Courier duty again?"

"How the hell should I know?" the admiral snarled, loud, so everybody could hear. "Maybe they still think you're a fucking hero for a simple rescue mission."

He had been to the White House twice before, picking up sealed pouches to deliver to the Pentagon, a glorified errand boy. Whatever this was, he was glad for the chance to get away from the asshole admiral.

He went to the Pentagon parking lot, opened the door of his turquoise

1965 Buick Wildcat, and undid the latches to the convertible top. As it was going down he took off his white saucer hat, examined his hairline in the mirror, and sighed. He was convinced it was the military code of uniformity, which mandated the incessant wearing of tight hats, hot or cold, rain or shine, that was making his hairline recede like the outgoing tide.

A Marine guard at the White House gate saluted and checked his ID; a valet took his car; a Secret Service agent escorted him inside. He assumed he would pick up a pouch and be on his way, and was surprised when the agent led him deep into the West Wing and pointed to a door. "In there."

The sign read: John Ehrlichman, Counsel to the President. He knocked, and from inside a grouchy voice bellowed, "It's open."

He went in, and Ehrlichman raised his egg-shaped, nearly bald head. "You Mulligan?"

"Aye, sir."

Ehrlichman flipped an intercom switch. "That lieutenant's here."

A female voice replied, "Come right down. I'll let him know."

Ehrlichman took him down the hall and past a U.S. Air Force colonel sitting on a chair by a narrow door. In the colonel's lap, handcuffed to his wrist, was an attaché case. Mulligan felt a creepy chill. Could it be what the Secret Service called the "football" with America's nuclear missile launch codes?

Ehrlichman knocked, appeared to count to five, and opened the door. "He's here, sir."

A familiar baritone voice said, "Send him in."

As the door closed behind him Mulligan's heart was thumping like Indian war drums. Across the room at a huge desk, silhouetted against sunlit windows and writing furiously, was the most powerful man in the world, Richard Milhous Nixon, the thirty-seventh President of the United States.

What was the protocol? Nixon was his Commander-in-Chief, but he wore no uniform. Mulligan went blank, unable to remember if saluting a superior out of uniform was optional or mandatory. Better safe than sorry. He gave a snappy salute. "Lt. Mulligan reporting, Mr. President, sir."

Nixon kept writing, muttered, "Fucking camel jockeys," and scratched something out.

Perhaps Nixon hadn't heard? Still holding the salute, Mulligan repeated himself, but louder, "Lt. Mulligan, reporting, Mr. President, sir."

Nixon glanced up. "At ease, Lieutenant. I'll just be a minute. Feel free to look around. There's a lot of history in here."

The office was indeed oval, no corners anywhere. Abraham Lincoln, Theodore Roosevelt, and Calvin Coolidge gazed down from the walls. He had been here before, in 1962 when JFK was President, with Troop 17 of the Milltowne Boy Scouts. He remembered that Franklin Roosevelt, Thomas Jefferson, and Woodrow Wilson hung on Kennedy's walls because his buddy McGill bitched that there wasn't a single Republican. McGill would be happy to learn there were no Democrats on Nixon's walls.

He was drawn to a bookcase filled with photographs of Nixon with dignitaries and celebrities—Eisenhower, Churchill, DeGaulle, John Wayne, Lana Turner, Bob Hope and Bing Crosby, Mickey Mantle, even Elvis Presley.

He heard a click, and looked up to see Nixon say into the intercom, "It's ready, Rose Mary."

"I'll be right in, Mr. President," replied a female voice.

Nixon took off his glasses and looked at him. "Good to see you, Lieutenant. How have you been?"

"Very well, Mr. President. I'd like to thank you for everything you've done for me."

"Nonsense," Nixon said with a wave of a hand. "You saved my daughters' lives. I could never repay you for that. It was a brave thing you did."

"We were never in danger, sir, and the crew—"

"Yes, yes, I know, I know…all in a day's work. That's the Navy way. And that's why I called you in, son. I have a job for you, if you're interested."

"Anything you want me to do, sir, I'll do it."

"That's what I expect from a Navy man. Annapolis, right?"

"Aye, sir. Class of '70."

"I'm Navy too, you know. Direct commission. Aviation supply. Spent most of my time in New Caledonia, in the Solomon Islands, outfitting our flyboys to fight the Japs by day and playing poker every night."

"Uh…poker, Mr. President?"

"We had a lot of time to kill."

The door opened and a tall, buxomy, middle-aged woman with short brownish-red hair came in. Nixon said, "This is my secretary, Rose Mary Woods. Rose Mary, this is Lt. Mulligan."

"My pleasure, Ma'am."

She acknowledged him with a nod as Nixon said, "Anything the

Lieutenant needs, anything at all, you make sure he gets it."

"Yes, Mr. President," she said as Nixon handed her his writing pad. "Nice meeting you, Lieutenant."

When the door closed Nixon put a finger to his mouth. "Ssshh." He walked to a small closet, opened the door, and stepped inside. Mulligan could hear clicking sounds, like switches on a tape recorder. Nixon came out, shut the door and said in normal voice, "Son, I'll get right to the point. I'm taking a lot of heat on this manifesto thing. That bastard Bobby's got his bull, bluff and bluster schtick down to a sound bite. He's killing me with it. Killing me."

"Aye, sir, I've heard him."

"The truth is, Nixon's working on it for the American people. Oh yes, Nixon's working on it. Things are brewing in the oven…which is where you come in. I'd like you to look into something for me."

"Uh…*me*, Mr. President?"

"Yes, but you can't discuss it with anyone, anyone at all. This is top-secret. Super top-secret. Is that understood, Lieutenant?"

"Aye, sir."

Nixon smiled. "Now let me show you something very interesting."

Nixon opened another closet, picked up two rolls of blueprints, and pointed to a footlocker on the floor. "Bring that to the coffee table, Lieutenant, and take everything out."

Mulligan placed the contents on the table—photo albums, books, and stacks and stacks of old reports.

Nixon said, "Take a look. It's mostly old experiments from the Ford and I.G. Farben companies. A lot of it's in German."

There were reports of ten, twenty, a hundred pages each, maybe four thousand pages in all. Most were labeled FORD MOTOR CO., Inc., and many of those were in German. Others were labeled I.G. FARBEN, G.m.b.H., and were all in German. Some dated before World War I. There were also U.S. government pamphlets from the Agriculture Department, and a book on something called "chemurgy."

"Now this stuff is pretty technical," Nixon said. "I'd evaluate it myself, but Nixon's not technically trained, Nixon's legally trained. That's why I called you in. If there's anything to this crackpot idea, I need to know it. The President of the United States can't be chasing a pot of gold if there's nothing at the end of the rainbow but a bucket of piss water. Understand?"

"I, uh…I think so, Mr. President."

"Good," Nixon said, rubbing his hands as if to warm them up. "Now, I can't go through channels on this. Can't afford leaks. It's you and me on this, Lieutenant, you and me alone. Nobody else is to know, and I mean nobody. Understand?"

"Aye, aye, Mr. President."

"Good. Now, you've had a lot of chemistry and engineering, and I saw German in your transcript."

"I read it better than I speak it, but I know my way around a laboratory and an engine room. Someday I'll go for a doctorate."

"Modesty and ambition. I like that, Lieutenant. Like it a lot. It's a good combination, taken me a long way. But let's get down to business."

"Aye, sir."

"Now, some people tell me that the key to energy independence is getting off an economy based on petroleum and into an economy based on carbohydrates from something called biomass. Does that make sense to you?"

"Aye, sir. Depending on the source, biomass can be burned by direct combustion, or processed by—"

"Save it," Nixon said with a wave of his hands. "Take a look at these...."

Mulligan listened as Nixon opened up an album and described photos of Model-T's, of Henry Ford hitting a car with a sledge hammer, and white-smocked scientists on ladders in fields measuring what looked like bamboo. "So from what they tell me, Lieutenant, Ford was serious about making cars that ran on alcohol, especially methanol. What do you think of the idea? Was Ford on the right track?"

"It's hard to say, but they use methanol for racing cars."

"So I'm told."

"Mr. President, I'm no farmer, but these plants look like...I don't know, bamboo or something."

Nixon gave him a knowing look. "It's called hemp, Lieutenant."

"You mean the stuff they use to make rope?"

"That's where things get very strange," Nixon said in a mysterious tone. "It's almost like somebody's tried to erase the word from the language, like it never existed."

"I...I don't understand."

"They taught you how to sail at Annapolis, didn't they, Lieutenant? Salt spray in your face, the wind at your back?"

"Oh, yes, sir. It's every Middie's favorite course. And the town of

Annapolis calls itself the sailing capital of the world. Everybody's a sailor."

"Do you know what sails are made of?"

"Excuse me?"

"What are sails made of?"

"I, uh...I believe they're made of Nylon, Mr. President."

The corners of Nixon's mouth turned up a smile. "Quite right, quite right. But before that what were they made of...back in the olden days?"

"Uh...probably canvas, Mr. President."

"Good! But what's it made from? A canvas tree, a canvas root...what?"

"I don't know, Mr. President, I'd only be guessing."

"Lieutenant, there's a dictionary on that shelf. I want you to look some things up. Start with canvas. Read it out loud."

Mulligan found it. "It's derived from the Dutch 'kanvass,' spelled with a 'k,' which comes from the Latin 'cannabis,' with a 'c' which in turn comes from the Greek, 'kannabis', with a 'k': 'A coarse hempen cloth used for tents, sails of ships, and other purposes.'"

"Now look up hemp."

He flipped to it. "'Cannabis sativa.' Oh, I see...so canvas gets its name from the plant it comes from. But, but sir,...isn't cannabis...isn't it marijuana?"

Nixon grinned. "You catch on fast, Lieutenant."

"Are you saying sails were made from marijuana, Mr. President?"

"I learned just last week that cannabis and hemp and marijuana are all different names for the same family of plants. They tell me it's like dogs. Like tiny toy poodles and big Great Danes are different varieties, but they're both still dogs. But you can see how it could create political problems if I were to propose doing what Henry Ford wanted to do and grow hemp for fuel?"

"Politics isn't my area, Mr. President."

"Well, it damn sure is mine...and I smell a rat. I don't know where the bodies are buried, but I smell a conspiracy so big and so wide and so deep not even Henry Ford himself could stand up against it."

"A *conspiracy*, Mr. President?"

"Yes, but don't trouble yourself over that, Lieutenant, leave that to Nixon. Your job is to evaluate the science. The President of the United States can't be pissing into the wind and having it blow back his face."

"Uh...no, sir, Mr. President."

"Lieutenant, if Henry Ford was right, we have a chance to bury the camel jockeys in the sandbox once and for all. If Ford thought he could do it in the Thirties, why can't Nixon do it in the Seventies?"

"It should be much easier now. There's been a lot of progress."

"My thinking exactly," Nixon said as he tilted way back in his chair, folded his hands and gazed at the ceiling, his mind a million miles away. "Energy independence is music to my ears," Nixon said, then he sang, "Happy days are here again…ha!"

"I saw you play that song on the piano on TV one time, Mr. President," Mulligan said with admiration. "You're pretty good, sir."

Nixon was shining with pride. "Let's just say Nixon can hold his own on the ivories."

Rose Mary's voice squawked over the intercom, "The Topeka Jaycees are here for the ceremony, Mr. President."

"Be right there, Rose," Nixon said, and pointed at him. "Lieutenant, your job is to see that I know everything there is to know about this before I decide whether to keep going or shit-can it. Now…are you the man for the job…yes or no? Look these over before you answer, and don't bull-shit me if you're not. I won't be long."

Mulligan found himself alone in the Oval Office with the ghosts of history. He leafed through the papers: the chemistry was fairly simple, and the engineering blueprints were four decades out of date.

Twenty minutes later Nixon returned and closed the door. "So what do you think, Lieutenant? Are you the man for the job…yes or no?"

"Sir, my German isn't what it could be, but from what I can see the science is basic. Aye sir, I can evaluate it for you. But I'll need a little time."

"How much time? A week?"

"There's a lot here."

"A month? Can you do it in a month?"

"I…uh…I think so, sir."

"Not good enough, Lieutenant. Can you do it—yes or no?"

"Yes, sir. I'm sure of it."

"Good. That's the kind of can-do spirit that's made this country great. Now I'm going to be doing a lot of traveling in the next few weeks. When you're the President and you're in trouble…travel. People kiss your ass everywhere you go and the press forgets about your problems. Remember that if you ever get to be President."

"Aye…uh, I will, Mr. President."

"Good. So, we'll meet here in a month. I've arranged for space across the street. If there's anything you need, anything at all, you just let Rose know. I want you to eat, sleep and dream this mission till you get it right."

Mulligan unrolled one of the blueprints as wide as his arms could go. "I'll need a drafting table, someplace I can spread out, and—"

There was a knock at the door, and exactly five seconds later Haldeman poked his head in. "Sir, *Army One* is landing."

"Be right there, Bob." Nixon rose to his feet. "Now, remember, Lieutenant, no one, and I mean no one, is to know what we've discussed."

"Aye, aye, Mr. President. You can count on me."

Nixon patted him on the shoulder. "I know I can, son, because you're a Navy man, just like me."

Chapter 8

The Duck Test

R OSE MARY WOODS SAID, "I'LL HAVE SOMEONE SHOW YOU TO YOUR NEW office, Lieutenant." She flicked an intercom switch. "Catherine, would you come in here, please."

A tall, athletic woman with auburn hair came in. Rose Mary introduced her as "Miss DeWolfe," explained the task, and handed her a set of keys. Mulligan walked beside her as she led him through the White House corridors and across the street. She was about his age, and while not exactly beautiful, she was attractive, dignified, and moved with a graceful, equine self-confidence he found oddly compelling. Her badge read "Catherine DeWolfe." Could she be one of *the* DeWolfe's?

"What is it you'll be doing, Lieutenant?" she asked in a soft, husky voice as she took him up the steps and into the EOB.

"I'm not at liberty to say."

"Well, whatever it is, Miss Woods says we're to take good care of you." She led him down to the sub-basement, showed him to a door, and used the keys to open it. The bare-bones office was Spartan and windowless. "You don't have much of a view, Lieutenant."

"I'll be too busy to notice."

She handed him the keys. "Well, if you need anything, be sure to call Miss Woods' office."

"Should I ask for you?" he said.

"You can if you like, but I'm sure anyone there will be able to help."

He busted butt twenty hours a day, evaluating blueprints, translating German experiments, trying to make sense of the mish-mash of research projects. He slept on the couch in his EOB office, played pickup basketball in the EOB gym, ate in the EOB cafeteria, got a haircut in the EOB barbershop, even bowled on the EOB lanes.

Rose Mary's office supplied everything he asked for, from chemistry texts to pepperoni pizzas, and when he was lucky, it was the husky-voiced Miss DeWolfe who took his request and delivered it. At night after turning in, scrunched up on the too-short couch, he would fantasize about making love to the delightful, delicious, delovely Miss DeWolfe.

A month later, report in hand, he entered Rose Mary Woods' office.

"The President is in a bad mood, Lieutenant. Try not to upset him."

"What's the matter?"

She pointed to the headline in the *Washington Post:* "Dollar Hits Record Low" and switched on her intercom. "Lt. Mulligan is here."

An angry voice barked, "Send him the hell in."

He strode through the door and came to attention and saluted in front of Nixon's desk. Nixon dispensed with pleasantries. "At ease, Lieutenant. Just let me have it."

"Aye, sir." He handed Nixon his seventy-eight-page, double-spaced report: *ALTERNATIVE FUELS: Sources and Solutions.* "I apologize for the typos, sir, but you said not to let anyone know, so I typed it myself."

"Quite right," Nixon said as he leafed through, not reading a word. He removed his glasses. "So was Ford right? Is it do-able…yes or fucking no?"

"Yes, sir, Mr. President. Absolutely. With an all-out effort, we could convert to a carbohydrate economy in three or four years."

Nixon wrinkled his forehead, obviously skeptical. "That's pretty damn fast, Lieutenant, even for a can-do optimist like Nixon."

"I came at it from a military perspective, Mr. President. I assumed we were at war, with a command economy, like World War II."

"A command economy? Yes, it sure would be fun to be President in times like that," Nixon said. "I could really get something done without the damned Congress getting in the way all the time. Three or four years you say?"

"Aye, sir. Five, tops."

"Hmmm…."

"Mr. President, it's not like we have to reinvent the wheel. New cars can be easily modified right on the assembly line, with almost no increase in production costs. The big problem is older cars. Alcohols are more corrosive than gasoline, so seals and hoses would have to be replaced with something more resistant, like stainless steel. And there are plastics that can do the job. We're only talking a few hoses and a couple of hours for a mechanic to install a conversion kit. There would be some cold-weather starting problems, but there are ways around that. Alcohol isn't as good in miles-per-gallon, so you'd have to fill up more often, but in miles-per-dollar, the cost of driving will be about half as much as with gasoline."

Nixon raised his hand, like a kid in a classroom. "So it's a trade-off? You'd have to fill up more often, but it would be cheaper?"

"Aye, sir…a lot cheaper, so for most people it'll be worth the trade off.

And both ethanol and methanol have higher octane ratings than gasoline, they don't pollute, and—"

"I don't give a rat's ass about the goddamned pollution," Nixon said, waving his hand as if shooing away a fly. "How much will it cost?"

"Well, sir, we would need processing and delivery systems—"

"How damned much?"

Mulligan took a breath and gave it his best guess. "Less than putting a man on the moon, Mr. President."

"Ha!" Nixon laughed. "Now you're thinking like a politician, Lieutenant. So say I'm Joe Sixpack, with an average car. What's it cost me?"

"I gave that a lot of thought, sir. I learned cars have a maximum average life of about fifteen years. I wasn't sure where to start until I remembered what my best friend's father used to say. They owned a car dealership, Chevrolets and Cadillacs, and his dad used to say the average car on the road was a six-year-old Pontiac, so—"

"How in the hell did he figure that?"

"I never asked, but he knew cars, and it seemed like as good a bench-mark as any. I looked at every six-year old Pontiac in the line, asked twenty different mechanics and car dealers to make a guess as to what it would take to convert them, and averaged the guesses out. I think a safe estimate is $160 per car, for both parts and labor."

Nixon was quiet for a moment. "So are you telling me that cars already on the road could be converted for $160?"

"Aye, sir, on average."

Nixon tapped his pencil on his desk. "That's not bad when you think about it. Easy enough to do with tax credits. Voters love tax credits, and if they thought they were getting back at the camel jockeys, it could even be good for the country's morale. Hmmm..." Nixon put on his glasses and leafed through the report like a ten-year-old with a new comic book. "Who did the drawings?"

"I did, sir. They're just engineering renderings, and a few diagrams."

"Looks professional to me. So $160 to convert a car?"

"Aye, sir, in that ballpark. It seems like a small price to pay in time of war, but in peacetime you're talking politics, and that's not my area."

"It may not be your area, Lieutenant, but it damn sure is mine."

The next morning, Nixon was gazing out of the Oval Office window, observing with satisfaction as the new, loyal gardeners spread bags of God-knows-what on the lawn. Haldeman brought in the daily newspapers and the Presidential Daily Briefing, the PDB. "Good morning, Mr. President."

"Anything besides the damned gas lines in the news, Bob?" Nixon asked as he took the papers. "A flood maybe, or a tornado somewhere?"

"Sorry, Mr. President. There are no catastrophes to report."

"Shit," Nixon said as he spread out the newspapers on his desk. Angry motorists glared off the front pages. "Dammit, I want some good news."

"There is one thing, sir. Gridley reports Timothy Leary fell out with the Black Panthers and fled to Switzerland, and some rock stars may go there to make a record with him."

Nixon snorted with contempt. "Like that time they all sat around naked in that asshole John Lennon's hotel room singing 'Give Peace A Chance.' A 'bed-in' they called it. What a crock of shit. So, will the Swiss extradite him so we can put his ass away for good?"

"Uncertain, sir. They have a reputation for harboring political exiles."

"Dammit Bob, Leary's a druggie. There's no politics involved."

"I know, Mr. President, but the Swiss can be assholes."

"Well, do everything we can. Back Gridley to the hilt. I want the bastard behind bars!"

"Yes, sir. We should go over your schedule."

"Oh, if we have to," Nixon said. "What piss-ants are sucking up today?"

"You meet with the presidents of Exxon and Chevron at nine about drilling in the Arctic Wildlife Preserve, then the Fed chairman on the currency crisis, then Senator Dirksen—he'll try to twist your arm on the farm bill—then lunch with the Saudi ambassador—"

"Why the hell am I eating lunch with that asshole?"

"So the public will think you're working on the oil crisis."

"Yes, yes, it's all in the damned perception."

It was time, Nixon thought, to let Haldeman in on the secret. But he did not want the conversation recorded. Nixon sidled up to Haldeman, who, being ignorant of the secret taping system, thought Nixon was exhibiting one of his quirky forms of intimacy. "Bob, I've stumbled over a conspiracy. I've suspected it for a while, but now I'm sure of it."

"A conspiracy, Mr. President?"

"Shhh. Keep it down. I need to know how deep it goes."

Haldeman lowered his voice. "I'll call the F.B.I., and—"

"No, since Edgar died, I don't know who to trust over there."

"The C.I.A. can—"

"No, those Ivy League twits are all Kennedyites. If they get wind of this, they'll squeeze me like a ripe tomato. Don't go through channels, Bob. I want my own people on this, people I can trust."

"What is it you want done, sir? And who do you have in mind?"

"I want a team of boys like I had when I nailed Alger Hiss with *The Pumpkin Papers*. We took on the whole damned Truman administration, and we beat their asses fucking purple."

"Will this be a dirty tricks operation, Mr. President?"

"No, that can come later. What we need is gumshoe detective work. A few good boys with brains, boys who can keep their mouths shut. But keep it away from our main people. If we let anybody in on it, there'll be turf wars out the ass…and that means leaks. And if this leaks, it will be Nixon who gets pissed on…understand?"

"Not exactly, sir."

"You don't need to, not yet anyway. Now, I've got a young Navy officer who can oversee the job on the technical side, but I don't know about his political skills. He seems like a good conservative, Annapolis and all, but his father's a union man. Steel, I think."

"Not good, Mr. President. Next to coal, steel's the worst."

"My point exactly. He couldn't possibly understand how conservative backs get scratched. We need somebody who knows how things get done in the party."

"I have just the man on my staff. You've met him. Rudy Duberman."

"Is he always combing his hair like he's a movie star?"

"That's him, but you'll like him, Mr. President. He understands how Republicans think. Sir, may I ask, just what kind of conspiracy is it?"

Nixon cupped his hand over his mouth and whispered, "Energy, Bob, energy. It's about America's energy supply."

"But the Arabs—"

"No, this is an all-American affair. It's got dollar signs all over it."

"If you told me more, sir, I could advise you better."

Maybe it was time to let somebody else in on it? "You promise you won't think I'm taking some of that LSD and, oh, what do the hippies call it—'traveling?'"

"I believe they call it 'tripping,' Mr. President."

"Whatever. Bob, I've learned somebody went to a lot of trouble to shut down Henry Ford's research on new sources of energy back in the 1930's.

I need to know who they were and how they did it so I'll know whose balls we have to crush if I move on it."

"Sir, that was a long time ago. Won't the trail be cold?"

"Yes, but the stink's still in the air. So, who's going to be against me?"

"The oil companies for sure."

"Yes, it could cost us the oil patch."

"Perhaps you should look at who might be on your side."

"I'm ahead of you there. With the right incentives, Detroit will lead the parade. Hell, Michigan will almost offset Texas by itself, plus the whole damned farm belt will be with us—two hundred percent."

"Why is that, sir?"

"Because when the oil patch loses, the farm belt wins. Every time."

"I don't under—"

"You know what the last straw was for me, Bob?"

"No, sir, I—"

"When I learned they use methanol in the Indianapolis 500."

"I don't—"

"Dammit, Bob, if methanol is good enough for Indy cars, why isn't it good enough for your car? I'll tell you why, money…m-o-n-e-fucking-*y*. Money. That's why there's gasoline in your car and not methanol…money!"

Nixon stretched a kink out of his back. "We have to find out who pulled it off, how they did it, and what kind of conspiracy it was. Was it like the Hiss case, with drop-offs and passwords and code names? Or was it a wink-and-a-nod kind of conspiracy? Those work the best."

Haldeman seemed worried. "You're sure about this, Mr. President?"

"Dammit, Bob, I know conspiracies," Nixon said. "Put it to the duck test. If it walks like a duck, quacks like a duck, and smells like a duck, you can bet your sweet-and-sour ass—it's a fucking duck."

"Yes, sir."

"And if I'm right about this, and we can pull this off.…"

Nixon fell silent, sipping coffee as he imagined millions of prosperous farmers across the Great Plains, from Ohio to Colorado, from Texas to North Dakota, all of them wearing straw hats and blue overalls and driving shiny red tractors as they harvested towering fields of energy plants and carted them to market in horse-drawn wagons—no, not right—in semitrailer trucks—and endless trains of railroad cars, and fleets of barges on the rivers of the Mississippi watershed delivering energy crops to spanking-clean factories where hundreds of thousands of highly-paid, nonunion workers in white hardhats converted America's bounty into fuel for two-hundred million motorists. It was a grand vision, as wondrous as any he had ever dreamed, in which all of America, even New York City, loved their cars, breathed clean air, and gratefully voted Republican, election after election after election.

———————————

Chapter 9

Follow the Money

MCGILL PRACTICED HIS SALES PITCH AS HE DROVE HIS VAN TO VINCE'S. HIS Grampa Art had always told him he'd make a hell of a salesman if he ever came into the car business, and growing up he endured many of his grandfather's lectures on the art of salesmanship. It wasn't love that made the world go round—it was sales. And it wasn't scientists or politicians or capitalists who made America great—but its salesmen. According to Grampa Art, without salesmen, the wheels of commerce did not turn, and civilization came to a standstill.

He felt infused with the can-do mentality Grampa Art must have felt in the Roaring Twenties, back from victory in the "war to end all wars," when the business of America was business, and a good salesman could do no wrong. If he could close the sale today, it would change his life.

He drove past the Bay Bridge exit for San Francisco and continued south through Oakland, taking the off-ramp at San Ricardo and using a map to find the house. Vince's mom answered and sent him around back to a shop in the garage. The big door was wide open, and Vince was at a workbench, wearing welding goggles, enveloped in smoke, holding a hissing acetylene torch in one hand and a wire rod in the other. On a nearby shelf, Birds stood in rows, like a platoon of soldiers in formation. McGill called out, "Hey man, what's happening?"

"Hang on a sec," Vince said. "I'm just finishing up on this one."

McGill walked over to watch as Vince brazed on the alligator clip, turned off the torch, took off the goggles, loosened the vise and proudly handed McGill the finished Bird.

"Looks good," McGill said.

"Yeah, I'm gettin' better," Vince said. "A lot depends on the fork. Good forks are tough to find."

McGill walked to the shelf and examined a few of the other Birds in the flock. Each was unique. "How long's it take to make one?"

"You can do 'em pretty quick once you're all set up and have the parts ready to go," Vince said as he pointed to the bins at the front of the bench.

"Looks like a production line in a car factory."

"Yeah, pretty close."

It was time to start the pitch. He began with a subject he knew scared the living crap out of most people—the law. "You know, Vince, I've been thinking a corporation is the way we ought to go on this. It'll make it easier to bring in investors, and there are tax advantages."

"What do you mean, *we?*" Vince said, flushing an angry crimson. "What the hell makes you think I need you for anything?"

"Come on, man, you don't really think you can pull this off by yourself, do you? And I'll save us big on legal stuff. I believe in this sucker. It's like the American Dream. You know what the Kaiser cement trucks say about getting rich, don't you?"

Kaiser Construction's fleet of cement trucks, with their eye-catching *FIND A NEED AND FILL IT* slogan rotating on the cement tanks, were a familiar sight all over Northern California.

Vince was puzzled. "Everybody's seen those trucks. What's it have to do with getting rich?"

"It's a take-off on what Henry Kaiser said about making money, that's what. What he really said was, 'The way to make money in America is to identify a need, and then fill that need.'"

"Yeah? So?" Vince did not seem to be impressed.

"Look man, there's a real need out there for a better roach clip. You've heard the saying 'Build a better mousetrap and the world will beat a path to your door,' haven't you?"

"I've been saying all along it's the world's best clip."

McGill quickly agreed. "And you're absolutely right. Nothing else is even close. Problem is, how do we make money off it? That's the key. Now between you and me, if I thought I could go out and make Birds on my own, I wouldn't even bother talking to you. I'd just go do it."

Vince's shoulders hunched up, like a cat about to scratch your eyes out, or a boxer ready to counter-punch. "What do you mean? It's mine!"

It was precisely the reaction McGill was hoping for. "Look, you own the clip, but you don't own the idea. That's in the public domain."

"The *what?*"

"The public domain. Look man, you found a clip made out of a fork that looks like a bird, but you didn't invent it or even know who did. Now, it looks to me like the guy who made the first one didn't know what he had. The dumb-ass put it up for grabs, which means you can come along and make 'em, and he can't do shit about it. But anybody else can too."

Vince calmed down a bit, lost in thought. Time to set the hook.

"Look, Vince, if somebody's got a patent on the design, we're shit outta luck. Now are you sure you don't know who made it?"

"How many times I gotta tell you? *No!* And quit saying *we.*"

McGill backed off, let him run with the line for a bit, let the reel play out. "Okay, so say it's a one-of-a-kind somebody made for an art class, or say there's some hippie cranking 'em out over in Haight Ashbury. It doesn't matter, because he's put it up for grabs. You don't want to screw up like he did, do you?"

Vince's facade of bravado was cracking. "So you're telling me anybody can just come along and make 'em?"

"It's what you're doing, isn't it?"

Vince sighed and took a deep breath. Time to reel him in. "Look, Vince, you need a partner who can take care of the legal stuff so you're not throwing money away on shysters. I'm your guy."

"If anybody can come along and make 'em, then what do I need a lawyer for? And you're not even a real lawyer."

"I am too, I just haven't taken the bar exam yet, that's all. I can do anything any lawyer can do except represent a client before a judge. But I'm a hell of a lot more than just a lawyer. I've got a plan to make this work. And I say we start with a strategy that will cover our asses when somebody tries to copycat us. I say we go the trademark route."

Vince gave him a wary stare. "The trademark route?"

"Yeah. We protect the name with a trademark. Costs three hundred bucks."

Vince was incredulous. "Three hundred…for a *name?*"

"Man, that's *cheap.* It's like Coca-Cola. Anybody can make a cola, but they can't call it Coke. That name's worth, what, maybe a billion dollars? It's why Coke's number one and Pepsi's number two. It's the name. Same thing with The Bird. If we protect the name, nobody but us can use it on roach clips. They can make a clip out of a fork, but they better not call it The Bird, or we'll sue their asses off. See what I mean?"

Vince grunted as he reached in his pocket and pulled out a pack of Marlboros. "So this trademark thing protects me?"

"Lawyers have a saying that copyrights, patents, and trademarks are only worth as much as you have to defend 'em. And I'll defend us for free. The name will be ours. Vince, if we do this right and get the Bird out before anyone can copy us, we can corner the market on roach clips."

Vince laughed and flashed a grin. "I like the sound of that."

Vince was stubborn as a rusty hinge, but McGill had his foot in the door. After thirty minutes, McGill closed the deal. They went partners, fifty-fifty. They each would come up with $1,000 to capitalize BirdCo, Incorporated, to manufacture and market the world's greatest roach clip—The Bird. McGill took his portable Remington out of the van and typed up two identical contracts. They signed on the dotted lines, shook hands, cracked a couple of beers, and fired up a joint to seal the deal.

McGill filed the paperwork to set up the corporation. They kept their jobs pounding nails and put half their paychecks into the BirdCo account. Vince spent evenings making Birds in the shop while McGill read up on ad design and the nuts and bolts of mail-order. The ad had to be catchy. A slogan, a photograph, maybe a graphic. He wasn't sure.

He spent a lot of time on the manufacturing problems. The key was raw materials: clips, bases, and forks. Alligator clips were readily available by the gross for 25¢ each. Bases were harder, but after spending a week of lunch hours in phone booths, he found a company in Fremont that made electrical switch boxes which had thousands of two-inch-diameter scrap steel slugs they would sell at 5¢/pound.

The crucial part—the fork—was harder to find in quantity. Much harder. Short-tined salad forks did not work at all. Birds required a dinner fork, and only ones with two-inch tines. On weekends, they scrounged at Goodwill stores, flea markets, and garage sales, but only about one used fork in twenty made a decent Bird.

One Monday, McGill took a day off work, put on a jacket and tie, and made the rounds to every restaurant-supply wholesaler in the Bay Area, but nobody had the right kind of fork. One gray-haired salesman told him flatware styles had changed, and that the forks he wanted had not been produced since the 1950's. American dinner forks were still seven-and-a-half inches long, tip to tip, but now they had a thicker stem and shorter tines, just a skimpy inch-and-a-half long. The new forks were fine for eating, but they made ungainly Birds, with stubby wings and waddly legs. The extra half-inch of tine made all the difference between a Bird that resembled a graceful egret or a squatty duck.

America's two major silverware manufacturers, Oneida, and Reed and Barton, were back in New York and New England. He inquired about old inventory. No luck. He asked about a production run from old dies, and they gave him estimates ranging from $10,000 to $20,000, cash up front. He said he hoped to see them soon.

He was determined to send the Bird into the marketplace with all the legal protection possible. He had a tool-and-die shop make a die and run five thousand bases stamped with the imprint:

THE **BIRD**™
WORLD'S GREATEST CLIP
MADE IN USA
By Genuine Hippies
© 1974 BirdCo, Inc.
San Ricardo, CA

Meanwhile, Vince developed an artisan's touch with the torch. He had a feel for heating the various types of metals just enough to be pliable. He could feather a fork handle into a tail with ease, and for the most delicate task, he used needle-nosed pliers and just the right amount of flame to spiral the outer tines into elegant, curly-cued wings. McGill was all thumbs with a torch, especially on the tines, which he often heated past the flashpoint, watching helplessly as they liquefied, dripped, and puddled up in a molten goop. Too many of his came out gimpy, broken-winged, or both, wasting precious forks. There was an art to making a Bird, and if they could get the process down to where even a klutz like him could make them consistently, anyone could be trained to do it.

One night, McGill went to the shop and found one of Vince's girlfriends sitting on stool, sketching him on an artist's pad as he made Birds. She was pretty good, and McGill asked her, "Think you could draw us a logo?"

"Maybe," she said. "What do you want?"

"I'm seeing a cartoon, halfway between Woody Woodpecker and the Roadrunner."

She picked up a Bird and held it at arm's length, studying it. "How will you use it?"

"For business cards, letterheads, magazine ads...you name it."

"Then you need a simple line drawing, so it will look good small."

McGill wrote up a two-sentence work-for-hire contract on a notepad, paying her $25 to design the logo. She began to sketch, like a carnival artist doing instant portraits. A line here, a stroke there, and The Bird came to life. The friendly, eye-popping logo fired them up all over again.

Vince was ecstatic. "Man, this sucker kicks ass!"

"I can change whatever you don't like," she said. "When you're happy with the sketch, I'll do a master with a precision pen."

With the logo out of the way, McGill got serious about ads. He phoned *Rolling Stone*, *High Times* and *Playboy* for their advertising media kits. He had learned how to do layouts working on his college newspaper, so he went to an art supply store for paste-up boards, glue sticks, and sheets of press-type. He made copies of the logo in many sizes at a copy shop and came up with layouts for several ad formats.

He bought a hand-cranked calculator at a Goodwill store to crunch numbers in a spreadsheet. The how-to books said an ad to the right target audience should produce a response rate of between .002 and two percent. So at ten dollars per order, an ad in *Rolling Stone*, with eight million pot-smoking readers, should generate a minimum of 16,000 orders and gross $160,000. How many magazines were there? How many issues a year? The results were mind-boggling—millions and millions. The Bird was the next Hula-Hoop, the next Frisbee. They'd be millionaires by Christmas. Easy.

He showed Vince the ad he thought would be the most cost-effective.

Vince looked it over. "I gotta admit, McGill, this is pretty good. Maybe I'll keep you around after all."

He showed Vince the spreadsheet for how the ad might do in *Rolling Stone*. "Now, if the mail-order books are right, this ad should pull between .002 and two percent."

"So how many Birds is that?"

"Somewhere between 16,000 and 160,000. Even on the low end, that's a hundred and sixty grand!"

"I like the high end better," Vince said as he looked over the projections. "But do you know how long it'd take us to make 160,000 Birds even if we had the parts? Years and years and years."

"Don't worry about it. With that kind of cash-flow, we'll farm everything out to Hong Kong or Japan."

It was time to unleash the Bird on an unsuspecting public. For the trial run, they chose the big Sunday flea market in Sausalito, across the road from the hippie houseboat colony. They had 187 Birds, and McGill wanted to bring his screw-ups and sell them cheap, but Vince was adamant. "No way, man. They make us look cheesy. Birds are classy."

At five A.M., they hit the road in McGill's van to make their fortunes. After paying the toll for the San Rafael Bridge, they fired up a doobie, put the Beatles' *Abbey Road* in the eight-track, and "Here Comes the Sun" came blasting out of the speakers as the first rays of dawn touched the peaks of Mount Tamalpais.

"It's gonna be a good day, McGill," Vince said. "I can feel it."

"Yeah, me too."

As they approached the Marin shoreline, McGill got an uneasy feeling at the sight of the bleak outcropping of San Quentin prison, its floodlights glowing eerily in the twilight mists. They got off the freeway and rode by the prison, so close they could see figures moving in the guard towers.

"Man, I never want to see the inside of that place," Vince said as he passed the Bird to McGill.

"I went in there a few times for a law-school seminar," McGill said in a pinched voice as he held in a toke. "It's way worse than you think."

Ten minutes later they arrived at the flea market, which was already bustling with energy. As Vince set up the table, McGill took a felt marker and wrote on a piece of cardboard—*World's Best Roach Clip, $10.*

The gates opened at seven, and The Bird was an instant hit. People crowded around, ooohing and aaahhing and forking over money.

"Oh, they're so cute," said the women.

"Really cool," said the men.

They sold out before noon, netting $1,570 after expenses.

McGill drove to the fanciest restaurant on the Sausalito waterfront, where they splurged on caviar and abalone. When the waiter popped the cork on an $80 bottle of Dom Perignon, McGill held his glass up and said, "Here's to The Bird, and to fuck-you money."

Vince shot him a quizzical look. "What in the hell is fuck-you money?"

"You've heard of Humphrey Bogart, haven't you?" McGill said.

"You mean Bogey, from *The Maltese Falcon* and *Casablanca*?"

"Yeah. He said fuck-you money was having enough in the bank to tell anybody you want—*fuck you!*"

Vince grinned. "Then here's to Bogey, the Bird, and to fuck-you money," and he tinked his glass against McGill's.

A few days after delivering his report to Nixon, Mulligan received a call summoning him back to the Oval Office. Ehrlichman was sitting in one corner of the couch reading what looked like a legal brief, and Nixon's speechwriter, Bullcannon, was doing a crossword puzzle on the other end. Nixon and Haldeman entered through another door with a guy Mulligan didn't know. Nixon motioned him over and introduced them. "Lt. Mulligan, Rudy Duberman. You two will be working together."

Mulligan shook Duberman's hand. He was about his own age, five-ten and athletic, like a tennis player, with dark, straight hair that touched his ears, not a hippie's hair, but very long by Nixonian standards.

Nixon called over to his speechwriter, "Bart, come on over here. This is the young Navy officer I've been telling you about. Lieutenant Mulligan, Bart Bullcannon."

Bullcannon came over and put out his hand to shake.

"Bart's my wordsmith," Nixon said, "my Thomas Paine. Makes the words sing right out of my mouth, don't you, Bart?"

Bullcannon chuckled. "I certainly do try, Mr. President."

"All of you, pull up some chairs," Nixon said as he went behind his desk and sat down. When everyone was settled, Nixon said, "Now I've kept this under wraps long enough. What you hear today must not go beyond this room. Is that understood?"

Everyone nodded.

"Good. Now, this damned embargo has brought to light a conspiracy, a threat to our national security."

Bullcannon bobbed up like a cork. "A conspiracy, Mr. President?"

"Lieutenant!" Nixon said, completely surprising him. "You know what I'm talking about, don't you?"

Mulligan gulped, caught off guard. "Uh, you mentioned a conspiracy a few weeks ago, but you told me not to worry about it."

"Worry about it now. Tell them what you've been doing."

Mulligan paused, taking a deep breath. "The President has asked me to evaluate alternative sources of energy to foreign oil, so—"

"Oh, Mr. President!" Bullcannon shouted. "You're working on your manifesto! This is great, sir. I'll write you a manifesto that will put you on Mount Rushmore."

"I hope you get the chance, Bart," Nixon said. "But first we've got a big problem to solve. Go ahead, Lieutenant."

"Aye, sir." Shit, where to start? He had no idea he would have to make a presentation. "Uh, the Agriculture Department estimates we have sixty million acres of arable farmland lying fallow. We're even paying farmers not to grow crops on a lot of it. If that land were planted with energy crops, we could grow our own fuel. The drawbacks are not scientific but political, because it's against the law to grow the one crop that can do the job."

"Ha!" Nixon said, thumping his fist on the desk. "Tell 'em about Henry Ford, Lieutenant."

"Ford wanted to make fuel from biomass. He wanted—"

Bullcannon interupted, "What's this thing called?"

"Chemurgy," Mulligan said. "It's the branch of chemistry that deals with turning plants into industrial products."

"No, not that," Bullcannon said. "What is it that's illegal?"

Nixon jumped in. "It's called hemp, Bart. Know much about it?"

Bullcannon paused, reflecting. "You mean what's used for rope?"

Nixon leaned back, grinning like teenager in on a prank. "That was my response when they told me. And the Lieutenant's when I told him. You and I call it by another name. Know what it is?"

Bullcannon's face tightened in thought. "No, Mr. President, I don't."

Nixon grinned. "We call it...*marijuana*."

Duberman smiled; the corners of Bullcannon's mouth turned down on a frown; Haldeman remained expressionless; Ehrlichman chuckled and said, "I can see why it must seem like a conspiracy."

Nixon leaned forward. "It doesn't seem like a conspiracy, John, it is a conspiracy. Or it was. I can *feel* it. Now Bob, I want you to get the boys whatever they need. John, you run interference in case anybody gets in their way. Bart, you listen in from time to time, keep track of what they're up to. If the press gets wind of this, I want you up to speed for damage control. And all of you, not a word outside this room. No leaks. I'm not saying I'll move on this, because if it's not a sure bet, Nixon won't play the hand. That's how you win at poker. You only bet the hands you know you can win. Understand?"

Everybody nodded.

"Good. Now boys, there's a trail there, it's old, but it's too big to hide. And no one must know Nixon is looking into it. If we're going to pull off this little caper, surprise will be crucial. When we find out who they are, Nixon will deal with them in his own way, in his own time. Your job is to track down who they are and how they did it without anybody knowing what you're doing. Is that perfectly clear?"

"Aye, Mr. President," Mulligan said.

"Absolutely, Mr. President," Duberman said.

Nixon spoke in his gravest voice. "Nixon understands conspiracies better than anyone, and when Nixon says these bastards are dug in deep, you can take it to the bank and toast it. Understand?"

"Yes, Mr. President," Duberman said.

"Aye, Mr. President," Mulligan said.

Nixon said, "Boys, taking on camel jockeys is one thing, but taking on the American establishment is a bigger sack of potatoes. But they can be beaten, because I've done it. I was just a sophomore in Congress when I took on Truman's White House, and by God, I won. I won! And do you know why I won? National security. Nixon had national security on his side then and Nixon has national security on his side now."

Nixon swiveled toward Haldeman. "Bob, give the boys some walking-around money out of the slush fund. And they'll need a cover that won't arouse suspicions. Any ideas?"

Ehrlichman looked up and said, "We need to staff the new Presidential Policy Commission pretty soon, or Congress gets the money back."

In his last year in office, Bobby Kennedy had convinced Congress to create an agency to "conduct research on such policy options as the President may deem necessary." Nixon could delay appointing a director, but he had to fill staff slots or give the money back to Congress. "I like it, John. Get the boys all signed up and give them whatever they need."

"Yes, sir."

"Now boys, you go wherever your leads take you. If somebody tells you something's off limits, give John a call and he'll set them straight. And keep a low profile, stay off the radar, and don't step on any toes. If anything sensitive comes up, let John or Bob know. They'll tell me, and I'll make the call. Understand?"

Duberman said, "Yes, sir, Mr. President."

Mulligan said, "Aye, aye, Mr. President."

"Good. Now, you're going to need some help. Rose Mary has picked out résumés of solid Republican boys, screened them all for loyalty. Loyalty is the primary consideration for this operation. I want boys who can keep their mouths shut, like the boys I had at HUAC when I bagged Alger Hiss. I won that one in the press with *The Pumpkin Papers* because I knew how to leak and my boys knew how to keep their mouths shut. Nobody knew what cards I was holding. Bluffed Truman good. Ha! That's poker, boys, poker. I was the best damned poker player in the South Pacific, and when I came home from the war, I had five thousand dollars in my wallet, a lot of money back then. Seven years later, I was the goddamn Vice President of the United States. Understand?"

"Aye, sir," Mulligan said.

"Yes, sir," said Duberman.

"Good. Now you must tell no one what we're up to, no one. And don't go mumbling in your dreams to the women you're balling. If I haven't appointed them myself, they're out of the loop. Is that perfectly clear?"

"Aye, Mr. President."

"Perfectly clear, Mr. President."

Nixon's gaze landed on Bullcannon, who had been so enthusiastic at first but was now sitting with his arms crossed, pouting like a sour-faced Halloween pumpkin. "What's the matter, Bart?"

"Mr. President, I'm worried we could lose the war on drugs if we back off now. We're so close to victory."

Nixon spoke like a concerned uncle. "We're not backing off, Bart, we're putting first things first. This energy mess is the worst crisis since Korea. We all know it's a long shot, but if Nixon can hit a home run out of the end zone, America wins the race."

Bullcannon sighed. "I suppose."

Nixon tried to buck him up. "I need you with me on this, Bart. For this caper to work, we've got to catch 'em on the shitter with their pants down and blow them away before they can wipe their assholes. Slice 'em and dice 'em and serve up their balls on a silver platter before they even know they're missing. That's the way to do it. Understand?"

"I understand the need for secrecy, Mr. President," Bullcannon said.

"You can count on me."

"Good. Now boys, there's two things to keep your eyes out for. I'm told finding the right kind of seeds will be a problem, so make that a priority. And there's a World War II movie out there somewhere called *Hemp For Victory* the government made for the war effort. See if you can track it down."

Haldeman's wristwatch beeped. "It's time, Mr. President."

Everyone stood up. Nixon handed his yellow legal pad to Haldeman, and gave them a final word of advice. "Boys, there's one thing you can count on with conspiracies, and that's money. When you don't know which way the bastards went, follow the money, boys, follow the money."

———————————————

Chapter 10

Back East

Spring 1974

ONE MORNING, ROSE MARY WOODS CAME OVER TO HER DESK AND SAID, "Catherine, you told me once you wanted to stay on after your internship is over. Do you still?"

"Oh yes, Miss Woods. Why?"

"Well, there's a new office starting up that needs temporary clerical help. If they like you, they could ask you to stay. Would you like to give it a try?"

To have any chance of bringing Nixon down, she had to find a way to stay on. "What do they do, Miss Woods?"

"It's very hush-hush. It's called the Presidential Policy Commission."

It was worth a look. She took her personnel folder and walked over to the EOB, Room 420. It was a typical suite, with a reception counter, two private offices, six cubicles with government-gray chairs and desks, and a conference room with a big table, a dozen chairs, and a splendid view of the White House across the street.

Two men were going over stacks of file folders.

"Hello," she said. "Miss Woods sent me over."

"Come on in here," one called. It was the Navy officer with the curly red hair and freckles she sometimes delivered packages to. His office was always a mess, blueprints everywhere. She had seen the other man in Haldeman's office and knew his family from the Social Register: Duberman, Beverly Hills social climbers, real-estate money. He was perfectly coifed, every hair in place, the kind who thought he was God's gift to women and bragged about the size of his pecker.

Duberman looked her up and down and snatched her file out of her hand. "I hope you can type, sweetums. My last intern could barely read."

Sweetums? She felt a fast burn coming on.

Duberman leafed through. "Let's see who you are, honey pie. You went to Vassar, you have a BA in Social Psychology, whatever the hell that is. And look at this—Yale Law. And you're a DeWolfe. Hells bells. Why's someone like you an intern?"

"You get to see a lot of different aspects from this angle."

He handed her back the folder and said, "Now, Miss DeWolfe—"

If she were going to work in one office, day after day, and didn't take control—*right now*—it would be too late. "I'd prefer to be addressed as Ms. DeWolfe, if you don't mind."

Duberman snorted. "Whatever you want, *Mizzz* DeWolfe."

She held her temper. "Thank you. What is it we do?"

"That's on a need-to-know basis," Duberman said, "and until you make the team, *Mizzz* honey buns, you have no need to know."

The Lieutenant was more helpful. "We can tell you we're putting a team together and will be needing a secretary. Miss Woods said you might be interested in staying on full time."

"Yes, I might, but I'd have to know what I'd be doing."

Duberman butted in. "All in good time, *Mizz* sweeetums."

"So, which of you is the boss?" she asked. The question seemed to make them uncomfortable.

The Lieutenant said, "We both are. I'm senior on the project—"

"But I'm senior in the administration," Duberman said.

"I see," she said. And she did. A typical power trip, both of them vying to be the Alpha Male. So predictable. "What would you like me to do?"

"First things first, honey pie," Duberman said. "How's your coffee?"

It occurred to her that Freud could have written a case study on Duberman as the archetypal male chauvinist pig. The Lieutenant, on the other hand, seemed respectful and courteous, even a gentleman. She wanted to be treated as an equal, but she would settle for courteous. She had never been drawn to uniforms, but he had always had a smile for her, and a friendly word. And he was three, maybe four inches taller than she was. She didn't find that very often.

After their spectacular success at the flea markets, the BirdCo entrepreneurs redoubled their quest for forks. Like conquistadors closing in on the golden city of El Dorado, they spent Friday nights in the university library poring over the classified ads of every Bay Area newspaper, looking up the addresses on Thompson's Guide maps, and plotting routes to every garage sale and thrift shop within a two-hour drive. On Saturday mornings they split up: one went west to San Francisco and down the Peninsula to Mountain View and Palo Alto, while the other went north to Vallejo, Fairfield, and over to Santa Rosa, or east to Sacramento, Stockton, and Modesto, or south to Fremont, Hayward, and San Jose. After a day of scrounging, they returned to the shop on Saturday nights with their raw materials, fired up the torches, and made Birds for the Sunday flea markets.

They tested various price points. Birds flew off the table at $10, did okay at $15, but only a few special Birds, made from sterling-silver forks with extra-fancy curly-cues, could fetch $20.

They devised two business plans: Plan A was to keep scrounging, selling at flea markets, and saving up for a production run of forks. Plan B—quitting their jobs and making Birds full-time—kicked in if they lucked out and found a few thousand forks somewhere.

After a few weeks, they had made and sold more than eight hundred Birds and banked over $11,000. They had also cleaned out the silverware sections of every second-hand store in Northern California. One Sunday afternoon, they came back to McGill's bungalow from the Alameda flea market. Once again they sold out early, and once again they were out of the critical raw material—forks.

"We gotta find a way to get more, McGill," Vince said as he finished the last of a beer. "Imagine how much we could be making?"

"A lot more than I'd make as a rookie lawyer."

Vince crushed the beer can and tossed it in the trash. "I gotta run. Can't let Susie get too horny. Tomorrow's your day to drive, so be on time."

The phone rang; McGill picked it up. "Hello."

"Hey Stick," said a familiar voice. "What's happening?"

"Mulligan Man? Is that you?"

"Yeah."

"I gotta go," Vince said as he opened the screen door. "Don't be late."

"Hang on," McGill said into the phone and put his hand over the mouthpiece. "Vince, wait a sec, man. Where is this new job?"

"Down by San Jose. I got directions. Don't be late."

The door banged shut and McGill went back to the phone. "How the hell you been, Mulligan?"

"Great. Who's there?"

"My partner, Vince. He just left."

"A partner? You in another band?"

"No, we started a business."

"A business? Doing what?"

"You'll have to see it to believe it. It's one of those picture's-worth-a-thousand-words kind of things."

"Stick, listen up. I've got a deal for you."

"The Mulligan Man's got a deal…for *me*? Now that's a laugh. There's a lot of things you're good at, Mulligan, but sales is definitely *not* one of them. Remember when you tried selling encyclopedias, and—"

"Listen up, asshole, this is important."

"Sheeesh, okay. Shoot."

"How would you like to come to Washington and work for me and President Nixon?"

McGill picked Vince up at six-thirty. Vince rode quietly, smoking a cigarette, drinking coffee from a thermos, and listening to the radio. Keeping him happy would not be easy. McGill turned off the radio.

"Hey, what are you doing?" Vince said.

"We gotta talk. Something's come up."

"Yeah…what?"

"My buddy Mulligan called yesterday—"

"The Navy guy in the magazine?"

"Yeah. He's working on a project for Nixon and, well, remember that résumé I told you I sent to Washington last year?"

"Sort of."

"Well, it popped up on Mulligan's desk. Shocked the shit out of him. I sent it right after Nixon won, but I never heard anything back. I figured they shit-canned it, but it turns out they'd put it in a special category. Pretty far out, huh?"

Vince flicked his butt out the window, sipped his coffee, pushed in the lighter, and took out another cigarette. "Cosmic." His cold tone hung in the van like a thick Tule fog in the Sacramento Valley, the kind that starts fifty-car pile-ups on the freeways. Vince was no Einstein, but he was no dummy. He had not gone to college, so the Army drafted him, but he came out a sergeant, he knew bullshit when he heard it, and had his own offbeat brand of common sense. McGill wanted him to get mad so he could go into his spiel. "Mulligan says he can get me a job at the White House."

The lighter popped out, and Vince lit up. "What kind of job?"

"All he could tell me is I'd be working directly for Nixon."

"Why in the hell would you want to do that?"

McGill tried to frame his answer in terms Vince would appreciate. "Man, do you have any idea how many chicks there are back in Washington? With all those secretaries, it's five to one back there."

"What's your friend say about the Bird?"

"I didn't tell him. Mulligan never took a toke in his life. He wouldn't understand the Bird."

"What about your bar exam?"

"I've been thinking of bagging it this round. Too busy making Birds."

"So you gonna break our deal?"

"Are you crazy? No way. Look, the way I see it, we need an East Coast operation. Think about it. We've cleaned out every Goodwill and Salvation Army from Santa Cruz to Santa Rosa. There's way more back there, in Washington, Baltimore, Philly, New York, all the way up to Boston. And I'll be able to talk face-to-face with the big silverware companies."

"I don't like it. We have a deal."

"We still will. You'll run BirdCo West, and I'll run BirdCo East."

"I don't like it."

Time to play his ace. "Look, you've been saying you want to move out of your mom and dad's and get your own place, right?"

"So?"

"And BirdCo will need an office, right?"

"So?"

"So I was thinking, what if I sublet my place to the company? BirdCo pays the rent, and you can crash there for free until I need it back."

"You mean me and Susie could move in?"

"Yes and no. It'll be our office, and you can crash till I need it back."

"I don't like you splitting."

"Are you crazy? I'll keep us in forks, maybe make a deal for a production run. I'll be way more valuable to us back there than out here. I'm telling you, this is the kick in the ass we've been needing to really make the Bird *fly*!"

Three days later McGill took the redeye from San Francisco, landing at Dulles International at six-ten A.M. He took his briefcase down to the carousel and got his suitcase, sleeping bag, and guitar case. He also had $5,000 in cash for BirdCo East in a money belt around his waist. He used the men's room, shaved, brushed his teeth, and changed into his summer-weight khaki suit and wing-tip shoes. He looked in the mirror and sighed. There was no way around it. He would have to get a haircut.

"Been a while," the airport barber said in a sarcastic tone as he tucked a towel around McGill's neck. "How much you want off?"

"I'm starting a new job at the White House in an hour. Make me look like a Republican."

The barber laughed. "That's easy." He fired up his clippers and turned the chair so McGill couldn't see the damage. Ten minutes later the barber spun him around, full on in the mirror. "That Republican enough?"

McGill hadn't seen his ears in years. The dorky straight-arrow staring back at him would not have a prayer of getting laid in Berkeley. He went outside, smoked the last of a roach in a parking lot, whistled down a taxi, and told the cabbie, "Pennsylvania and Seventeenth."

He felt a thrill as the driver let him out in front of the White House. He walked up the steps of the EOB and asked an MP, "I'm looking for the Presidential Policy Commission."

The MP checked a directory. "Room 420. They're just moving in. You can leave your bags in the cloak room if you like."

He left everything but his briefcase and took the elevator. A woman about his age, her auburn hair up in a bun, was standing behind a counter. She was very tall, just an inch shorter than he was. He looked for a wedding ring, and seeing none, gave her a once-over. She wore low heels, a pleated skirt, and a clinging white, not quite see-through blouse that stretched across a pair of melony breasts. If she let her hair down, she'd be a real fox.

"May I help you?" she asked.

"I'm Art McGill. Lt. Mulligan is expecting me."

She marked him off a list and handed him a packet. "You can use the table in the conference room to fill these out, Mr. McGill."

She was too young for him to address as "Ma'am," so to be polite he used his best country-club manners. "Thank you, Miss."

She flashed him a scowl. "I'm not a Miss, Mr. McGill...I'm a Ms."

The women's lib movement was doing all it could to purge English of "sexist" terminology, and every woman in Berkeley had embraced the new term—'Ms.' But he was surprised to hear it here, among Republicans.

"I'm sorry. Thank you, *Ms.*" He turned to leave but paused, unable to stop himself from saying, "Did you hear how ridiculous that sounded?"

"Excuse me?"

"'Thank you, *Ms.*' It hurts your ears to hear it, know what I mean?"

"I don't know what you're talking about."

"Well, to my ear 'thank you Ma'am' or 'thank you Miss' sound right. But 'thank you, *Ms.*' sounds all wrong. What's it short for, anyway? Sounds like slaves talking in *Gone With The Wind.*"

"It's not short for anything, Mr. McGill. And to my ear, 'thank-you-Miss' sounds like you're talking to a waitress...I mean a waitperson."

A waitperson? Uh-oh, this chick was a radical. Time to exit. "I'm sorry, and it won't happen again, but I can't see your name badge, Ms...."

She turned so he could read it.

"...DeWolfe. Thank you, Ms. DeWolfe."

Holy cow. Was she one of *the* DeWolfes? He went to the conference room wondering if Mulligan was balling her but forgot her completely at his first glance out the window at the White House across the street.

He filled out forms until a simple question on the F.B.I. questionnaire stopped him cold: "Have you ever used or sold dangerous or illegal drugs?"

He bit the pen as he thought about it. He had dropped acid a few times in college—kiss-the-sky "purple haze," and the great "orange sunshine" at Woodstock. But that was years ago, so he was okay there. And like every guy in Milltowne, as he turned sixteen he got a phony ID saying he was eighteen so he could get into the college bars across the Ohio line to drink three-two beer and hear live music.

But that was old news. He was twenty-five now. He'd quit cigarettes...again, hadn't had one since New Year's Eve. The Surgeon General said tobacco killed, but tobacco was legal...so it didn't count as dangerous. He despised needles...so shooting heroin or anything else was out of the question. He'd popped dexedrine pulling all-nighters for finals, but dexies were made by drug companies...so they didn't count. More and more cocaine was showing up at parties, and he tooted up to be polite, even chipped in a few times, but he couldn't understand why people were so eager to pay exorbitant prices for the same buzz he got from two cups of coffee and a cigarette...so that didn't count. The peyote he took in Mexico was legal down there...so that didn't count. As for marijuana, Nixon's own commission concluded it was harmless and should be decriminalized...so that didn't count. As for selling, he went halves on a pound of Panama Red with Dombrowski one time, but he had been a terrible dealer, paranoid, jumpy, always looking over his shoulder. He had hated it and never dealt again...so that didn't count. When he signed his signature beneath the UNDER PENALTY OF PERJURY notice, he was satisfied that, with all the mitigating circumstances, there was not a single outright lie on the entire F.B.I. questionnaire.

Chapter 11

Secret Missions

FOR DAYS, CATHERINE HAD DONE NOTHING EXCEPT MAKE COFFEE AND SIT IN an empty office listening to the radio. What was the point of being a spy if there was nobody to spy on? Had she made a mistake?

Four new men were to join the staff today, so maybe she would learn what it was all about. The first to arrive, a guy about her age from California named McGill, was filling out forms in the conference room. His haircut told her all she needed to know: cookie-cutter conservative.

The nine o'clock news reported that Timothy Leary had been arrested in Switzerland and was being held pending extradition hearings. She wondered if Gridley was involved, and wished Leary a silent good luck. Three men walked in, two whites and a black. The black man broke into a wide grin. "Catherine...is that you?"

Oh my God. "Chester Thompkins?"

"Yes. Good to see you."

He still wore his hair in a neatly-trimmed Afro that stuck out half an inch from his very round head. He was well-muscled, like a boxer, and his deep black skin glistened like polished ebony. He stood about five nine, and wore a blue suit with a striped tie and a yellow, button-down shirt. His thick-rimmed, Buddy Holly glasses gave him a studious look.

"Catherine and I went through Yale law together," he told the others. "So what are you doing here?"

"I'm a White House intern."

"An intern? You should be clerking somewhere. You had the grades."

Men just did not get how it was for women, but she didn't want to start anything. "I thought you were with Judge Horsham on the Tenth Circuit?"

"I was, but he had a stroke and retired early. It looks good on the résumé, though, and that's what counts. I'm starting here today."

One of the other men introduced himself in a well-bred, Southern drawl, "Lee Backwater, at yaw service, Ma'am."

Backwater was a lean five-ten, good-looking, with wavy black hair, brown eyes and an ingratiating smile that oozed Southern charm.

The third man was also about five-ten, thin, with curly, dishwater blonde hair, squinty blue eyes and a boyish face. He stretched out his hand

and said, "George Branche."

"Nice to know you. That's Mr. McGill. He's new too."

McGill came in, and they introduced themselves. It was always amusing watching men trying to size each other up and establish a pecking order.

"Anybody know what we'll be doing?" McGill asked.

Backwater said, "All they told George and me was that we'd be working directly for the President."

"So what is it all about, Catherine?" Thompkins asked.

She must insist on respect, right now, or it would be too late. "I think we should observe the formalities here at work, Mr. Thompkins."

Thompkins' jaw dropped. He looked crestfallen. "Well, sorreee...."

She hated herself when she didn't think. She had embarrassed him, and he hadn't done anything. "Look, I just feel that it's better if here in the office you're Mr. Thompkins and I'm Ms. DeWolfe, that's all. If some of us are on a familiar basis and others are not, it could become awkward for those of us in subordinate roles because of our gender. How about we have a drink after work and catch up. Okay?"

A half-smile crossed his face. "I understand. Ms. DeWolfe it is."

"So what is the job all about, Ms. DeWolfe?" McGill asked.

"They haven't told me a thing," she said.

She pretended to be busy, listening in as they filled out forms and swapped personal histories—schools, degrees, home towns, favorite sports teams—all the male basics. She learned McGill had a law degree from Berkeley and was the Lieutenant's high school pal, Backwater had a Masters in Political Science from Clemson and had worked with Duberman, and Branche had a Harvard MBA and was the son of a Congressman from Texas Nixon had just named ambassador to China.

Mulligan and Duberman were in the Oval Office, watching as Nixon chewed out somebody over the phone. "I don't give a rat's ass about ethics. Fuck ethics! I'm telling you to sic the I.R.S. on the Kennedys like they did to me. Make the bastards pay, do you hear me, *pay!*"

Nixon slammed down the receiver, looked up, smiled and said with utter calm, "So are you getting set up over there?"

"Aye, sir," Mulligan said. "The team is to report this morning."

"Good, good. Bob, did you take care of background checks?"

"Yes, sir. They all passed Level Two F.B.I. profiles. There's the question of converting the intern to a permanent position." Haldeman turned to them and asked, "Do you want her, or should I get somebody from the secretarial pool?"

"She's overqualified," Mulligan said. "I say we're lucky to have her."

"She's a bit of a bitch," Duberman said, "but I can live with her."

Haldeman jotted himself a note.

"Anything else?" Nixon asked.

"Yes, sir," Mulligan said. He opened his briefcase and took out a motion picture film canister and handed it to Nixon. "We think we found the movie you wanted. It's under seal. The label's dated August 21, 1945."

"That's just a week after the Japs surrendered," Nixon said. "Who authorized it? And why?"

"We don't know why," Duberman said, "but it's signed by Frederick W. Vinson, Secretary of the Treasury."

Nixon examined the canister. "Vinson? Why, Truman made him Chief Justice, in '47 I think it was. So why was the Treasury Secretary sealing a movie from the Agriculture Department?"

Nixon took a pair of scissors from his desk and snipped the seal himself. He opened the lid and removed the film. "Doesn't look like it's too long," Nixon said. "Let's take a look at it. Is there time, Bob?"

"The U.N. arms control delegation will be here in an hour."

"Good," Nixon said. "Alert the screening room."

Mulligan seized the chance. "Sir, the team hasn't been briefed on the mission. Maybe now might be a good time?"

Nixon waved his hand in hurry-up circles, like a spastic traffic cop. "You're right. Get their asses the hell over here. And Bob, give John a call. Bart too. Everybody in the loop. Ten minutes. And make sure there's popcorn. And fresh-squeezed lemonade."

Duberman came bursting through the office door. "Are they all here?"

"Everyone on the list is in the conference room," Catherine said.

"Come on, everybody," Duberman called. "Follow me, we'll take the stairs, it's faster. You too, honey buns. You're in if you want in. If you're going to bail, do it now. Are you in or out?"

Duberman did not have a clue how badly he pissed her off, but she couldn't pass up a chance to land a permanent assignment. "I'm in."

They hurried down the four flights of stairs and across the street to the White House, where Duberman passed them off to a Secret Service agent, saying, "I'll see you in there."

The agent took them to the basement of the West Wing and showed them into a small movie theater, not far from the copy room where she had briefly worked. It had maybe fifty seats and a lectern off to the side. "Sit in the back," the agent said. "When the President enters, stand, don't speak unless you're spoken to, and never sit if he's standing."

A minute later the door swung open, and they jumped to their feet. Nixon did not notice them as he strode down the short aisle, followed by Ehrlichman, Haldeman, Mulligan, Duberman, Bullcannon, and two butlers wheeling a serving cart.

Everyone waited until Nixon sat; Lt. Mulligan went to the lectern. "Good morning, Mr. President, everybody. You're here because the President asked us to track down this film. It's a World War II film, but the Pentagon knew nothing about it. The Library of Congress had a record of it in their catalog, but to their embarrassment, their copy seems to have been misplaced. This may be the last copy of this film in existence. We don't think anyone has seen it since it was officially sealed in 1945."

Mulligan motioned to the projectionist, the lights dimmed, a film flickered to black-and-white life, and *Hemp For Victory* splashed across the screen.

The movie opened in the ruins of ancient Greece, with the narrator explaining that when the Greeks built their temples, hemp cultivation was already 3,000 years old. In 1940's documentary style, the movie explained the importance of hemp in American history, showing clips from early Hollywood movies of sailing ships in battle, and oxen yoked to canvas-covered "prairie schooners." The narrator explained that every sailing ship on the seven seas used canvas, lines, and caulking made from the hemp plant. "The sailor, no less than the hangman," intoned the narrator, "was dependent upon hemp to do his job."

The film showed America's most famous warship, the *Constitution*, nicknamed "Old Ironsides," as an example of how sailing ships used sixty tons of sails, lines, and caulking made from hemp every time they put to sea. It explained that hemp cultivation nearly disappeared after steamships and railroads eliminated the need for canvas for ships and covered wagons, and that fiber for rope was replaced by cheaper abaca, jute, and sisal from the Philippines and India.

When the Japanese took the Philippines, they cut off America's supply of fiber. The military needed fiber for ships' lines, tents, fire hoses, knapsacks, boot laces, parachute webbing, the list went on and on. Without vast amounts of fiber, the war effort would unravel. It was the patriotic duty of American farmers to come through for the country by growing the one crop that could supply the military with all the fiber we needed—*hemp.*

The film showed a crop cycle on a hemp farm, from planting to harvesting. In 1942 after Pearl Harbor, farmers in Kentucky planted an emergency crop of 43,000 acres of hemp for the war effort, and increase of several thousand percent over 1941. Now, in 1943, Uncle Sam needed farmers across the country to plant the seeds from that crop to grow the 300,000 new acres of hemp for the fiber needed to win the war.

The grand finale showed tens of thousands of troops marching in formation, driving home the point about bootlaces, then cut to a parachute drop, with hundreds of airborne soldiers filling the sky like snowflakes thanks to their hempen rigging. But best of all was the aerial view of a fleet, hundreds of warships as far as the eye could see, steaming to meet the enemy as a stirring rendition of "Anchors Away" played in the background and the narrator called out, "Hemp for *VICTORY!*"

The lights came up, and Catherine saw Nixon use the back of his hand to wipe something from his cheek. A tear? Was Nixon...crying?

Everyone was silent, waiting for Nixon, and when he spoke there was a patriotic quaver in his voice. "A movie like that makes you proud to be an American. Very, very proud. I was a supply officer in the Solomons, you know. I disbursed everything from parachutes to boot laces to our flyboys every day. So I was a dope dealer and didn't even know it. Ha! Did it work? Were we able to do it?"

"Yes, sir," Duberman said. "By 1944, we were growing all we needed."

"It's a testament to America's can-do spirit," Nixon said, visibly bursting with pride. "By God, this is do-able, boys, it's fucking *do-able!*"

Catherine sat still, taking it in. What was 'do-able?' Why was Nixon showing them a World War II movie about rope?

There was a beep; Haldeman looked at his watch. "Mr. President, we should go."

"Mr. President, sir," Mulligan interjected. "Before you leave, the new team members are here. If they heard how important this is from you, it would mean a lot."

"Yes, of course it would," Nixon said as he turned around and saw them for the first time. "Come on down here."

She followed the men down the aisle. Duberman introduced them as they approached. "Mr. President, this is Chester Thompkins, Lee Backwater, George Branche, Arthur McGill, and Ms. DeWolfe."

Nixon ignored the men and took her hand. "I have a Ms. working for me? Ha! You're not some kind of bra-burning women's libber, are you?"

"I believe in equality for everybody, Mr. President."

"Well, so do I, so do I. Did I hear your name right...*DeWolfe?*"

"Yes, Mr. President."

"Any relation to Edward, or Harold, or—"

"Edward is my father."

"Then you must be all right. He's one of my biggest supporters."

Nixon brought her hand to his lips and kissed it, European style. She would have slugged any other man for being so presumptuous. Instead, she smiled. "It's an honor to work for you, Mr. President."

"Good to have you aboard. And say hello to your father for me."

"I will, Mr. President."

Nixon turned to the men and shook their hands—man-to-man, no kissing. "Boys, this is either the jackpot of the century, or it's a total crock of shit. Now I don't want bullshit—I want the truth. The future of America may depend on you. If there's been a conspiracy, I need to know who the players were and how they did it. And no one must know what you're doing. Your mission must remain totally secret. Is that perfectly clear."

They all nodded, but she had no idea what Nixon was talking about.

Haldeman pointed to his watch. "Sir, the U.N. arms-control delegation is waiting."

"Let 'em sweat," Nixon said. "Peaceniks bore the piss out of me. So...any questions? Suggestions? Anybody. Go ahead, speak up."

Bullcannon said, "Every secret mission needs a code name, Mr. President."

"Yes, good code names make things fun. Any ideas?"

"Yes, sir," Bullcannon said. "You just said it could be the jackpot of the century. How about Operation Jackpot?"

"Ha!" Nixon said. "Operation Jackpot it is."

When Nixon's entourage left the theater, Catherine watched the Lieutenant and McGill shake hands and slap each other on the back. Male friendship rituals were fascinating. Women would have hugged, but men never did. McGill gave the bigger, stronger Lieutenant a surprise noogie on his scalp, rubbing furiously with his knuckles right on the balding spot. "Gonna be a chrome dome by the time you're thirty, Mulligan Man."

"Cut it out, Stick," Mulligan yelled, grabbing McGill's wrist and twisting his arm away. "Thank God you got a haircut. I was afraid you'd show up looking like a refugee from Woodstock."

"I forgot I could be this dorky," McGill said as he ran his fingers along the white sidewalls above his ears. "So what's this top-secret gig all about? It can't be about rope, can it?"

"We'll brief you in the office," Mulligan said.

An agent came in and said, "They want me to escort your people through credentialing after lunch. You can eat in the White House mess."

As they stood in line, Catherine noticed McGill taking a long time at the silverware bins, staring at a fork, turning it over and over, as if it were a priceless work of art. She couldn't believe it when he casually slipped two more forks out of the bin and into his suitcoat pocket when he thought no one was looking. If they had been valuable pieces of silverware, she might have said something, but they were cheap stainless-steel, with "U.S. Government" on the back. What did it say about the character of some-body who would steal forks from the White House?

After lunch, the agent took her and the four new men to be photographed, fingerprinted, and lectured about the stiff penalties for violating espionage and national-security statutes. They took an oath to uphold the Constitution and were sworn in as staff members of the Presidential Policy Commission.

They spent the afternoon at the conference table listening as Mulligan and Duberman briefed them on ethanol, methanol, and the plans of Henry Ford to grow fuel from plants. What had she fallen into?

Branche was skeptical. "So Nixon really thinks there was a conspiracy?"

Duberman nodded. "Yes. He wants answers and he wants them fast."

"So what are we supposed to do?" McGill asked.

"We're the President's eyes and ears," the Lieutenant said. "Our job is to prove his hunch right or wrong, one way or the other."

"But it was decades ago," Branche said. "What's the point?"

"Yeah, anybody involved is probably dead," Thompkins said.

"They may be gone," Mulligan said, "but if he was right, somebody's benefitting today because of what happened back then, and we're all paying the price. The President is determined to make Project Independence succeed, and knowing who helped to ban hemp and how they did it means he'll be a step ahead when they line up against him. And who knows…maybe we'll get lucky and find a smoking gun."

"You all need to get up to speed," Duberman said as he passed out a report in identical three-ring binders. "Lt. Mulligan has done the heavy lifting on the science. Read this tonight, so we're all on the same page by morning."

Just before five, a courier dropped off an envelope with their new photo-IDs and letters-of-introduction. Catherine felt a surprise sense of pride swell up at seeing her name on gilt-embossed, White House stationery, above the signature of Richard M. Nixon.

Backwater said, "Excuse me, but Ah just have to know. Which one of you is the number one bossman?"

The Lieutenant shuffled, uneasy. "Consider us co-equals. Rudy's job's the political side, I'm the technical side. Of course, if he tells you one thing and I tell you another, do it my way."

Even Duberman chuckled. With his easy-going assumption of authority, the Lieutenant had just taken charge.

The Lieutenant said, "Let's get acquainted over dinner. Any suggestions?"

"What's that place the *National Review* always says has the best political action?" McGill said.

"Pachyderm's," Duberman said. "On 'K' Street."

Gridley walked into Pachyderm's, the hippest conservative watering hole in Washington, to meet his old friend Bullcannon for dinner and strategize how to maximize the PR for his new project. Known for its thick steaks and Republican decor, Gridley especially liked its famous Double Tusk Bar, with the pair of giant mastodon tusks above the mirror. High-powered horse-trading in Pachyderm's booths had been a staple of Republican politics since the presidency of William McKinley.

He heard Bullcannon calling his name through the din. "Grayson!"

He was with some people, a Navy lieutenant and—whoa, what do you know—Miss Moneybags.

Bullcannon started the introductions. "This is Grayson Gridley, director of the Office of Narcotic Operations. Grayson, this is Rudy

Duberman, Lt. Mulligan, and some of their people from the new P.P.C."

Gridley extended his hand to Moneybags. "Yes, Miss DeWolfe and I have known each other for years. Nice to see you again."

"It's always a pleasure, Mr. Gridley," she said, shaking his hand. He could tell she was faking. He had her crapping her pants.

Bullcannon said, "So Grayson, congratulations on your Operation Intercept idea. The President thinks it's a winner."

"Thanks. It kicks off tomorrow."

"What kind of operation is it?" Duberman asked.

Gridley loved talking about it. "The O.N.O. is sealing off the border from Brownsville to San Diego in the first joint operation between the D.E.A., Customs, F.B.I., Coast Guard, C.I.A., I.N.S., A.T.F., and the Border Patrol. We'll nail druggies and wetbacks at the same time."

A tall, skinny guy from Bullcannon's group said, "Say, aren't you the same guy who busted Timothy Leary for peat moss a few years ago?"

Gridley hated wise-asses. "There was a lot more to it than what you saw in the news," Gridley said as he took a last drag off his cigarette, crushed the butt out with his shoe, reached in his pocket for his pack, and lit another. "Somebody had to break up Leary's druggie heaven, and I did it."

Another man in the group said in a Southern accent, "Mr. Gridley, Ah've never heard the inside scoop on that. Can you tell us about it, suh?"

He glanced at Moneybags and gave her a wink. "I was a DA up there when those hippie Mellons gave the bastard a sixty-room mansion to play in. Well, nobody pulls that kind of druggie shit under E. Grayson Gridley's nose. So I went after him, you bet I did. Harassed his ass right out of town."

A black man in the group asked, "What what the charge he finally went to prison for?"

"Possession," Gridley said with satisfaction. "Got thirty years. And don't you worry. We'll bring him in. He can't run forever."

The wise-ass asked, "Is it true the cops planted the evidence?"

"I wasn't in on that one," Gridley said, "but so what if it was? We have to send a message in the war on drugs. Zero tolerance, that's what I say." He took a deep drag on his cigarette. "If it were up to me, I'd line every druggie in the country up against a wall and shoot 'em."

The maitre d' called, "Duberman, party of seven. Duberman."

As they started to leave, he gave Moneybags a wink and said, "Au revoir, Miss DeWolfe. Washington's a small town."

Catherine had never been more glad to get away from anybody in her life. Gridley's little wink at her sent shivers up her back. What did he want from her? What was he planning? He seemed to be everywhere.

The maitre d' seated them under a photograph of Teddy Roosevelt in a safari outfit, a rifle slung over his shoulder, his foot on the mane of a very dead lion. After the waiter left, McGill asked her, "So, Ms. DeWolfe, how come that narc gets to call you Miss?"

This McGill was a real pain. "I don't have to work with him every day."

Dinner was pleasant, and when the waiter brought the check the Lieutenant said, "I'll take it."

McGill feigned a gasp. "Mark your calendars, everybody. Hell has frozen over. The Mulligan Man is *buying*."

"No, not on my Navy pay," the Lieutenant said with a laugh. "This outing is courtesy of Nixon's discretionary fund. Think of it as a morale builder, like a Bob Hope show for the troops."

Backwater gave a hearty, "Hear, hear" and stood up, tapping his spoon on his water glass: tink-tink-tink-tink-tink. "Attention, may Ah have your attention, puhleeze." He tinked at the glass again, louder, like a master of ceremonies. He tinked a third time, completely taking charge of the room as the other patrons stopped talking. When he had their full attention he declaimed in his aristocratic, Charlestonian drawl, "Ah propose a toast…to Richard Milhous Nixon, the President of these Ewenited States."

He held his glass high, and as if by command, everybody else in the room held theirs up too. "To the President…hip, hip…"

"Hooray," she said along with the crowd, quietly, not together.

"Hip, hip…"

"Hooray," she went with the crowd, louder, more in synch.

"Hip, hip…"

She was ready this time, and yelled loud and in synch with a cheer that vibrated the room—"HOO-*RAAY!*"

When they stepped out into the warm April evening, McGill put two fingers in his mouth, gave an ear-piecing whistle, and pulled over a taxi. The others were all going back to the office for their cars and she said, "I don't live far, and it's a beautiful evening. See you in the morning."

She strolled up lively 'M' Street, with its vibrant mix of students, government workers, tourists, and professionals. After a few blocks, she turned up the hill, into her leafy historical neighborhood, where Mother Nature and U.S. history conferred at every corner. Cherry, dogwood, and apple blossoms filled the trees as daffodils, pansies, and tulips thrust out of the ground to demand their time in the sun.

Her plan was working so well it was scary. She had penetrated to the heart of the administration and landed a job that brought her into contact with Nixon himself. She was in a position to strike a blow for feminism, or for environmentalism, but she had no idea what that blow might be.

Her immediate problem was the peacock, Duberman. She could not abide his preening male chauvinism. Now that Nixon knew who she was and that she was on the team, it would be much harder for Duberman to fire her when the time came for her to put him in his place.

Thompkins worried her too. They had been acquaintances at Yale, and if he ever saw her file, he would know she lied about her membership in Yale's Young Republicans. She liked Backwater's Southern manners, and Branche seemed like a harmless preppie. McGill was an odd one—quirky, devious, a kleptomaniac who swiped forks. But he had popped that acid-tongued question to Gridley about arresting Leary for peat moss. As for the Lieutenant, so far there was nothing about him she didn't like. And then there was Gridley; at least she didn't have to work with him.

She opened her gate and picked some lilacs. When she was a girl her grandmother always took her to Mackinac Island's Lilac Festival, which celebrated the three-hundred-year-old lilac bushes planted by French missionaries, but these lilacs were her very own; she had never known any quite so sweet.

She took a bath and climbed into bed to read the Lieutenant's report: *ALTERNATIVE FUELS: Sources and Solutions.* All she knew about hemp was that rope was made from it, and she had never connected it with marijuana. She knew to watch out for grain alcohol used in Purple Passion punchbowls at fraternity parties, and she knew ships and boats like her own *Athena* used wood alcohol in galley stoves because its fire could be put out by water. DeWolfe Forest Products made it as a sideline, but she didn't know any details.

She hoped to find something wrong, something bogus, but the more she read, the more it seemed this was something she could believe in, even work for. But her mission was to bring Nixon down, not to help him. What if she could help Nixon make America self-sufficient in energy *before* she brought him down? Would it absolve her of five generations of her family's bad karma for raping the environment? She had never been so confused.

Chapter 12

A Secret Weapon

MCGILL GOT HIS SUITCASE, GUITAR CASE, AND SLEEPING BAG FROM THE COAT room at the EOB while Mulligan went to the garage and pulled his car around to pick him up. They went to the nearest deli and Mulligan put the top down while McGill ran in and came back with a couple of six-packs. He passed Mulligan a beer and sat back to enjoy the warm spring air as they drove along Independence Avenue. "How in the hell did you ever get this gig, Mulligan?"

"Right place, right time. What can I say?"

"It's like you beamed into the *Twilight Zone*. I mean, first you save the Nixon chicks in the Bermuda Triangle, then you get a cushy job at the White House, then you come across my résumé, and here I am. One week I'm pounding nails, the next I'm working for the President of the United States. And what's my job? I'm helping him grow pot."

"Don't think of it like that, Stick. Nixon's got a war on drugs to win too. He has to neutralize the drug aspect, separate it from energy."

"How's he going to do it?"

"That's the million dollar question. He's hoping we can figure it out."

The words "million dollar" brought the Bird to mind. McGill had three with him, and bases and alligator clips to make two hundred more if he could find the forks and rent time in a welding shop. But what to tell Mulligan? He had known him since the first day of junior high, when they sat next to each other in the back row in Miss Crowne's homeroom, the two tallest M's. In all that time he had never seen Mulligan smoke a cigarette or toke on a joint. He wouldn't tell Mulligan about the lid of Panama Red stuffed in his blue socks, but he couldn't help bragging about the Bird. When they came to a stop light, McGill reached over the back seat, opened his suitcase, and took one out. "Mulligan Man, meet the Bird."

Mulligan examined it as they passed the Lincoln Memorial and started across the bridge over the Potomac River. "Looks like it's made out of a fork. What's it for?"

McGill could only shake his head. "It's a roach clip, asshole. We're gonna make big bucks with this sucker. You watch."

"You mean it's...it's for smoking...*marijuana?*"

"You are so out of it, Mulligan. Where have you been since high school? Mars? Pluto?"

Mulligan's face turned red. "Shit, Stick, how could…I mean…what if somebody finds out? Do you know what it could mean to the President?"

"Jeez, Mulligan, don't freak out on me. It's just a chopped-up old fork with an alligator clip on the end. Lighten up."

"*Lighten up my ass*! We're not in junior high any more. You know how you always got me in trouble?"

"*Me?*"

"Yeah…*you*! Every time I got swats, it was because of you. Every time! When your résumé came up, I called you because I want somebody around I know I can trust. But if you're making roach clips, I mean it's…it's the country's future we're talking about."

"But it's totally legal. The Bird's legit."

"I don't give a shit. Do you know how embarrassing it could be to Nixon if the press found out somebody working at the White House was making these things?"

"Well…maybe you've got a point."

"*Maybe* I've got a point? Now listen up, Stick, and listen up good…you drop this Bird business—right *now*—or you're out. I won't have you endangering the mission. Understand?"

"Okay, I'll cool it. I promise."

McGill sat back, sipping his beer and taking in the sunset as they cruised the George Washington Parkway along the Potomac river, past the Pentagon and National Airport to Mulligan's third-floor apartment in the old town section of Alexandria.

He was not surprised to see blueprints and engineering drawings covering Mulligan's furniture. "Would you look at this mess. It's like your room back in Milltowne. Where's your guitar?"

"I don't have time for it any more."

"You mean there's nobody to play with. We'll change that real quick."

McGill opened the door to a small balcony and stepped outside. He was impressed with Alexandria's tree-lined, brick-paved streets and nineteenth-century gaslight lampposts, nothing at all like Berkeley or Milltowne. There was a lively bar across the street. The Eagles' "Take It Easy" blared from a jukebox.

"Nice neighborhood, Mulligan. So I'm not gonna be in your way crashing on your couch, am I? I brought my sleeping bag, but can I use some of these blueprints for a pillow?"

"Very funny, Stick. Ha, ha. Sometimes you are really lame. I've put the word out to find you a one-bedroom apartment. Let's hope something turns up before I kill you. Did you get out of your lease out there?"

"Nah. We can use it as an office for the Bird."

"Not one more word about the stupid Bird. Drop it…understand?"

"Okay. Not another word…except, you just gave me an idea for a radio jingle," and he launched into the chorus of the old novelty hit that was famously made on a bet that anything could be sold to the American public, no matter how bad it was.

"The bird-bird-bird
The bird is the word—"

Mulligan rolled his eyes, shook his head, and yelled, "*Drop it!*"

"Okay, okay. If we can't talk about birds, then how about chicks? Is it really five to one back here?"

"I didn't bring you back here so you could get laid."

"I'll consider it a fringe benefit. And speaking of getting laid, what's the story on DeWolfe? You balling her?"

Mulligan shot him a glare. "No."

"Good. I'd hate to snake her from you. She dating anybody?"

"I don't know, but keep your hands off."

"Don't go weird on me in your old age, Mulligan. Remember that time we took your dad's boat up to Erie and spent the night halfway to Canada with those chicks from Ohio State?"

"We never had to see them again, and we work with DeWolfe every day. Why do you think it's against regulations for women to be on ships?"

"Uh…bad luck, because there's not enough to go around, right?"

"That's right. You can't have a ship out at sea for months at a time when a few guys are getting laid and the rest aren't. You put women out there with men, discipline and unit cohesion go right down the shitter. It's the same in an office. Mixing women with work is nothing but trouble. So just forget her. This is too important."

"Jeez, Mulligan, you got it bad, don't you?"

"What are you talking about?"

"You got it bad for DeWolfe."

"You're crazy."

"Don't you even try to bullshit me, Mulligan. I've known you too long.

You got it bad all right."

The next morning Catherine filled an empty coffee can with water for the lilacs she had picked on the way to work. She turned on the radio and started the copier as the men argued about whether to cut cards, flip coins, or arm-wrestle for the best cubicles.

As she bent over to open the paper tray she heard Duberman's voice behind her say, "So how's my favorite honey buns this morning?" Suddenly she felt a hand palming the right cheek of her buttocks, like it was testing a cantaloupe for ripeness. Without thinking she grabbed the wrist in a judo hold and forced her attacker to his knees, pinched his ear and gave it a sharp twist, like Moe does to Larry and Curly in Three Stooges movies.

"Ow!" Duberman cried. "Stop. Ow!"

"I will not have you pawing me," she yelled as the others watched in stone cold, granite silence. "It won't happen again, will it?"

"Ow! No, no, I swear. Let go, please."

"And the next time you call me honey buns or sweetie pie or sugar puss I'll feel free to call you whatever I want. Let's see…how does Doobs sound? Or Dubious? Yes, Mr. Dubious." She tweaked his ear again.

His face was squinched in pain. "Stop, please. I'm sorry. I swear it won't happen again!"

"It won't happen again *who*?" she said.

"Ms. DeWolfe. It won't happen again, Ms. DeWolfe."

"It better not." She gave him one last tweak and went to her desk. Her chest was heaving, her heart pounding. She had planned to confront him, but not like that.

Duberman was rubbing his ear. "Jesus H. Christ."

Backwater said in his aristocratic drawl, "As we say down where Ah come from, you have done gone and stepped in it, Mr. Dubious."

The others broke into guffaws. "Mr. Doo…Doo…Dooobious," Branche said, doubling over in laughter.

Thompkins was laughing so hard he could barely speak. "It's p…p…perfect."

She was seething. "What I said goes for the rest of you too. I will be your secretary and I will make your coffee, but I will not be treated like a servant or a sex object. Is that understood?"

Branche clicked his heels as he gave a Nazi salute and shouted in a horrible German accent, "Jawohl, mein Fräulein!"

"Knock it off," Mulligan said. "She's right. From now on, she is Ms. DeWolfe, and that's an order."

Nobody said anything; Duberman massaged his ear.

"Maybe this is the time to lay down a rule," the Lieutenant said. "There's an old saying that a smart dog doesn't crap on its own porch. What it means for us is no dating anybody we work with. In the military it's called nonfraternization. Got it?"

"Bow wow, bark bark," Thompkins said with a grin.

As they took their seats around the lunch table for the briefing, McGill asked, "So where do we start?"

"Not where," the Lieutennt said, "when. In 1937, the year Congress passed the ban, and work backwards. How far back, I don't know. Use any source—newspapers, magazines, trade journals, government reports, anything. Rudy and I made a list of assignments to get started. Rudy's going to take the old Federal Bureau of Narcotics—"

McGill held a hand to his mouth like a bugle. "Dut-dut-dut-dut, dut dah. Hark! Hark! Into battle, sallies forth…Mr. Dubious."

Duberman glowered as the others chuckled.

"Knock it off," the Lieutenant said. "Act your age, all of you. And that goes double for you, Stick."

Branche smiled an impish smirk. "What are you going to do to us, Lieutenant…drop us for push-ups? I'm dubious."

"No, you're Branche," Thompkins said as he pointed at Duberman. "He's Dubious."

They went into yet another laughing spasm, even the Lieutenant. Men were so strange.

When the laughter subsided, Mulligan said, "There's one name that's going to keep cropping up, Harry Anslinger. He was the commissioner of the Bureau of Narcotics from 1930 until 1962. He's retired now, living outside of Altoona, Pennsylvania, but he has a lot of friends in high places, so tread lightly. The President doesn't want to tip anybody off.

"Backwater," Mulligan said, "you start with the Congressional hearings. We need to know whose ox was being gored."

"Right up my alley," Backwater said.

"Branche, you take the government medical studies. The British did one in the 1890's in India, the U.S. Army did one in Panama in the Twenties, Mayor LaGuardia had one in New York in the Forties, Britain did another a few years ago, and so did Canada. The most recent is the Shafer Commission report that's been in the news."

"So what am I looking for?" Branche asked.

"Truth, lies, connections. What adds up, what doesn't."

The Lieutenant pointed at McGill. "McGill, you know the Pittsburgh area, so your focus is Andrew Mellon. You'll probably have to go up there and nose around. He set up the Narcotics Bureau when he was Treasury Secretary, and he had some kind of personal relationship with Anslinger. It was Mellon who appointed him, and like Nixon said, when in doubt, follow the money."

"Hot damn, the Burgh on an expense account," McGill said, grinning and rubbing his hands in mock glee.

"Thompkins, you take the media," the Lieutenant said. "Especially William Randolph Hearst. In his day his newspapers were bigger than all three TV networks combined."

"Ms. DeWolfe, you will be our nerve center. The President has ordered frequent progress reports. All of us, Rudy and me included, will have a report on your desk every morning by 09:00, detailing what we did the day before, as well as copies of relevant documents. You will edit them into something presentable and type them up."

"What will you be doing?" Branche asked.

"I'll take a trip up to Delaware and nose around at DuPont."

Branche asked, "Why not start with the oil companies?"

"Because," the Lieutenant said, "after the *Hemp for Victory* movie I asked myself, who's making money on sails and rope now that there's no hemp? In the Navy, its all made out of Nylon—"

"And DuPont makes Nylon," Thompkins said.

"That's right," the Lieutenant said. "It came out just after they banned hemp."

"So you think there's a connection?" Branche asked.

The Lieutenant shrugged and said, "Don't you?"

Rose Mary Woods gave everyone in the loop a white three-ring binder with TOP SECRET in big red letters on the cover so they could easily add the latest installments, which they immediately nicknamed *The Hemp Papers*. The bi-weekly reports, cogently organized and neatly typed, quickly became a highlight of Nixon's routine.

Ever since boyhood, Nixon had been fascinated with seafaring and its role in history; he was astonished to learn that without hemp there could have been no Age of Discovery. Sails made of cotton, wool, flax, or animal hides disintegrated after a few months at sea because of what they called "salt rot," while sails and cordage made of hemp lasted two or three years. Without hemp, trans-oceanic travel would have been next to impossible. If hemp did not exist, Columbus could not have discovered the New World and there would be no United States. Why had the history books overlooked it? Did the conspiracy run so deep it could erase history itself?

Nixon found the variety of its uses astounding. He learned that the Diesel enginre was designed to run on hemp oil; that the thirteen American colonies lit their lamps, not with whale oil, but with hemp oil, and that a young Abe Lincoln studied in his log cabin by the light of hemp oil. He learned hemp oil makes the best paints and varnishes and that all great painters, from DaVinci to Picasso, painted on hempen canvas. He learned it was hemp, not flax, which made the finest linen, and that books printed on hemp paper survived for centuries. He learned that hemp seed was eaten by people in many cultures in a kind of porridge, like oatmeal and that it made an excellent cattle feed. Nutritionists called it "the world's best vegetable" because it contained the most complete proteins of any plant. Agronomists claimed if it were widely cultivated for human consumption, it could eliminate hunger in the Third World because it grew so fast and so easily in practically any climate. For millennia, its fibers had clothed half of humanity. Even Christ's robes were woven from it. How could it be that he, Richard Nixon, an avid student of history and the leader of the Free World, had never heard any of this before? By any standard, it was a miracle plant, arguably humanity's single most important crop. Something was rotten. Nixon could smell it.

One night, he climbed into bed, plumped up a pillow against the headboard, and being careful not to wake his slumbering wife, settled back with the most exciting installment of the *Hemp Papers* yet. There was nothing a history buff like Nixon loved as much as an epic tale of war and peace, deceit and diplomacy, and the centuries-long conflict between England and France—the Limeys and the Frogs—was the most blood-tingling, back-and-forth Great Power saga of them all.

The key had been the British Royal Navy. "Rule Britannia, Britannia rule the waves" went the rousing song of imperial conquest. But the British Navy had an Achilles Heel. Like "Old Ironsides," a British man-o'-

war gobbled up a hundred tons of hemp every year for sails, lines, and caulking. But only czarist Russia had the millions of serfs needed to do the backbreaking labor to harvest the massive crop on which the world's shipping depended. Nixon was shocked to learn that Russia controlled eighty percent of the supply, giving the czar a choke-hold on that era's key strategic commodity far worse than the choke-hold the Arabs had on today's key strategic commodity—oil.

He switched off the light, kissed Pat on her forehead, and pondered the problem from Napoleon's point of view. If Napoleon's armies could have cut off the British hemp supply, in a couple of years the Royal Navy would have withered and died. No hemp, no sails; no sails, no ships; no ships, no navy; no navy, no empire on which the sun never set. End of game. Frogs win, Limeys lose. At last Nixon understood Napoleon's reasoning. But why had it been left out of the history books?

It was routine for everyone in the loop to meet in the Oval Office with Nixon for half an hour every Friday morning.

"Good morning, boys," Nixon said as the butlers and Secret Service agents left. He opened his desk drawer, made sure his secret taping system was on, took his coffee mug, and walked to his giant globe. He turned the globe until the Baltic Sea came into view, then spun it to the Persian Gulf, then back to the Baltic. Both bodies of water were choked off, bottled up. Same damn thing. He tapped his finger on Moscow and said, "Invading Russia makes perfect sense."

Bullcannon puffed up and said, "I'd love to write that speech for you, Mr. President. I can hear you now—*roll back the Iron Curtain.*"

Sometimes Nixon couldn't tell when Bullcannon was joking. "Not me, Bart. Napoleon. It made sense for Napoleon to invade Russia."

Bullcannon deflated like a leaky balloon. "Oh."

"I don't understand, Mr. President," Ehrlichman said.

"It's simple, John," Nixon said. "If Napoleon could have choked off the hemp supply, he would have driven a stake through the heart of the British navy. That's why he risked it."

He was surprised nobody said anything. He sighed, and gave the globe a spin. "Hells bells, boys, don't you see? That damned plant was what oil is to us today, the world's key commodity, worth fighting a war over. In Napoleon's day, hemp was the ball-breaker. In Nixon's day, oil's the ball-breaker. Napoleon tried to use it as a weapon, but he blew it. Nixon will not blow it. Not Nixon. Ha! A secret weapon has been dumped right in my lap—and nobody knows I've got it! Ha! I love it. Fucking love it! It's kind of, oh, I don't know...."

Nixon reflected, gently spinning the globe. "Napoleon and Nixon, two great strategic minds, a hundred and sixty years apart, and both of us with the same damn weapon. Ha. There should be *Twilight Zone* music playing." He tweedled the fingers of his right hand on the globe, like he was picking out the melody on the piano, and sang the notes to *Twilight Zone's* famous theme song, "Do doot do doo, do doot do doo."

"It is an amazing coincidence," Bullcannon said.

McGill blurted out, "Hippies would say it's cosmic, Mr. President."

Nixon gave him a quizzical look. "Cosmic? Did you say cosmic?"

"Uh, yes, sir."

"It certainly does seem as though it's part of something bigger," Nixon said. "But how do you know what the hippies would say? Are you a hippie, Mr. McGill?"

His young aide smiled as he raised his hands to his ears and pointed his thumbs at the sides of his head. "Not with this haircut, Mr. President."

Nixon chuckled. He liked the boy, and with all the toadies constantly sucking up to him, he appreciated a little irreverence now and then. "Boys, I've got a question I can't get out of my head. Now, I'm about as well read in the subject of history as anybody. So can somebody please tell me why in the hell I'd never heard about this damned plant before now?"

"Mr. President," the Lieutenant said, "we've been asking the same thing. In the early-America exhibits at the Smithsonian, it isn't mentioned once. They have exhibits on clipper ships and covered wagons, but there is not a single mention that all the canvas and ropes were made of hemp."

McGill added, "It's kind of like the un-persons in *1984*."

"Or like magic," Nixon said. He threw his arms upward, like a kid simulating an explosion, and said, "POOF—gone, in a puff of smoke. No pun intended. Ha!"

Everyone laughed. "Boys," Nixon said, "the more I learn about this the more it reminds me of how Stalin air-brushed photos of Trotsky right out of their history books like he'd never existed. Somebody's air-brushed this damned plant right out of American history and I'm going to find out who and why or my name isn't Richard Milhous Nixon."

Chapter 13

Go! Susannah

SUSANNAH, LA COWGIRL AMÉRICAINE, HAD IT DOWN. ALL THOSE YEARS OF dance lessons and diving competitions were finally paying off. Jenny had learned to go for the zone, to ignore distractions and to enjoy the feel of the coins tapping on her body. When she stepped into the go-go cage, she imagined herself in a diving meet doing a triple-back flip off the ten-meter platform. She was surprised how happy she was with her secret double life—graduate student by day, go-go dancer by night. She was getting straight A's and banking money, more than she had ever earned in her life. As for men, she just didn't have time for men.

One night, she was in the go-go cage, halfway through the last song of her set, The Who's "My Generation." She had just tossed off her halter top and was into her tassel-twirling routine when there was a commotion below her on the floor. She could see flashbulbs popping, so she knew it wasn't a bar fight. Must be celebrities. The Olympique got a lot of them. They were good tippers, with gawkers and groupies trailing along and spending money. Oskar would be pleased. She felt safe in the cage, loose, good. She was shocked when the deejay stopped the song in the middle, and the organ intro to "Light My Fire" by the Doors came blasting over the speakers, throwing her out of the zone. More flashbulbs popped. It was hard to see who it was with the spotlights glaring up. She could make out eight or ten men, with glitzy women on their arms. Oskar's bouncers were keeping the rest of the patrons at bay, giving the celebrities room.

A tall man in a cowboy hat, with muttonchop sideburns and a pony-tail, was getting a lot of attention. Behind him, another celebrity, dressed in what looked like black leather, was getting even more. He lifted his head and fixed his eyes on her. Oh my God…it's the Doors' singer, Jim Morrison. She had read he was in Paris, resurrected after hoaxing the world with a phony death stunt. Even his parents thought he was dead for over a year. The cocky slouch, the dangling cigarette…it was him all right, the dark poetic genius, the baddest bad boy in all of rock 'n' roll who called himself "The Lizard King." She could guess what that meant.

From beneath her cage, a loud voice yelled up, "Hey, cowgirl, wanna ride my horse!" A surge of shame ripped through her like a bullet. Despite her pasties and bikini bottom, she felt totally naked. Why did Americans always make her feel so vulnerable, but the French never did?

As "Light my Fire" rocked to a finish, she matched the driving beat with a bravura performance of the crazy-windmills.

Her theme song, "Oh! Susannah" came on, the end of her set. As her cage began to rise Morrison rushed to the deejay's booth, took the mic from the deejay and sang:

> *"Go Susannah,*
> *Go-go-go for me*
> *'Cause I come from Alabama*
> *With a hard-on to Paree!"*

The celebrity with the sideburns laughed, whooped, and began waving his cowboy hat high in the air, beckoning the cage back down as the other celebrities and their entourage joined in singing:

> *"Go Susannah,*
> *Go-go-go for me*
> *'Cause I come from Alabama*
> *With a hard-on to Paree!"*

She kept up her exit routine, praying the cage would rise faster, as the crowd, incited by the rockers, hurled coins and wadded-up bills at her so hard it hurt. Then she heard Oskar, hoping to milk it for all he could, call to the cage operator, "Encore! Encore!" No, Oskar, please, noooo—

The cage jerked to a stop, swung for a moment, and started back down. For the first time she felt scared, imprisoned, humiliated, no longer protected by the cage, and totally out of the zone. It was all she could do to keep from bursting into tears as the tall cowboy and Morrison and the entourage and the deejay and Oskar and the bartenders and the waiters and the bouncers and the whole crowd sang, "With a hard-on to Paree!"

When the cage stopped, the deejay announced, "Susannah, La Cowgirl Américaine!" The crowd gave her a cheer and another shower of tips. A new song came over the speakers, "One Way Out," by the Allman Brothers. Another cheer went up. The rockers were smiling and waving as the tall cowboy took off his hat and tipped it to the crowd. Now she recognized him—guitarist Duane Allman.

The dance floor was packed. She was grateful people forgot about her as they earned a lifetime's worth of bragging rights for dancing with the stars. She kept performing, catching glimpses of Morrison, sullen, staring. She had heard the rumors of his heavy drug use, of voodoo parties with sacrificial chickens, and secret recording sessions with everyone from John and Yoko to Janis Joplin to Jimi Hendrix to now, apparently, the Allman Brothers.

Allman was dancing with a slinky fashion-model type. Jenny detected no hint of the motorcycle accident that had almost killed him a couple of years before. He looked up, caught her eye, and smiled at her. The woman he was with saw their eyes meet and bared her fangs, ready for a cat fight. Jenny just smiled and looked away. No problem, sister. The customer is always right.

Finally, "Oh! Susannah" came on, and her cage went up to a cacophony of hoots and hollers and everybody singing, "With a hard-on to Paree!"

The other dancers mobbed her as she climbed out of the cage and came off the narrow walkway. They were thrilled that the biggest stars in rock 'n' roll had been serenading one of their own—who could believe it?

They escorted her to the dressing room like she was visiting royalty. Little Nicole stayed behind to keep an eye on the cage operator as he scooped up the money from the cage floor and put it in the tip sack. The dancers plumped up the pillows on the couch and handed her a tall Pernod. She needed it. She was exhausted.

Nicole burst in with the sack and emptied the money onto the carpet. Everyone gasped at the size of the pile. Jenny was numb as she watched them separate the currencies: francs, dollars, pounds, marks, lire. The dancers counted as Nicole scribbled in her notebook and consulted the exchange rates in *La Monde*. After some calculating, Nicole announced, "Four thousand, one hundred and twenty-two francs."

The room went topsy-turvy with shrieks of amazement. Her share came to over five hundred dollars!

Somebody passed a hash pipe. She took a hit, loosened her robe, and peeled off her pasties. She hated the flaky white residue of glue they left stuck to her nipples, like dried milk in a cereal bowl. All she wanted was a long, hot bath, and a bed.

Suddenly there was pounding on the door, and Oskar was yelling in French, "Susannah, you have a visitor."

"Oh, Oskar, do I have to?"

The other dancers insisted with a loud, "*Mais oui!*"

She sighed, closed her robe, tied the sash tight, and leaned back on the pillows as the door opened.

It was Morrison, in skin-tight black leather pants, a cigarette dangling from his lips. The dancers twittered as he sauntered in and said in English, "I very much enjoyed your performance, Susannah."

The dancers were whispering and giggling, awestruck to be in the presence of a legend. She was embarrassed, managing only a tiny smile as she said, "Thanks."

Morrison pointed to the couch. "I love what you do with your tassels. Does it take a lot of practice?"

She looked down at her pasties on the couch. She'd forgotten all about them. She forced a smile, picked up the pasties, casually spun the tassels with a flick of her wrist and said, "It's easy once you get the hang of it," then slipped them into her bathrobe pocket. She had no intention of discussing her breasts with a man she'd never met, no matter how famous he was.

Morrison grinned. "So, Susannah, are you a real cowgirl?"

"Not until I came to Paris." God, what a dumb thing to say.

"So where are you from?"

It had been easy keeping her history from the others at the Olympique. Chicago, Pittsburgh, Podunk…it didn't matter. If it wasn't Manhattan or Hollywood, the French didn't care about her hometown, where she went to college, what her father did for a living, none of it. She hardly had to lie to them at all, but Morrison could trip her up in a heartbeat. Where was he from? She had read his father was a Navy admiral, and Navy brats grew up all over.

Before she could answer, a voice called through the door, "Hey Jim, come on, man. Mick and Keith are already back at the hotel with the stuff. You know how they are. If we don't get there soon, it's gonna be *gone!*"

"Yeah, just a sec," he called, then he spied Nicole's notepad and asked in bad French, "May I have a piece of paper?"

Nicole gave him the pad and blurted out in English, "Can I have your autograph? My name's Nicole. It's spelled N-i-c-o-l-e."

The dancers gasped at her childish audacity, as Morrison was famous for being rude to autograph hounds. He took the pen and spoke in English, very slowly, writing as he went. "For… Nicole… whose… English… is… better… than… my… French." He signed with a flourish.

Nicole held up her prize, showing it off. "Oh, merci, merci bien!"

Morrison wrote something on a second sheet, folded it in quarters, and bent over her, close enough for Jenny to smell brandy on his breath as he whispered, "There's a session tomorrow. Five o'clock. It could be very special. Call, and I'll send a driver."

He pressed the folded paper into her palm and wrapped his fingers around hers, sending shivers up her spine as he squeezed her hand closed and said, "Au revoir, Susannah."

In the morning, Nicole and the dancers bugged her and bugged her until she finally called the number just to get them off her back. A limousine took her to a studio; a guard led her to a booth. Morrison was sitting behind a massive mixing board with banks of knobs and lights and sliders and VU meters. He was watching as Duane Allman, who was wearing a set of headphones, tuned his guitar on the other side of the glass.

Morrison flicked a switch and spoke into his microphone, "Yo, Duane, look who's here."

Allman looked up and saw her, grinned, and ripped off a blistering slide guitar riff of "Oh! Susannah" that started her blushing.

Morrison stood up and greeted her, not like a self-absorbed rock star, but like the well-mannered son of a U.S. Navy admiral. "Susannah, I'm so glad you could make it."

"I'd have never heard the end of it if I didn't come," she said, testing his sense of humor.

"We'll try to make it worth your while. Ever been in a studio before?"

"They recorded our sixth-grade Christmas pageant for the radio, but I don't know if that counts."

"Of course it counts. So you're a singer?"

"I've sung in choirs all my life."

"Great. We're doing a scratch track. Why don't you go in the studio with Duane and help us test the mics while I work the board?"

There were half a dozen mic stands in the studio. He gave her a set of earphones and she went to the first mic, switched the button up and said, "Testing. Testing."

"Okay, it's working," Morrison said. "Now sing something."

"What?"

"Anything at all, just to get the levels."

The first song to come to mind was "With a Little Help From My Friends." She sang a few a bars as Morrison worked the console; to her surprise, Allman's guitar began to accompany her. He was playing and smiling, encouraging her to keep going, so she sang the entire song. When it wound up Allman said, "Hey Jim, this girl can flat out *sing!*"

Soon the other members of the two bands arrived. It was a jam session to loosen up and get comfortable, maybe write a song or two. They let her sing a few back-ups and when they heard what she could do, assigned her to her own microphone. She had never had so much fun.

Morrison's plans were bigger than a mere album. He wanted this to be a political statement, a musical tour de force that would shake the foundations of civilization. When the Rolling Stones went on tour, the Doors and the Allman Brothers would quietly borrow Mick Jagger's chateau and private recording studio on the Riviera. A *Who's Who* of superstars were planning to secretly drop in and add their talents for a song or two. Janis Joplin was to join Morrison on a rock duet; Jimi Hendrix would add his high-energy guitar to Duane's sweet slide on a couple of tunes; John and Yoko, Jerry Garcia, Carlos Santana—even Bob Dylan—had all promised to contribute.

But the biggest coup of all would be a session with the world's most dangerous man, Timothy Leary, who was sitting in a Swiss jail pending a hearing on his request for political asylum. The Swiss were proud that it was a Swiss scientist who had discovered LSD and a Swiss drug company which owned the patents. Switzerland also had a long history as a haven for political refugees, so there was every reason to believe asylum would be granted. The plan was to move the project to Geneva for a session with Leary when it was approved. Morrison was exultant at the prospect. "If we can pull this off, Nixon will shit his pants."

When Jenny woke up in Morrison's bed the next morning, she couldn't help wondering what on Earth had made her sleep with a man on a first date. She had never done that before, ever, not once. Had she sold out in a moment of weakness, become a rock-star groupie, the antithesis of the ardent feminist she thought herself to be?

No, she had told herself that morning…and every morning for the past two weeks. She wasn't a groupie. Groupies hung out at stage doors and threw perfumed panties and hotel keys at the stars. Morrison had pursued her, asked her out on a date. She had given in because…because it felt right. What was wrong with that?

As the time for the big session on the Riviera approached, stars would pop over from London for a couple of days of get-acquainted jamming and song-swapping. Since meeting Morrison, she had spent most of her free time with him, much of it at the studio, singing backup for Janis Joplin one day, harmonizing with John and Yoko the next. No matter who was jamming, whenever a song needed a harmony or an ooh-wah or a shooby-doo, she was there, right on key. And when she wasn't singing, she was in the booth, watching and listening and soaking up all she could about the process of making music.

Unfortunately, there were some negatives. Big negatives. The wild, drug-crazed, debauched rock 'n' roll lifestyle had never appealed to her, but she had been in the fast lane since that first night with Morrison, and it was taking a toll. A little pot or hash with a couple of beers or glasses of wine while collaborating on songs would have been fine. But there was an endless river of hard liquor, and halfway through the night, somebody would break out the white powders and screw the music up.

Morrison claimed he was going straight as soon as the album was in the can. She didn't believe it for a second. She tried to look beyond the drugs and the lifestyle and see him as a person. Even if he were to go on the wagon and quit everything, cold turkey, she could tell they would never truly click as a couple. She liked him. He was cute and talented, but underneath the bravado he was just another guy, certainly not "The Lizard King." But sex was never a priority for her. Synergistic companionship and mutual respect were what she wanted in a man—someone simpatico. She found him deep and poetic when he was sober, but even then he had a dark side—morbid, melancholy, macabre. His flat was filled with books and artifacts of the occult—black magic, witchcraft, and especially...voodoo.

She had thought his interest in it was harmless, like Catherine's infatuation with astrology. Then last night he took her to what he said was a "mojo party," which turned out to be a voodoo ceremony with candles, chanting and drumming, coconut cups of liquid potions, and an aged Haitian woman in a mask throwing bones like a soothsayer in a cheap horror movie. Jenny found it exceedingly creepy, and had been appalled when they killed a live chicken and cut out its still-beating heart.

She turned away, unable to watch, whispered, "Jim, I can't take this," and got up to leave.

He put his hand around her wrist, whisked her into the hall, and led her down to his limousine. "I'm sorry," he said as he opened the limo's door. "I should never have brought you. I'll see you back at my place."

"Aren't you coming?"

"No. My turn's coming up."

"Your turn for what?"

He grinned. "To get my mojo rising."

"Then I want to go to the Olympique."

"I'll send for you tomorrow, at noon. It's the last session before we head down to Mick's." He gave her a perfunctory kiss and raced back in.

As the chauffeur drove to the Place Pigalle she was amazed to realize that for Morrison the voodoo was real. It gave her goosebumps to even think about it. She hadn't given up the priests and rituals of Catholicism just to get involved with the witch doctors and blood-sacrifices of voodoo. No, thank you, Mr. Morrison.

The next morning she had a long talk with herself. What exactly do you feel for him, Jennifer? What? She concluded it was not the yearning of a woman for a man but something closer to sympathy, what a nurse might feel for a patient. For once in her life, she was glad she wasn't in love.

So if it wasn't love, what was motivating her? The fun of singing...was *that* it? Did she have an addiction to music like Morrison had for white powders? If so, it was time to kick the habit.

She knew her life was about to change, no matter what. Classes were over, she had written her term paper, and only needed to neatly type it and turn it in. Soon she must decide between returning to the States or accepting a job offer from U.N.E.S.C.O., the Red Cross, or Greenpeace. No matter what, when Jennifer Marie Abruzzi, JD, began her professional life as an attorney, Susannah, La Cowgirl Américaine, would vanish without a trace.

It was time to break it off with Morrison...but how to break the news? It must be done early in his day, before he started drinking. How would he react when she told him she just wanted to be friends? If he took it well, it was possible they really could be life-long friends and someday she could tell him her real name. If he freaked out, she would walk away and Susannah would disappear. A postcard to Oskar, wishing everyone at the Olympique a fond farewell, would be all the explanation necessary.

It would be best if she could manage it one step at a time, make it a process with no ugly scenes. She would start by telling Morrison she couldn't go with him to the Riviera.

She was trembling as she rode up to his flat in the building's tiny elevator. She crossed her fingers and hoped he hadn't started drinking. She rang the bell. The door opened a crack and Morrison stuck his head out, looked up and down the hall, and said, "Anybody following you?"

What a strange comment. "No, why?"

He let her in, then stuck his head back into the hall to make sure no one was there. He was always alert for crazed fans or paparazzi, but she'd never seen him this jumpy.

"Jim, what is it? Is something wrong?"

"No, but I've got a surprise for you."

He closed the door and called toward the bedroom, "It's okay. It's Susannah. She's going to help us."

The bedroom door opened and a man emerged. He wore jeans, a turtleneck sweater, and carried a sailor's cap and a navy peacoat. He had gray hair, was quite handsome, and was beaming a broad, elfin smile.

"Susannah, say hello to Dr. Timothy Leary, the world's most dangerous man," Morrison said with a laugh. "We're going to help him get to Afghanistan."

Chapter 14

Gay Paree

WITH SIX MEN AND ONE OF HER, THE OFFICE OF THE PRESIDENTIAL POLICY Commission soon resembled a football locker room. Catherine did her best to ignore the incessant male banter—the bragging, the constant razzing, the childish pranks. *Playboy* centerfolds went up in the cubicles, and an AutoChamp Spark Plugs cleavage-of-the-month calendar hung by the water cooler. There was no law against being a man, though she often wished there were.

She had been surprised to feel a surge of pride when she opened her first pay envelope. She had never seen a paycheck, much less ever earned one. What were the deductions all about? FICA—what was that? Her trust fund gave her more in a month than she would earn working forty-hours a week for an entire year. She was amazed that the other secretaries could live on it.

She made coffee, kept the copier filled with paper and toner, edited, typed, and took messages. The days flew by until one Friday morning she was alone in the office, and in walked Gridley. He set his briefcase on the counter. "Ah, Miss DeWolfe, we meet again."

Trapped. "Nice to see you, Mr. Gridley," she said, lying as sweetly as she could. "What brings you here?"

Gridley's eyes flitted about, casing the room, almost like a burglar. "I'm looking for your Mr. Duberman."

"I don't expect him until late this afternoon. Would you like to leave a message?"

"Maybe you can help. He's been nosing around over at the D.E.A. and Treasury, requesting access to old Bureau of Narcotics records. That agency doesn't even exist any more, so there are jurisdictional issues all over the map. Since I'm Nixon's drug czar, they asked me to sort it out. So here I am."

"So you are. What may I do to assist you?"

"Tell me what you're looking for, and maybe I can save everybody some time."

She didn't mind lying to Gridley; she could lie to him all day long, even if she were telling the truth. "I'm only a secretary, Mr. Gridley. Questions regarding our operations must go to Lt. Mulligan or to Mr. Duberman."

"Yes, of course. The odd thing is, they're looking into the files of somebody you and I both know."

"I...don't understand."

"Commissioner Anslinger. You met him at the memorial dinner for Secretary Morganthau, the same time we first met. Remember? We were all at the same table."

Her skin crawled at the memory, but she couldn't place him. "I'm sorry, but all I remember is sitting with J. Edgar Hoover."

"Well, anyway, your people want access to his files from the early days of the old F.B.N. in the Thirties. Now, if you can tell me what you're looking for, I'll give him a call. He's getting on in years, but he's sharp as a tack. We could make an outing of it, go up there together. I'm sure the Commissioner will remember you. Would you like that?"

The notion of an outing with Gridley repelled her; she dodged his question. "But why on Earth would he remember me?"

"You were in college down the road from Leary's playpen, and he was worried you'd be like the Mellon brats and finance Leary's orgies. The Commissioner is tight with the Mellons, so it was personal. He wanted us to tail you full time, but we didn't have the manpower."

"What? You followed me...*in college*?"

"You and every other rich girl at Vassar. You were just the richest and the wildest. Do you really find that surprising?"

Don't get angry, stay calm. "My father always said I'd be watched because of my name, but I never imagined it would be by the police."

"We had quite a dossier on you. And you'll be interested to know that your name popped up on an INTERPOL report not too long ago."

"*My* name?"

"When you were in college, your lawyers filed a complaint against a scam artist from Romania for credit card fraud. The case is still open."

She hadn't thought about it in years. "It's something I prefer to forget."

"I can't blame you. My office in Poughkeepsie handled the paperwork, and they keep me up-to-date on all my old cases. Whenever his name comes up, you and a dozen others come up too. Seems he's made quite a career for himself. I'll let you know when they get him."

She couldn't believe how much Gridley knew about her. "Thank you, I'd like that very much."

"So it seems you've been promoted?" Gridley said. "Perhaps now you'll reconsider my offer for dinner?"

"I'm flattered, but like I said, I don't date co-workers."

Rejection seemed to embolden him; he leaned over the counter and said in a whisper, "I have some news about your drug-guru friend."

"Dr. Leary was not my friend, Mr. Gridley. I hardly knew him."

He looked over his shoulder, checking to be sure they were alone. "Between you and me, I'm going to nail him this weekend. I really shouldn't be showing you these, but...."

He opened his briefcase and pulled out a folder of 8"x10" black-and-white photographs. He showed her a grainy blow-up of a man with gray hair looking out a window. "That was taken just a few days ago."

She couldn't help being curious. "It does look a little like him. I thought they set him free?"

"The assholes refused to extradite him, but they said he was there illegally and gave him a month to find a country to take him or they'd deport him back here. Nobody wants the bastard, so he's got to keep running. He thinks he gave us the slip, but I'm going over there to nail him."

He handed her a second photo of people in swimsuits around a pool. "Recognize anybody?"

Two faces jumped out. "John Lennon and Yoko Ono?"

"And that's not all." He slid another across the counter. She recognized Jimi Hendrix, Duane Allman, Janis Joplin, and in the back by the diving board, Jim Morrison, with his arm draped around Jenny. *What?* She gasped and did a double-take. Her heart was booming like the kettledrum canons in *The 1812 Overture.*

Gridley tilted his head, concerned. "Anything wrong, Miss DeWolfe?"

"No, no, it's just...just all these stars...in one place."

"Yes, it's a real collection of dirt bags, all right."

She needed to know more. "Where...where is this?"

"I'm afraid I can't answer that. But watch the news this weekend, and you'll see me strike the biggest blow ever in the war on drugs. Nixon himself just gave me the okay. And can you imagine the headlines if I nail Leary along with assholes like Lennon and Morrison and Hendrix?"

She could imagine all right. "What..." she said, pausing, not wanting to appear too eager, "what about the others? Are you going to arrest them too?"

"If it was up to me, I'd haul 'em all in, but the Frogs aren't as gung-ho in the war on drugs as they ought to be. It depends what we find, but

I'll settle for Leary if I have to. The others will be icing on the cake."

Now, instead getting rid of Gridley, she wanted to keep him talking. "You seem confident you're going to get him."

"This time his ass is grass."

"How did you find him?"

"I've been playing cat-and-mouse with him for so long I know how he thinks. He loves the spotlight, and I knew he'd try a stunt like this. I've had people on the inside watching the rockers for a while."

She had to be sure it was Jenny and not a look-alike. "This is so exciting, Mr. Gridley. May I see the other photographs?"

Gridley slid the folder across the counter, smiling and stroking his mustache as she looked through. She tried to appear star-struck, so he wouldn't guess she was pumping him for information. "I recognize Janis Joplin, but who are the other women? Anyone famous?"

"Nah, riff-raff, groupies. The one with Hendrix is a model from Argentina, calls herself Cilantro. The one with Morrison's a go-go dancer in Pig Alley, calls herself Susannah, La Cowgirl Américaine. That one...."

Jenny...a go-go dancer? In Pig Alley? He must mean the Place Pigalle, in Paris. It was too crazy. She looked again to be sure; it was Jenny all right, wearing the same tank suit she'd seen her in dozens of times when they worked out together in the Yale pool. If she weren't seeing it with her own eyes, she would never have believed it. Jenny, always-careful, always-practical Jenny, using a phony name and partying with rock stars at the hideout of the world's most wanted fugitive? What had she gotten herself into? What about the Sorbonne? Was she sleeping with Morrison? What if she got caught in Gridley's bust? Did Jenny even know Leary was there?

The only good news was that Gridley didn't seem to know or care who Jenny was. He was after bigger fish. Could she warn her?

Gridley took a leather organizer from his inside pocket. She noticed a Pan Am ticket envelope in it as he handed her a business card and said, "I've got some things to wrap up, then I'm off to nail the bastard. Give this to Duberman. Tell him to call me next week so we can see about setting up an interview with the Commissioner."

"I'm sure he'll be very pleased to hear that, Mr. Gridley. Good-bye."

"Not good-bye, Miss DeWolfe, au revoir. And be sure to watch for me on the news this weekend."

"I will," was all she said, pointedly not wishing him luck.

What to do? She had an address for Jenny, but no phone number. A telegram? No, too risky. Besides, there was the phony Susannah name. What was that all about?

She called Jenny's home in Pittsburgh and reached her mother. "Mrs. Abruzzi, this is Catherine DeWolfe, Jenny's friend from law school. Remember me?"

"Of course, Catherine, how nice to hear from you. How have you been?"

"Very well, thank you. I'm trying to get hold of Jenny. I have an address, but would you happen to have a phone number?"

"They don't have phones in the rooms, so we stay in touch by mail."

"Is she still at the Sorbonne?"

"I think she's finished with classes, but she has a term paper left."

"How is she doing? Does she like Paris?"

"She sounded a little depressed around Christmas, but she seems much happier in her last letters."

"When's she coming home?"

"She's not sure. She's been interviewing for jobs with the United Nations and the Red Cross and something called Greenpeace."

It was obvious Jenny's mother knew nothing about go-go dancing or rock stars or Timothy Leary. Those were not subjects any twenty-five-year-old single woman in her right mind would ever discuss with her mother.

She remembered Gridley's ticket envelope and called Pan Am. The agent said the next flight left Dulles at 7:15 this evening, arriving at Orly Airport at 6:53 Saturday morning. Chances were Gridley would be on it.

"Is there any way to get there sooner?"

"Well, you could catch a shuttle to New York and take a flight out of Idlewild. And Air France has the new Concorde, but it's very expensive."

She always did her best not to be the stereotype of the spoiled rich kid, but what good was being a DeWolfe if you couldn't throw a little money around when you needed to? She called Air France. The Concorde left Dulles at 1:10 her time and arrived at Orly on Friday night at 10:45, Paris time, crossing the Atlantic in just three-and-a-half hours for a round trip fare of only $10,624. If Jenny was a go-go dancer, she wouldn't get off until very late Friday. There might be time to warn her.

She booked the flight on a credit card and left a brief note to the Lieutenant and Duberman saying she had to leave early. She took a cab home, stopping at her bank for $5,000, half in dollars, half in francs, in a zippered money pouch. She would travel light, just an overnight bag with a change of clothes and a few toiletries. She changed into jeans, sneakers, a cotton blouse, and a cashmere sweater. Spring could be rainy in Paris, so she wore a waterproof jacket with a hood. Thinking that a picture of Jenny might be useful, she took the snapshot off the refrigerator of the two of them hugging like sisters in front of the fireplace at Lib House and put it in her jacket pocket.

On the cab ride to Dulles she remembered from Criminal Procedures class that police preferred to raid early in the morning, when suspects were in bed, naked, hung-over, and less likely to resist. If Gridley got in Saturday morning, the raid would probably come Sunday morning. She had less than a day to track Jenny down and warn her.

And what about Leary? His prison sentence was a gross injustice, but would she be risking everything by flying off to Paris to warn him if Jenny weren't in jeopardy? No. The "happenings" at Millbrook all those years ago had been fun, but she had hardly spoken to him even then.

On the other hand, did she want to warn him if she could? Yes. Would warning him, even indirectly, make her guilty of aiding and abetting a fugitive? What if she warned Jenny but not Leary? If she warned Jenny, and Jenny warned Leary, would both of them be committing felonies? What if, what if, what if? And under whose law, Napoleon's or Nixon's? She would need a week in a law library to even begin to be sure.

She must keep her involvement secret, or her days in the White House and her chance to bring Nixon down were over. Only Jenny could know, but it would be better if even she was in the dark. Perhaps she could warn her anonymously, so Jenny didn't even know where it came from, and let her warn Leary? Did Jenny even know Leary was there?

She had not used her passport since the summer of 1967, when they met on the Seven Sisters Debate Club's tour group, when Jenny was on Bryn Mawr's debating team, and she was on Vassar's. As she stood in line at the ticket counter she leafed through her passport looking at old entry and exit stamps and visas of a dozen countries. Memories flooded in, good and bad. She winced at the reminder of her infatuation with the phony Romanian count on a motorcycle who had ripped off her credit cards.

She was concerned about her rusty French. She had spent three summers in Montreal with some cousins when she was in grade school and had taken advanced French, so at one time she knew it pretty well. But except for practicing with Jenny at Lib House once in a while, she hadn't used it in years. Don't worry, she told herself. It will come back.

She breezed through customs, jumped in a cab and said, "Place Pigalle!" She was afraid Jenny would be hard to find, but a marquee under a flashing orange neon sign reading OLYMPIQUE AU-GO-GO proclaimed in lights: "Susannah, La Cowgirl Américaine."

There was a crowd milling about on the sidewalk like they were waiting for somebody. She could feel the eyes of the men undressing her as she walked up and paid the doorman.

Inside, a huge dance floor was flanked by two go-go cages dangling by cables suspended between elaborate theatrical curtains. It was past midnight at the hottest disco in Paris, and desperate men, knowing they were going home alone if they didn't get lucky soon, hit on her in French: A dance? A drink? A toke of hash? A toot of coke?

Men were the same in any language. She brushed them off like ants from a picnic table and ordered a glass of wine at the bar, asking the bartender in French, "When's Susannah come on?"

He glanced at his wristwatch. "Tout suite."

Thank God she was in time. She relaxed and moved to a corner to watch. Soon, a deejay's voice announced, "Susannah, La Cowgirl Américaine." A go-go cage descended from the overhead curtains as a rocked-out "Oh! Susannah" came over the speakers.

She got goosebumps seeing her friend descend in the cage, suggestively riding a broomstick pony and shooting off a toy cap gun. She had on a Lone Ranger mask, a white ten-gallon hat, a skimpy halter top, a miniskirt, a gun holster around her waist, and red-leather cowboy boots with silver spurs. It was a side of Jenny she would never have guessed at, not in ten million years, the polar opposite of the dedicated feminist she thought she knew.

With each new song Jenny teased the crowd on. One by one, off came her hat, holster, mask, miniskirt. Twenty minutes later, glistening with perspiration and down to only the halter top, leather boots, and sequined bikini bottom, Jenny slipped off her top, going bare-breasted except for a pair of star-shaped pasties with silver tassels she somehow spun in a blur, like airplane propellers. Men whooped and showered her cage with money.

Catherine didn't know whether to be proud of Jenny or ashamed for her. The deejay said, "Susannah, La Cowgirl Américaine," and "Oh! Susannah" came over the speakers as the cage started up.

Just when she thought there could be no more surprises, the crowd began singing *With a hard-on to Pareee!* in bad English as Jenny waved and blew kisses. If Cornelia had been there, she'd have excommunicated Jenny from the women's liberation movement on the spot.

When Jenny's cage disappeared into the overhead curtains, Catherine started toward the back of the bar, planning to bribe her way into Jenny's dressing room. She was inching through the crowd when a man's voice said in English, "So, Little Butterfly, again we meet."

Terror clamped her by the throat as the biggest mistake of her life flashed before her like it was yesterday. "Andrei?"

"The world is small, Little Butterfly, is it not?"

It had been 1967, the Summer of Love. She and Jenny and two others had left the official Seven Sisters Debate Club tour group to travel on their own. They arrived at the hostel in Florence around midnight, and in the morning she let them sleep in while she went out to take photographs of the piazza while the light was soft. She shot a roll of film, bought a copy of *Time* from a kiosk, sat at a sidewalk café, and ordered a cappuccino.

She read about the big rock festival she'd missed at Monterey. She would have gone to California instead of Europe if she'd known it was going to be the Summer of Love. Backpacking around Europe with her new friends on the Eurail train pass was fun, but out in California the Summer of Love was half over, and she was missing it.

She heard the roar of a motorcycle and looked up to see a bullishly-built man, darkly handsome, on the same bike Marlon Brando rode in *The Wild Bunch*, a black Triumph 650. He had a rakish mustache, bushy eyebrows, and dark, curly hair that covered his ears like a helmet. He raised his silver sunglasses high on his head, and straddling the motorcycle's seat, scanned the café's patrons. He put down the kickstand and unzipped his leather jacket, revealing a V-cut shirt showing off a gold-link chain and a bristly chestfull of hair. There was no free table, so in the European custom he took a chair at hers and pointed to her magazine.

"You American?" he asked in heavily-accented English.

"Yes."

"On holiday?"

"Yes."

"From California?"

"No, I'm from Michigan."

"I from Bucharest, in Romania, but no can go. If communists catch," and he slid his finger across his throat, like a knife, and made a slicing sound through his teeth. "Thiiiit."

"They'd kill you?"

"Si, like zat," and he snapped his fingers–*click*. "How long you here?"

"About a month so far, with another month to go."

"Where you seen?"

"So far we've been to Paris, Heidelberg, Vienna, Budapest, Istanbul, and Athens. We just got in from Venice."

"Ah, like a little butterfly, going here, going there. Where next you go, Little Butterfly?"

"Tomorrow we go to Rome, then to the South of France and Spain."

He dismissed the idea with a wave of his hand. "España? Why? Franco's fascists belong to past. You want future, go Copenhagen. You been?"

"There won't be time. Maybe next year I'll do the north."

"Next year too late, future gone. Come, we go. I show you future."

Had she heard him right? "You want me to go with you to Copenhagen?"

"Si. Future is good in Copenhagen."

The Danish capital had a reputation as a rock 'n' roll Valhalla, a counter-culture heaven-on-earth with a Scandinavian accent and no-hassle cops. It didn't have the warm Mediterranean sun, but artists, writers, poets, musicians, hippies, revolutionaries and freethinkers of all stripes summered in Copenhagen. Copenhagen was copacetic.

"What matter, Little Butterfly? You scared of motorcycle?"

"No, I love motorcycles. But…I don't even know your name."

He stood up, clicked his heels, and bowed. "Count Andrei Antonescu." He took her hand in his, and kissed it.

He was about ten years older, late twenties or early thirties, and almost as tall as she was. She was drawn to his vitality, his raw masculinity, and his motorcycle. At last, here was a man, a real man, a count no less, who would know how to treat a woman, not like the immature American college boys who were always hitting on her on the trains and in the hostels. The Summer of Love was half-gone, and until that very instant she hadn't met any man she wanted to see a movie with, much less make love to.

She rode with him back to the hostel and went upstairs to get her things and tell the others.

Jenny was dumbstruck. "You're going *where*?"

"To Copenhagen. Why don't you come and meet me?"

"But what about Rome. And Spain?" one of the others asked.

"Rome will always be there, and Andrei says Copenhagen's much better than Madrid."

"Who is this Andrei?" Jenny asked.

"He's a count…from Romania. We're going on his motorcycle."

"Are you insane?" Jenny said. "You can't go riding off on a motorcycle with some stranger you just met on the street."

"We met in a café, and I'm nineteen and I can do anything I want. Besides, I'm tired of police and soldiers everywhere we go. Hungary, Turkey, Greece, they're all dictatorships. Andrei says Spain's even worse. I want to see the future before it's too late."

Jenny spread out a map on the bed. "Copenhagen, huh?"

"Why don't you come meet me, and we'll go to Amsterdam and London together. You wanted to see England more than Spain, anyway."

After a brief discussion they agreed to meet in Copenhagen in a week. They went down with her, and she introduced them to Andrei. He put their packs on the motorcycle's rack with bungee cords; two people, two backpacks, somehow it all fit. She had everything she needed: backpack, sleeping bag, passport, credit cards, and a six-week supply of birth-control pills to get her through the Summer of Love.

Soon, they were cruising the twisting roads of the Italian Alps, the wind in her face. She clung to his muscular body, anticipating her first real man, not the fumbling, heavy-handed boys she'd known all her life.

They took a room at an alpine inn near the Austrian border, and he told stories over a seven-course Italian dinner and a bottle of Chianti. He ordered a second bottle, which he drank mostly by himself, and topped it off with a few cognacs. When they went to bed, he paid no attention to her needs or desires as he quickly satisfied himself and fell asleep, snoring like a carpenter's saw. She lay awake for a long time, staring at the ceiling, worried she had made a mistake.

The next day they crossed the Alps over the spectacular Brenner Pass, stopping so she could take photos. That afternoon they rode through Austria, had lunch in scenic Innsbruck, then into Germany's lush green Bavarian countryside. In the evening they checked into a cheap Munich hotel, and he took her on a tour of the city's famous sing-along Ratskeller. She had a few beers, but Andrei preferred schnapps. About midnight he got into a shouting match with two men over some ancient tribal grievance, screaming in Romanian about Hapsburgs as they yelled in Hungarian about Dracula. They would have come to blows if the German bouncers hadn't intervened.

Back in the hotel room, Andrei pulled a flask from his pack.

"Haven't you had enough?" she said, disgusted with his boorish behavior.

He let out a grunt and roughly pulled her to him.

"No…not when you're drunk."

She winced as his fingers dug into the back of her arm.

"You say no to Andrei?"

"Stop. You're hurting me!" She used a simple judo move to twist out of his grip. His eyes went wild and he raised his hand to slap her, but she deflected it and stepped back in a judo crouch.

He lunged and tried to grab her by the neck. She judoed him around, and he cried out a surprised "Aaaggh!" as she flipped him over her back, slammed him face-first to the floor, and pinned him to the shabby carpet. He struggled, cursing in Romanian. She controlled him by his wrist and elbow like her sensei had taught her. "Be quiet, or I'll break your arm. I swear it. You want somebody to call the police, I'll tell them you attacked me. You want that?"

"I get you for this, Little Butterfly. I pick off you wings."

He outweighed her by fifty muscular pounds, and she wouldn't catch him by surprise a second time. How to disable him without breaking bones? His belt? No, too hard to get off. A cord from a lamp? No, the cheap room only had an overhead. By the backpack—the bungee cords.

She forced him to scoot along the floor until she could reach the cords, and tied his wrists behind his back. Now she could control him by adjusting his little finger…just so.

"Owww!"

She forced him to the bed, made him lie flat on his belly, took off a pillowcase and tied it around his mouth to gag him. She bound his ankles with another bungee and hog-tied them to his wrists like a buckaroo roping steers in a rodeo.

He growled through the gag, thrashing around on the bed. His eyes were glowing with rage, so she took another pillowcase and blindfolded him. She hooked more bungees together and threaded them under the bed and over his torso, strapping him tight so he couldn't roll off.

She sat on the chair to catch her breath and think, watching as he thrashed to get free. The bungees were holding. Now what?

If he was an example of a real man, they weren't worth it. She would just have to miss the Summer of Love. "I don't date men who attack women, Mr. Antonescu," she told him as she packed her things. "I'll tell the clerk you do not wish to be disturbed until noon. I'm sure the maid will turn you loose when she finds you."

He redoubled his thrashing, rocking the bed. She took out her camera, snapped some photos of her handiwork, turned off the light and waited in silence until he'd worn himself out and could only growl muffled curses through the gag. She left, locking the door, and hiked the empty streets of Munich to the train station. It wasn't until weeks later, back at college at Vassar, when her credit card bills came in, that she discovered he had stolen her credit card numbers and had gone on a $20,000 spree.

As she looked at him now in the dim light of the disco, she could see his hair was graying, and he had grown a beer gut. What had she ever seen in him? She started to move away, but he bumped up against her in the press of the crowd. "So why ze Little Butterfly at ze Olympique? Come to fuck a rock star?"

"I don't need this." She tried to leave but was surprised to find herself pinned, immobilized by two men, one on either side of her, disguising their attack in the close crush of the crowd. Something sharp jabbed in her back.

"No, Little Butterfly," Andrei said, "we must, how you Americans say…catch up. Smile, like you having fun. And no judo tricks. My friend, he fast with ze knife."

They forced her through the crowd, out the door and into the night. Andrei led them down a side street and into a dark, narrow alley, looked around, and said, "We have netted a rare butterfly, my friends, very rare." He gave his accomplices a nod, and they slammed her up against the brick wall. The knife-man flashed a blade as the other brandished a leather blackjack, stripped her bag off her shoulder, and tossed it to Andrei.

He removed the bank's money pouch and unzipped it. His eyes bulged as he thumbed through the bills. "Still ze rich one," he said with a smirk as he held up the wad of money to the approval of the others. "What I tell you? A butterfly with wings of gold and tears of diamonds. Take her jewelry."

They stripped her watch from her wrist, and the knife-man yanked the chain off her neck and held up her great-grandmother's diamond pendant for the others to see; they all stared at it, grinning.

"Take it," she cried. "Take everything, just let me go. Please. There's something I have to do. I won't tell the police, I swear."

Andrei sneered. "What you hurry, Little Butterfly? Maybe ze Beatles come, and you can fuck zem all. Zay no come, Andrei make you happy."

"With what? Your teeny little pecker or your new beer gut?"

His eyes blazed as he slapped her hard across the mouth. "Maybe we keep you for ransom, like Getty? You people cheap like his, we cut off you ears, send in mail. You like you ears, Little Butterfly?"

The year before a grandson of J. Paul Getty, the richest man in the world, had been kidnapped and held for ransom. When the grandfather refused the demands, the kidnappers cut off one of the grandson's ears and sent it to him in the mail. Getty paid up, the one-eared grandson was released, and the kidnappers were still at large.

Suddenly, a voice yelled in French, "Let her go, Romanian swine."

Andrei snarled and yelled back, "Stay out, Hunky. Not you business."

"You come my club, you make my business."

Another man showed himself, one of the bouncers, and they charged up the alley. She took her chance, hooking her foot inside the knife-man's instep and sending him sprawling to the ground. She caught a flash of her diamond pendant skittering down the alley, and everything went black.

Chapter 15

Freedom Fighters

CATHERINE WOKE UP ON A COUCH, UNDER A QUILT. A DIM LAMP LIT THE room like a night-light. She could see a desk, a stereo system with giant speakers, a wall of shelves stacked floor-to-ceiling with records, and an upright piano. Everything reeked of cigarettes.

She tried to sit up, but a throbbing pain in her head forced her back down. She groaned and felt the top of her skull, wincing as she touched a lump the size of a chicken egg. She quickly felt the side of her face to be sure she still had both of her ears.

"You shouldn't move too much," said a girl's voice in sleepy French. The girl was in a nightgown, curled up under a blanket in a big leather chair. She stood, put down a teddy bear, stretched, poured a glass of water from a pitcher, took four aspirins off a desk, and handed them to her. "Uncle Oskar said to take these when you woke up."

Catherine forced herself to sit up and gratefully gulped down the water and the aspirins. "Thank you, very much. Where am I?"

"In Uncle Oskar's office. He's not my real uncle, my mom just makes me call him that because he's like an uncle. Are you Susannah's friend?"

"How did you know that?"

"From the picture." The girl held up the photo of her and Jenny at Lib House. "We found it in your pocket. It's the only thing you had with you. They took everything else."

"Does she know I'm here?"

"Oh, no. She left before they brought you back. Oskar gave her time off to make an album with Jim Morrison. She's his new girlfriend. Jimi Hendrix and the Allman Brothers are going to be on it too, but nobody's supposed to know."

"I have to find her, right away. Do you know where they went?"

"It's supposed to be a secret, but Claudine's boyfriend's a paparazzi, and he says they're at Mick Jagger's chateau on the Riviera."

She tried to stand up, but the room swirled around her, and she sat back down. "Oh, my head. What time is it?"

The girl walked to the window and pulled back the drapes, flooding the room with light. "I don't know, but it's Saturday, so I don't have to go to school."

"Who were the men who saved me?"

"Uncle Oskar and Laszlo. He says you're a fool to get mixed up with men like them."

"He's right about that."

"What's your name?"

"Catherine."

"You have a funny accent, not like Susannah's. Are you sure you're American?"

"I learned French in Montreal, when I was about your age."

"Oh, Quebec! Are they going to quit Canada and join France, like DeGaulle said?"

This was not the time to debate Franco-Canadian politics. "I don't know enough about it to say. What's your name?"

"Nicole. My mom's a dancer, like Susannah. How much did they steal from you?"

Reality was sinking in. She was in Paris, with no passport, no return ticket, no checkbook, no wallet, no cash, not even a credit card. What a mess. She felt for her great-grandmother's pendant under her blouse. Gone. Her mother would kill her.

"What they took from me doesn't matter. What's important is that I find Susannah, right away, or it will be too late."

"Too late for what?"

How much to tell her? "Look, Nicole, Susannah's in trouble and she doesn't know it. If I can talk with her today, I might be able to save her."

"What kind of trouble?"

"Grown up trouble. Can you help me find her? What about the paparazzi? Would he know where it is?"

"I think he went to the film festival in Cannes to shoot movie stars."

"Is there anybody else who would know?"

"Maybe Uncle Oskar."

"The one who saved me last night?"

"Yes. He comes in at eleven."

"I don't remember much. What's he look like?"

Nicole went to a wall, took down a framed photo, and pointed to a husky, handsome young man in a leather coat with a rifle slung over his shoulder being awarded a medal by a man in a top hat and a tuxedo with a ceremonial sash. "That's Uncle Oskar before he lost his hair. Laszlo says he's a hero, but he won't talk about it."

"Who's giving him the medal?"

"The President of Hungary. Laszlo says the Russians murdered him."

Catherine deduced that this Oskar owned the disco and was probably a refugee from the Hungarian uprising of 1956, when Soviet tanks rolled into Budapest and killed thousands. "Why do you think your Uncle Oskar would know where Mick Jagger's chateau is?"

"He knows everything. And if he doesn't, he knows how to find out."

There was nothing to do but cross her fingers, wait, and hope Oskar would help. "Is there someplace I can clean up, maybe take a hot bath?"

Nicole pointed to a door. "That's the bathroom. Do you have a skin disease too?"

"No. What makes you think that?"

"Because Susannah does. She has to take a bath every day."

Nicole started the water running and gave her a towel. Catherine took stock in the mirror as the tub filled. The aspirins weren't helping much, and the lump on her skull throbbed at the slightest touch. Her lip was swollen where Andrei backhanded her, and the bags under her blood-shot eyes drooped like a pair of saggy hammocks. All she had to wear were the torn and rumpled clothes on her back.

When she finished the bath, there was a carafe of coffee waiting, along with one croissant, a miniscule portion of marmalade, and a small glass of orange juice—a typical "continental" breakfast.

"I got you breakfast from the kitchen," Nicole said.

"Thank you, that was very kind." She gulped down the glass of juice and was grateful for the carafe of coffee, but she yearned for bacon and eggs and hash browns with ketchup. It mystified her why the French, so famous for their cuisine, couldn't make a decent breakfast.

"Nicole, I really need to find Susannah. It's so important. What makes you think your Uncle Oskar can help?"

"He was a freedom fighter in Hungary and he's a count, with a castle and everything, but the Russians killed his family. They say he smuggles people out from behind the Iron Curtain, and everybody goes to him when they need something fixed." She pointed to a heraldic shield on the wall. "That's his coat-of-arms. Want to see his castle?"

It would be good to know as much about Oskar as possible if she hoped to convince him to help her. "Sure."

Nicole went to a shelf and took down a thick album filled with fading black-and-white photos of elegantly-dressed nobility, ox-drawn carts, and folk-dancing peasants. Many had hand-written captions in a language with funny marks that she couldn't begin to decipher. "That's it," Nicole said, pointing to a photo of a manor house on a hill above a village.

Catherine looked on as Nicole turned the pages until one photo caught her eye. It was of a score of peasants in a field, wielding long-handled scythes, and cutting down plants twice their height.

"Wait, Nicole. Stop. What's that? What are they doing?"

"I don't know. They're just old pictures."

Just then the door opened and Nicole jumped to her feet. "Uncle Oskar, we were right...she is Susannah's friend. Her name's Catherine."

The well-dressed man gave a bow and did not offer his hand. European men never did. "Oskar Prokrazny." His baldpate was ringed with a thick fringe of curly salt-and-pepper hair, and his thick, meaty hand suggested a man of considerable strength.

"Catherine DeWolfe," she said. "I'm in your debt, Mr. Prokrazny. It was very brave what you did last night. Are you and your friend all right?"

"No hurt," he said with a dismissive wave. "Please, my name Oskar. How you feel?"

"I've felt better, but I'm okay."

"Ze pig, Andrei, you know him, oui?"

"Many years ago I made a big mistake. I never dreamed I'd ever see him again."

"He think he Casanova, prey on tourists, not my business. When he take you from my club, he make my business. You lucky my man see. What you lose?"

"My passport, my wallet, jewelry...everything I had with me."

"No, not all," Oskar said as he reached in his pocket, held up her diamond pendant, and offered it to her. "Ze clasp, it broke. I fix."

"Oh thank you!" she cried as she took it. "Thank you, thank you. It was my great-grandmother's."

"You lucky Oskar find. You say you name *DeWolfe*?"

"Yes."

He paused, tilting his head in thought. "Like ze forest DeWolfe?"

She hesitated a second, and said softly, "Yes."

"You rich, oui?"

"Yes."

"Andrei, he know you rich?"

"Yes. He stole a lot of money from me once."

"He know you come to Olympique?"

"No, I didn't even know I would be here. I just ran into him. He threatened to hold me for ransom and cut my ears off."

Nicole was tugging at Oskar's sleeve. "Susannah's in trouble, Uncle Oskar. We have to help her."

Oskar looked down and placed his thick hand on Nicole's head. "Trouble? What kind of trouble?"

"Catherine can't say, but we've got to find Susannah so she can warn her before it's too late."

Oskar looked up, right at her. "Too late for what?"

"I can't tell you," Catherine said, "but I have to find her...*today.*"

Oskar glanced down at Nicole and gave her a gentle smile. "Nicole, would you leave us alone, please."

Nicole's eagerness evaporated. "No, please, Uncle Oskar, please don't make me go. Please. I can help too. I'll be good, I promise. I won't talk, or ask questions, or anything."

Catherine knelt down beside her, face to face. "It's not a matter of being good. Your Uncle Oskar and I need to have a grown-up talk. You can understand that, can't you?"

Nicole sighed as she picked up her teddy bear. "Will I see you again?"

"I hope so. But if I can't, will you do me a big favor and don't tell anybody I was here, no matter what? If anybody asks, say I was a customer who got in trouble, but don't ever tell anybody my name, or that I was a friend of Susannah's. No matter what. Can you do that?"

"Playing stupid is easy."

"Thank you, Nicole, you've been wonderful." She gave her a hug, wondering what it would be like to have a daughter like her some day. "Thank you for watching over me. Good-bye for now."

When the door closed Oskar got to the point. "What kind of trouble?"

"I can't tell you, but Nicole says she's with Jim Morrison, probably at Mick Jagger's chateau. Can you help me find her? I'll pay whatever it takes."

"How? Andrei take you money, no?"

"My bank can arrange for me to get as much as I need. And thanks to you, I have the pendant. I can pawn it."

He walked behind his desk and sat in the chair, lit a Gauloise cigarette, took a deep drag, and leaned back. "What you tell police?"

"I don't want the police involved."

"Why? You want Andrei steal more?"

"I'll close my accounts and cancel my credit cards. Nobody was hurt, and the money isn't that important. I just don't want them involved."

"What trouble Susannah in?"

"I can't tell you, but if I don't warn her today, it will be too late."

"Drugs, no?"

"Not exactly."

"What mean 'not exactly?'"

"I can't say."

"Who after her?"

"Nobody. That's the problem. She's in big trouble, and she doesn't even know it. All I'm asking you to do is to help me find her so I can warn her."

"Who trouble with? Police? Dealer? Lover? Who?"

"I can't tell you. Please, just help me find her."

He stubbed out his cigarette, turned both his palms upside down, hunched up his shoulders in an exaggerated shrug, and said, "You no can tell, Oskar no can help."

If he didn't help, she had no way to warn Jenny. If he were a real Hungarian count, and not a phony Romanian count like Andrei, he might have a noble's code of honor. He had rescued her without knowing anything about her and returned her very valuable pendant when he could have kept it. She had a good feeling about him, and little choice. It was trust him, or fail. "Have you heard of Timothy Leary?"

"Leary? Ze LSD man?"

"Yes. The authorities think he's hiding out with a bunch of rock stars, including Jim Morrison. They're planning a raid, tomorrow, I think, and I don't want her caught up in it."

Oskar leaned forward, keenly interested. "How you know?"

"The man who's chasing Leary works in my building, in Washington, and yesterday he was bragging he was going to arrest him this weekend. He showed me some photos to impress me. I almost died when I saw her with Morrison in the same place Leary's hiding. I didn't know what else to do, so I came to try to warn her."

Oskar leaned back, deep in thought. He lighted another cigarette, took a drag and slowly blew a string of perfect smoke rings. "What if American police know you tell Susannah?"

"It is hard to say. If I warn her and she warns Leary, it gets into obstruction of justice and conspiracy. We could all go to jail."

"Why you take so big a risk?"

"Because she's like a sister to me."

"Does Susannah know Leary there?"

"I don't know."

He stubbed out the butt in the ashtray. "Last week Susannah act strange. My people say she buy passport, visas, but not for her. Could she make Leary look like woman?"

She remembered how much Jenny enjoyed making everybody up for Halloween and costume parties. "She loves the theater and working with make-up. It would be just like her."

"American police want Leary bad, oui?"

"Oh yes. Nixon calls him the most dangerous man in the world."

"Nixon," he said with a derisive sneer. He opened a drawer, took out a *Time* magazine, and slid it across the desktop. It was the 1956 Man of the Year issue, and on the cover was a drawing of a band of grim-faced men with submachine guns—the Hungarian Freedom Fighters. "Nixon lie, promise America help, so we throw Russians out of Budapest. Two weeks we wait, we beg, but no Americans come. Russians come back with tanks, kill thousands my people because Eisenhower lie. Nixon lie."

She knew little about that Cold War incident, except that the Soviets took over by force and Hungary was still behind the Iron Curtain. "I'm sorry, Oskar, but I was only eight years old in 1956. All I know is my best friend is in big trouble. Will you help me help her? Please."

He sighed and asked, "What about Leary?"

"Saving her is what I care about, but I'd like to help him if I could."

"Susannah, she nice girl…I like. You pay ze bribes, Oskar help. No fee."

"Yes, of course I'll pay, whatever it takes."

"Leary, I no care, but if Nixon hate, I like. You have money, Oskar maybe can help. Could cost much."

"How much?"

"Impossible to say. Where Leary want to go?"

"I don't know for sure, but I read an article in *Rolling Stone* that he's trying to get to Afghanistan."

"Why Afghanistan?"

"There's no extradition treaty, and the crown prince was a student of his at Harvard. The story said he's promised Leary asylum."

"When we know more, we make plan. First, what Susannah do if we help her, but no help Leary?"

"What do you mean …would she walk away to save herself?"

"Oui."

"Not if she thought she could make a difference."

"Police want her too?"

"No, that's the thing. They're only after Leary. She hasn't done anything, and I don't think they even know her real name. All they know is she's dating Morrison. I'm hoping to keep her out of it so she can go back to the States and nobody will ever know."

Oskar picked up the phone, dialed, and spoke for several minutes to somebody in a language she assumed to be Hungarian. When he hung up, he lit a cigarette. "Now we wait, and I must work, pay bills." He spun in his chair, opened a cabinet, turned the tumblers on the combination lock to a safe, and took out an accountant's ledger and a stack of papers.

She sat on his couch and read *Time's* account of the 1956 uprising, the slaughter of the Freedom Fighters, the scattering of 200,000 Hungarian refugees all over Europe. Oskar and tens of thousands of others had settled in France. When she finished the article, she picked up the photo album and leafed through until she came to the picture of peasants in the field, hand-harvesting something that looked very familiar. "Oskar, what is that they're cutting?"

She held up the picture. He glanced over and said, "Chanvre."

"Is that what's called hemp in English?"

"Oui."

"What do they use it for in Hungary? Rope? Canvas?"

"In most of Hungary, oui, but Prokrazny make linen. For three hundred years my family make ze finest linen in all of Europe. Hapsburgs, Bourbons, Romanovs all make bed with Prokrazny."

"Do people in Hungary smoke it?"

Oskar chuckled and shook his head. "No, give headache."

So Oskar knew about hemp. Was it the kind used in Henry Ford's experiments? She was struck with a crazy idea. "Oskar, could Hungarian hemp grow in America?"

"You have good land like in Hungary. Should grow good."

She remembered the photo of soldiers guarding stacks of hemp seeds in a Kentucky warehouse, and Nixon's admonition to them to give priority to finding seeds. "Oskar, how hard is it to get hemp seeds?"

"Easy."

"Would you have to go all the way to Hungary?"

"No. After Russians come, many people come here and make farms."

"You mean, it's growing right here in France?"

"Oui, but not so much like in Hungary."

She wondered what Lt. Mulligan and Duberman would say about using Hungarian hemp from France in the project?

The phone rang. Oskar answered in Hungarian, put his hand over the mouthpiece, and said to her in French, "We can bribe police radio girl."

"Yes, of course, whatever it takes. Keep this as collateral." She put the pendant on his desk.

He gave some orders and hung up. "We know more later. Now I must work. What you want to do?"

"I should check into a hotel and call the embassy about my passport, cancel my credit cards, and let Air France know my ticket was stolen."

"What hotel you like?"

"The Antoinette. I've stayed there with my parents. Could you lend me a little money until I can get things straightened out?"

He opened his safe, put her pendant inside, removed a bundle of cash with FF10,000 on the band, and handed it to her.

"Oh, but I don't need this much."

"Oskar know many rich woman. You no zink good when you broke. You go, take hotel, buy what a woman need. Come back in three hour. Maybe we know more, have plan."

Chapter 16

Sex & Drugs & Rock 'n' Roll

LAST SUNDAY WHEN SHE WENT TO MORRISON'S, IT WAS WITH THE INTENTION of easing out of the relationship, telling him she wouldn't be going to the recording sessions at Mick's chateau on the Riviera. Instead, she found herself in the middle of a conspiracy to smuggle the world's most wanted fugitive to safety in Afghanistan.

Leary had shown up at Morrison's door out of the blue, looking for help—money, a place to hide, and a new fake passport. They listened spellbound as he told the story of his trumped-up conviction, draconian sentence, and his high-wire acrobatic escape from prison with the help of the Weather Underground. They had shaved his head and gotten him out of the country on a fake passport. His first stop was Cuba, where he was too psychedelic for Castro, then he went to Algeria as a guest of the Black Panthers' "embassy in exile." The Panthers' leader, Eldridge Cleaver, demanded Leary endorse his anti-American diatribes as the price of his hospitality. Leary declined, was accused of being insufficiently radical, and the Panthers announced they had placed him under "house arrest."

He escaped to Switzerland, where he lived openly for a short time until the U.S. embassy pressured the Swiss to arrest him on an extradition warrant. Leary requested political asylum, and though the Swiss refused to grant it, they also refused to extradite him. Instead, they ruled he had entered Switzerland illegally and gave him a month to find a country which would accept him, or they would deport him back to the one country that wanted him.

They released him from custody, and Leary took off, ditched his C.I.A. tails, and went on the run, destination unknown. He snuck across the French border in a delivery truck under a shipment of Ementhaler cheese and made his way to Paris in hopes of connecting with Morrison. Every cop in Europe was on the lookout for him, and France would have no compunctions about shipping him back to Nixon's clutches.

"I can help you with money, and you can hide out here for now," Morrison told him. "And we have the use of the record label's Lear jet for the sessions. How about if we fly you straight to Afghanistan? The publicity will guarantee the album goes multi-platinum."

"A private jet sounds good to me," Leary said. "But they don't have much range. We'd have to refuel once or even twice where they don't check passports, and you'd need permission to fly though all those other countries' airspace so we don't get shot down."

"I'll talk to the pilot tomorrow and see what the alternatives are," Morrison said.

"I'll still need another passport," Leary said. "The crown prince will vouch for me if I can get to Kabul, but if something goes wrong and I have to run for it, at least with a passport I'll have a fighting chance."

Jenny said, "The first thing is to get you a disguise, Dr. Leary."

"That's for sure. All I have now is a false mustache and a pair of sunglasses."

"They aren't looking for a woman," she said.

"You're suggesting I travel in drag?"

"Why not? Remember *Some Like It Hot,* the Marilyn Monroe movie where Jack Lemmon and Tony Curtis dress up as chorus girls to hide from the mob? With a wig and make-up, I can make you up so no one would ever know you're a man. You'll just have to be careful with your voice and how you walk."

"I've always wondered what it would be like to be a woman," Leary said with a smile. "Why, this could be fun, and heaven knows, I need some fun."

"And I may be able to help with the passport," Jenny said, knowing she would be digging herself in deep by aiding and abetting a fugitive.

Leary cocked his head. "You?"

"I'm a dancer at a disco in the Place Pigalle. Everybody who works there is into one thing or another. Passports are a staple. What nationality do you want to be?"

"I think German, or Austrian," Leary said. "My German is quite good. Being in the same field as Freud and Jung, it has to be."

The recording sessions started the next day, and schedules could not be changed. Morrison would fly to the Riviera with a plane full of stars, and she would stay behind with Leary to make him a disguise and get him a passport, then drive him down in Morrison's car. They would hide him in the maid's room, keeping his presence a secret. Morrison would set everything up for the escape, and when the time came he would bring Leary down to the studio for a surprise with the other superstars, then whisk him off in the jet to Kabul.

The next day, Morrison left for Mick's, Leary stayed hidden in the apartment, and she took the cash Morrison gave her and went shopping for a passport. She imagined herself an engineer on the underground railroad, an abolitionist violating the Fugitive Slave Act by helping escaped slaves get to freedom. Like the abolitionists, she was obeying a higher law.

She looked up the bartender who dealt in passports and told him what she wanted—a foolproof passport for a fifty-year old German-speaking woman with visas for the countries which required them. He told her it would be 4,000 francs, half down, half on delivery. He gave her an address to take her friend for a photograph and a thumb print, and told her to bring cash. He would deliver it to her on Friday night, at work.

She went shopping for the wigs, make-up, and clothes that would turn Leary into a dowdy German Hausfrau. She stopped at American Express and talked to one of their travel agents, picking up airline, boat, and train schedules and a list of airports with direct flights to Kabul if the Lear jet getaway plan fell through.

Leary shaved his face, legs, and armpits, and she plucked hairs to clean up his eyebrows to make him appear more feminine. She showed him how to apply eyeliner, makeup, rouge, mascara, and lipstick. They chose a curly-brown wig, fitted him with a padded bra stuffed with toilet paper, a frumpy dress, and a fake pearl necklace and matching earrings. He was completely convincing as a female.

"Hey, I'm pretty cute," he said in a falsetto as he stood up and admired his new identity in the full-length mirror, then he turned to her and placed his hands on her shoulders. "Thank you, Susannah, but I have to ask, why are you doing this? There's nothing in it for you."

"We all have an obligation to fight injustice, Dr. Leary, and you got a raw deal. Your sentence was a clear violation of the Eighth Amendment prohibition against cruel and unusual punishment."

"Tell me, Susannah," he said, "why are you lying about who you are?"

She was stunned. "What…whatever do you mean?"

He smiled and spoke in a calm, soothing tone, "If you're Susannah from Chicago, then I'm Tinkerbell from Never-Never Land."

"But—"

"Don't try to deny it. I know a Pittsburgh accent when I hear one. I was stationed near there during the war. I don't care who you really are. I'm just curious why you're lying."

She couldn't believe he'd found her out. "You've heard of stage names, haven't you?"

He smiled. "Ten dollars says you're a lawyer. I bet you're not a year out of law school. Am I right?"

How could he know? She faked a little laugh. "What on Earth makes you think that?"

"Your demeanor, the way you evade questions, the way you're trying so hard, right this very second, to make me think you're telling me the absolute truth when we both know you're lying through your teeth. My guess is you got involved with Jim because rock stars are glamorous. But you're a serious woman, and now that you've seen the lifestyle, you're scared of it, and you're bored with it."

He was right about all of it. She was scared of the drugs, sick of the drinking, and bored with the nonstop partying. But she had never had so much fun as when she was in the studio singing backup for Jim and Duane and Jimi and Janis. If only there was a way to have one without the other.

"And you've decided you're not in love with Jim, haven't you?"

He was right about that, too, but she only said, "Come on, we have to get your picture taken."

She drove him to the address, a small camera store in a seedy neighborhood. An elderly man took Leary's photo and thumb print, and told them her bartender friend would deliver it to her Friday at the Olympique. She gave him 2,000 francs, with 2,000 due upon delivery.

They left Paris in Morrison's car and headed to the Riviera. As she drove she wondered if Leary's presence might be a good thing for Morrison? It couldn't hurt to have a world-class psychologist evaluate him. Leary had impeccable academic credentials, and she had never been around anyone so relentlessly upbeat and intelligent. She remembered Catherine's description of him as the happiest person she had ever known. Given his thirty-year frame-up, his optimism was remarkable. If anyone could get through to Morrison, it was Leary.

"Dr. Leary, I'm really worried about Jim. He's pushing to see how high he can get, how much he can take, always quoting Rimbaud about the rational derangement of the senses, and Blake about how the road of excess leads to the palace of wisdom. It's like he wants to get as high as he possibly can in hopes of seeing God or something. He's taking it right to the edge. I'm afraid he's going to kill himself."

Leary was somber. "His is a very interesting case. That death hoax he pulled last year has a deep psychological meaning."

"I've only known him for a few weeks, but he's getting worse. He's got a mystical belief in voodoo...coming back after death by taking over somebody else's body. At first, I thought it was a joke, but the other night he took me to a mojo party where they killed a chicken. Now I think he really believes in it."

"And what do you think about it, Susannah?"

"The voodoo is kooky, but it's the drugs that really scare me. I'm no prude, Dr. Leary. I drink and I smoke pot now and then, but watching them tie those rubber things around their arms and shoot up makes me sick to my stomach. Did you know some of the Stones had to get their systems flushed out before they could tour the States?"

"Flushed out?"

"Yes. They call it the 'vampire treatment.' A doctor replaces all their blood with a total body transfusion so they come up clean on the drug tests. I don't want Jim ending up like that. Is there anything you can do?"

"Perhaps, if I had time, but I'm on the run, and a rock-and-roll recording session is not a good environment for psychotherapy."

"So you do think he needs help?"

"We all do from time to time. What about the others. They aren't into voodoo too, are they?"

"No, just Jim. For them it's a party. Snort a couple of lines and ten minutes later come back for more. It's all a big joke about Vitamin C."

Leary shook his head and let out a heavy sigh. "It's not like it was back in the Sixties, Susannah. Cocaine has ruined drugs, and Nixon's making the addiction problem ten times worse. He's equating cocaine and heroin with things as harmless as pot and as enlightening as LSD, and he doesn't even mention alcohol and nicotine. Kids know pot is harmless, and when they see Nixon lying about it, they assume he's lying about the others too."

She and Leary arrived at the chateau about midnight, and Morrison was able to sneak him up to the master bedroom without anyone knowing. She stayed Tuesday and Wednesday, singing backups and lounging by the pool, and returned to Paris on the Wednesday night train. She turned in her term paper, worked on Friday night and completed her transaction with the bartender for Leary's passport. After her final performance, she went to Oskar and told him she needed some time off, starting tonight. He gave her a hug and told her to come back whenever she wanted.

She slept a little on the train, arriving at the chateau in a taxi just before sunrise, at the tail end of what had been a drunken coke-fest. She'd read about parties called "snow balls" and wondered if this qualified.

The sun was dawning when she came upstairs to the master bedroom. She tossed a blanket over Morrison, who was sprawled on the bed, snoring, with his clothes and shoes still on. She heard a motorcycle roar to life and went to the window to see Duane Allman tearing down the driveway with Janis Joplin on the back. She drew the drapes to darken the room.

"Leave it open, will you please," Leary said as he came in from the maid's room. "My whole time in prison I never saw a sunrise. We only get so many in this life, and I don't want to miss a single one."

She did as he asked. The room filled with light. Morrison stirred, let out a nasally *snork,* and continued snoring.

"I'm so glad you're back, Susannah," Leary said quietly, being careful not to wake Morrison. "You sparkle like a Roman candle, a bright and shining beacon of hope in a bleak and dismal fog of self-indulgence and excess. It's clear you're not the type."

"What do you mean…not the type for what?"

He came over to her, smiled, and took her hands in his and gave them a gentle squeeze. "Not the type to let herself become addicted to anything but universal love."

Was he coming on to her? No, it couldn't be…could it? He was her father's age, but he was handsome and energetic and charming, with a notorious reputation as a ladies' man, and for robbing the cradle.

She withdrew her hands and asked, "Do you have everything you need?"

"Everything except human companionship. I'm going crazy here, Susannah, and I'm a psychologist, so I know. Jim's kept me holed up ever since you left. At least in prison I had a library and people to talk to. Here it's just Jim…when he's awake and sober. It's been like solitary confinement. So tell me how it went. Did you get me a passport?"

His eyes lit up at his Hausfrau photo in an official Federal Republic of Germany passport. He laughed and said in a falsetto, "Guten Tag, ich bin Frau Helga Kaulbeck, aus Frankfurt-am-Main."

She laughed and said, "I haven't talked to Jim since I left. What's the latest on the plans?"

"The last of the musicians come in tonight, and my session is set for tomorrow. Jim will bring me down, surprise everybody, and I'll sing and play tambourine or congas on a few tracks. Then he and I will take the producer's jet out of Nice, refuel in Athens and Abu Dubai, and then fly on to Kabul. If nobody leaves the plane, we won't have to deal with customs or passports."

"That's great news, Dr. Leary. You don't want to have to use this passport if you don't need to."

"No matter what happens, I'll always be grateful for your help," Leary said. "If there were more people like you in the world, bastards like Nixon wouldn't be running things. Thank you, Susannah, or whoever you are," and he leaned over and kissed her on the forehead.

Chapter 17

Over There

MULLIGAN PULLED HIS CAR UP TO THE CURB, SHIFTED INTO PARK, GRABBED his briefcase as he got out, and told McGill, "Don't waste your time looking in Georgetown, Stick. You can't afford it. Your best bet for a decent one-bedroom is Arlington or Alexandria."

McGill slid behind the wheel. "You never know. Thanks for the car."

"Be here at sixteen hundred sharp. Don't keep me waiting."

"You got it," McGill said, and took off to go apartment hunting.

It was Saturday, and he would have the office to himself. He walked up the EOB's steps wondering who Ms. DeWolfe was with, why had she left early? She wasn't in the Navy, but he was her superior, and officers and enlisted personnel were forbidden by military regulation to fraternize. Besides, mixing work and romance was poison, and her super-rich family put her way out of his league anyway. Focus on the mission, Mulligan, focus on the mission. A smart dog doesn't crap on its own porch.

He had just opened the door when the phone rang. "Presidential Policy Commission."

"Oh, Lieutenant, I'm so glad I caught you."

"Ms. DeWolfe, is that you?"

"Yes."

"Speak up. The connection is terrible. Where are you?"

"I'm in Paris."

"Paris? What are you doing over there?"

"I came over to…to go shopping. But I've had some trouble, and I wanted to let you know I won't be in on Monday. I'm not sure when I'll be able to get back."

"What kind of trouble?"

"I was mugged, and—"

"*Mugged*! Are you all right?"

"Yes, just a bump on the head, but they stole my passport, and I don't know when I'll be able to get it straightened out. I hope you and Mr. Duberman won't be too mad. I don't want to lose my job."

"Mad? No, of course not. I'll talk to Ehrlichman to make sure the embassy takes good care of you. Where can I reach you?"

"I'm at the Hôtel Antoinette, on the Champs Elysee, room 565. But something else has come up…something about our project."

"Oh?"

"The President wanted us to find a source of seeds. How are we doing on that?"

"That's Backwater's area, but if he'd had any luck I'm sure he'd have said something. Why?"

"I think I might have found a source, right here in France…."

———————————

Nixon had two lazy days planned, his first break in months. A round of golf at Burning Tree with pals Bebe Rebozo and Bob Aplanalp, followed by a night of poker with the boys, not a politician among them. He didn't give a damn about the golf, only played to be social, but he hadn't cleaned anybody's clock in poker in years. He was looking forward to some old-fashioned, poker-table fun. He hadn't heard a good joke in ages.

He was finishing his favorite breakfast combo—corned beef hash and poached eggs on toast—and scanning his Presidential Daily Briefing.

—Another steel mill was shutting down, this one in Youngstown, putting ten thousand out of work. The Industrial Belt was turning into a Rust Belt, but unions voted Democratic, so it didn't matter politically.

—Russian and Chinese army units continued the standoff in their border dispute. He relished the prospect of Ruskie commies fighting Chink commies in Siberia. He would speak with the C.I.A. and Kissinger about how to provoke them to really get into it, maybe get them to shed a little blood so he could step in, broker a deal, and win a Nobel Peace Prize.

—The C.I.A. reported a possible Soviet coup was brewing in Afghanistan. Not good, but it was on their border and too far from America to be of any real concern.

—Pittsburgh's District Attorney was found with his guts blown away by a shotgun at the estate of his wife, a Mellon. Hmmm…Petey and Richie Mellon were hosting a big conservative pow-wow and fund-raiser up there this summer. He hoped this didn't screw that up.

His trusted personal valet, Manolo, put a telephone on the table. "Señor Haldeman's office, Señor Presidente."

Nixon picked up. "Yes."

"I hate to bother you, Mr. President," Haldeman's aide said, "but a Lt. Mulligan is requesting a meeting with Bob or John. They're both out of town, and he said if he couldn't talk to them he had to speak to you. Bob told me your orders were to honor all his requests. Should I try to contact Bob, or would you like to speak to him?"

Maybe his boys had come up with something? "I've got some time. Send him on up."

———————————

Mulligan was astonished when the Secret Service agent escorted him up the White House stairs to the second floor. There was Nixon, in the Lincoln Sitting Room, in slippers, plaid pajamas, and a blue silk robe with the Presidential Seal on the breast. A diminutive Filipino man in a white steward's uniform was clearing dishes. Since the Spanish-American war it had been traditional for U.S. Navy officers to employ Filipino servants.

Nixon glanced up. "Good morning, Lieutenant. Like some coffee?"

"Why, yes, thank you, Mr. President."

"Pat and the girls are in San Clemente for the weekend, so I have the place to myself. Going to play a little golf this afternoon, then some poker tonight with the boys."

"Sounds like fun, Mr. President."

Nixon stood up. "Yes, even the leader of the Free World needs a little R-and-R now and then. We'll take coffee on the balcony, Manolo."

Nixon led Mulligan through the First Family's private quarters to the Truman Balcony and motioned for him to take a seat at the patio table. Manolo followed with a tray, poured two coffees, and departed.

"So, Lieutenant, what brings you over here on a Saturday?"

"Sir, we may have a chance to solve the seed problem, but it's a foreign source, and if we bring them into the country, we'd be breaking the law. I thought I should inform you before we went any further."

"Petty legalities have never stood in Nixon's way. Tell me more, Lieutenant."

"I don't know the details, but Ms. DeWolfe informed me that Hungarian refugees in France grow hemp for tablecloths and sheets and such. She thinks we might be able to buy seeds from them to get started."

"Hmmm...Hungarian hemp. In France, you say?"

"Aye, sir."

"But is it what we need for energy? That's what's important. I don't give a rat's ass about fucking tablecloths."

"It's hard to say for sure, but if they use it for linen it means the fibers must be exceptionally long, and that means the plants must be very tall, exactly what we need for biomass. And sir, if we don't start soon, we'll miss the growing season. George Washington always sowed his at Mount Vernon no later than early May."

Nixon leaned back, drumming his fingers on the glass table. "So you're saying if we're going to grow our own pot, it's time to shit or get off the pot? Ha! Send me to the punitentiary."

Mulligan smiled and chuckled.

"Lieutenant, I may be the most powerful man on the goddamned planet, but even I can't change the seasons. The bottom line is if we don't move on this when we've got the chance, we're just farting in the ocean."

"Uh…aye, sir. Sir, if we get the seeds, we need a place to grow it."

"Where do you have in mind?"

"The area around here was a major hemp-growing region, from colonial times right up to the Civil War. If we're going to use Jefferson's and Washington's timetables at Monticello and Mount Vernon as our blueprint, it seems to me we should grow it around here."

"Washington and Jefferson tell you how to grow it, do they?"

"They both left farm journals, so we know when they planted and harvested and some of the problems they had. But it doesn't give us the hands-on experience we need. Sir, to put it frankly, I don't think any of us on the team has ever grown so much as a tomato."

"So none of you knows hay from horseshit?"

"No sir, I don't think so. But look at this." He handed Nixon a pamphlet. "In World War II, the Kentucky 4-H clubs handed this out as part of the Hemp For Victory program. It has step-by-step instructions, from preparing the ground in the spring to harvesting in the fall. If we go by Washington and Jefferson's timetables and follow the 4-H Club guidelines, even a bunch of newbie farmers like us can't go too far wrong."

Nixon put his coffee cup down and riffled through the pamphlet. "Hmmm…how much land are we talking about?" Nixon waved his hand in an arc, gesturing to the South Lawn. "As much as we're looking at here? They tell me it's about fifteen acres."

"It depends how much seed we can buy and how many of us can work it. Jefferson reported sowing a bushel an acre and it took one slave to tend three acres. The hardest part was the harvest, when the whole plantation came out to help. But that was long before mechanized equipment."

"So say you go over there and bring some seeds back. Then what?"

"We'll plant half for seed and half for fiber, enough to give us a base to estimate what this variety could yield. It will also give us some experience in the two types of cultivation. If we get a good crop, we take the seeds and move south, to Florida, or Arizona, and put them in the ground. Each plant produces about six hundred seeds, so we'll be able to increase the supply geometrically."

"But didn't your reports say it grows taller in the north?"

"Yes, sir, but in warm climates we can grow year-round and get two or even three crops a year. The old Agriculture Department studies from before World War I say it matures in anywhere from ninety to a hundred and forty days, depending on variety and soil and climate. Our goal should be three seed crops by spring. We'll have hundreds of millions of seeds for thousands of farmers, and you'll have the Arabs on the run."

Nixon thumped his fist on the glass table, rattling the coffee cups. "I like it, Lieutenant, I like it a lot. And I think I know just the place to get started. I don't know what the ground up there is like for farming, though. I'll have somebody look into it."

"Sir, it would help if you could have them plow it up and spread fertilizer so we can get started as soon as we get back."

"I'll get the best people on it. How much is it going to cost?"

"Ms. DeWolfe said there's no drug value in this variety of hemp, so the seeds should be cheap."

"Will the hippies be able to use it to get high?"

"No, sir. They won't like it at all."

"Good, we've got a war on drugs to win too, you know. How are you going to get it into the country?"

"I'm hoping you can set something up. Maybe in diplomatic pouches."

"Hmmm...so did you send Ms. DeWolfe over there to find seeds?"

"No, sir. She went over to go shopping and came across them by accident."

Nixon chuckled. "It's uncanny how things fall into place on this project. How did she find them?"

"She was mugged, sir, and the people who rescued her are Hungarian refugees who grow it."

"Mugged? Is she all right? What happened?"

"She says she has a lump on her head, but otherwise she's fine. They stole her passport though, and she's worried she'll lose her job."

"Why the hell would someone like that worry about a job? Her family's worth more than the goddamned Kennedys."

"She's very idealistic, Mr. President, and extremely proud to be working for you. I'm sure it has nothing to do with money."

"So she just flew over there for a weekend of shopping?"

"I think it's what she does for relaxation."

"Women are like that," Nixon said with a sigh. "I can't imagine getting on a plane just to go shopping. I hate shopping."

"Me too, Mr. President."

"It's a female problem all right, like periods. Something to do with the moon is all I can figure. But I wonder what it's like growing up and having that kind of money and knowing that you've done absolutely nothing to deserve it? How do you look at yourself in the mirror?"

"I wouldn't know, Mr. President. My father's a millwright."

"Mine was a corner grocer and a small-time farmer. Oranges and lemons. I'd light the smudge pots and sit out in the orchard all night to keep them going to keep the frost off. Hard way to make a living. We never had two nickels to rub together. It toughened me up, though. I'd hate to think what I'd be like if I'd been born rich. Not where I am today, that's for sure. Big money spoils a man rotten. Look at what it's done to the Kennedys. Rich Republicans are bad enough, but there's nothing worse than Democrats with real money. Don't get me wrong, rich is all right if you make it yourself, that's different. But who the hell could respect anybody who starts out like that? Sure, people are going to kiss their asses, that's what being rich is all about. But respect? Only way anybody born rich deserves any respect is if they give it all away and start from scratch. Then they'd get respect."

Nixon stood up, walked to the railing and looked out at the South Lawn. "Imagine growing America's first energy crop right here. Would that send a message to the Arabs, or what?"

"It would sure show them you meant business, Mr. President."

"Yes, but I'm not ready to commit political suicide. Before I let anybody know what I'm up to, I've got to find a way to neutralize the drug problem. So, Lieutenant, first things first. You get your ass over there, bring back those seeds, and get 'em in the goddamned ground."

"You want me to go to Paris, Mr. President?"

"We don't want to miss the growing season, right?"

"Uh...no, sir."

"And we don't want Ms. DeWolfe dealing with this by herself, do we?

She's a woman, for crying out loud. I want you to get your ass over there and let her do her shopping while you take care of business."

"Aye, sir."

"I'll call the C.I.A. and get you diplomatic passports. They'll work up some kind of cover, make you a businessman of some kind, make her your wife or your secretary. Wife would be better, she's too cute for a secretary. And they have a half-day spy school for boys on missions like yours I want you to take before you go. But don't tell anybody at the agency what you're up to. They'd love to get the goods on me so they can leak it to the Kennedys. They'll try to wheedle it out of you, make you think they're on my side, but they're not. So keep your wits about you. Understand?"

"I…uh…aye, sir."

"That's the spirit. I'll get you some money from the slush fund to take care of business. Just make sure nobody knows what you're up to when you're over there, or that you work for me, because if this gets out Nixon's ship of state will spring more leaks than the goddamned *Titanic*."

"Aye, sir."

"Ah, Paris in the springtime," Nixon said, his eyes glazing over. "Thomas Jefferson smuggled hemp seeds from Paris in diplomatic pouches, the same thing we're about to do. He once said that the greatest service that can be rendered to a country is to add a useful plant to its agriculture, and those plants of his spread all over the country and made the canvas and rope that won the American West. Remember that when you're over there, Lieutenant. Jefferson did America a great service, and two hundred years later, we're about to do it all over again with the same damned plant. We're treading in the footsteps of a giant, Lieutenant. Don't let Jefferson and Nixon down."

"I'll give it my very best, Mr. President."

"I know you will, son. You're a Navy man…just like me."

Chapter 18

Hide and Seek

OSKAR'S BRIBES BOUGHT THE LOCATION OF MICK JAGGER'S CHATEAU AND THE timetable for the raid. They learned the phones were tapped and the roads were under surveillance. The Americans wanted to go in at dawn on Sunday, but the French were insisting on a more civilized eight o'clock.

The prospects seemed bleak. "Is there anything you can do?" she asked.

"Maybe," Oskar said. "Susannah, she nice girl…I like. You pay expenses, I try to help, no charge. But she must go home to America. No come back."

"Oh, I'm sure that won't be a problem, and I'll cover all the expenses."

"Leary, I no care, but if Nixon hate…I like. You want I try to save him, 50,000 francs. You want him go to Afghanistan, 50,000 more."

"You can save him and get him to Afghanistan?"

"I try. No guarantee."

She considered the offer. Nicole said Oskar smuggled refugees to freedom from behind the Iron Curtain all the time, so he must know what he was doing. And 100,000 francs wasn't too much, only $33,000, more or less. She asked, "Can you keep my involvement secret?"

"Oui."

Her brain told her it was crazy, but in her heart it felt right. "Yes, I'll do it. I'll talk to the Paris office of my bank first thing on Monday."

They sealed the deal with a handshake.

"Oskar, one more thing. After you told me about the hemp seeds, I called a friend of mine, and he wants to come over and buy some."

"Why you want? No make high, and you go to jail, like Leary."

"Well, my friend and I came across some old experiments to make paper out of the part that's always thrown away. But the government made it illegal before the idea could ever be tried. We want to test it, at my farm…in Michigan. But there are no seeds left in America, and if the idea works, it…it could help me get control of the company from my cousins."

She couldn't believe the lie that had just come out of her mouth.

Oskar nodded, satisfied with her answer. "You cousins like mine, zay want everyzing. When Leary business over, maybe we see."

Oskar picked up the phone, talked for a long time in Hungarian, hung up and said, "We have plan, better you not know. I have my man take you where Susannah stay when she not Susannah and get her zings. Monday you go to bank, get cash, go to hotel, and wait."

A man named Laszlo drove her to Jenny's address, a shabby fourth-floor student walk-up. He picked the lock, and they packed her clothes, books, typewriter, passport, and papers and put it all in the trunk of his car. It was after two when she got back to her hotel. There was a note in her mail slot written in garbled English: "Hungry seeds good. I come in you soon. Mooligin."

She laughed and read it again. Wait, could it mean he was coming here? No! She had to stop him. She went to her room and placed a person-to-person transAtlantic call, but it was Saturday night, so she left a message with the EOB switchboard telling him not to come. She got his home number from information and called every half-hour. Finally someone picked up, and McGill's voice growled, "Hullo."

"It's me, Mr. McGill, Ms. DeWolfe. I must speak to Lt. Mulligan."

"The connection's terrible. Where are you? Speak up."

"I'm in Paris," she shouted. "I have talk to the Lieutenant. Please put him on."

"He's not here. I dropped him off at the office yesterday morning, and when I went to pick him up, an MP said he'd gone on a mission. I figured it was Navy maneuvers or something. Any idea what it's about?"

She ducked the question. "If you see him, tell him not to come over here. Okay? And don't tell anyone you've talked to me, not Duberman or Haldeman or anybody. Okay?"

"Huh...."

"Promise you won't say a word to anybody, no matter what. Promise?"

"I guess, but—"

"Thanks, I have to run," and she hung up.

———————————

It was ten to seven on Sunday morning as Jenny helped keep a groupie she found wobbling down the hall to Duane Allman's room, from falling on her drunken ass. She felt like she was sixteen, a counselor at Camp Tioshango, making sure all the little kiddies were safely tucked in. She just wanted some sleep, but a maid came to her and said, "Mademoiselle, there's a delivery for you."

"A delivery?"

"Oui, Mademoiselle. Flowers."

"Take care of it, will you?"

"The girl insists she will give them only to you."

Flowers. At seven o'clock on a Sunday morning? Morrison must be trying to make up for being a jerk, but it wasn't going to work. As soon as Leary was safely on his way, she was gone.

She went downstairs, crossed the courtyard and swung open the big iron gate. A girl with a scarf over her head, hiding her face, was standing next to a bicycle with a bouquet of roses in its basket.

"You have flowers for me?"

The girl looked up and whispered, "Susannah, it's me."

"Nicole! What are—"

"Shhhh. You're not supposed to know me. Uncle Oskar says to tell you the police are watching, and they're going to raid the house at eight o'clock. At seven-thirty someone is coming for you in a taxi."

"But, but...how, how does he know?"

"Uncle Oskar knows everything. He said it's safer if you come alone, but if you bring your friend, disguise him good and hope you don't get caught, because if you do he can't help you. You're supposed to give me a tip, so the police don't get suspicious."

How had Oskar found her, and how did he know what the police were doing? Or about her "friend." Her knees went wobbly, and it was all she could do to reach into her jeans and give Nicole a few coins for the benefit of whoever was watching.

Nicole handed her the roses and curtsied. "Oskar says be careful. Somebody inside is a spy." She climbed on the bicycle and peddled off.

Jenny was tingling with fear as she looked at her watch: ten to seven. She rushed to the bedroom, where Morrison was passed-out. Good.

She opened the door to the maid's room and shook Leary awake. "The police are coming. Don't ask questions, just shave and put on your wig and your dress. I'll be back in a minute to help with the makeup."

She gathered up Morrison's bags of white powders and flushed them down the toilet. She collected the syringes, needles and rubber tourniquet, rolled him over and slipped off the silver coke spoon he wore on a chain around his neck. She wiped off fingerprints, wrapped it all in a newspaper, and stomped on it a few times to crush the glass for good measure.

Leary was calm and collected, almost jovial as she helped him put on make-up for his disguise. "You function well under pressure, Susannah, an excellent quality in a litigator. Are you scared?"

"Of course I'm scared. Aren't you?"

"Yes, but I'm used to it."

"I could never get used to it."

"You don't want to. Fear is a natural defense mechanism. Never trust anyone who says they don't get scared."

They wiped the tables, chairs, windowsills, toilet, doors, sink, bedposts, anywhere he might have left fingerprints. She heard a honk, and soon a maid called, "Mademoiselle Susannah, a taxi for you."

They went out the kitchen door, and she tossed the newspaper in the big dump bin. As they got in the taxi the driver said, "Oskar say no talk."

Two gendarmes blocked the first intersection, inspecting cars. One looked them over and asked the cabbie questions, the other opened the trunk and poked around. They let them go just as a helicopter passed overhead, followed by the high-pitched WHEEP-WHEEP-WHEEPing of European police sirens.

Leary turned to her and whispered, "Who is Oskar?"

"He owns the disco where I work."

"Did you tell him about me?"

"I didn't tell anybody about you."

"How did he know about the police?"

"I don't know."

"Where are we going?"

"I have no idea."

They sat in nervous silence until they came to signs for the on-ramp to the AutoRoute. The cabbie pulled off on a gravel road, where a black Mercedes waited under a row of sycamore trees. Next to it was a blue Renault, with Laszlo behind the wheel. Oskar hopped out of the Mercedes and began waving "come on."

The taxi skidded to a dusty stop, they got out, and the driver sped away.

Oskar pointed to the Mercedes. "Susannah, there. You, there," and he ushered Leary into the Renault and shut the door. Laszlo hit the gas and peeled out, spitting clouds of dust and gravel. She and Oskar followed, and when they came to the cloverleaf, the Renault went south to Marseilles, as Oskar headed north toward Lyons and Paris.

"We're not going with them?" she asked.

"Not safe."

"What about Nicole?"

"She go on train."

Jenny was as grateful as she was confused. How did Oskar know, and why was he risking so much? She leaned over and kissed him on the cheek. "Oh, Oskar, thank you. But how did you know about the police? And what I was planning? And why are you helping?"

"It my business."

She tried another tack. "Where's Laszlo taking him?"

"Better you not know."

"Well, where are we going?"

"Le Havre. You take ferry to England, fly to America. No come back."

"You want me to leave France?"

"When police no find Leary, zay come for you. I make big lie."

"But I don't even have my passport."

He reached into the door's map pocket and handed her the manila envelope she kept hidden under her mattress with her passport and documents.

"How'd you get this?" she asked.

"It my business. I send you other zings in mail."

The envelope now also included ferry and airline tickets for each leg of a journey to Pittsburgh. She was dumbfounded. She had never uttered a peep about who she was. "How...how did you know?"

"It my business."

"What about Dr. Leary?"

"We hide till—how gangster movie say—heat off."

"I think I understand why you're helping me, I mean, I'd do the same for you. But why are you helping Dr. Leary? You don't know him, do you? What's in it for you? Is someone paying you?"

He laughed. "Oskar have many clients."

After talking to McGill, Catherine was able to get a few hours sleep, waking up in the early afternoon. She turned on the TV and the radio. About four came the first news bulletin: Jim Morrison, Jimi Hendrix, Janis Joplin, Duane Allman and others had been arrested in a drug raid at Mick Jagger's chateau on the Riviera. Police would not comment on a rumor that Timothy Leary was among those in custody. A hearing was set for the morning, and the stars would spend a night in a French provincial jail.

Had Jenny been arrested? Had they caught Leary? There was no way to know. A thunderstorm rolled in, lighting up the sky. She sat on the tiny balcony and waited for Oskar's call, sipping wine, monitoring the news, and watching lightning strikes hitting the Eiffel Tower.

Jenny had peppered Oskar with questions on the day-long drive from the Riviera to Le Havre, but he just lit another cigarette every time she tried a new approach, refusing to say what he intended to do for Leary, how he had known about her plans, or who was paying her passage to the States.

They arrived in time to catch the last ferry to England. "We miss you," Oskar said, "but you no come back. No call. No letter."

"So I'll never know what happened?"

"Maybe when Nixon gone."

"But that could be another six years."

Oskar arched his brow and shrugged—*C'est la vie*.

She hugged him, boarded the ferry, climbed into her tiny berth, and slept. In the morning she cleared customs at Portsmouth and took a train to Heathrow, reading in the British tabloids about "The Superstar Bust." She waited for her flight watching the TV in an airport pub filled with Yanks on their way home and Brits heading across the pond on a cheap holiday while the dollar was in the tank. The crowd grew quiet when the TV cut to a story on the bust. A police spokesman said paraphernalia had been found in a dump bin, but a search had uncovered only tiny amounts of drugs, not enough to bring charges, and rumors that Timothy Leary was in custody were not true. All the suspects were being released.

A roar went up in the pub, the young people clapping in a spontaneous hooray as the older patrons shook their heads in disgust. The TV showed the rock stars leaving the courthouse, with Morrison screaming obscenities at the bald-headed American drug czar, E. Grayson Gridley, who was fuming like a dirty chimney as he got into a car. The reporter said the French were blaming the fiasco on bad information from Gridley.

She felt relieved and thankful she wasn't in love with Morrison. This made it easier. She had left without a good-bye, so she bought a postcard of the Eiffel Tower and wrote him an unsigned note:

> Jim,
> *I'm sorry I had to leave without saying good-bye, but it's*
> *better this way. I'm sure you understand.*

It was concise, more or less told the truth, and didn't give anything away in case the police saw it. She wiped off her fingerprints and popped it in the mail.

Now she must be practical. Her dreams of a globe-hopping U.N. job were history, and her law-school debt loomed on the horizon like the Himalayas. Passing the bar exam and paying off her loans were her top priority. Corporate law—had she sunk that low?

She thought of her friend, Catherine, who always told her it was her Capricorn rising that made her so practical and steady, a sure-footed mountain goat climbing relentlessly to the top. She also said your rising sign was how others saw you, but it was your sun sign that signified the type of person you really were. What would Catherine say if she knew the kind of life she'd been living in Paris? She'd probably blame it on her sun in Scorpio—the Sign of Sex—and say it was a manifestation of her true inner-self, or some such Age of Aquarius malarkey.

She would need a plausible excuse for coming back early. Fooling her family would be easy, but it hurt to know she couldn't tell her friends about her adventures until the statute of limitations expired. Maybe she could blame it on the energy crisis and the plummeting dollar? Yes, of course. She just ran out of money. Even Catherine would believe that.

———————

On Monday, Catherine took a taxi to her bank's Paris branch. Her famous name garnered instant respect, and a phone call to her account manager in Detroit quickly settled everything. Old accounts were closed, new ones opened. She cashed a check for $40,000 and took the currency in francs, more than enough to pay Oskar what he'd lent her plus his fee and Jenny's travel expenses. She zippered it into her new purse, took a cab to her hotel, turned on the TV and radio, and waited. From time to time she paced around the telephone yelling, "Ring, dammit—*ring*!"

Finally, the evening news: All the rock stars were being released, no charges were filed, and Timothy Leary was not arrested. She yelped a happy squeal and held her breath as Gridley hurried down the courthouse steps with Morrison hard on his heels shouting and screaming. Then the other prisoners filed out the door, stars first, followed by roadies and groupies. Jenny was nowhere to be seen. Oskar's plan had worked!

She let out a big *yahoo* and jumped around, whooping and clapping. She'd done it! If she hadn't acted, Leary would be in custody, Jenny would be in trouble, and Gridley would be strutting like a peacock.

She felt terrific. Exultant! For the first time ever, the fabled DeWolfe fortune, founded on the obliteration of Michigan's ancient white pine forests, had been used in a noble cause. Perhaps great wealth wasn't such a curse after all?

She opened a bottle of Remy Martin from the mini-bar, poured a shot in a snifter, and toasted, "Here's to you, Oskar Prokrazny, wherever you are!" She slugged it down in a single gulp, her whole body involuntarily shivering. She poured another, wishing that there was someone besides Remy Martin to help her celebrate. She had never felt so totally alone.

When her phone finally rang five hours later, she pounced on the receiver like a kitten on a ball of yarn. "Hello."

"Susannah go home. Other friend safe."

"Oh, Oskar, that's really, really super. When can I see him?"

"I no understand. You say you no want him to know you pay, oui?"

"Oh, that's right. I forgot."

"Forgot? You drunk?"

"Me? No, I never get drunk. I just celebrated a little when I saw the news tonight, that's all. And when—"

"You drunk. Be quiet, listen. Susannah give him passport and make him disguise."

"You mean, she was trying to help him escape?"

"Oui. You go to bank?"

"Yes."

"Good. Tomorrow we meet, two o'clock. Brasserie Bleu Giraffe, Rue Marchais. You know?"

"I'll find it. Oh, and Oskar, about that other thing.…"

"What zing?"

"The seeds. Remember?"

"Why you talk so drunk?" he said, sounding exasperated.

"Please, it's very important."

"We see. Tomorrow. Two o'clock."

———————

Chapter 19

Honey Bear

MULLIGAN HAD FOLLOWED AS NIXON PADDED DOWN THE WHITE HOUSE staircase in his slippers and bathrobe, went into Haldeman's office, and opened a safe. His eyes had popped when Nixon handed him five bundles of bills with $10,000 on the bands and said, "This should buy you a lot of cooperation. Good luck, Lieutenant."

A driver took him to the C.I.A. complex at Langley. They measured him for a wardrobe and a custom-fitted holster, and he qualified on the firing range with a 9mm Smith & Wesson with a silencer. They gave him a series of lessons in rudimentary espionage skills: bugging, hot-wiring, lock-picking, and issued him a briefcase filled with accessories: knockout drops; a small, one-eared stethoscope for eavesdropping; a cigarette-pack camera; a mace pen; a mechanical pencil with a powerful explosive charge.

His new identity was James Thornton Bennington III, a commodities broker specializing in grain futures at the Chicago Board of Trade. His custom-tailored suits included secret pouches in the sleeves for the lock-picking tools. It was an axiom that the best spies never stood out in a crowd, and his handlers warned him that his red hair, height, and Navy haircut all set him dangerously apart in a long-haired, hippie world.

They drove him to Dulles and put him on a TWA 747 for Paris, but halfway across the Atlantic the pilot announced a wildcat strike by French airline unions would force them to land not in Paris, but in Brussels. From there he took a train to Paris, and it was not until 01:30 Tuesday that his train pulled into the City of Light.

He called her room from a pay phone, no answer. He passed a newsstand and picked up *The International Herald Tribune,* hailed a cab and told the driver, "Hôtel Antoinette." He flicked on the light. Vice President Spiro Agnew had just arrived on *Air Force Two* for a conference. There was a story about a botched raid to catch Timothy Leary at Mick Jagger's chateau. The French were blaming the head of the O.N.O., E. Grayson Gridley, who in turn was blaming a stripper at a disco for helping Leary escape. Hadn't he met Gridley that time at Pachyderm's?

The lobby of the Antoinette was adorned with the finest crystal chandeliers and attended by bellhops in red uniforms with shiny brass buttons. He asked for a room on the fifth floor, and as soon as the bellhop left he went to Ms. DeWolfe's door and knocked. No answer. Could she have checked out? The hallway was deserted; he put his stethoscope to the door. A TV was on. He took out a lock-pick out of his sleeve, and after a little fumbling, the tumblers clicked, and he slipped inside.

She was passed out on a couch; a nearly-empty bottle of brandy was on the coffee table. He kneeled beside her, avoiding the puddle of puke on the carpet, and gently shook her shoulder. "Ms. DeWolfe."

She moaned, but didn't wake up.

He would need her at her best in the morning, and remembered McGill's theory about hangovers being caused by dehydration. If you had the presence of mind to drink a huge glass of water and take a double dose of aspirin before going to bed, the next day wouldn't be too bad.

He had aspirin in his shaving kit. He searched for her room key so he wouldn't have to pick the lock again. He found it in her purse, along with a zippered bank pouch stuffed with currency. When this girl went shopping, she really went shopping. There was also a photo of her with a gorgeous woman with long dark hair. A friend from college?

He went to his room and brought his bags to her room. He slipped his arms under her knees and shoulders, girded himself—one, two, three— lifted her up and carried her to bed. As he laid her down he discovered a golf-ball sized lump on the back of her skull and felt an overwhelming rage.

He wiped the puke off her chin and sweater with a wet towel, then pulverized four aspirins in a hotel envelope with the butt of his gun. He dissolved the powder in a glass of water, sat her up, braced her head in the palm of his hand, and put the glass to her lips. "Drink up, Ms. DeWolfe. You'll thank me in the morning. There you go...."

She sputtered and coughed. He held the glass to her mouth until she finished every drop, then tucked her in, stroked her hair, kissed her on the forehead, and whispered, "Sleep tight." He left the bathroom light on, closed all the drapes, took blankets and a spare pillow from the closet, stripped to his skivvies, and crashed on the couch.

Catherine was shocked to find herself in bed, fully dressed; she never slept with her clothes on. And how did her blanket get tucked in? She never tucked herself in. She stumbled to the bathroom, noticing the smell of vomit on her sweater. She hadn't had a hangover since a toga party at a

Cornell fraternity her freshman year at Vassar. She remembered the French saying about a hangover—*my hair hurts*. It was true. Never again.

She started the water for a bath and brushed her teeth. The toothbrush made her gag, and she threw up a little in the sink. She soaked in the tub like a prune. It helped, but not much. She put on the thick terry-cloth hotel bathrobe and went to call room service for coffee. As she made her way to the phone a voice said, "How are you feeling?"

She shrieked—"Aahh!"—jumped back and braced in a judo stance. The drapes were drawn, and the room was in shadows, but she could see the outline of a man, sprawled on the couch, his feet sticking out the bottom of a blanket. "Who are you? What do you want?"

"Take it easy, Ms. DeWolfe. It's me."

"Lieutenant? What are you doing here?"

"I left you a message with the hotel clerk. Didn't you get it?"

"Yes, but I called you right back and left messages with the switchboard and Mr. McGill telling you not to come."

"I saw Nixon right after I talked to you. When I told him about the seeds, he gave me some money and ordered me to come over and take charge. You were passed out when I found you, so I put you to bed."

"*You* put me to bed?"

"You were pretty out of it."

"How did you get in?"

He stood up, keeping the blanket around his waist, took his suitcoat off the chair, sat back down on the couch, and pulled something out of the cuff of the sleeve that looked like a dental tool with a long, thin needle, with a hook on the tip. "Nixon sent me to spy school. I aced lock-picking."

He was brimming with enthusiasm as he opened his briefcase and handed her two passports, the normal light-green one everyone carried, and another with a white cover and DIPLOMAT embossed in gold. "We're to use the diplomatic passports to get the seeds through customs, and the regular ones for everything else."

She opened them up. Both used the photo from her ID card. Her new identity was Margaret Frances Bennington, from Evanston, Illinois.

"I'm a commodities broker," he said, "and you're my spendthrift wife. It's a tighter cover if we're married."

"We're married?"

His face reddened. "Only until the mission's over."

He was so cute when he was embarrassed, and so masculine with his curly red chest hairs popping out all over from beneath his T-shirt. She eased herself down on the couch. "I don't know what to say."

"You should be proud. Based on your information, Nixon gave me a lot of money to get what we need. Have you talked to your contact about the seeds?"

She must be careful. "I asked him to check, but we haven't discussed details. I never expected you to come all the way over here right away."

"Are you kidding? This could solve our biggest problem. What's his name? Can you trust him?"

"His name is Oskar. And yes, I trust him."

"When are you going to see him?"

"I'm supposed to meet him this afternoon, at two."

"Will he have the seeds?"

"No. We're meeting on...on another matter."

"Is that what all the cash is for?"

"You were in my purse?"

"I needed your key. Why so much money?"

He was so matter-of-fact about violating her belongings. She tried to control her anger. "My private life is none of your business, Lieutenant."

"Ms. DeWolfe, we're on a mission, so everything you do is my business. Now, why do you need so much money?"

Think fast—a rich girl routine. "It's...really not that much. I do it all the time. You get much better deals with cash, you know. And I...I'm buying something from him...a pendant. For my mother."

"It must be very nice."

"Oh, it is." Change the subject. "I'm not sure you're meeting him is a good idea. He's very...shy."

"Does he know how rich you are?"

"He knows all about my family."

"Does he know you work for Nixon?"

"He knows I work in Washington for the government, that's all."

"We have to make sure he doesn't make a connection with the White House. Why does he think you want the seeds?"

"He knows my family's in the paper business, so I told him we came across those old paper-making experiments and need seeds to test them out."

"Good thinking. He said it's no good for smoking, right?"

"Yes. They grow it to make linen."

"So what makes you think you can trust him?"

"He was a freedom fighter in Hungary, and he smuggles refugees out from behind the Iron Curtain. And he might have saved my life."

"I like him already. Tell me about the mugging. That's a real goose egg you've got."

She felt the lump. "It's not as bad as it was."

"How did he get involved?"

"I was at a disco he owns, the Olympique Au-Go-Go, and—"

"The one in the news?"

"What do you mean?"

"It's in the paper, something about Leary's escape." He reached in his briefcase, removed the Herald Tribune, and found the headline on the bottom of page one: "Drug Czar Blamed."

She reached for it, but he tossed it on the table. "You can read it later. I need to debrief you first."

"Yes, of course."

"So. You were at this disco, and...."

"And a man I used to know recognized me."

"You know who mugged you?"

"I met him years ago when I was in college, backpacking around Europe on trains."

"Tell me about him. Everything."

"His name is Andrei, Andrei Antonescu. He's Romanian. He said he was a count, and he had a motorcycle, but he was a lout, so I ditched him. After I got home I discovered he'd ripped off my credit cards for a lot of money. When he recognized me, he thought he could cash in."

"Cash in? You mean hold you for ransom, like the Getty kid who had his ear cut off?"

"Something like that."

"So it's a copycat kidnapping?"

"No...I mean yes...I mean I had no idea I was even going to be there until I got there, so he couldn't have planned it. I was just in the wrong place at the wrong time."

"What were you doing there?"

She hated lying, but she had no choice. "I was...I was there to dance. It's a disco."

"And this Oskar saved you?"

"Andrei and two men forced me outside with a knife. They'd just taken my things when Oskar and his man came along. There was a fight, and I got hit with a blackjack and woke up in Oskar's office."

"Why would he stick his neck out for you?"

"Honor. He couldn't let someone be kidnapped from his club."

"Hmmm....So how did you learn about the seeds?"

"That was an accident. His, uh, niece, a girl named Nicole, was showing me photos of his village in Hungary, and there were pictures of peasants harvesting what looked like hemp. I asked him a few questions, and when he said they were growing it here in France, I called you."

"Very heads up, Ms. DeWolfe. So, tell me, is this Andrei still after you?"

"He wouldn't dare."

"What did the police say?"

"I don't want them involved."

"But he stole your money and your passport?"

"It wasn't that much, and the last thing my family wants is publicity. Kidnapping is a real worry for us. Please, Lieutenant, let it drop. Okay?"

"I can't tell you how to live your life, but I won't let anybody cut off your ears on my watch. Until this is over, you're not leaving my sight."

"That's very gallant of you, Lieutenant, but I can take care of myself. I have a black belt in judo."

He smiled. "I remember you took care of Duberman pretty good."

"I've been taking lessons since I was ten. My father insisted."

"You're full of surprises, Ms. DeWolfe."

"So what do we do?"

"For now we'll play it safe and check into another hotel under our new names. They even gave you a wedding ring." He took a ring case out of his briefcase, opened it and slipped an expensive diamond band on her finger.

She quivered, a swirl of feelings. She noticed a second ring in the case, a man's gold band. "Why aren't you wearing yours?"

"I don't wear jewelry."

"Oh? Why not?"

"I don't believe in it."

"You don't believe in it?"

"No."

"What about your Navy uniform? All those medals and ribbons and fancy thingamajigs are just male jewelry."

"That's not true at all."

"But of course it is. How is it any different?"

"It's…it's just different, that's all."

Ooohh, she'd touched a nerve. This could be fun. "I'll bet you haven't even tried your ring on, have you?"

"Men don't wear wedding rings."

"That's nonsense. Of course they do."

"Not where I come from. They're dangerous around machinery, and against work rules in the steel mills."

"Maybe a steelworker in a hard hat has rules about jewelry, but a commodities broker has fancy cuff links and a diamond tie clasp." She removed the gold band from the box. "Now, give me your hand."

He folded his arms, tucking his hands under his armpits, as if he were protecting them from attack. This was fun; she really had him going.

"You want to do what's best for the mission, don't you Lieutenant?"

"Of course."

"Then you're obligated to wear it. Do you know why?"

He tensed up, as if he were expecting to take a punch. "Why?"

"Because women won't be throwing themselves at your feet if you're wearing a ring. You'll be much more efficient and focused if you're off the market and not wasting valuable spy time bedding the ladies like James Bond. Now give me your hand."

He gave her a dirty look. She just smiled, holding out the ring. He held firm for a few awkward seconds, finally stretching out his hand. She slipped the ring on his finger. "Perfect. Not too tight, not too loose."

He glared as she put her hand next to his, so their rings were side by side. "You know what they say, Lieutenant…abstinence builds character."

He huffed a big sigh. "You shouldn't call me Lieutenant until the mission's over. We're supposed to be married."

"So what should I call you? Dear? Sweetie? Snookums?"

"Our passports say James and Margaret, so why don't you call me Jim, and I'll call you Peggy?"

Without thinking she took his hands in hers and in the cartoon character Tweety Bird's voice said, "How about if I caw you my BIIIG, wed Honey Bear?"

He flushed a deep crimson, from his receding hairline down to the freckles on his broad shoulders, even the chest hairs bristling out the edges of his T-shirt seemed to turn redder than they already were. She reached out and tickled the bottom of his chin and ran her fingers up and down his cheek, like in an after-shave commercial. "Oh my, so skwatchy. Da big wed Honey Bear needs a shavy wavy. Kitchy-koo, Honey Bear...."

Mulligan was happy to let her have her fun, but as she kitchy-kooed in her soft, husky voice and ran her fingers along his cheek her robe came open a bit and her right breast peeked out, her nipple coyly winking at him. He squirmed, rearranging the blanket on his lap. "I think you're right. Ms. DeWolfe, I'd better clean up."

Keeping the blanket around his waist, he picked his clothes off the couch, grabbed his shaving kit, waddled awkwardly to the bathroom, closed the door and began repeating the workplace mantra under his breath, "A smart dog doesn't crap on his own porch, a smart dog doesn't crap on his own porch," over and over. He took a cold-water Navy shower which, in addition to saving precious hot water at sea, was supposed to decrease intense horniness. It didn't work. The fire ignited by her soft kitchy-koos and a flash of her succulent nipple was far too hot to be doused by a little cold water. The only way to put it out and get back to normal was to quit fighting it and gave in. After a few quick strokes, he came all over shower, but didn't quite get back to normal.

Chapter 20

Hands and Knees

WHEN THE BATHROOM DOOR CLOSED CATHERINE SNATCHED THE PAPER OFF the table and read the article. Gridley was claiming Leary escaped with the help of a stripper at the notorious Olympique Au-Go-Go. Thank God there was no picture. Jenny should be safely in the States by now.

She called room service for coffee and put on jeans, sneakers, and a blouse. Fifteen minutes later the Lieutenant emerged from the bathroom tying his tie and barking orders. "Ms. DeWolfe, better take off the ring until we get you checked out of here. But first we need to be sure you're not being followed by the muggers, so here's what we'll do…."

He was worse than her father: Do this, Ms. DeWolfe, do that, Ms. DeWolfe. He actually insisted they synchronize their watches, in military time. "Oh nine-fifty-two hours, check."

When he left she stormed out on her tiny balcony and shouted into the wind and rain, "I'm not in the goddamned Navy!"

She took the elevator at exactly 10:30 hours—as ordered—while he observed from the mezzanine to see if anyone was following her. She talked to a desk clerk, feigning stupidity over a map—as ordered—and poked around the shops—as ordered—buying an umbrella. At 10:50 she exited— as ordered. She put up the umbrella, walked for five minutes in the driving rain, made a show out of forgetting something, and rushed back at exactly 11:00—as ordered. He was still watching. She shook water off her umbrella as she waited for the elevator, happy to end the charade. He'd better be pleased with her performance, because if he wasn't, he could stick it.

Two men with mirrored sunglasses were standing in front of one of the elevator doors, as though they were guarding it. It opened, and out came Spiro Agnew, the Vice President of the United States, with half a dozen others, including the speechwriter, Bullcannon. No, please no, don't let him recognize her.

He stopped as he walked by. "Why it's Miss DeWolfe, isn't it?"

"Mr. Bullcannon, what a surprise."

"What are you doing here?" he asked.

"I'm stuck here because of the airline strike."

"Say, this could be your lucky day. You have a White House security clearance, don't you?"

"Uh, yes…why?"

"How's your French? Pretty good, I'd bet. How would you like to do something interesting for a change?"

She didn't like where this was going. "I don't understand."

"Half our staff was flying commercial, and with the strike, we're scrambling for help."

"I'm sure the embassy has people who do that sort of work."

"We need our own people, and you've got a clearance. You'd be doing us a big service. Be a real feather in your cap."

"But I already have a job. They're depending on me."

"This is just a few days, and you're stuck here anyway. Besides, it'll be fun. You can start tonight at the reception at the embassy for the Vice President. We can really use you."

"But I have nothing to wear, and—"

"Oh, come now. You'd be ravishing in an old dishrag. You run out and get whatever you want and we'll put it on the embassy's tab. I'll tell Spiro's people you're pitching in, and they'll let your people in Washington know what's going on. And don't worry about the strike. You can hop a ride back with us on *Air Force Two*. I'll send a driver for you at eight."

She rode up in the elevator and went out on her little balcony, her thoughts racing between Leary and Gridley and Oskar and Jenny and Nixon and the Lieutenant and now, out of the blue, Bullcannon and Agnew and an embassy reception. A lightning bolt flashed, crackled, and boomed, triggering a long-ago memory exactly like this.

She must have been nine or ten, and fishing from the dock at Timber Crest on Lake Charlevoix as a thunderstorm approached, the best time to catch the really big ones. She was choosing among the two dozen lively black crickets that the groundskeeper, old Jonas, had brought her from Holton's Bait and Tackle. She opened the screened lid and reached in for a fat one when another cricket landed on her arm, scurried up her sleeve, and squiggled down the front of her blouse, all itchy and scratchy and yucky. She shrieked, slapping like crazy to get the awful thing out and knocking over the pail. It rolled around the dock in a clatter, and the crickets bolted for freedom, springing every which way and landing on her face, her legs, in her hair. She crawled franticly around the dock, screaming, "Come back! Come back!" grabbing and missing and missing again, scraping her knees and filling her hands with splinters. How many crickets did she catch back in the pail? One? Two?

She heard a click, and saw the door open. The Lieutenant had picked her lock again.

"I didn't spot anybody tailing you," he said, "but that was bad timing with Bullcannon. What did he have to say?"

"I'm supposed to go to work for him tonight."

"What?"

"His staff didn't get here because of the strike, and he wants me to fill in. I'm supposed to buy a dinner dress and be Miss Congeniality at an embassy party for Agnew. How do I get out of it?"

"Damn." He clasped his hands behind his back and began pacing, lost in thought. He reminded her of actor Gregory Peck in *Captain Horatio Hornblower*, pacing stone-faced in his British uniform on the deck of his ship. He stopped, wheeled toward her and said, "You have to do it, Ms. DeWolfe. You have the right M-O-S. It's your duty."

"I have the right *what*?"

"Sorry, I forget you're a civilian. It means Military Occupational Specialty. In the Navy, you'd be a 27-Alpha, a clerk/typist. I'm not sure what the M-O-S for linguists is, but you'd have one for French, too."

This was insane. He's playing Captain America, and she has to deal with Oskar and rescue Jenny and smuggle Leary to Afghanistan and hemp seeds to America and now go to work for Agnew and Bullcannon? She had to get out of it. "But I have to meet Oskar about the seeds."

"Introduce us, and I'll take it from there."

"No!"

"What do you mean *no*?"

"My business with him is personal."

"Now you listen up, Ms. DeWolfe. The stakes are far higher than you can imagine. The seeds Jefferson smuggled back won the West, and it could be the seeds we smuggle back that power America for the next century...."

He was so earnest, so quaintly patriotic, trying to save America by being Thomas Jefferson, Thomas Edison, John Wayne, and Johnny Appleseed all rolled into one. Wasn't Jefferson tall, with red hair?

"I don't see why you are in such a tizzy, Lieutenant. When's your birthday?"

"Huh?"

"When's your birthday?"

"May 18th. Why?"

"Well that explains it then."

"Explains what?"

"Why you're such a brick wall. You're a Taurus. They're very fixed. And the sun's in Taurus now, which makes it even worse. There's not much hope of getting through to you when your mind's made up."

"You don't believe that crap, do you?"

"I'm only trying to understand why you're so discombobulated. The seeds aren't going anywhere."

He began pacing again, waving his hands and spittering like a garden hose when it's first turned on. "If we don't get them in the ground soon we'll miss the growing season."

How to calm him down? "Let me see what Oskar says."

"I have confidence in you, Ms. DeWolfe, you're officer material. But I have questions about equipment, fertilizers, all kinds of things. Maybe I should go to that disco of his and see him on my own?"

"No!"

"Why not?"

"Because...because the police are watching it, right? Look, he trusts me. Let me finish my business with him, then I'll see what he says. Okay?"

"Does he speak English?"

"I don't know. We've only used French."

"If he doesn't, tell him I can get by in German. And drop a hint we might pay him to grow some seeds for us, see how he reacts."

Hooray, she won a round! "I'll try, Lieutenant. What will you do?"

"I should get out of here. A Secret Service agent I play basketball with is on Agnew's detail, and if he sees me, my cover's blown too."

"What do we tell Duberman and the others?"

"We tell them the truth."

"Uh...the truth?"

"From now on, your story to Bullcannon or Duberman or anyone but Nixon is you came over to go shopping, got mugged, and were stuck by the strike. But you haven't seen me."

"McGill knows I called from Paris, but I made him promise not to say anything. Think he'll keep quiet?"

"McGill can be an idiot, but you can trust him." He closed his suitcase and put it by the door. "How long will your business with Oskar take?"

"I hope not too long," she said.

"Where can we meet? A park, something easy to find."

"How about the benches along the Seine, just up from Notre Dame? Around four…I mean sixteen-hundred."

He opened the door, glanced up and down the hall, then back at her. For a breathless moment he seemed to hesitate, as if he might sweep her up in his muscular arms and give her a big Hollywood kiss. Instead, he sighed, picked up his bag, said, "Sixteen-hundred hours," and was gone.

How did she get into this mess? It was as if she were crawling all over Paris on her hands and knees trying to catch crickets. What was wrong with her? And what did he mean by "officer material?" Is that how he thought about her, just another Navy recruit? *Damn him!*

An hour later she took a cab to the Brasserie Bleu Giraffe for her meeting with Oskar. After days of rain the sun brought out a crowd, and people were sitting and sipping drinks, chatting and reading under the sturdy blue canvas awning that stretched over the rows of sidewalk tables. She couldn't help wondering if the canvas were made of hemp.

She bought a copy of *Le Monde,* took a table, and ordered a cappuccino. Her newly-synchronized watch said ten-to-two, though he would have said 13:50 hours. Why couldn't she stop thinking about him?

The streets were filled with puddles, and the tires of passing cars hissed in harmony on the wet pavement. The dampness kept the warm, bready aromas from a nearby boulangerie lingering in the air like a freshly-baked cloud. It was oh-so-very Paris-in-the-springtime, but she was too frazzled to enjoy it.

Oskar arrived, dapper in a leather jacket, a gray turtleneck and a black beret.

"The Olympique's in the paper," she said, pointing to the article.

He chuckled. "Police ask about Susannah. I make big lie. Easy."

"Are they safe?"

"Susannah in America, other friend on way to Afghanistan."

She took an envelope from her purse and slid it to him. He looked inside, smiled, put it in his jacket pocket and slid one to her. She opened it. Her pendant. They both smiled.

"Oskar, about the seeds. Can you help us?"

"Maybe. How you get to America?"

"My friend has it figured out. You'll have to talk to him about the details, and he has a lot of questions about farming techniques, tractors, all that kind of thing. Oskar, will you come and talk with him? Please."

Chapter 21

Red Tape

MCGILL HADN'T EXACTLY LIED TO MULLIGAN ABOUT WANTING TO BORROW his car to go apartment hunting. He really and truly did *want* to go, but scrounging forks was more important, and Mulligan would have hit the ceiling if he knew.

It had been a good day. He had scored 107 forks and he was looking forward to his first real night on the town. He and Mulligan had reservations at Pachyderm's for dinner and were planning to hit the Georgetown clubs later. They hadn't gone chick-hunting together since high school.

He pulled up to the corner of Pennsylvania and Seventeenth only a few minutes late. An MP walked over and said, "Lt. Mulligan told me to tell you he's been called away and not to worry if you don't hear from him for a few days."

"Did he say where he was going or what it was about?"

"Nope. Just not to worry."

"How long's he been gone?"

"Since before noon."

What could it be? Maybe Navy war games?

He went to Pachyderm's and dined alone, feeling a glow of fulfillment at being in the same room with Senators and Congressmen and K Street power lobbyists making deals and plotting strategies. He strategized too, plotting the road to riches on street maps to the Sunday garage sales listed in *The Washington Post*.

Later in the bars, he discovered the five-chicks-to-every-guy story was a myth. It was the same as everywhere he'd ever been: three guys to every chick. The pickup lines were different, though. Back East "What-do-you-do?" got things going. Out West "What's-your-sign?" broke the ice. He was amazed how women's interest in him perked up when they heard he worked at the White House. By last-call he had a pocketful of phone numbers, and not one woman had asked him his sign.

Back at the apartment he drank a big glass of water, took four aspirins, and set the alarm for seven to get an early start. He had just nodded out when the phone rang. He expected Mulligan, but it was DeWolfe, calling all the way from Paris. All he could figure was that Mulligan must have been secretly balling her on the side and they had a spat.

He had Mulligan's car, so Sunday he went scrounging, scoring eighty-nine forks. He got back at seven and called Vince.

"Where the hell have you been, McGill?"

"I been trying to get you, man. You're always gone. We need one of those new answering machines. A lot of people here are getting them."

"Don't bullshit me, McGill. You've only sent one fucking fork the whole time you been gone. How are we supposed to get rich on that?"

"Gimme a break. I've been out scrounging all weekend. I'm sending almost two hundred tomorrow."

"That's nowhere near what we need. You talk to any factories about production runs yet?"

"I've been getting settled in. How did the one I sent work?"

"It's like the ones we had in the Army. Why?"

"But did it make a good Bird?"

"Yeah, the size is right and all. Only problem is that the U.S. Government stamp comes out under the tail. It's kind of cool, actually. Makes the Bird look like it's made by the government. Why?"

"Because if you tell me it works, I'll pull some strings and see if I can track down who made 'em. Are they good enough or not?"

"I see what you're saying. Yeah, plenty good."

In the morning, McGill stood in line at the EOB post office to mail the forks, making him late. The others were all waiting for him.

"Dammit, McGill, you're late for everything," Duberman said. "What do you know about Mulligan and DeWolfe and a special assignment?"

"Nothing," he lied as he set his briefcase on the counter. "I dropped him off Saturday and borrowed his car. When I came to pick him up, an MP told me he'd been called away."

"Called away?" Duberman said. "Where?"

"That's all the MP knew. I figured it was Navy war games."

"The switchboard took this Saturday night," Duberman said as he handed him a message slip. "Know anything about it?"

> Lt. Mulligan,
> Please don't leave until you hear from me.
> C. DeWolfe

"Beats me," he said. "Who says they're on an assignment?"

"Haldeman," Duberman said.

"Mulligan we can do without," Branche said, "but if DeWolfe's gone who's going to type and answer the phone?"

"Haldeman doesn't think they'll be gone long," Duberman said, "and Nixon doesn't want anybody new coming in and risking a leak. So we'll rotate. Who's first?"

"Me," McGill said. "I need phone time to track down apartments."

He made a show of looking in the classifieds, but when the others left he opened the Interagency Governmental Directory. His credentials cut through the red tape even on the phone. "I'm with the Presidential Policy Commission, and we're looking into a matter for the White House...."

A few calls led to the Defense Reutilization and Marketing Service, the D.R.M.S. An Army captain there asked, "How many do they want?"

"All I was told was to find out what you have, where they are, and what they cost. They don't want any special favors. Treat this like a civilian inquiry. They just want to know what's available."

The captain called back two hours later with the answers: There were almost half a million surplus sets of military cutlery in the U.S., Okinawa, West Germany, the Philippines, Panama, Hawaii, and Diego Garcia. Sets were comprised of a teaspoon, a soup spoon, a salad fork, a dinner fork, and a knife. There were five thousand sets on a pallet, and the price was $500 per pallet, plus freight.

McGill had been hoping to find a thousand or two—but half a million? "How come there's so many?"

"They were procured for the Vietnam build-up, but Kennedy ended the war before it ever really got going. We'd make a deal on the whole bunch if you were to take them off our hands."

"How much just for the dinner forks?"

"We can't sell them separately. What good's half a million table settings with a fork missing?"

"I see what you mean. But what if they paid for the full sets, and you just shipped the pieces they wanted? You could sell the rest for scrap."

"I guess it'd be okay."

"I'll let them know, but half a million sounds like a lot. I doubt they'll want more than a pallet or two. And I'm sure they'll want to inspect them before they make a commitment. Where are they?"

"All over. I have the list right here. Got a pencil?"

The nearest warehouse to Washington was at the Naval Supply Center in Newport News, with four pallets, 20,000 sets. McGill winced when the captain said, "Oakland Army Base, twelve pallets, sixty-thousand sets." The sprawling base had been a debarkation point for troops sailing to the Pacific since World War II and was ten minutes from his Berkeley bungalow. *Ten minutes!* If he had used his head, they would have had all they needed right from Day One, and they'd already be rich.

McGill talked Duberman into giving him tomorrow off to check out apartments. He got up at five and cruised in Mulligan's car to the supply depot in Newport News, three hours away. A Navy chief showed him pallets in a corner of a huge warehouse. He slit open a carton and handed him a box marked FORKS, DINNER, 20 PIECES. McGill took one out—Bingo!

"We'll take all you have if you consolidate the dinner forks in a crate and truck it to Railway Express. You can sell the other pieces for scrap."

He paid in cash, got a stamped receipt with two Xeroxed copies, followed the truck to the railroad yard, and shipped the pallet to BirdCo, San Ricardo, California.

"You *what*?" Vince said when McGill called with the news.

"I just got us twenty thousand forks exactly like the one I sent you."

"You're shittin' me?"

"Nope. You'll see 'em in a week at the Oakland REA station. The pallet weighs thirteen hundred pounds, so you'll need a truck. I mailed you the manifest and the receipt."

"So is it time to run an ad?"

"Yeah. I say we go for the eighth of a page in *Rolling Stone*. If you send a check and the artwork first thing tomorrow, it should be out in about six weeks. That gives you a month to find some help and crank out Birds."

"I'll drop it in the mail on my way to the job site," Vince said. "And help won't be a problem. There's a lot of guys out of work."

He worried Vince was in over his head. "You'll have to set up a production line," he told him, "and you'll need a secretary and somebody who can type and do bookkeeping. It'll get crazy when orders start coming in, and I won't be there to help."

"I can deal with it, McGill. I ran a whole platoon in the Army. And Susie's taking bookkeeping at the JC. We got it covered."

McGill was three time zones away, so all he could do was cross his fingers and hope for the best. He'd done his part, and if Vince did his, they'd be rich by Christmas. Easy.

Chapter 22

Farmers in the Dell

MULLIGAN SPENT TWO DAYS IN THE NORMANDY COUNTRYSIDE WITH OSKAR and the Hungarian refugee community learning about hemp cultivation. He bought seeds, a semitrailer, and specialized equipment, whatever they said he needed. To maintain the cover, he told Oskar to ship everything via the St. Lawrence Seaway to the port of Detroit, near Ms. DeWolfe's farm. After he and Oskar watched the trailer loaded onto a ship at Le Havre, he said good-bye to Oskar and the Hungarians, took a train to Brussels, and flew back to Washington using his diplomatic passport.

"Good morning, Mr. President," he said as he set two suitcases on the Oval Office floor.

"I hope you have good news," Nixon said. "I could use some. It's been nothing but gas lines for weeks now."

"Aye, sir, I do." He opened a suitcase and took out a twenty kilo burlap sack marked CHANVRE and hoisted it onto Nixon's desk. "This is prime Hungarian hemp seed, Mr. President. They sold me forty bags like this and all the equipment we'll need. Everything is in a trailer on the docks in Le Havre. The ship sails the day after tomorrow. You'll have to move fast to divert it, or we'll miss the planting season."

"I'll get people on it right away. They have no idea you work for me, do they?"

"No, sir. We made up a story about wanting it for paper-making experiments at Ms. DeWolfe's farm."

"Is she with you?"

"No, sir. We've been out of touch for security reasons. The last I heard she'd gone to work for Mr. Bullcannon."

"Bob mentioned that. How the hell did that happen?"

"She bumped into him in the lobby and he asked her to help out. I told her it was her duty, and she pitched right in."

"Good for her. Shows she's a team player."

"Aye, sir, she is. Did you arrange a place for us to get started?"

"You bet I did. A company of Seabees is up there right now fencing it off and setting up a bivouac area. Some boys from the Agriculture Department went in there and plowed it up, trucked in cow manure, and plowed it up again. You can fly up with me this afternoon."

That evening, McGill was in Mulligan's apartment watching the news when the phone rang.

"Stick, it's me."

"Hey, Mulligan Man. Where the hell are you?"

"I can't say, but write down this number. Got a pen?"

"A 710 area code?" McGill said as he wrote. "Where's that?"

"It's the nationwide military area code."

"How about DeWolfe? What was she doing in Paris?"

"She went shopping."

"You with her?"

"No."

"She called both me and the switchboard to tell you not to go. Is that where you are…Paris?"

"No. Did you tell anyone you talked to her?"

"No. She made me promise."

"You sure?"

"I've been playing dumb, but Bullcannon's office called and said she's temporarily assigned to them. When are you coming back?"

"Haldeman's going to brief you."

"Come on, gimme a clue. A week…a month…Christmas? Should I keep looking for my own place? Should I open your mail and pay your car insurance? There's all kinds of practical stuff."

"Okay. Give the bills to Haldeman. You'll have the place to yourself for a few weeks, but we have to be able to stay in touch. Get one of those new answering machines and hook it up. I've got one on this end."

"I was going to check out the Mellon angle up in the Burgh pretty soon. You want me to forget it?"

"No, just be sure to call when you go, and check your machine twice a day in case I need you to do something and your not there. But only call from pay phones so you can't be traced."

McGill could contain his curiosity no longer. "So Mulligan, you getting any nookie?"

"Knock it off, Stick."

"Those long legs must be something."

"I said knock it off!"

"Jeez, listen to you. You got it worse than I thought."

"What are you talking about?"

"Don't even try to bullshit me, Mulligan Man. I've known you too long. You got it bad. Admit it."

"You're full of shit."

"Just be careful. You can't trust chicks with that kind of dough."

"Why don't you mind your own fucking business?"

"Because you're my best friend, jerkoff, and that makes it my business. Besides, if you really want to pluck her heartstrings, try lilacs."

"Lilacs?"

"Haven't you noticed? She's got a thing about them."

It had not been easy keeping all her lies straight: to the Lieutenant about Oskar; to Oskar about hemp seeds; to Bullcannon about everything. At Le Bleu Giraffe she had persuaded Oskar to come with her to meet her friend, "Jim." She left them on the benches along the Seine talking in German about "Hanf" while she went to work full-time for Bullcannon, and had not seen or heard from either of them since.

On her way to the last day of the conference she stopped for her usual copy of *Le Monde* in the newsstand. The headline read: "Coup à Kabul."

My God, wasn't Kabul the capital of...*Afghanistan*! Her stomach churned as she read about Soviet paratroopers dropping out of the sky to help the rebels, and of rumors the Royal Family had been executed. If Leary had made it to Kabul and been with them, could he be dead too? If she hadn't helped him escape, he might be in prison, but he would be alive.

She called the Olympique and was told Oskar was out of town. She somehow made it through the day, and after the final event she went to her hotel room to prepare for the flight to Washington on *Air Force Two*, when she heard a knock on her door.

"There's been a change in your plans, Mrs. Bennington," a man in a suit informed her.

She was surprised he used her C.I.A. name. "A change in my plans?"

"The Air Force has diverted a C-5 from Wiesbaden to pick up you and your shipment."

"My shipment?"

"Yes, Ma'am. We've informed Mr. Bullcannon that Ms. DeWolfe won't be returning with him."

He drove her to a French military base outside Paris, where a giant U.S. Air Force C-5A cargo plane sat on a pad outside a hanger, its nose popped open like a flip-top cigarette box. A powerful tractor was pulling a double-door semitrailer into the plane's belly. She went up the ramp and was greeted by an Air Force sergeant and a French customs agent. She showed the diplomatic passport, and the agent gave it an exit stamp.

"Where is my shipment?" she asked the sergeant.

"Right there," and he pointed to the semitrailer being secured by a team of airmen. "It's under diplomatic seal."

The windowless cargo plane was stacked high with crates, but in the front section were a few rows of seats filled with Army and Air Force servicemen, many with wives and children, maybe sixty passengers in all.

They landed at 02:10 at Dover Air Force Base, Delaware. She walked down the ramp hoping to see the Lieutenant, but a Marine sergeant with an MP brassard approached her. "Mrs. Bennington?"

"Yes."

"Would you please come with me, Ma'am."

He escorted her to an olive-drab sedan with a blue police bubble on the roof and a heavy mesh screen between the front and rear seats. He opened the back door and locked her in. "I won't be long."

She watched as he talked to a Marine behind the wheel of a big-rig truck. A few minutes later, a huge forklift pulled the trailer down the ramp and over to the big-rig. They hooked it up and the sergeant returned, opened the trunk, took out a blanket and a pillow, and handed them to her. "You may want to catch some sleep, Ma'am. It's a few hours drive."

"Where are we going?"

"I'm sorry, Ma'am, I'm not at liberty to say."

The two-vehicle convoy headed out. When they got on a freeway, she stretched out on the back seat and closed her eyes. She woke up two hours later as they exited a freeway off-ramp. Through the early morning mists she saw a road sign: Frederick 22. They took a secondary road wending through rolling, forested mountains. She saw another sign: Catoctin Wilderness Area 15. They turned on an unmarked road and came to a gate with a guard house manned by Marines with M-16's. She glimpsed what looked like log cabins through the trees, then they turned on to a rutted dirt path, hardly a road at all, bouncing along until they came to a chain-link fence topped with razor wire. A red skull with lightning bolt crossbones warned: DANGER HIGH VOLTAGE!

The sergeant picked up the radio transmitter. "Trader Joe to Farmboy. Over. Trader Joe to Farmboy. Over."

She felt a warm rush of affection at the sound of the Lieutenant's voice squawking over the speaker, "Farmboy to Trader Joe. Over."

"Cargo and passenger at your gate. Over."

"On my way. Farmboy out."

A few minutes later she felt a surge of excitement as he came to the gate in blue jeans, work boots, and a red flannel shirt. He was wearing the C.I.A. wedding ring he had been so dead-set against and practically stuck it in her face as he got in the car and said, "How was your trip, dear?"

She played along. "Very tiring, Honey Bear," and she gave him a kiss.

They went through the gate and rode through the woods for another hundred yards and stopped in a clearing. The Lieutenant hopped out and opened her door like a perfect gentleman. "This is it, dear."

She climbed out and looked through wisps of fog up a little valley into a long, narrow meadow. The dank morning air was heavy with the pungent aroma of cow manure. She saw a compound of tents, large and small, like in the TV show *M*A*S*H*. Nearby were a backhoe and a forklift painted in military camouflage, and an old-time, hand-operated water pump right out of *Death Valley Days*.

The sergeant asked, "Where do you want the trailer, Mr. Bennington?"

"By the big storage tent."

After the driver parked and unhitched the trailer, the sergeant said, "Anything you need, Mr. Bennington, you call."

As they watched the big-rig and car drive away, she asked, "Why are we still using our phony names?"

"Because Nixon's worried about leaks. He doesn't want anyone to know anything about who we are or what we're doing."

"What's with him? Why is he so paranoid?"

"I don't know, but he's the President, so to the Marines and the staff up here, we're with the Agriculture Department."

"Where exactly are we?"

"The most secure piece of real estate on the planet—Camp David."

"Camp David?" she echoed softly, tingling at the news.

"And that, Ms. DeWolfe," he said, pointing to a newly-plowed field that stretched up the valley, "is National Strategic Hemp Patch Number One."

"It doesn't look very strategic to me."

"Give it a couple of months. According to Washington's farm diaries, we should be right on time. The elevation here is eighteen hundred feet higher than Mount Vernon, but I don't think it will make much difference."

"What's in the trailer?" she asked.

"Seeds and equipment. If they said we needed it, I bought it. Oskar thought he was shipping it to you in Michigan. Your tent's on the left—"

"What do you mean *my* tent? Why do I need a tent?"

"Nixon wants us to stay up here until the crop's in."

"*Me*? Who does he think I am, Old MacDonald? I don't know a thing about farming."

"Neither do I, but we have all the equipment we need, and the how-to pamphlets from the 4-H club and the Agriculture Department. And you'll have a complete office, everything you need."

"An office?"

"Nixon wants you to keep editing the reports. They'll send a courier up with the team's notes every day."

"I can't stay here. I've got a bar exam coming up, and—"

"It's all taken care of. They brought your mail and study materials, and Miss Woods went through your clothes and picked out what she thought you'd need. The C.I.A.'s worked up a cover story for your family, and—"

"But why me? Why not one of the others?"

"Because this is on a need-to-know basis, and right now only you and I and Nixon need to know. We'll get the others up here when it's time to bring in the harvest."

"I don't think I like this, Lieutenant. I already feel like a prisoner."

"Think of it as an honor, like being at Los Alamos during the Manhattan Project. And you couldn't ask for a nicer spot. When Roosevelt made this the presidential retreat, he named it Shangri-La."

She was too jet-lagged to think clearly.

He seemed to sense her fatigue. "You must be tired. How about some bacon and eggs, and then you can nap as long as you like?"

"That would be nice."

"Why don't you freshen up and I'll make it. The outhouse is up the path, just behind those trees. I'll heat some water so you can wash up."

"There's no hot water?"

"The Seabees will set up a field shower tomorrow along with the irrigation system and the generator. Meanwhile, we have the hand pump."

He found a two-handled cooking pot in the mess tent, went to the water pump, and picked up a coffee can next to it that was half-filled with water. "You have to prime this baby to get her going. Always remember to leave some water in the can for the next time." He poured water down the pump's throat as he worked the handle. She'd never seen a hand-pump in use except in the movies and on TV. He pumped vigorously—*squeak-squeak-squeak*—like he was Marshall Dillon on TV's *Gunsmoke*.

He went to the mess tent to start the water and showed her to her tent, politely holding the wood-frame screen door for her. A bouquet of lilacs waited in a vase on a one-drawer desk. She bent over and took a deep whiff. "Oh, they're wonderful, Lieutenant."

"They're from your yard. I asked Miss Woods to pick you some when she was there."

"Thank you. That was very thoughtful."

The tent was about as big as a dorm room, with a portable wardrobe closet with drawers filled with her own clothes, a week's worth of mail on a folding chair, a table with a wash basin and soap, and blankets, sheets, and a pillow on the folding cot.

He brought the hot water. She washed up, brushed out her hair, and joined him in the mess tent. He was turning bacon when his walkie-talkie squawked, "Sentry Three to Farmboy. Over."

He picked it up. "Roger, Sentry Three. Over."

"C-I-C is on foot with King Timahoe. E-T-A at your A-O is three minutes. Over."

"Copy, Sentry Three. Farmboy out."

She had no clue what they'd said. "What was that all about?"

"Nixon's on his way."

"How can you tell? What did all the initials mean?"

"C-I-C is short for commander-in-chief, E-T-A means estimated time-of-arrival, and A-O is area-of-operations."

"Who's King Timahoe?"

"Nixon's dog."

Soon she heard a bark and looked outside to see an Irish setter bounding across the meadow. The dog raced up and cautiously stuck its head into the tent. She petted him and said, "Hello, King," thinking how similar the coloring of his coat was to the Lieutenant's hair, both a shade or two redder than her own. An unexpected thought of what color their children's hair might be like sent a shiver up her spine.

Nixon emerged from the woods, hailed them with a wave, then turned and said something to the Secret Service agents. One of them handed

Nixon a large plastic bag.

Nixon walked the last hundred yards alone, carrying the bag over his shoulder like Santa Claus. "Good to see you, Ms. DeWolfe. I can't tell you how excited I am about your discovery. You've done a fine job, a fine job. I brought you both something to make you feel at home."

Nixon removed two navy-blue, silk warm-up jackets with CAMP DAVID embroidered beneath the Presidential Seal on the breast. He checked the label on one, handed it to the Lieutenant, then held the other up by the shoulders for her to try on. "Let's see if this fits. Rose Mary says it should be about your size."

She slipped her arms in the sleeves. "Thank you, Mr. President."

"Looks good on you," Nixon said. "Now, I'm sure you haven't had time to settle in yet, so I'm sending you down a batch of Pat's homemade potato salad and a rack of Filipino spare ribs. Do you like spare ribs, Ms. DeWolfe?"

"Yes, sir, but—"

"Then you'll love these. My valet Manolo does them in a special pineapple-and-papaya sauce that's just out of this world."

"But—

"Now, I want you and the Lieutenant to see this through to the end. Your country is depending on you, Ms. DeWolfe. But I don't want anybody else in the loop but us, not even your own people. None of them know about it now, right, Lieutenant?"

"No, Mr. President," Mulligan said, "It's just the three of us."

"Good. Keep them in the dark till the time's right. I haven't even told Bob or John what's going on up here. This is too sensitive to risk leaks."

"But Mr. President, I can't stay up here," she said as King Timahoe licked her hand. "I have a house to take care of and a bar exam coming up, and my family is expecting me to—"

"Don't worry," Nixon said. "I'll get a proctor up here to administer the test whenever you're ready, and the White House gardeners will take care of your property. And I'll have a talk with your father, let him know how proud we are of you. You might be a woman, Ms. DeWolfe, but you're one of the boys. And you, Lieutenant, remember you're an officer and a gentleman, and treat Ms. DeWolfe like a lady. You'll be in close quarters up here."

"Aye, aye, sir."

"You see that he behaves himself, Ms. DeWolfe."

"Oh, don't worry about that, Mr. President. Lieutenant Mulligan is like King Timahoe," she said, scratching the dog behind its ear.

Nixon gave her a quizzical glance. "How's that? I don't understand."

"He's a very smart dog, Mr. President."

Mulligan's face flushed a bright rosé as Nixon flashed her a puzzled look. "You're right about that, Ms. DeWolfe," Nixon said as he scratched behind the dog's other ear. "I've had a few dogs in my time, but King here is the smartest. A lot smarter than that stupid cocker spaniel Checkers ever dreamed of being. Checkers was good with the girls when they were little, and he saved my political ass back in '52 when I used him in the speech, but King here's a lot smarter. Doesn't obey worth a damn, though. Must be the Irish in him. Well, I'd better be going. When you're President, there's always something. Come on, King."

After breakfast she went to her tent, made up the cot, lay down and pulled the gray U.S. Navy blanket up over her shoulders. What was she doing here in the middle of nowhere? Was she working to bring Nixon down, or was she helping him solve the energy crisis? And what about Leary? Was he dead? Had she been responsible?

Chapter 23

Ollee Ollee Outs in Free

THE WHOMP-WHOMP-WHOMPING OF NIXON'S HELICOPTER WOKE CATHERINE up as it passed overhead. She looked outside and saw the Lieutenant working in the field like a hayseed farmer. God he was so…so…she didn't know what he was, only that she felt lonely, and guilty about Leary, and all she wanted to do was wrap her arms around his broad, freckled shoulders and hang on tight. What was wrong with her?

She put on a pair of jeans and a blouse, brushed out her hair and tied it in an efficient ponytail. Rose Mary had packed her western boots, so she put them on and walked out to where he was breaking up clods of dirt with a garden spade. "What can I do to help, Lieutenant?"

He pointed to the trailer. "We need to unload. It's a two-man job."

He swung open the double-doors. The interior was jam-packed with farm implements: a tractor, a plow, and big metal thingys on fat tires whose name and function she couldn't begin to guess. Behind the machinery in the front half of the trailer were stacks of crates. "How are we going to get all this stuff off, Lieutenant?"

"We have a forklift. I'll drive, and you do the rigging." He handed her a pair of leather work gloves. "Put these on so the steel splinters from the cables don't eat your hands up."

It took almost three hours to empty the trailer. The last two crates were marked CHANVRE. He moved them into the storage tent and shut down the fork lift. He grabbed a crowbar, pried the boards of a crate open, removed a burlap sack, cut a small hole in the corner, and said, "Cup your hands."

He poured out dozens of shiny-brown, oblong seeds, about an eighth of an inch long. "These could be more important than the seeds Jefferson smuggled back that won the West, Ms. DeWolfe, and it wouldn't be happening if it weren't for you. You should be very proud."

His quaint, gung-ho, All-American enthusiasm was catching, and she felt an unfamiliar surge of patriotic pride.

They rinsed off at the water pump. He worked the handle as she kneeled by the spout, then she pumped for him. He went to the mess tent and emerged with a cooler, set it on the picnic table, took out a six-pack, handed her plastic silverware and a paper plate, and served up Pat Nixon's potato salad and Manolo's Filipino spare ribs.

They sat on top of the table, perching side-by-side, their feet on the bench, sipping beers as the clouds turned orange and pink in the sunset. Soon, lightning bugs began to flicker in the gathering dusk, and an evening star appeared over the valley. Venus, she guessed, Planet of Love.

She felt a sense of contentment as she surveyed their new domain, and wondered what he was thinking. "A penny for your thoughts, Lieutenant."

He sighed, and a look of resignation crossed his face. "It won't be easy up here, Ms. DeWolfe. It's going to be almost like being at sea."

"What do you mean?"

"There are sound reasons why the Navy prohibits women on warships, and they have nothing to do with the old superstition that women on a ship are bad luck. And it's not because they're weaker and not suited for war or life at sea. It's because they're a disaster for morale."

"That's total macho baloney. When the Equal Rights Amendment passes, all that tired old male chauvinist crap is going right down the toilet."

"I wish it were that easy, Ms. DeWolfe, but you can't repeal biology with an amendment. Jealousy over women on a ship undermines unit cohesion worse than anything."

He was Mr. Oh-So-Sincere, the kind you could really goof on. She tried to lighten things up. "So are you saying that my being here is detrimental to your unit cohesion?"

"Huh...."

"Maybe you're worried you're not a smart dog like King Timahoe but a dumb dog like Checkers? Is that it, Lieutenant?"

She shot him a smile to show she was pulling his leg, but he missed the joke completely.

"Look," he said with a deep sigh, "besides the morale issue, it's against regulations for officers to fraternize with enlisted personnel. We eat in separate messes and drink in separate clubs. It's a court-martial offense to even attend the same parties. This is like that. We work together, but I'm your superior. Plus your family is—"

That pissed her off. "You leave my family out of this. And I am not in the goddamned Navy, and I will fraternize with anybody I please, including you if I feel like it." She leaned over, gave him a surprise kiss on the lips, pulled right back, and glared at him. "So there!"

He sat for a moment stunned, like he couldn't believe what had happened, then enveloped her in his arms. After a long kiss he eased her back on the table. She felt his hand sliding up her side, so she shifted a little to make it easier for him.

It was immediately obvious that the splintery top of the old wooden picnic table wouldn't do at all. He whispered, "Don't move a muscle," and raced to his tent, rushing back with pillows and blankets. He picked a spot by a big oak, tromped down the tall grass, and spread the blankets. He ran to her, scooped her up, and carried her to his love nest as if she were light as a feather. He laid her down and began stroking her hair, kissing her forehead, her eyes. He unhooked her bra and slipped off her blouse, and soon he was sucking, licking, massaging.

She unbuttoned his shirt and ran her hands all over his broad shoulders, his furry chest, his sinewy forearms, and his thick biceps. She explored every ripple of his rock-hard abdomen, and when she could go no further, she loosened his belt.

They made love for what seemed like forever, then nestled up in the silent afterglow. After a while he said, "Hey, look at that."

Across the valley, the pointed tip of a pale-orange crescent moon was peeking over the mountain. They watched as it slowly curved up like a golden scimitar and into the starry sky as if in a fairy tale.

She said, "I think that's the most beautiful thing I've ever seen."

He gazed at her and said, "Second most." She cuddled closer and he gave her a long, grateful kiss, pulled the blankets around them to ward off the chill, and like most men, he soon fell asleep.

She wondered what she would call him now that they were lovers…Mike? Michael? Mikey? She couldn't very well keep calling him Lieutenant, except maybe at the office. Honey Bear wouldn't be appropriate in public, and definitely not at the office.

She woke up a few hours later to a pair of owls hooting in call-and-response, first one, nearby, then the other, like an echo. She wondered if they were mates, or courting? Maybe they were rivals? Some things would always be a mystery.

The now-silvery scimitar moon was high overhead. She lay still, cuddled up with her very own Honey Bear under the starry sky, listening to the hooting of the owls and the chirping symphony of crickets. With every shooting star she made the same wish: "Please, God, let this be real."

Too soon, she had to pee. She glanced at the luminous dial on his Navy wristwatch: 03:55. She rolled out from under the blankets, being careful not to wake him. She put on her jeans, boots, and her new Camp David jacket, took his flashlight, and went up the path to the outhouse.

Coming back, she heard something odd—*tap-tap-tap*.

She froze. A few seconds later, there it was again.

Tap-tap-tap.

She switched off the flashlight, hurried back and gave him a shake, whispering, "Mike, wake up. Mike...."

He stirred with a grunt. "Huh?"

She cupped her hand over his mouth. "Shhh...there's something out there."

Tap-tap-tap.

She felt him stiffen as he came alert. "Hear that?" she whispered.

"Yes."

"What is it?"

"I don't know."

Tap-tap-tap.

"Is it an animal?"

He didn't answer but got up, slipped on his clothes, and took the flashlight from her. She followed him to his tent, where he picked up his gun.

Tap-tap-tap.

"I think it's coming from the storage tent," he said. "You wait here and don't move."

He snuck off in a silent crouch, like an Indian; she quickly caught up.

"I told you to stay put," he said in an angry whisper.

"Not on your life."

They quietly entered the big tent. He shined the flashlight all around and said, "Whatever it is, it's not in here."

There it was again—*tap-tap-tap*—definitely outside. He took the crowbar they'd left by the crates and gave it to her. "Stay behind me."

There it was again—*tap-tap-tap*.

"I think it's coming from the trailer," she said. Its double-doors were swung wide open.

He chuckled. "See what happens when there's a woman around? I was distracted and forgot to make final rounds. If this was a ship, we could be in Davy Jones Locker because of my dereliction of duty, and all because there's a woman on board."

For an instant she felt that he was blaming her, but he whispered, "You can come on board me any time," and gave her a kiss.

Tap-tap-tap.

He broke it off. "It must be a deer or a raccoon or something."

"Do they have bears around here?"

"Maybe. Okay, here's the plan. Whatever it is, we want to lock it in the trailer so we can get it out of the compound in the morning. You take the left door, and I'll take the right. I'll shine the light in to see what it is, and when I say *go* you swing your door closed, and I'll shut mine and slip the pin down to lock it in. Understand?"

"Yes."

"You afraid?"

"A little."

"Me too."

They snuck up to the trailer. She gripped her door, ready to slam it. They poked their heads up, and he flicked on the flashlight and shined it all over. Empty. She whispered, "I don't understand."

There it was again: *Tap-tap-tap*. It was definitely coming from inside. But how? From where? It was empty!

He flicked off the light, took the crowbar from her, handed her the gun, and said in a whisper, "You know how to use this?"

"My father insisted I learn all about guns. I'm a good shot."

"This time, you wait here. Promise?"

"Okay."

He climbed in the trailer, stealing to the front like a cat burglar.

Tap-tap-tap.

He felt with his fingertips all over the trailer's front wall.

Tap-tap-tap.

After a minute he came tiptoeing out, as if he were counting his steps. He signaled hush with his finger to his lips, hopped to the ground, took the gun, gave her the crowbar, and measured his paces along the outside of the trailer. A few feet from the front he stopped and put his lips to her ear. "The inside wall is here. When it's full, nobody'd ever notice. We sure didn't."

"You mean…there's a secret compartment?"

He nodded, handed her the flashlight, and with the gun in one hand and the crowbar in the other, he went to the front of the trailer and pounded on it with the crowbar—*BAM-BAM-BAM*. "We know you're in there. Come out, with your hands up. We have guns." *BAM-BAM-BAM*.

"Don't shoot! Don't shoot!" pleaded a voice. "I'm unarmed!"

"Come out with your hands up."

"I can't get the hatch open. It's stuck."

Mulligan crouched low; she kneeled beside him, shining the light at the underside of the trailer so he could see. He handed her the gun, crawled underneath, found something, and began working the end of the crowbar into a crack on the underside of the trailer. He pushed, leveraging, straining, grunting...hard, grunting, grunting—SNAP.

"I think that got it," called the voice from inside.

Mulligan scurried out, took the gun from her and gave her the crowbar. He went to one knee, gun in one hand, flashlight in the other. "Come out with your hands up."

A pair of legs dangled down, struggling to fit through the opening. A figure dropped to the ground and crawled out on hands and knees.

"Stand up, real slow," Mulligan said. "Or you're dead."

The three of them rose to their feet in a ballet of slow motion. Mulligan shined the light at the face of a willowy man in sneakers, jeans, a peacoat, and a narrow-brimmed seaman's cap. The man held his hands up in front of his face, shielding his eyes from the flashlight, so she couldn't see his features very well, and said, "Is this really Camp David? Are we really growing pot for Nixon? What fun."

That voice...could it be? Her spirits soared—over the moon, beyond the stars! Then it dawned on her how much trouble she was in, and her gut tore loose like a runaway anchor chain, whipping around her ankles and yanking her down to the darkest depths of the deep blue sea.

Mulligan brandished the gun at the newcomer. "What do you mean 'we?' Who in the hell are *you*?"

The man grinned ear to ear—a Leprechaun's smile—and gave a little bow. "Dr. Timothy Leary, at your service."

Chapter 24

Reunion

CATHERINE FOLLOWED A FEW STEPS BEHIND AS MULLIGAN WALKED LEARY TO the office tent at gunpoint. He pushed Leary into a chair and handed her the gun. "If he blinks," he told her, "shoot him."

She was trembling as she held the gun on Leary while Mulligan lit a lantern and bound Leary's hands to the arms of the chair. Would she go to prison? Was she in love? Did he care about her? Would he turn on her when he learned what she had done? She leaned against a desk, feeling woozy as he bound Leary's ankles to the legs of the chair.

"Haven't we met before?" Leary asked her.

"M...me?"

"Yes. You look familiar, Ms. DeWolfe. I suspect you're one of *the* DeWolfe's, aren't you? And I'll bet it was a DeWolfe farm in Michigan Oskar thought he was sending the trailer to, wasn't it?"

"Don't answer him," Mulligan ordered.

She didn't. Maybe she could bluff her way through this.

As Mulligan tied him down, Leary kept up a cheerful banter. "I remember a tall, high-spirited DeWolfe girl from Vassar who came out to the happenings at Millbrook a few times. Hmmm...Catherine, isn't it? Yes, of course. Nice to see you again. How have you been?"

She was dumbfounded he remembered her. They had only spoken a few sentences at most, and it had been, what, seven years? Eight?

Mulligan tightened the knot with a hard yank, stood up, and took the gun from her. "Okay, Buster, I want answers."

Leary exhibited a nonchalance which implied that he, though tied to a chair with a 9MM Smith & Wesson in his face, was in control. "My name isn't Buster, Lieutenant, it's Tim, or Timothy, or Dr. Leary if you prefer to be formal. Now from the way you tie your knots, I'd say you're Navy. Annapolis, right?"

Mulligan brandished the gun. "I'm asking the questions here."

"If you're going to shoot," Leary said calmly, "we should go outside. It will take you forever to get the blood splatters off everything in here."

"We're going to turn you over to the authorities." Mulligan said.

"No, I don't think you'll want to do that," Leary said with a smile.

"And why the hell not?"

"Because I'll sing like a canary. I heard everything from the time you paid Oskar at the docks in Le Havre to Nixon and his dog and your disquisition on Thomas Jefferson. Imagine if the press knew Nixon was growing pot, at Camp David no less. If you want to keep it secret, you have two choices. You can shoot me and get it over with, or you can help me get away. We're in this together now."

Mulligan shouted, "We're not in anything together!"

"Oh, but we are," Leary said, "whether we like it or not, and I certainly don't, but what can you do except try to make the best of it? So what's the National Strategic Hemp Patch for, anyhow? Why is Nixon growing pot? It sounds very exciting."

"None of your damn business!" Mulligan shouted.

She had to ask Leary, "You heard…*everything*?"

Leary chuckled. "I'm not a voyeur, Catherine, but you two are—how shall I say it—*enthusiastic* lovers. I'm sure you woke up every squirrel and chipmunk and porcupine for miles around."

She felt a flush of embarrassment as Mulligan screamed, "What the hell are you doing here?"

"It's not my fault," Leary said. "You're the one who lied to Oskar, not me."

Mulligan glared at him. "I want the whole story. *Now!*"

"Well," Leary said, "as you may know, I've been on the run, and the crown prince of Afghanistan, if he's still alive, was a student of mine. He promised me asylum if I could get there. I had to leave Switzerland or be deported to the States, and I knew Jim Morrison was in Paris. He'd promised to help, so I snuck into France and looked him up. He hid me out, but he had a recording session about to start. The plan was for me to record a few songs with them, then he'd fly me to Kabul on a private jet. Gridley pulled his raid before we had a chance."

"How did the police know where you were?" Mulligan asked.

"Oskar said one of the roadies is a narc."

"So you were there?" Mulligan said.

"Someone helped me get out just in time."

"The stripper?" Mulligan asked.

"Susannah's not a stripper, she's a go-go dancer…a fine girl. I think she's a lawyer too, though she wouldn't admit it. She's very idealistic. Idealism is a hallmark of your generation. You seem to have some of it too,

Lieutenant, misplaced though it may be."

"How did she know about it?"

"Oskar got a warning to her."

"Oskar?"

"Yes, she was a go-go dancer at his disco. But I'm worried about her. Has there been any news?"

"The last I read she'd disappeared," Mulligan said, then paused, thinking. Catherine felt a chill when he cast a glance at her, turned and asked Leary, "So who tipped Oskar?"

"He wouldn't tell me," Leary said.

"How much are you paying him?" Mulligan asked.

"Paying him? Why...nothing."

"Oskar isn't the type to work for free. Why'd he help you?"

"To tell you the truth, it's a mystery. Susannah didn't know either."

"So when did you last see her?"

"Oskar separated us in the getaway, and I haven't seen her since. I kept asking about her, about how he knew and why he was helping, but he wouldn't tell me anything except she was safe and refugees were his business. He seems to be very good at it. I was just hours from leaving on a boat from Marseilles to Beirut and a flight to Kabul when we heard about the coup. He asked where else I could go, and I said my second choice was Canada."

"Why Canada?" Mulligan asked.

"They're much more civilized up there than we are, and I've met Prime Minister Trudeau a few times. His wife Margaret and I are old, uh...friends. I'm betting he'll give me asylum just for the fun of sticking his finger in Nixon's eye."

"So Oskar figured he'd get you into Canada in our trailer?"

"Yes. They drove me to Le Havre and put me in the secret compartment. He told me it was a shipment of farm implements. I had plenty of water, beans, sardines, a sleeping bag, an oil lamp, books, a radio and plenty of batteries. Even an airtight can to go to the bathroom in. The peepholes aren't bad, and you can hear what's going on outside. It's cramped to be sure, but comfortable enough, considering."

"So you thought you were going to Michigan?" Mulligan said.

"They were supposed to take me off in Montreal. They loaded me on the freighter, then two hours later some men came along and bribed the first-mate, and the next thing I knew they hoisted the trailer off the ship with me in it, hauled me halfway across France, and put me on an Air Force cargo plane. I thought Oskar had sold me out, but it turns out you were hoaxing him. And now, here I am, in Camp David of all places. So why is Nixon growing pot, anyhow?"

"None of your damned business!" Mulligan yelled.

"Oh, but you've made it my business, Lieutenant. You should look on the bright side. I can help until we figure how to get me out of here. I have a green thumb. Gardening was my prison job. I'll be very useful."

Mulligan said, "We don't need any help, and the only way you're leaving is in handcuffs."

"Once you've had time to consider the situation, I'm sure you'll see things differently." Leary turned and looked her in the eye. "So, Catherine, would you thank Susannah for helping me when you see her?"

A spurt of fear surged through her as she blurted out the literal truth, "But I don't know anybody named Susannah."

"No, of course not," Leary said. "So what is her real name?"

"How...how should I know?"

"You're not a poker player, are you, Catherine?" Leary asked.

"What makes you say that?"

"Because you don't lie very well."

Mulligan was staring at her, his brow furrowed in thought. He asked Leary, "Does this Susannah have long black hair?"

How would he know that? Uh, oh, he must have seen the photo of her with Jenny by the Lib House fireplace when he searched her purse.

"Why, yes, she does," Leary answered. "A beautiful girl. She can sing too, you know, a wonderful voice. Is that the same one?"

Mulligan scowled, took a towel from a drawer and tied it over Leary's mouth to gag him quiet. He opened the tent flap, held it with one hand, and motioned her out. "We need to talk."

She followed him across the compound in the pre-dawn night, zipping up her new Camp David jacket as tight as it would go to ward off a feeling of dread as cold and miserable as a Michigan sleet storm.

———————

Mulligan was seething as he lit the oil lamp in her tent. She'd been lying to him the damned whole time. "I want answers, and I want them now. You knew all about this, didn't you?"

"No, I swear, Mike, I had no idea."

"So you don't know Susannah?"

"I don't know anybody named Susannah."

"Leary sure as hell thinks you do." He looked around for her purse, grabbed it off the chair, turned it upside down, and dumped everything on the cot.

"Mike, what are you doing? *Mike!*"

He picked up the photo. "Is this her? Let's go ask Leary?"

"No, I…uh—"

"No more games. You didn't go to Paris to go shopping, did you? This woman is Susannah, and you know all about Leary. I want to know what the hell is going on. All of it. We're in big trouble here, and I won't be able to think us out of it until I know the whole story. Do you understand?"

"Yes, but—"

"Out with it…*now!*"

And what a story it was, from lying to get into the White House intern program to Gridley showing her photos of Leary and her friend Jenny to Leary popping out of the trailer like a jack-in-the-box.

"And that's the whole story, Mike, I swear. I'm sorry I lied to you, but I didn't see any other way."

A tear streamed down her cheek. He wiped it away and gently wrapped his arms around her in a bear hug. "It's going to be all right."

"Oh Mike, what are we going to do? You're not going to hurt him, are you? And you can't turn him in. And if they find out what I've done, they'll send me to prison. And Jenny too."

"I'll figure us a way out of this, Cate, I promise."

He rocked her, back and forth. What a mess. The only course of action that made any sense at all was to take her back to the sleeping bags in the meadow and ball her eyes out until the sun came up.

———————————

Chapter 25

Points of No Return

Six Weeks Later

AS MULLIGAN CAME UP THE PATH, HE STOPPED TO WATCH CATHERINE SETTING sprinklers for the bushy seed plants in patch #1. Dressed in a flowing Earth Mother dress, the highlights in her auburn hair shimmering like sequins in the gentle morning sunlight, she could have stepped out of a painting of nineteenth-century French country life by Millet. Despite her blue-blooded upbringing, she was down-home, country-girl beautiful, a real woman who loved making love and could dig in the Earth and get her hands dirty and not worry about breaking a fingernail.

Along the tree line at the edge of the meadow, Timothy Leary was pushing a wheelbarrow to the burn pile. Ever since Leary popped out of Oskar's trailer, he'd had them over a barrel. If they handed him over to the authorities, Leary would blow Operation Jackpot sky high. Even worse, aiding and abetting a fugitive was a felony, and he would not let Catherine go to prison. It was up to him to make the operation succeed while keeping them all out of jail. It wouldn't be easy.

If his temperament were different, he could have ended the Leary problem that first day. All he would have had to do was dig a deep pit with the backhoe in the middle of the newly-plowed hemp patch, put the silencer on his Smith & Wesson, walk Leary to the edge, pop him, push him in, backfill the pit, spread seeds over the top, and Timothy Leary would have joined Amelia Earhart, Judge Crater, and Jimmy Hoffa on the short list of famous Americans who had disappeared without a trace from the face of the Earth.

He might have just let Leary go on his merry way, but it wasn't an option. "Why don't you drive me out to the highway and let me take my chances?" Leary had suggested. "I don't mind hitch-hiking, and Canada's not that far. And I promise I won't say a word if I get caught."

"The Marines have orders not to let us leave," Mulligan told him. "We're stuck here, same as you."

"Then give me a backpack and some food and water and I'll go over the fence. I'm in excellent shape, and I was an Eagle Scout, and I had Army survival training during the war. I can take care of myself in the woods."

"The fence has nothing to do with security," Mulligan said. "It's just to keep out deer and any guests who might wander over. This whole mountain is honeycombed with TV cameras, microphones, motion detectors—you name it, they've got it. You wouldn't get half a mile."

It was the classic Mexican standoff, two desperadoes, each holding a loaded gun on the other.

So they struck a deal. Mulligan agreed to hide Leary and come up with a plan to smuggle him into Canada. In return, Leary swore to never say a word about Nixon's operation, or that he had ever been to Camp David. All Mulligan had for a guarantee was Leary's handshake, but his gut told him Leary could be trusted. Leary was Irish, of the same generation as his dad and Uncle Danny, and as full of high-spirited blarney as they were. He couldn't help but like the guy. Besides, he had no choice. Like an airplane low on fuel, he was way past the point of no return.

For now, the secret of the existence of National Strategic Hemp Patches was safe. Deep in a mountainous wilderness, guarded by U.S. Marines and hi-tech Secret Service gizmoes, Nixon's Camp David meadow was also the perfect location for an under-your-nose hide-out for the most dangerous man in the world.

Mulligan couldn't say whether Leary was the victim of a police frame-up as he claimed, but guilty or framed, thirty years for two roaches seemed disproportionate. He was astounded when Catherine informed him Leary's sentence was not cruel and unusual punishment under the Eighth Amendment because of a new legal principle, the "meter maid doctrine," promulgated by Justice Rumpquist.

Mulligan rolled out highly-detailed U.S. Army Corps of Engineers maps on a drafting table and evaluated the risk factors of various routes for getting Leary into Canada. Dressed in his disguise, they could drive him over, though there was always a risk that his papers would be questioned. Other options were to backpack through the backwoods of Maine, canoe through the boundary waters of Minnesota, ride horseback across the plains of Montana or North Dakota, sail across Lake Huron in Catherine's sailboat, or rent a speedboat and zoom up Lake Champlain under a new moon like bootleggers during Prohibition. Perhaps the safest would be to drive Leary to Milltowne, borrow his dad's pick-up truck and outboard, haul the boat up to Presque Isle, and motor fifty miles across Lake Erie to a small port or a beach on the Canadian shore?

He showed them the maps, but Leary cut him short. "The Weathermen told me the best way is on the *Maid of the Mist,* the sight-seeing boat that goes under Niagara Falls. They don't check identification, it stops on both sides of the border, and there are no guards. You just buy a ticket for the tour, and when it stops on the Canadian side, get off and keep walking."

They agreed it was the best idea. Now all they had to do was figure an excuse to drive the trailer out of Camp David. He would need a plausible reason to convince Nixon. It would take thought and planning.

He divided up cooking and housekeeping chores between the three of them, and they settled into a routine. Nixon had ordered the Marines to provide Mulligan with anything he wanted, so he requisitioned a Nikon camera with a complete set of lenses, lights, umbrellas, and a darkroom. Every morning at 08:00 Catherine would shoot, develop, and print a roll of film documenting the daily growth. Leary's knowledge of agriculture was greater than his or Catherine's, and for the remainder of the morning they would both help Leary in the fields, doing whatever he instructed. After lunch, he would meet a courier at the compound gate and pick up a sealed pouch of yesterday's P.P.C. team's reports for Catherine to edit. She spent her afternoons in the office tent editing and typing, Leary worked in fields, while he worked on various projects in the Lab tent.

In the evenings they relaxed—reading, playing gin-rummy, hearts, and Scrabble. They often built a campfire, roasting marshmallows and singing songs as he strummed the new Martin guitar he requisitioned. And when atmospheric conditions were right, there was baseball on the radio. Catherine didn't care much for the game, and she would read or work in her darkroom when games were on. But Leary was as rabid a Red Sox' fan as he was a Pirates' fan, and they would play chess and drink beer, listening to broadcasts from Boston and Pittsburgh and arguing which team would win if both made it to the World Series this year. The teams were in different leagues and had not played an official game against each other since the very first World Series, in 1903, won by Boston. He and Leary were in complete agreement that the American League's new designated-hitter rule would ruin the game.

At bedtime, he and Catherine would say good night to Leary, who would retire to his secret compartment, while he and Catherine would put two sleeping bags together and make love under the stars.

In some respects they were Nixon's prisoners; in others they were totally free. There were no social conventions to conform to, no military regulations to adhere to. As Mulligan had stood in front of the mirror one morning the first week, he realized that he was not required to scrape his face with a razor for the first time since he entered the Naval Academy. When he said, "Maybe I'll grow a beard," he was shocked when Catherine said, "Good, because I don't want to shave either."

"But women like to shave, don't they?" he asked.

"No," she informed him with great indignity, "we don't. I didn't touch a razor for seven years until I applied for Nixon's job. Most women in Europe don't shave. Women are much freer over there."

As they sat roasting marshmallows that evening, Catherine recited a long, fiery poem she had written in college: "Women Under Arms!" in which she railed against "the tyranny of the razor" and how American women—brainwashed since the 1920's by the relentless advertising of Schick and Gillette—must take back control of their bodies so as not to be mere objects of sexual gratification for male chauvinist pigs.

Leary laughed, nodding in agreement as she recited from memory, but Mulligan could only listen in dumbfounded silence. When she finished, Leary applauded, "Bravo! Bravo!" He could barely clap and pretend to smile.

"You know," Leary said, "it's amazing how social conventions vary from era to era and culture to culture. In America, beards can be the height of fashion in one era, crude and barbaric in the next. Did you know that during the Civil War military officers on both sides were required by regulation to grow a beard or a mustache? I mean, can you imagine Lee or Grant without their beards? But today, a beard in the military is a court-martial offense. Sailors even have to shave when they're out at sea. Have you ever heard of anything so utterly stupid?"

"It is pretty dumb," Mulligan agreed. "Sailors hate it."

"And you're right about the history, Catherine," Leary said. "American women only picked up the shaving habit in the Twenties after hemlines went up and Schick and Gillette set out to double the market for disposable razor blades. It was one of the first great triumphs of mass-media advertising. And then there are the rigid Islamic societies. They have some very peculiar notions about shaving."

"I know in some countries men have to let their beards grow," Catherine said. "But the women cover up from head to toe, so why would they need to shave their legs or their armpits?"

"No, not their legs," Leary said as his lips curled up in an impish grin. "Their pubic hair."

Catherine drew back, startled. "You're joking?"

"No, I'm quite serious," Leary said. "It probably started as a means of controlling lice and crabs."

Mulligan glanced at Catherine, imagining what a certain part of her anatomy would be like if it were as smooth and silky-soft as the rest of her.

She scowled and wagged a scolding finger at him. "Don't you dare even *think* about it, Michael Patrick Mulligan!"

Leary broke into a laugh. "Sometimes you two are just so darned cute. But it's not just the women, Mike. Men have to shave too."

He was astonished. "Men grow their beards and shave...*their pubes?*"

"Indeed they do. They're not supposed to go over forty days."

Mulligan rubbed his fingers over the new growth on his chin, wondering what it would be like to be required by military regulation to grow a beard but shave your pubes every forty days. What would plebe inspections at Annapolis have been like?

Later, as he cuddled up to Catherine after making love under the stars, he admitted to himself that McGill had been right. He did have it bad, *real* bad. Catherine—Cate—was strong, graceful, statuesque, the personification of a Greek goddess, halfway between Demeter, goddess of the Earth, and Diana, goddess of the hunt. Plus she was funny, kind, smart...and brave. You didn't find that in a woman very often. She truly was officer material. The only negative he'd seen so far was that she could be completely out-to-lunch and over-the-top on the topics of sexual equality and women's rights. But what worried him most was that she was so obscenely rich. Could an aristocrat like her ever be serious about a guy like him? He was in over his head, light years past the point of no return.

Chapter 26

An Extra Beat

July 4, 1974

NIXON ROLLED HIS CHAIR AWAY FROM HIS DESK AND TOLD HIS YOUNG AIDES gathered around, "I spoke to Lt. Mulligan this afternoon. He asked me to say hello to everybody for him and Ms. DeWolfe."

"Can you tell us when they'll be returning?" one of them asked.

"Yes, I can," Nixon said, smiling. "They'll be back when they've completed their assignments."

The dean of the White House domestic staff, a silver-haired Negro butler named Jeffers who had served every President since Silent Cal Coolidge, was making drinks at the portable bar. He removed a frosty martini glass from a silver ice bucket, poured a clear liquid from a pitcher, speared three plump olives with a toothpick, and presented the drink to Nixon on an ornate silver tray.

Nixon took a sip…aahh. Its cool bite was just right. "Perfect as usual, Jeffers. That will be all."

Ehrlichman was in a chair next to Bullcannon. Haldeman was on his feet, flipping through his appointment book.

Nixon looked at his watch: five-thirty. In a few hours he would be off for a long weekend at Camp David, his first break in months. He wanted this briefing recorded for posterity, so he opened his bottom-left desk drawer and checked the on/off switch for his secret taping system. The green light glowed. He closed the drawer, put his feet up on his desk, took another sip of his martini and said, "Okay, boys, what've you got?"

Duberman, the one who was always combing his hair, stepped forward. "Mr. President, we think you were right. There was a high-level conspiracy to ban hemp. The circumstantial evidence is very strong."

"I told you so," Nixon said. "It's been hanging in the air like a fart in church ever since this thing started. So, who the hell is it? Big oil? Those candy-assed Rockefellers again?"

"Not exactly," Duberman said. "You said to follow the money, and the evidence points not to the oil industry, but to the paper industry."

Nixon wasn't expecting that. "The paper industry?"

"Yes, sir," Duberman said. "It was the big paper companies that stood to take the biggest hit if hemp made a comeback."

Nixon stretched his legs way out on his desk and leaned back in his reclining chair. "Big paper? Hmmm…You mean like in newspapers?"

"Yes, sir," Duberman said, "and cardboard, toilet paper, and—"

"Toilet paper!" Nixon shouted. "Ha! I love it. Fucking *love* it."

He swung his feet off the desk and sat up straight. "Oh, this is going to be good. I can feel it. There's nothing like a good old-fashioned conspiracy, and this one runs right up everybody's asshole. There's no way around it, everybody's got an asshole. Ha! Toilet paper…who'd have guessed? Bart, fix the boys a drink, and pour me another while you're at it. This could be more fun than bagging Alger Hiss. Toilet paper. Ha!"

Nixon loosened his tie as Bullcannon poured and his boys got ready. One adjusted an easel, another arranged a series of drawings on poster boards, and two prepared items in some boxes.

Duberman said, "I'll start with an overview, if that's all right?"

"It's your show," Nixon said.

"The value of hemp," Duberman began, "traditionally came from the fibers, called 'bast.' These run lengthwise around the outside of the stalk, surrounding the woody core, called the 'hurd.' Hemp has been prized for thousands of years because its fiber is the longest and strongest of all natural fibers, far superior to cotton, flax, or wool. In addition, hemp oil has been used for cooking and illumination since the dawn of history."

As Duberman described the anatomy of the hemp plant, Thompkins, the black one, changed the illustrated cards on the easel and Branche, the son of his new ambassador to China, used a rubber-tipped pointer to identify the various parts.

"What's so important about how long they are?" Ehrlichman asked.

"You can do more things with long fibers than short ones, and do them better," Duberman said. "We've brought examples of some of the uses."

McGill, the skinny one, and Backwater, the one with the accent, passed around the items as Duberman described them: an old pair of bluejeans; a swatch of canvas sail; a pack of cigarette papers; an artist's canvas on a frame; a set of art paints; an exquisite table cloth that felt like silk; a strand of rope; a section of four-inch thick naval hawser; a square of carpet backing; a U.S. Army knapsack; a Bank of England ten-pound note; photographs of the Constitution and the Declaration of Independence; a King James Bible; a sheaf of crinkly-white Bible paper.

Bullcannon let out a harrumph at the mention of the Constitution, and when Duberman said Bibles were printed on hemp paper, Bullcannon roared, "How dare you desecrate the Word of God and our nation's most hallowed documents by associating them with *drugs!*"

"We're only pointing out the plant's traditional uses," Duberman said. "When the Constitutional Convention adopted the final document, they printed copies on hemp paper and sent them to the states for ratification. It's because of hemp's durability so many exist today. And Bibles have been printed on hemp paper since the time of Gutenberg, but we have to import our Bible paper because of the ban on growing hemp."

Nixon could see Bullcannon was fuming. "Bart, the boys are just explaining the historical context."

"If you say so, sir," Bullcannon said.

"Go ahead, Mr. Duberman," Nixon said.

"Yes, sir. In 1912, scientists at the Bureau of Plant Industry in the Agriculture Department set out to find a use for the hurds, which throughout history were either burned or plowed back into the soil. Hurds comprise seventy percent of the weight, and are over seventy-five percent cellulose, almost double the cellulose content of the average tree."

They passed Nixon a pamphlet, Department of Agriculture Bulletin 404, *Hemp Hurds As Paper-Making Material.* "Mr. President," Duberman said, "this is the result of their experiments. It was published in 1916."

Nixon read the credits: Lyster H. Dewey, Botanist in Charge of Fiber-Plant Investigations; Jason L. Merrill, Paper-Plant Chemist, Paper-Plant Investigations. He chuckled and asked, "Fiber-plant and paper-plant investigations? Are you making this up?"

"No, sir," Duberman said. "Both had been operating for many decades, but they were abolished in the 1930's, and the research terminated. We suspect it was the work of the conspiracy."

"I'm confused about this paper thing," Nixon said. "You just showed us papers for cigarettes, Bibles, and currency. How is this different?"

"Those were made from the fibers," Duberman said, "not from the hurds. Hemp fiber has always made the finest paper, but it's expensive because it has so many other uses. What they were after was cheaper paper made from the cellulose in the hurds, which had always been a waste product. It was evident to them that a new source of cellulose would be a valuable natural resource. The idea was to give farmers a profitable new reason to grow an age-old crop."

"Sounds like a hell of a good idea," Nixon said. "Did it work?"

"Yes, sir," Duberman said. "And to prove it, they printed the report you're holding on paper they made with the new process. Notice how well it's held up."

Nixon fanned through the pamphlet, held it up to his nose, and gave it a good long sniff. "Doesn't have that old-timey smell. So this lasts longer than regular paper?"

"Centuries longer, Mr. President," Duberman said. "Extracting cellulose from hurds doesn't require the highly acidic chemicals that extracting it from wood does, so it doesn't leave the paper acidic. Most books since the 1930's are printed on paper made by a process DuPont patented, and as a result, our heritage is crumbling on library shelves. If our books had been printed on the paper you're holding, it would not be a problem."

"So let me get this straight," Nixon said. "Are you saying we wouldn't need to cut down trees?"

"Not for paper," Duberman said. "Their experiments showed that in a twenty-year span an acre of hemp could produce as much paper from the hurds as four acres of trees. And the fiber could still be harvested for all its traditional uses. At today's prices, an acre of hemp would be four or five times more valuable than an acre of corn or wheat."

Nixon smiled. "Sounds like they hit a grand slam. It's good to see tax dollars well spent once in a while."

"Do you have any samples?" Ehrlichman asked.

His aide with the Southern accent, Backwater, said, "Ah wanted to have some to show y'all, but neither the Smithsonian, nor the National Seed Herbarium, nor the Agriculture Department have any samples. They are supposed to archive our agricultural heritage, but it's almost as if hemp had never been grown in America at all."

Bullcannon looked up from his notepad. "I'm sorry, but it all sounds like a bunch of crap to me. If this process was such a breakthrough, why didn't anything come of it?"

"One more problem had to be solved," Backwater said. "The method for harvesting hemp was called 'dew retting.' Farmers would cut it down and let the stalks rot in the fields for a few weeks until the fiber separated from the hurd, like in the movie we saw. But retted hurds are a slimy mess, good for nothing. The process would not be practical until a machine called a 'decorticator' was developed to separate the fiber from the hurds when they're fresh. A decorticator, combined with the new process, would have revolutionized American agriculture just like Eli Whitney's cotton gin had done a century earlier. When the scientists announced their discovery, they issued a call to America's engineers and inventors to turn their skills to the decorticating problem. But the newspapers and magazines of the day never got the word out. The world would have to wait another twenty years for a decorticator, and by then it was too late. Show the President the *Popular Mechanics* article, would you, Art."

As McGill passed a magazine Backwater said, "Mr. President, suh, that is the March, 1938, issue of *Popular Mechanics.*"

Nixon put on his glasses. "Sure, *Popular Mechanics* has been around forever. Every backyard inventor in the country reads it."

"Yes, suh, they do," Backwater said. "The lead article is 'Billion Dollar Crop.' It reports on a decorticator that was almost perfected and predicted that it would make hemp America's first billion-dollar crop and end the Depression on the nation's farms. It was written a few months before hemp was banned, but due to publishing schedules, it did not appear until after Congress had already outlawed it."

Nixon was puzzled. "So this idea sits around for twenty years, and just when the machine to make it practical comes along, Congress goes and makes the damned plant illegal? Do I have that right?"

"Yes, suh," Backwater said. "That is precisely what happened."

Nixon took a sip of his martini. "That's one hell of a coincidence."

"Suh," Backwater said, "in the 1930's there were many articles in the trade journals of the paper, timber, and chemical industries about the decorticator and the threat hemp posed to the way paper was made. What happened to the decorticator entrepreneurs was capitalism using the power of the government to eliminate the competition. Imagine what it might be like if they hadn't killed it off. Once hemp was being grown in quantity for paper, it was bound to be used for fuel too."

Nixon nodded his head. "I see what you're saying. I wouldn't have an energy crisis and the Arabs wouldn't have us by the balls because we'd have been growing our own for the last thirty years. Damn the bastards."

"We're calling it the Great Hemp Conspiracy, Mr. President," Duberman said.

"Names, I want names," Nixon said. "Who were the players? "

"We should start at the beginning," Duberman said. "Chester has been researching that angle."

Thompkins, the black one, cleared his throat. "Mr. President, we think it dates from about 1915, when William Randolph Hearst—"

"Hearst?" Nixon said, surprised. "The son-of-a-bitch was a one-of-a-kind. Started the Spanish-American War just to sell newspapers."

"Yes, sir," Thompkins said. "He was the biggest consumer of newsprint in the world, and owned pulping plants, paper mills, and vast tracts of timberland. He wanted to control every aspect of his business, like Henry Ford with cars. It's a business model economists call 'vertical integration.'"

"Hearst was an old man when I met him," Nixon said. "Helped me when I ran for Congress, and when the Hiss case came along, he printed everything I leaked like it was gospel. And he got all his California papers behind me to whip the Pink Lady's ass. I doubt I'd be here today if it hadn't been for Hearst. Go ahead, son, I'm all ears."

Thompkins spoke precisely, enunciating every syllable in a slow, rumbling baritone, as if he were trying to make sure that no hint of black dialect crept in. "From the 1880's to the 1950's, Hearst's papers used racial smears to sell papers, calling blacks darkies and niggers and jigaboos...."

As Thompkins detailed Hearst's history of fomenting racial bigotry, his breathing grew heavier and his diction quickened, chugging faster and faster, like an accelerating train. Sweat beaded up on his cheeks and forehead as the mood in the room turned somber.

"...and for decade after decade, in story after story, in city after city, Hearst's papers portrayed blacks as subhuman beasts driven to rape white women. More than anyone, he fed the public the lies that stoked the fires of racial hatred that led to thousands of lynchings."

Thompkins paused to pull out a handkerchief and wipe his face.

"Lynchings were bad, son, very bad," Nixon said, commiserating like a bartender. "I went to law school down South in the Thirties, and some poor black bastard was always getting his ass strung up down there. But those days are in the past, son. America has progressed. What do lynchings have to do with our problem today?"

Thompkins breathed deep, trying to compose himself. "Mr. President, the association of drugs with blacks, Mexicans, and Chinese that Hearst pounded into the public mind is still with us today. He started with Chinese and opium in the 1880's, switched to blacks and cocaine about 1900, and when Woodrow Wilson sent General Pershing and 10,000 troops after Pancho Villa, he switched to marijuana."

"Hmmm...Pancho Villa," Nixon said. "Now there's a name you don't hear any more. Never did get him, did we?"

"No, sir," Thompkins said, "but the troops brought back a Mexican folk tune, 'La Cucaracha,' which—"

Nixon clapped his hands, said "Ha, I know that one," and sang:

> "La Cucaracha, la cucaracha
> Ya no puedo caminar
> Por que no tiene, por que no tiene
> Marijuana que fumar."

Bullcannon applauded. "Nicely done, Mr. President."

"That sure brings back the memories," Nixon said. "We all sang it when I was a kid, but nobody knew what the hell it meant."

"Mr. President," Thompkins said, "the song is a fatalistic folk tale about a soldier who expects to die in battle. 'Cucaracha' is Spanish for 'cockroach,' a nickname Villa's soldiers gave to themselves—like our doughboys and dogfaces and grunts. But the soldier is not worried about dying. He's mad because he's out of marijuana. It's like one of our campfire songs, where you take turns making up verses and everybody sings the chorus. The night before the battle of Torreón they sat around singing it for hours. After they won, it became a good-luck anthem, and they sang it before every battle. I'd translate it like this," and Thompkins sang in a deep, bluesy baritone:

> "The cockroach, the cockroach
> He is not able to walk
> Because he has no, because he has no
> Marijuana he can smoke."

Nixon smiled and said, "Imagine that. I was singing about drugs when I was a five years old and didn't even know it. Ha! Go on, son, go on."

"Marijuana is Mexican slang for a variety of what Americans had always called hemp. Hearst scared whites into thinking it turned the 'lower races' into murderers and rapists. Fear sold a lot of papers."

"Fear, not love, is what motivates people," Nixon told them with assurance. "They don't teach you that in Sunday school, but it's true."

"But you've been telling us hemp was an important crop," Ehrlichman said. "Wouldn't farmers have noticed?"

"Ah can answer that," Backwater said. "Ah've been studying the agricultural history, and for five thousand years the hemp plant was the world's most valuable agricultural commodity. There was even a Civil War battle in Missouri named after it, the Battle of the Hemp Bales, where the heroic Confederates used 200 pound bales of hemp as mobile fortifications to defeat the damned Yankees. But with the coming of the steam engine, hemp's glory days were coming to an end. Steamships replaced sailing ships, and railroads made covered wagons obsolete, a one-two punch that knocked the market for canvas on its ass. And the first oil wells were coming in, and hemp oil, which like alcohol and whale oil had been widely used as an illuminant in lamps, was replaced by kerosene."

"So the shit hit the fan all at once?" Nixon said.

"Yes, suh," Backwater said. "After five thousand years, the market for hemp collapsed in just a few decades. As late as 1850, hemp was second only to cotton in its value to American agriculture. Kentucky alone produced 40,000 tons that year. The industry slowly declined until 1915, when Congress pulled the rug out by abolishing the tariff on imported fibers. After that, inferior fibers from places where labor was cheap—jute from India, and abaca from the Philippines, called Manila hemp—took over most of the market for rope and twine.

"Only a few hundred American hemp farmers hung on, mostly in Wisconsin, where they grew it for high-quality uses like fishing lines, and in Kentucky, where they grew it for birdseed and hemp oil, which was used as a drying agent for paint. By the time Hearst started changing the name, most Americans didn't even know what hemp was, and by 1937, he'd confused things so much the man in the street would have told you hemp and marijuana were as different as pineapples and poison ivy."

"So Hearst was like Big Brother in that novel, *1984*," Nixon said, "changing the language to vilify Mexicans and sell more papers?"

"Whether or not he set out to change the language, that's what he did," Thompkins said. "We don't think it's a coincidence that his papers started lying about marijuana just when the Agriculture Department published the discovery about making paper from hurds. The lifting of the tariffs at the same time may be involved too."

"It does seem too coincidental to ignore," Nixon said

Thompkins handed him a folder filled with old newspaper clippings. "Mr. President, these are typical of Hearst's headlines."

Marihuanha Makes Fiends of Boys in 30 Days!
Marihuanha Smoker Identified as Wild Gunman!
Hashish Goads Users to Blood Lust!

"Hearst wrote many of his papers' editorials himself," Thompkins said. "He claimed it made blacks uppity and gave us the gall to refuse to step aside for a white man, and the audacity to step on a white man's shadow."

Beads of sweat were again forming on his young aide's coal-black forehead, reminding Nixon of old black-and-white movies of Southern life. In his mind's eye he could see the master in a white suit, sitting high on a black stallion, a coiled whip on the pommel of his saddle, a pistol at his side, sipping a cool mint julep while watching hundreds of slaves picking cotton and singing work songs in the blazing noonday sun.

"Hold on a second, son," Nixon said as he leaned toward Thompkins. "I just want to assure you that the Negro race has my full support. I saw Jim Crow up close when I was in law school down South at Duke, and I want to end it as much as anybody. But my election strategy depends on taking the South from the Democrats. The Democrats stuffed Civil Rights down their throats, so segregationists are flocking to us in droves. Those people aren't ready for change, son, you know that. It goes to the heart of the states-rights issues we conservatives hold dear. You're a rock-ribbed conservative, aren't you, son? That's why you're working for me, isn't it?"

"Yes, sir, of course," Thompkins said.

"So as a rock-solid conservative, you support states' rights over individual liberty and human rights, don't you, son?"

"I know I have to, sir, and I do, but it's just that sometimes, well...."

"It's all right, son, I understand. Some day, true equality will come to the races, but right now race is a wedge issue that can make Republicans dominant for generations. It's politics, son, politics."

"I understand, Mr. President," Thompkins said.

"So," Nixon said, "we need to focus on our current problem. Hearst is dead and gone, so I don't have him to worry about. So who do we worry about? Who's going to try to stop Nixon if he moves on this?"

Duberman said, "The DuPont Corporation for one. They control the patents used in the wood-pulping process."

"Shit," Nixon said. "Talk about biting the hand that feeds you. They run that dinky-assed state of theirs like it's a medieval duchy and they're the goddamned Dukes. They rake in another fortune every time there's a war somewhere. Everybody called them merchants-of-death when it came out they'd made hundreds of millions in the First World War."

"They'd always made money on gunpowder," Duberman said. "After the war, they got control of I.G. Farben's most important patents as part of Germany's war reparations, which made them more diversified. They patented a pulping method in the 1930's that's still the industry standard.

When you drive by a paper mill, it's DuPont you're smelling."

"Paper towns stink worse than cow towns," Nixon said, remembering pulp mills belching clouds of fumes, and drain pipes pouring effluent into rivers and turning them neon green for miles downstream. "There was a paper-town in Pennsylvania, up the road from Altoona, where the yellow mist got trapped in the valley so thick it made your eyes burn and stunk worse than cabbage in a Polack kitchen. What was that place?"

One of the young aides, McGill, the skinny one, pinched his nostrils and said in a nasally voice, "Tyrone, Mr. President."

"Yeccch, that was it, all right," Nixon said. "So that crap that turns rivers green is what the tree-huggers say is killing all the fish?"

"Yes, sir," Duberman said. "Using hemp instead of wood pulp to make paper would eliminate that source of pollution."

"Well, I don't trust tree-huggers," Nixon said, "and this isn't about pollution, it's about conspiracy. Who else was in on it?"

Duberman pointed to McGill. "Art, you're up."

McGill opened a slim binder with a yellow legal pad, looked down at his notes, and took a deep breath. "The key to the conspiracy, Mr. President, was the Federal Bureau of Narcotics and its commissioner, Harry Anslinger. It's odd you just mentioned Altoona, because he's from Holidaysburg, about ten miles away."

"It's *Twilight Zone* time again," Nixon said, and he sang the opening bars of the show's theme song, "Doo doot doo doo, doo doot doo doo."

McGill passed him two photos. "I only wish it were that simple, Mr. President. That's Anslinger in 1962, just before he retired. And that's him in the 1930's, testifying before Congress."

Nixon said, "Sure, I know Harry. Good law-and-order man. He was big buddies with Joe McCarthy. Joe told me once that he got his rock-'em, sock-'em, commie-bashing style right out of Harry's druggie-bashing playbook. Harry was his, oh what do shrinks call it…his role model. I used to hear rumors McCarthy was hooked on morphine and Harry kept him supplied on the sly, but I never knew for sure."

"I don't know about that," McGill said, "but the style of Anslinger's campaign to demonize marijuana in the Thirties and McCarthy's red-baiting style in the Fifties are identical."

"So how is Harry the key?" Nixon asked.

"Compared to the F.B.I., the F.B.N. was small potatoes," McGill said. "There were only about three hundred people in the whole agency. They called themselves 'narcs,' and were proud of it. Anslinger did everything he could to get his agency more agents and a bigger budget, and—"

"Nothing wrong in building up your agency if you're a bureaucrat," Nixon said. "They all do it. It's part of the job."

"Yes, sir. There wasn't much of a drug problem at the time, so he needed a new menace to go after if he wanted Congress to authorize more agents. His bureau helped make movies on the evils of marijuana to stir things up. *Reefer Madness* is the most famous. It's a cult comedy today, but back then people actually believed it was true. He traveled all over giving speeches. People would hear him rail about how the country was going to hell because of marijuana, and he'd tell them to go home and write letters to newspapers and politicians. And they did. The press called them 'Anslinger's Army.' He could bring a lot of pressure when he wanted to."

"I remember Harry could get a crowd going," Nixon said. "All the drys who were still pissed off about the repeal of Prohibition loved him."

"Yes, sir," McGill said, "and when the Court ruled Congress could tax machine guns, he used the same logic in his marijuana bill. Congress passed it thinking they were fighting drugs and had no idea they were criminalizing the plant Jefferson called America's most valuable crop."

"Ha, so Harry bamboozled 'em, did he?" Nixon said with admiration. "That's the way to go when you don't want anybody to know what you're up to. Hard to do now with the goddamned liberal press. It's not like in the old days when we had the press in our pocket."

"Art," Duberman said, "why don't you tell the President about Anslinger and music."

"Music?" Nixon said.

McGill flashed him a grin. "Yes, sir. Since you play piano, we thought you'd appreciate a musical angle."

"I'm only interested in good music," Nixon said. "Jazz, you know, Benny Goodman, Louis Armstrong, Tommy Dorsey. Swing. Not that crap you young people listen to. So what's music got to do with it?"

"Well, sir," McGill said, "Anslinger played piano too, but unlike you he despised jazz, claimed it was the devil's music. He was always talking about how jazz ruined morality and made white women easy prey for black predators. He told audiences that marijuana was responsible for jazz because it changed a musician's sense of time."

"Changed the sense of time?" Nixon said.

"He claimed that smoking marijuana lets jazz players slip an extra beat into a measure."

"An extra beat?"

"Yes, sir. In 1943, he got *Time Magazine* to write a story on it after he arrested Gene Krupa." He passed Nixon a copy of the article with a slow-shutter-speed photo of jazz drummer Gene Krupa blazing away.

"Harry must have known Plato's dictum," Nixon said.

Bullcannon glanced up. "Excuse me, Mr. President...*Plato*?"

Nixon grinned, relishing a rare opportunity to show off his knowledge of philosophy. "Yes. I think it goes: 'Never are the measures of music altered without affecting the most important affairs of the state.' Makes me wonder if Harry wasn't on to something. I mean, I can't figure out how they do it either, and Nixon's no slouch on the ivories. What do you boys think? If Nixon were to smoke some marijuana, could I slip in an extra beat? Could Nixon be a jazzbo?"

McGill grinned. "I could run over to Lafayette Park and score you a lid if you want to give it a try. Only take a few minutes."

"Ha! Score me a lid," Nixon said. "I just love those hippie terms of yours, Mr. McGill. You sure you're not a hippie?"

"Are you kidding, Mr. P?" McGill said with a grin as he pointed his thumbs at the sides of his head. "They'd have kicked me out of Woodstock with a haircut this dorky."

"Mr. P? Ha! You're a card, young man, a real card."

———

McGill flushed with pride—Nixon was laughing at his joke! But it also made him wonder what Nixon would have thought if he had seen him a few weeks before with his hair halfway down to his shoulders. Was it possible to be both a hippie *and* a conservative? Did it count toward his conservative credentials that he had founded his own business—a corporation no less—or would points for being an entrepreneur with a better mousetrap be negated by the nature of the product?

"So Harry was appointed by Roosevelt, right?" Nixon said.

"No, sir, by Hoover," McGill said. "Roosevelt reappointed him, and Truman and Eisenhower did too. He ran the Narcotics Bureau right up until 1962, when Kennedy forced him to retire."

"Just like Kennedy, kicking a good man out. Go ahead, son."

"Yes, sir. When the Narcotics Department started, it was part of the Prohibition Bureau, under the Treasury Department. There was a lot of corruption on the alcohol side, with agents taking bribes from bootleggers like Al Capone. When it looked like the wets would repeal Prohibition, they split Narcotics off into its own bureau. The Treasury Secretary, Andrew Mellon, had Hoover appoint Anslinger as commissioner. It's the Mellon connection to Anslinger that's at the heart of the conspiracy."

"Just how rich was Mellon?" Haldeman asked.

"A lot of people said he was the richest man in the world," McGill said, "richer than Rockefeller or Ford. Harding appointed him in 1921, and he ran the Treasury all through the Twenties. A joke back then was that he didn't serve under three Presidents, three Presidents served under him."

"You don't hear much about Mellon any more," Nixon said, "but when I was in school Republicans called him the greatest Secretary of the Treasury since Alexander Hamilton. If he said 'jump,' every one of those Presidents would click their heels and say 'how high?'"

"Yes, sir, and his belief in trickle-down economics and his policies of slashing taxes on the rich was popular with Wall Street. They called it the Mellon Plan. When the market crashed, people accused him of being responsible for the Depression. When the Democrats took over Congress in 1930, Hoover sent him to England as the ambassador to get him out of the country so he wouldn't have to testify before Congressional committees controlled by Democrats."

He handed Nixon a photo of Mellon, a slight man with keen, penetrating eyes and a wispy white mustache, in tails and a top hat. Then he passed him an "Advance to Boardwalk" card from a *Monopoly* game, showing the game's cartoon banker with the white mustache strolling along with his top hat and diamond-studded cane. "Mr. President, *Monopoly* came out in the 1930's as a kind of antidote to the Depression, and to me, the banker looks a lot like Andrew Mellon."

"Well, I'll be damned," Nixon said, his eyes lighting up as he compared the cartoon to the photo. "It's him all right. Has to be."

Nixon passed the photo and the card. Haldeman, Ehrlichman, and even Bullcannon agreed the resemblance was unmistakable.

"So let me get this right," Nixon said. "They think Prohibition's going out, so Mellon appoints Anslinger to head up a separate drug agency?"

"Yes, sir," McGill said.

"What year was that?" Nixon asked.

"1930, Mr. President," McGill said.

"Okay," Nixon said. "Then Mellon goes off to England because

Democrats are after his scalp for causing the Depression?"

"Yes, sir," McGill answered.

"But Anslinger keeps his job. Right?"

"Yes, sir."

"Then Roosevelt beats Hoover and takes over in '33, and Prohibition gets repealed. Right?"

"Yes, sir."

"But Anslinger stays on?" Nixon said.

"Yes sir."

"And when did Anslinger push the ban through Congress?"

"In 1937."

Nixon shrugged. "So by then Roosevelt had won a second term and Mellon was long gone from Treasury. How's there a conspiracy?"

"Anslinger was close to the Mellon family, Mr. President," McGill said. "His father-in-law owned coal mines and steel mills and was a good friend of Mellon, and his wife was a playmate of Mellon's daughter, even called him Uncle Andy. We think Anslinger was secretly working on the inside for Mellon interests, and DuPont was one of the biggest."

Nixon was skeptical. "Why didn't Roosevelt clean house when he came in? You don't leave your enemies running a government agency."

"It doesn't make sense to us either, sir," McGill said, "especially since the Democrats tried to pin a tax-evasion charge on Mellon."

"I was in college when they held those hearings," Nixon said. "They wanted a scapegoat for the Depression, and Mellon was it. But why would Roosevelt let Anslinger stay on? It doesn't make sense."

"No, sir, it doesn't," McGill said.

"Well," Nixon said, "it's an interesting theory. But can you prove it? Do you have hard evidence?"

"Not yet, sir," McGill said.

Nixon sipped his martini, chomped an olive, and drummed his fingers on his desk. "I don't know, boys, it's all conjecture. I need something concrete or I'm just pulling my pud. And I'm *not* happy to hear the Mellons are in on it with the DuPonts. Hell, Petey Mellon headed up my fund-raising committee, put the touch on every fat cat in the country. And Richie Mellon ponied up a million all by himself. And they're talking about bankrolling new conservative think-tanks and magazines and foundations to really stick it to the liberals. They're throwing a pow-wow at their Rolling Rock Club this summer to kick it off. But that was planned before that murder scandal came up. Bob, what's the latest on that?"

Like everybody from around Pittsburgh, McGill was fascinated by the explosive scandal rocking the world's richest family.

"As I understand it," Haldeman said, "a prosecutor up there was investigating the local District Attorney, a Republican named Duggan, on charges of taking bribes from the mob."

"So the Democrats went after him?" Bullcannon asked.

"No, the prosecutor's a Republican," Haldeman said. "Name's Thornburgh."

Bullcannon was incredulous. "What the hell's one Republican doing investigating another?"

"Apparently the charges were too substantial to ignore," Haldeman said. "Duggan was an old friend of the Mellons, grew up with some of them, and they were ready to finance his run for governor. But before he was to testify to a grand jury about all the money sloshing around in his bank accounts, he secretly married a Mellon heiress. The papers speculated it was so he could claim the money came from her. That turned some of the Mellons against him, and the day he was indicted, his body turned up in a field on his wife's estate, with his guts blown away by a shotgun."

Nixon grimaced in disapproval. "Messy, very messy. Not the way Republicans should handle things. Do they know what happened?"

Haldeman shook his head. "The police haven't determined if it was a murder, an accident, or a suicide. One theory says it was a mob hit, but some are saying one or more of the Mellons was behind it. The family's at each others' throats over the whole thing. It's pretty ugly."

"It just goes to show money can't buy happiness," Nixon said.

"Maybe not, Mr. President," McGill quipped, "but it can rent it."

Nixon chuckled. "Yes, I suspect it can. Isn't there something else going on with the Mellons right now, Bob, about LSD and that Leary bastard?"

"Yes, sir. A young Mellon bankrolled an LSD ring called the Brotherhood of Eternal Love, a kind of hippie mafia, and set up a banking operation in the Bahamas to hide the profits. They cornered the market on LSD for a while with something called 'orange sunshine.'"

They were interrupted by the ring of a muffled telephone. Nixon, Haldeman, Ehrlichman and Bullcannon all froze and glanced at each other. It rang again, from under Nixon's desk. McGill watched Nixon bend over, open the bottom drawer, and take out a red phone with a blinking red light—the Moscow-to-Washington hot line!

"Bob, see what they want," Nixon ordered. "And the rest of you, keep your assholes puckered. Don't go crapping your pants."

Haldeman picked up the receiver. "Oval Office…" He paused, probably for the translator. "May I ask what it's about, Mr. Chairman?…I'll see if he's available." He pushed HOLD. "It's Brezhnev, Mr. President."

"What the hell's he want?"

"He says he'll only talk to you."

"Damn," Nixon said. "Just when I was having a little fun. Bart, pour me another, and don't skimp on the olives."

"Shall I clear the room?" Ehrlichman asked.

"No, we're not finished yet," Nixon said. "Maybe he's just into his vodka. It's past midnight there, and you know how the Ruskies are."

Nixon slugged back the rest of his martini and traded Haldeman the empty glass for the telephone receiver.

"Leonid, nice to hear from you," Nixon said in a warm, friendly voice, as if Soviet Premier Leonid Brezhnev were an old college buddy. "How's the Mrs.?…Pat's fine, thanks. So, what's up? You haven't launched at us, have you? Ha.…What?…No…You're shitting me? When?…Yes.…Uh huh.…How many?…Uh huh…What about nukes?… Uh huh…I understand…Be sure to give my best to the Mrs…You keep your pecker wet too. Thanks for calling, Leonid."

Nixon hung up. "Bob, get Henry the hell in here, on the double, the Joint Chiefs, the whole security team. Bart, where's that drink?"

"Right here, Mr. President," Bullcannon said as he handed Nixon the martini, its toothpick skewered with three green olives.

Nixon took a sip and munched an olive. "Boys, I have to cut this short. But you're on the right track on this conspiracy thing. I can feel it."

"Sir," Bullcannon said, "can you tell us what's happening?"

"Oh, that asshole Mao's launched an invasion," Nixon said. "Tanks, bombers, the works. Commies killing commies. Who the hell are we supposed to root for? They can't both lose, can they? Ha."

Nixon sprang out of his chair, hurried to his giant globe, and turned it until the Far East came into view.

Ehrlichman said, "Mr. President, if China's attacking Russia, shouldn't the Pentagon go to red alert?"

"No, not Russia," Nixon said. "Vietnam. China's attacking Vietnam. That's only a slant-eyed yellow alert. Ha."

He stared closely at the globe. "Dammit. You know what this means, don't you? It means the whole damned Domino Theory is out the fucking window. Do you know how many elections it's won for us? Now the liberals will say it proves we've been blowing smoke out our assholes since day one. And they'll be right. Shit."

"I'd better get started on your statement, Mr. President," Bullcannon said. "Which way are we going to tilt?"

"Damned if I know," Nixon said in a growl. "Maybe Henry can figure a way to fix it so they knock each other out. That's the way to go."

Ehrlichman was skeptical. "It seems unlikely, sir. China's too big."

"Mr. President," Haldeman said as he hung up, "the C.I.A. says ten Chinese divisions crossed the border and are advancing on Hanoi."

Nixon sighed and gave the globe a spin. "Boys, I have to go, but you keep digging. Find where the bodies are buried. We need something physical, something people can touch and feel and see, even if it's total bullshit like *The Pumpkin Papers*. They were a pair of deuces, but I played that hand like I had a royal flush. I had six good boys just like you working for me back then, and we bluffed Truman right out of the White House. But now that I'm the President, I need a pat hand before I place my bets. Deal me aces, boys, aces. A smoking gun…that's what I need to sell this to the American people. And remember, when you don't know where the bastards went…follow the money. That's the key to conspiracies. And no leaks. National security is at stake. Am I perfectly clear?"

Filled with the exhilaration of being entrusted with the fate of the nation by the President of the United States himself, McGill yelled out in unison with the others, "*Yes, Mr. President!*"

Nixon flashed a broad smile. "That's the gung-ho spirit. If this hare-brained caper of ours is to have a chance, we've got to catch 'em with their pants down and their peckers up. Now tread lightly, keep below their radar. The DuPonts are the Dukes of Delaware. Why in the hell do you think all the fat cats incorporate up there? Because they have it fixed so nobody can touch 'em, that's why. And Mellons have been pulling strings behind the scenes for a hundred years. If either of them get wind of what I'm up to before I'm ready to move, they won't have to assassinate me or impeach me, they'll just laugh me out of office…ha!"

Chapter 27

Hail to the Chief

CATHERINE SLIPPED OUT OF THE COVERS, BEING CAREFUL NOT TO WAKE MIKE. She put on her boots and picked up the flashlight, but before she could reach the outhouse the nausea took over. She upchucked a little behind a pine tree, and covered it over with dirt and needles. Is this what morning sickness was like? Missing her period last month had started her worrying. Except for a craving for pickles and ice cream, she had all the symptoms.

How could it be possible? The slots in her birth-control dispenser said she should be all right, except she was foggy on what happened in Paris. All she could think of was the brandy made her take two pills the same day, then skip a day. But even so, after so many years on the regimen, could missing a single day make such a difference? Or was she just the unlucky one in a hundred who did everything right and still got pregnant?

Since arriving in the meadow life had been a happy-ever-after fairy tale. She was surprised at the back-to-nature satisfaction she got from working in the fields with Mulligan and Leary. And as she worked at her desk in the afternoons, organizing, editing, and typing the team's reports for *The Hemp Papers,* she felt she was making a difference, atoning for her family's crimes against the Earth. It was absolutely impossible for anyone to be any happier than she was right now. She wanted it to go on and on and on.

When she and Mulligan first made love she assured him she was completely safe, so he never bothered with what he called "damned raincoats." What would he say if he knew she might be pregnant? Would it be a boy, or a girl? What would they name it? What would it be like? They both had blue eyes, so it should too, and it should grow up to be very tall, with hair somewhere between his wiry carrot-top and her silky auburn. But what about its character, its personality? The baby should come in late February or early March…Aquarius or Pisces. Which did she want? Which would he want? And since the recent Roe v. Wade decision, she had another option, though it gave her chills to even think about it. And what about her parents? Her mother would be furious for diluting the DeWolfe bloodline with bog-Irish genes. And there were legacy questions. If she had a baby out of wedlock, the Heirs Committee would disown her, and all of her descendants would be forever ineligible for the J.C. DeWolfe Trust Fund. And if her father disinherited her, as he often threatened, she would have nothing but those few things in her own name, her house and her jewelry and her boat and her Corvette. Impoverished.

She was anxious, worried, and as desperate to get away as Leary. Of course he wanted to escape to Canada to avoid prison, while she only wanted to see a gynecologist to learn if she was having Mulligan's baby, make sure everything was all right, then rush right back to the meadow and live happily ever after.

At the mid-morning break she went to the mess tent, eager to try the new Italian-style coffee maker the Marines delivered yesterday. She hadn't had a cappuccino since Paris. She ground the beans and had started cinnamon buns warming in the toaster-oven when she heard a noise in the garbage cans. She glanced out the fly-screen and saw King Timahoe sniffing around. "King, what are you doing here?"

The dog turned to her and barked a hopeful "woof" just as a familiar voice called from a distance, "Ki*iing*! Here boy. Ki*iing*!"

Oh my God! Nixon! He wasn't due until tomorrow, and there he was coming out of the woods with two Secret Service agents. Had the Marines alerted Mulligan on the walkie-talkie? Had Leary been able to hide?

She had to distract Nixon while warning them. She hailed him, yelling and waving, "Yoo hoo, Mr. President! Yooooo hoo!"

Nixon saw her, waved back, and started in her direction. She cupped her hands and yelled as loud as she possibly could toward the fields, "Mi*iiike*. The President is here. Mi*iiike*...."

Nixon heard a woman's hails and saw Ms. DeWolfe beckoning him. "Wait here," he told his Secret Service detail. "I'll be an hour or so."

She came up the path to greet him in an old-fashioned dress that made her look like Maureen O'Hara in a John Wayne western. She certainly was a handsome woman.

"It's good to see you, Mr. President. How have you been?"

"Excellent, Ms. DeWolfe. And you?"

"Very well, thank you. But you're early. We aren't quite ready for you."

"Sorry to drop in like this, but this job is unpredictable."

"Well, you're just in time. I'll have hot cinnamon buns in a minute."

"Maybe next time. I came to see the plants for myself. Those photographs of yours are remarkable. I can't believe they're six feet high."

"Yes, they're averaging two inches a day."

"So does the rustic life agree with you? Fresh air and all that?"

"Yes, Mr. President, but…but do you think it might be possible for me to get away for a few days? I promise I won't tell anybody anything."

He hadn't been expecting that. "Why? Is something wrong? I gave orders to get you anything you asked for."

"Oh no, Mr. President, nothing's wrong, and we have everything we need…but I need to get away."

"Sounds like you've got a touch of cabin fever. Had it myself in the South Pacific during the war. What you need is a little fun with some people your own age. Julie and David are with me this trip. I'll have them invite you up to their cabin tonight. You can play charades, or whatever it is you young people do for fun these days. There's no worrying about leaks with Julie and David, but don't tell them what you're doing. Can't be too careful."

"Thank you, Mr. President, but that isn't the problem. My family's annual get-together is coming up, and—"

"Don't worry about that. I spoke with your father, told him you were on a personal assignment for me. He said to tell you he was proud of you, and he'd brag about you to your family. And he wrote a big check for my reelection campaign. I always did like your father."

"Mr. President. I missed an appointment with my doctor, and—"

"You feeling okay? My personal physician is up here right now. You can come up to the lodge and see him this afternoon. We have a complete medical facility here. An X-ray machine, test tubes, you name it."

"That's kind of you, Mr. President, but I really need my own doctor."

"Doctors schmocters. What is it with women and doctors? Pat and the girls are the same way. So was my mother. I'll never understand it. To me one doctor's the same as the other."

Her face drooped, the corners of her mouth curling down in a pout. She gave him a sad, doe-eyed stare and whimpered, "Please, Mr. President."

Damn it! He hated it when females played on his emotions to wheedle something out of him. "Oh, very well. I'll have somebody drive you down to see your doctor and bring you right back up."

"The doctor's only a part of it. I need to take care of some personal matters. This came up so suddenly, I left all my affairs up in the air. Just a day or two, please. I promise I won't leak anything, and I'll come back up here and work straight through to the very end. I promise." Her mouth turned up into a hopeful smile, and she batted her eyes at him. "Pretty please, Mr. President."

Why was it he could go toe-to-toe with a Krushchev or a Castro or a Kennedy, but a pouty-faced female pretty-pleasing him turned his better judgement into a bowl of cherry Jell-O? "Oh, very well, I'll look into it, see what I can do. Does the Lieutenant feel the same way?"

"He would never ask, but I'm sure he could use a few days off too."

"Men need their shore leave, there's no doubt about that. So he's treating you like an officer and gentleman, isn't he? He better not be trying any hanky-panky, or he'll have me to answer to, and that wouldn't be pretty. He's under direct orders to treat you like a lady."

"Oh, no, Mr. President! Lieutenant Mulligan is a perfect gentleman."

She seemed startled, almost defensive at his question. There was something she wasn't telling him. Perhaps he should not have left them alone together for so long? He sometimes forgot that not everyone could control their hormones like him and Pat. It wasn't for nothing that the Navy banned women from warships.

Just then a voice behind him called out, "Hello, Mr. President."

He turned to see a tall, red-bearded man in blue jeans and a red-and-black checked lumberjack shirt. "Lieutenant, is that you?"

"Aye, Mr. President."

"Between the beard and the shirt, you look like Paul Bunyan."

"I figured the Navy won't give me another chance to grow one until I retire."

"I can't grow a beard in my job either," Nixon said. "Voters wouldn't understand. But I felt the same way when I was on that godforsaken hellhole in the South Pacific. I'd have grown a damned good one if they'd let me. Never have understood why the brass doesn't allow it. Seems to me it goes against the seafaring tradition."

"It's never made sense to me either. You could really boost morale if you gave orders to let sailors have beards. You'd be a real hero to the men."

"Hmmm…maybe I'll look into it, but right now, let's go see those plants of ours."

Ms. DeWolfe stayed behind to putter in her kitchen while the Lieutenant took him and King Timahoe on a tour. As they walked up the path he asked the Lieutenant, "Ms. DeWolfe says she needs to get away for a few days. How about you? Do you need some shore leave?"

"Me? Oh, no sir. But what I could use is some time in a state of-the-art lab and some technical expertise. My workshop here is very primitive."

"A lab? Hmmm…Do you have somewhere in mind?"

"Aye, sir. The Air Force Institute of Technology at Wright-Patterson, outside Dayton. They've been in charge of the military's research into fuel since before World War I. Nobody knows more about fuel than they do. If you get me a big-rig, I'll haul my models over there in our trailer, and with their help I'm certain I can put together a prototype. There's not much to do here for the next few weeks anyway. It's up to Mother Nature now."

They came to a well-tended field of plants spaced in rows, each about three feet high. Nixon laughed at a wooden sign on a stake: *National Strategic Hemp Patch #1.*

"This is the seed patch, Mr. President. We followed the instructions in the Kentucky 4-H Club pamphlet to the letter. We planted in mounds a few feet apart, so they have room to branch out. We should get about six hundred seeds from every plant."

As they walked among rows of bushy, three-foot tall plants Nixon asked, "Smoking these won't get the hippies high, will it, Lieutenant?"

"No sir. Not this variety."

"But what if you were growing the kind that does get you high in the middle of this? How would you tell the difference?"

"Mr. President, if anybody tried to grow marijuana within ten miles of here the pollen from our plants would fertilize theirs and ruin it for smoking. It's a matter of genetics and dominant genes. Think of hemp as a kind of anti-marijuana. If hemp were growing everywhere, you couldn't grow marijuana anywhere."

"Why the hell don't the narcotics boys ever mention that when they talk about it?" Nixon asked.

"Maybe because if the public understood how the genetics work, they'd be out of a job."

"Hmmm…if what you say is true, it could be the key. If some Democrat tried to sell it like that, whimpering about science and dominant genes, there's not a conservative in the country who'd buy it. But everybody knows Nixon's a law-and-order man, so if I'm the one who tells 'em, they won't have any doubts."

"I…I don't follow, Mr. President."

He looked the Lieutenant in the eye, so it would be sure to sink in. "Son, politics is as much about who's doing the selling as about what's being sold. That's why every conservative in the country ripped Bobby Kennedy a new asshole for going Red China and meeting with Mao. Now imagine what would have happened if Nixon had been the one to go to China. Why, the liberals and the media would have called me a visionary and a statesman, and the conservatives would have gone along because it was Nixon who was doing the selling. Conservatives will go along on this because they know Nixon is a law-and-order son-of-a-bitch. But they'd never buy it from a liberal. Understand?"

"I, uh, I think so, Mr. President."

"I'll get you thinking like a politician yet, Lieutenant."

The sign in the next field read: *National Strategic Hemp Patch #2.*

"This is the fiber patch, Mr. President. We sowed the seeds thick, like grass seed, what farmers call broadcasting, so they grow tight together and straight up, with very few leaves or branches or seeds."

Unlike patch #1, this field was a thicket of skinny, six-foot tall plants, more like a jungle. "These look different from the ones over there. Are you sure they're the same plant, Lieutenant?"

"Aye sir, from the same batch of seeds. It's the method of cultivation."

"Which one do we want for fuel?" Nixon asked.

"This one, sir. It's the biomass aspect that's important as a feedstock for fuel. This field will produce three times more biomass than a corn field. No other crop is even in the ballpark."

Nixon walked up to the edge of the patch, stuck his arms in the dense growth, and pushed aside the thick jumble of spindly plants as though he were parting a bamboo curtain. "Look how thick these damned things are. The last time I was here this was nothing but mud and manure."

"Aye sir, it's the fastest growing crop there is. The average plant should be about fourteen feet tall when we harvest. If our Hungarian friends are right, we'll get ten tons of biomass per acre. And if we had a decorticator to process it, out of that we'd get six tons of hurds, two tons of high-quality fiber, and two tons of leaves and flowers. At today's prices, the fiber alone would bring four times more than an acre of corn or wheat. And the hurds should be perfect for making paper using the Ag Department process. Hemp will be a gold mine for farmers, Mr. President, and much better for the environment. It doesn't need the fertilizer or the pesticides or the herbicides crops like wheat and corn need."

"The environmental crap is icing on the cake when it comes time to sell it to the public, Lieutenant, but you can't sell a cake that's still in the oven. And what if this machine doesn't work as good as you think it will? We don't even have one yet, do we?"

"No sir, but if I go to Wright-Pat I'll take a trip up to Iron Mountain and talk to the guy who has Henry Ford's equipment in his barn. He may have one, and if he doesn't, he might know where to find one."

"What if we can't find one? How important is it in the big picture?"

"There's no need to wait for the decorticator. That can come later. The fuel aspect takes priority. If you declare war on oil, and we go all-out to win, we can be growing all our own fuel by the end of your second term."

"You're finally starting to think like a politician, Lieutenant. But a President has to be practical."

"This *is* practical, Mr. President. We can win a war on oil, but we have to go all-out to do it."

"A war on oil? Hmmm…it's got a ring to it, like the war on drugs. Okay, Lieutenant, lay it out. How do we win it?"

"First thing we do is distribute portable ethanol stills like we use in the military to every farmer in America so they can distill their excess crops into ethanol. Then we blend that with gasoline to stretch our oil reserves out an extra year. That will give us time to grow enough hemp seeds for full-scale production. At the same time, you put the Rust Belt back to work making things like storage tanks for service stations, and the infrastructure for cracking plants."

The Lieutenant took him to a big tent marked *LAB #1*, where he was met by a blast of hot air, like walking in to a restaurant kitchen. The interior was criss-crossed with pipes and tubes connected to an industrial oven the size of a horse trailer. Puffs of white smoke rose from some kind of thingamajig. "Is that a moonshine still, Lieutenant?"

"No sir. I'm trying to apply modern technology to Ford's experiments. But I need a real lab to do it right."

They went to a tent marked *DESIGN*. A free-standing blackboard filled with equations and calculations stood next to an elaborate model train set up on plywood sheets and sawhorses. "So this is how you're spending the taxpayers' money," Nixon said with a smile. "Growing pot and playing with toy trains?"

The Lieutenant laughed. "I'm trying to model the distribution system. I figure we'll need a medium-sized cracking plant every fifty miles or so." On a big bulletin board was a U.S. Army Corps of Engineers map— *Navigable Waterways of the Mississippi Watershed*—dotted with dozens of colored pushpins. On a drafting table was an architectural rendering of what looked like a railroad tank car on legs, with a row of gas pumps beside it. "What's that?" Nixon asked.

"It's my design for a methanol fuel tank for gas stations. It will fit on a flatbed trailer, and a crew should be able to install one in under a day."

"You're a jack of all trades, Lieutenant."

"No sir, but my dad's a millwright, and I majored in Mechanical Engineering at the Academy. I've been around machinery all my life."

"Why put the tank above ground?" Nixon asked.

"Because we're talking *speed*, Mr. President. We've got to go all-out from Day One. We can always bury the tanks after we've won the war."

Nixon pointed to the map. "What are the push-pins for?"

"The red ones are cracking plants, the blue ones are railroad terminals, the yellow ones are—"

Nixon cut him off with a laugh. "And I thought I was a dreamer."

"It's not a dream Mr. President, it's a vision. We can do it, sir, I know we can. We did it in World War II with the Manhattan Project when we made the atomic bomb, and we did it with the Apollo Program when we put a man on the moon. This will be easier and cheaper than either of those because we already have the technology, so it's not a scientific or an engineering problem—it's a political problem."

Nixon studied the map, which depicted every highway, railroad, and waterway from the Alleghenies to the Rockies. But it was the pushpins that unleashed Nixon's imagination, sent it soaring like an eagle across the boundless prairie skies, where tens of millions of acres of towering energy crops swayed in the Midwestern breeze, fleets of tugboats towed barges along America's mighty rivers, long trains rolled endlessly across the Great Plains, and thousands of tanker trucks delivered home-grown fuel to service stations in every city, village, and town from sea to shining sea. And gazing out from high atop Mount Rushmore was the image of the man whose wisdom had brought energy independence to America, the thirty-seventh President of the United States, Richard Milhous Nixon.

Chapter 28

The Home Team

WHILE WAITING AT NATIONAL AIRPORT FOR HIS FLIGHT TO PITTSBURGH, McGill called Mulligan's number and left a message. "It's four o'clock Friday, and I'm off to the Burgh to dig up what I can on Mellon and maybe interview Anslinger. I'll be in Milltowne at my mom and dad's until Monday, then downtown at the Hilton. Say hi to DeWolfe."

His brother, Tommy, seven years younger, was home for the summer after his freshman year at college and came to the airport to pick him up. McGill hadn't seen him for two years, and was stunned to be looking up at his "little" brother, who was suddenly an inch taller than he was.

"Jeez, Tommy, what have you been eating?"

"Doc Gibson said I had a late growth spurt."

Tommy was driving a red Chevy pickup with *McGill Motors* on the doors like the ones they both drove in high school working for their dad. When they hit the highway, Tommy opened the ashtray and took out a joint. "Smoke one, big brother?"

McGill felt old. Tommy was no longer the pain-in-the-ass younger brother in a Little League uniform.

"So what are you doing for Nixon?" Tommy asked.

"I can't talk about it. National security."

"My brother, the spy."

When the joint burned low McGill opened his briefcase, took out a Bird, clipped in the roach and said, "Tommy, meet the Bird."

Tommy broke into a broad smile as he looked it over. "Cool. Where can I get one?"

"Keep it. It's yours."

"Wow, thanks. Where'd you get it?"

"Made it. I'm getting pretty good with a torch."

"You mean…you invented it?"

"No. A guy out in California I was working with found one. I checked it out at the Patent Office, and when nothing came up, we started a company, even incorporated. We've sold fifteen grand worth of these puppies at flea markets, and we have an ad coming out in *Rolling Stone*."

McGill pulled out his BirdCo file from his briefcase and showed Tommy the ad. "We're gonna get rich off this sucker."

"This is really cool, Art. But how can you work at the White House if you get high and make roach clips?"

"What they don't know won't hurt 'em."

"Don't they make you take piss tests?"

"Nah, I'm too high up for that. So how about you. How's college? You pick a major yet? Did you get on at Sheet and Tube for the summer?"

Tommy sighed. "There's no jobs around here any more. Sheet and Tube's down to one shift, and they're saying it's shutting down next year."

Just a few years earlier Milltowne's factories ran three shifts a day, seven-days a week, and McGill and hundreds of other college kids worked as summer vacation replacements at union scale—over three dollars an hour—earning him enough to pay his Penn State tuition for a year. Now, the unemployment rate was at twenty percent, and Milltowne had become the archetypal poster city of the Rust Belt.

"So where are you working this summer?" McGill said.

"I'm washing cars and running parts for Dad at a buck and a quarter an hour, same as in high school. I'm lucky to have any kind of job. Things really suck around here."

Upon hearing Tommy's predicament, an idea struck him. "Tommy, do you want to make some real money this summer?"

"Sure. How?"

"Making Birds."

"Huh?"

"The garage has welding torches, vises, everything we need. What are you doing this weekend?"

"I work until noon tomorrow, and there's a kegger tomorrow night out at Rock Hill quarry. Why?"

"I've got parts for a couple hundred Birds with me, everything but forks. Tomorrow morning I'll scrounge every used fork in Milltowne, then I'll meet you at the garage and show you how to make 'em. If we have enough, we'll go to the Sunday flea market at the fair grounds and sell 'em."

"Talked me into it."

"Just don't tell Mom and Dad. They'd freak."

McGill scrounged through Milltowne's second-hand stores, scored fifty-two forks, and met Tommy at McGill Motors' shop, which closed at noon on Saturdays. After the mechanics had gone, they rolled two sets of oxy-acetylene tanks to a workbench with two big vises. McGill demonstrated the procedure, and Tommy followed along. Tommy was a natural, and after only a few screw-ups he was making Bird after flawless Bird like he'd done it all his life.

When they ran out of forks, they turned off the torches and admired the new flock of Birds on the table. Tommy said, "Why don't we try to sell them at the kegger?"

McGill had no interest in attending a teeny-bopper kegger, but selling Birds there was worth a try. "Go for it. You can keep half of whatever you sell. But don't stay out late. We have to get up early if we're going to the flea market."

That night he made the rounds of Milltowne's meager bar scene. He ran into people he knew, but he was eight years out of high school, and all his close friends had gone to greener pastures and usually only came back at Christmas. He felt like a stranger in his own home town.

Tommy shook him awake at three o'clock and stuffed a wad of cash in his hand. "Fuck the flea market—I sold every one. Two-hundred thirty dollars each. I don't make this in a month of working for Dad."

The next day McGill tried calling Vince to tell him the news and hook him up with Tommy, but there was no answer at the bungalow or at Vince's parents' house. He figured Vince must be in Santa Cruz. After one last try at midnight, he told Tommy, "You keep calling until you get him. Tell him who you are, and about the shop, and how it went at the kegger. Tell him I said you're our East Coast production guy, and to ship you enough parts to make a thousand Birds. Meantime, we'll scrounge forks and I'll come up Saturday. We'll make a bunch in the shop and hit the Sunday flea market."

In the morning he put on a starched white shirt, his gray pinstriped suit, and brought along his old *Milltowne Red Tornados* canvas gym bag for dirty laundry. Tommy dropped him at the Hertz office, where he rented a Chevy Impala on his government credit card.

On the drive into the city he spun the radio dial and came across a deejay he'd never heard before: "This is Rusty Limbergh, the Duke of Pittsburgh, and a WDTO good morning to everybody stuck in the gas lines. It's an even day, so only vehicles with plates ending in even numbers can fill up. And keep enough in your tank to make it to the Golden Triangle Music and Arts Festival this weekend. There will be arts and craft galore, exotic foods, and the Tri-State's top bands. And you can't beat the price…it's free."

A music festival across from his hotel sounded like a great opportunity to get laid. The desk clerk gave him a room on the top floor with a panoramic view of "The Point," where the confluence of the Allegheny and Monongehela rivers form the Ohio. He remembered from Pennsylvania History class that French explorers had considered the Allegheny and Ohio to be a single river, La Belle Rivière, "the beautiful river." In the French and Indian War, a young officer named George Washington knew The Point as "the forks of the Ohio," the strategic key to control of "the Ohio country" and the interior of the North American continent.

As he took in the view he remembered a grade-school field trip on a paddle-wheel riverboat on which they learned that Pittsburgh's river system was the world's busiest waterway in terms of gross tonnage, carrying more freight than the Suez or Panama canals. They saw dozens of tugboats hauling barges of coal, coke, limestone and finished steel that day. Today, there was not a tugboat in sight, only the new fountain at The Point shooting a stream of water 150 feet into the air.

He walked through Pittsburgh's compact downtown to the headquarters of Mellon Bank, America's sixth-largest financial institution, and presented the foil-embossed letter-of-introduction from the White House. When the receptionist saw Nixon's signature she asked, "Is it real?"

The letter opened doors as if by command, like a magic talisman out of *1001 Arabian Nights*, one after the other—open, *sesame*! When he got off the elevator at the top floor, a uniformed Pinkerton with a pistol escorted him to a double-door and rang a buzzer. A secretary appeared, read the letter, and led him through a corridor over carpeting so thick it felt like walking on a mattress. She opened a door with a sign reading: "Bradford A. Bannan, Executive Vice President."

Several people were sitting around a conference table on which paper plates and half-eaten sandwiches vied for space with file folders. A man with a full head of perfectly-coifed gray hair stood and extended his hand, "Welcome to Pittsburgh. I'm Brad Bannan."

"Art McGill. Thank you for seeing me so quickly, Mr. Bannan. I hope I'm not interrupting anything."

"Just a working lunch," Bannan said. "We're always ready to help President Nixon. This is Mr. Winter, our Vice President of accounting...."

"Nice to meet you," the man said as he stood up.

"My pleasure," McGill said as they shook hands.

"Mr. Ambrose, his assistant...."

They shook.

"And this is Miss Abruzzi, from our legal department."

She was about his age, with shoulder-length brunette hair. "Hello," she purred in a voice like melting butter. His heart ka-*thumped* as she extended her hand. What was the proper greeting upon meeting a beautiful woman in a business setting? Should his handshake be manly, businesslike, or gentlemanly? He *must* make a great first impression.

"The pleasure is all mine," he said, and gave her a limp-wristed fish-shake which was neither manly, businesslike, nor gentlemanly. She gave him an odd look, and he felt himself, and his chances, flushing like a toilet in embarrassment.

Bannan said, "So how may we help the President, Mr. McGill?"

Forcing himself to ignore the woman, he shifted into bullshitting mode. "President Nixon is looking for ways to pull us out of the recession, and my office is studying the policies of our most successful Treasury Secretaries…Alexander Hamilton, Albert Gallatin, and Andrew Mellon."

Bannan smiled. "Around here, we think Andy Mellon was the most brilliant economic mind this country has ever produced."

"The President thinks highly of him too, and I'm here to try to help him understand how Mellon made the Roaring Twenties really *roar*."

He laid it on thick, being careful not to mention that most historians said a root cause of the Great Depression was Mellon's trickle-down philosophy of giving enormous tax rebates from profits from the war years to the rich, which unleashed a spree of financial speculation that turned Wall Street into a massive Ponzi scheme. "We'd like to take a look at whatever you may have and talk to people who knew him—family members, friends, employees—anyone who might help President Nixon understand how Andrew Mellon worked his magic."

Bannan leaned back, thinking. "He was well into his eighties when he died, in 1937, if I'm not mistaken, so I doubt any of his close friends are still alive. As for his personal papers, the Mellons are very private. I don't know which of them has custody, but I doubt anyone outside the immediate family has ever seen his papers, or ever will. But the bank does have public archives, dating from about 1870 when it was founded by his father, Judge Thomas. And the Mellons still control Gulf Oil, you know, which is right across the street. They have a little museum which may have something. As for interviewing family members, let me see what I can do."

He dialed an extension. "Bannan here. A representative of the

President is in my office asking to speak with relatives and associates of Andrew Mellon…Yes, *that* President…Exactly. There may be secretaries still alive, so try Pensions. And call P.T.'s and D.K.'s offices…Yes, I know the Duggan scandal makes it difficult, but there's a lot of Mellons. Give the tree a shake and see who falls out…Tell them it's for Nixon…Right. Get back to me."

He put the receiver in its cradle. "You can't just pick up a phone and expect to talk to a Mellon, Mr. McGill. And this is a difficult time for them."

"I've been reading about it. Did they ever decide if it was murder?"

"No, but life goes on, and with a little luck, we'll have something for you by the end of the day. In the meantime, if you would like to research our public archives, they're on the second floor."

This was not what he needed. "Mr. Bannan, the President is interested in Mellon's methodology, how he picked his winners and fingered the losers. I think we both know it's the records which are not open to the public that will be the most useful to the President."

Bannan chuckled. "We bankers are trained to keep transactions private, Mr. McGill. It's in our blood. Take the Rothschilds. It upsets historians no end, but their records have never been made public. And Swiss banks have troves of transactions from the fifteenth century no outsider has ever seen, or ever will. Some things are beyond the purview of history."

McGill summoned up his best red-blooded, patriotic persona. "This is not for the public, Mr. Bannan, and it is not for history. It is for the President of the United States, the Republican Party, and the economic future of America."

Bannan pursed his lips and folded his hands. He looked around at his associates, and when his gaze landed on the woman a gleam flashed behind his eyes. "Perhaps we can make an exception for President Nixon. But we can't let you copy anything without my approval, and one of our representatives must be with you at all times."

"That's fair enough," McGill said.

"Very well. Miss Abruzzi, would you show our guest to the archives, and assist him in any way you can?"

The woman's mouth sagged open. "*Me?* But the Evans contract—"

"Leave it on my desk," Bannan said. "Sanborn can handle it."

"But—"

"This takes priority, Miss Abruzzi. We must do all we can to aid

President Nixon in these difficult times."

She let out a defeated sigh, said, "Of course, Mr. Bannan," and put a file folder on his desk.

Bannan glanced at his watch. "It's almost one. Why don't you come back here at four, Mr. McGill, and see if we have any news."

The woman led him to the elevators. He could feel anger spouting from her like water from a broken fire hydrant. She was definitely unhappy with her assignment.

He tried to break the ice. "Your boss said you're in the legal department, Miss Abruzzi. Are you a secretary, or a paralegal, or—"

"I'm an attorney, Mr. McGill."

"Hey, me too, but I haven't taken the bar exam yet. Where'd you go?"

"Yale."

He was hoping she would reciprocate, ask where he went, but the only sounds were the *click-click-clicks* of her heels on the marble floor. When they reached the elevator, she punched the DOWN button—hard.

She had given him a who-do-you-know opening, so he took it. "Some people I work with went to Yale. Do you know Chester Thompkins, or Catherine DeWolfe?"

Her body jolted, like she'd grabbed an electric fence. "You work with *Catherine*?"

"She's our secretary, or was. She's on special assignment for Nixon."

"You must be mistaken. It couldn't possibly be her."

"She's tall, kind of cute, with long, reddish-brown hair. And she's a timber DeWolfe. Money out the wazoo."

"That's Catherine all right. But I can't imagine her working for Nixon."

"She was a White House intern, and when our operation started up, they hired her full-time. She says it's for the experience."

"It's just not like her. What's she doing?"

"I can't talk about it. National security."

"I see."

"Do you know Thompkins too?"

"We had some classes together. I thought he got a clerkship?"

"His judge had a stroke and had to retire, so he came to work for us."

She was quiet, absorbed in her own thoughts. He tried to keep the banter going. "Do you have a first name, Miss Abruzzi?"

"Jenny…I mean, Jennifer."

"Sounds like you're not sure of your own name."

"This is the corporate world, Mr. McGill. I'm observing formalities."

"Me, I hate formalities. Mr., Miss, Ms.—they all get in the way. So why not call me Art, or my high-school nickname, Stick. Or just McGill, and forget the Mr. part? What do you say?"

"I prefer to be businesslike."

"Of course, I understand. Your friend said the same thing, except she made a big deal about everybody calling her Ms. So does being a Miss mean you're not a women's libber?"

"I believe in women's liberation, Mr. McGill, but Ms. isn't appropriate in the corporate world. Besides, my name comes out sounding like a beehive—Mizzz Abruzzi."

He chuckled as the elevator stopped, and minding his best ladies-first manners, he held the door and waited for her to exit. Somehow, some way, he would get to know this exquisite creature.

Jenny could not imagine Catherine working for Nixon. She was up to something...but what?

She sized up the guy from the White House as a troglodyte. He parted his straight brown hair on the left side in a "Princeton," like half the Republicans in the universe. He had a high forehead, an ingratiating smile, and was cute enough to look at twice, though his spindly wrists were a giveaway he was as skinny as a sapling.

"How do you like corporate law?" he asked on their way to the archives.

"It's a job. I'm just being practical."

"What would you be doing if you didn't have to be so practical?"

"If the election had gone the other way, maybe I'd have your job."

"So you supported Bobby Kennedy?"

"Yes. I worked for his campaign."

"So you wanted to end inequality and injustice, but ended up at a bank working for blood-sucking capitalists. It must be very difficult."

Was he trying to insult her? She fired back. "I have not 'ended up' here, Mr. McGill, I'm starting here. And may I ask how you got a job in the White House? Did Daddy make a contribution to the Grand Old Party?"

He grinned, unfazed. "Remember when Nixon's daughters almost died on that burning yacht in the Bermuda Triangle?"

"Yes, right after the election. Why?"

"My best friend from high school went to Annapolis, and he was in command of the rescue boat. After that, he got a plum assignment at the Pentagon, and a year later Nixon asked him to help start up our office. He was hiring staff when my application landed on his desk. He gave me a call, and here I am—*ta-daa!*"

He seemed to be a happy-go-lucky kind of guy, and she found his self-effacing demeanor refreshing. Unlike the ego-driven hotshots in the bank's legal department, he didn't take himself too seriously.

They entered a chamber that resembled a university library, with row upon row of floor-to-ceiling shelves filled with ledger books and bankers' boxes, tens of thousands of documents. She hadn't been in this part of the bank before. A bird-like woman in a corner office came out and said, "Follow me."

She showed them to a musty room filled with filing cabinets. "This is the catalog of all transactions since Judge Thomas founded the bank a hundred years ago."

When the librarian left Jenny asked, "Where do we start?"

"We'll work backward from 1937, the year Mellon died."

"What are we looking for?"

He took out a legal pad, wrote out a list, and handed it to her. "Start by looking up any references to these. I'll think of more as we go."

She read aloud: "'Ethanol, methanol, wood alcohol, grain alcohol, carbohydrates, hydrocarbons, oil, gasoline, diesel fuel, threshers, timber, paper, wood pulp, Southern pine, Prohibition, refineries, distillation.' What a strange list. So what do these have to do with economic policy?"

"I'm only looking for what you've got. Somebody higher up will decide what to do with it."

Like a Magic Fingers vibrator on a motel bed with a broken OFF switch, the presence of the beauteous Miss Abruzzi induced a continual, low-voltage tingling sensation beneath McGill's skin. It was as if Cupid, the impish God of Lust, had spent the afternoon gaily flitting about and shooting an entire quiver of arrows into his hapless victim for target practice. By the time they took the elevator to the four o'clock appointment, McGill was head-over-heels, hopelessly smitten.

"You're in luck," Bannan said. "Some of the Mellon family have agreed to meet you tomorrow at one of their estates out in Sewickley Heights. Miss Abruzzi will accompany you. And we've arranged a meeting for you on Wednesday with executives across the street at Gulf."

"That's great," McGill said. "I can't thank you enough."

"You're quite welcome," Bannan said. "Did you find anything useful?"

"We've only started. There's a lot there."

"Take all the time you need. I've informed Miss Abruzzi's department that she will be assisting you for as long as necessary."

"She's been very helpful. And please, bill my office for any expenses, especially for her time."

"We have no qualms about billing the government, Mr. McGill, you can be sure of that. So how might you spend your free time in our fair city? Pittsburgh is quite cosmopolitan, you know. We have fine museums, a world-class symphony, and—"

"I thought I'd catch the ball game tonight. The Cubs are in town."

Bannan perked up. "Are you a Cubs fan?"

"Oh no, I grew up in Milltowne. *Beat 'em Bucs.* But I've been away at law school and haven't seen the new stadium yet."

Bannan's mouth turned up in a genuine smile. "Then you must use our box at the Allegheny Club. There's nothing quite like dining at a four-star restaurant while watching a ball game."

"Oh, I couldn't…."

"But I insist. How many tickets do you need?"

"I'm here by myself."

"A baseball game's no fun alone," Bannan said, then turned to her, "Miss Abruzzi, could you possibly accompany our guest this evening?"

McGill thought it sounded more like an order than a request, but it didn't matter. Say yes, please say yes!

"I…I don't know," she said. "Let me make a call."

Bannan handed her his phone; she took an address book out of her briefcase and dialed a number. McGill knew he should be gallant and say, "Please don't change your plans for me, Miss Abruzzi." Instead, he put his hands behind his back, crossed his fingers, and mentally chanted: please say yes, please, say yes, please….

"Hi, Rusty, it's Jenny. Some bank business has come up. Can I take a rain check…I'm sorry. Tomorrow, I promise…I'll meet you right after work. Thanks for understanding."

She hung up, said, "I can go," and McGill's heart *ka-POPPed* like a champagne cork.

She glanced at her watch. "But I would like to run home and change."

"Take the rest of the day off," Bannan told her. "I'll make sure that the will-call window has tickets and the maitre d' has our table waiting. Now if you don't mind, Mr. McGill, I'd like to borrow Miss Abruzzi back for a few minutes before she leaves."

"Of course," McGill said. "Shall I pick you up, Miss Abruzzi?"

"Where are you staying?" she asked.

"The Hilton."

"I'll call you from the lobby, say around six. It's a short walk to the stadium."

The instant the door closed her boss said, "I don't buy that cock-and-bull story of his for a second, Miss Abruzzi. Not one damned second. What's he have you doing down there?"

"Here's a list of what we're searching for, Mr. Bannan."

He looked it over. "Ethanol, methanol, timber, paper…there must be hundreds of documents dealing with some of these. Hmmm…. Well, it's obvious he's a low-level flunky who doesn't know what the hell he's doing, and *that*, Miss Abruzzi, gives us an opportunity. There's something big going on here, I can smell it. Now I want you to cooperate with him, give him whatever he wants, but keep me informed of every detail. Whatever the government is up to, it could be worth millions if we're the first to know about it, and your job is to find out what it is."

"But—"

"No buts, Miss Abruzzi. The only reason I'm letting him snoop around is because he practically came in his pants when he shook your hand. Now I'm sure a woman like you knows how to get what she wants out of a loser like him. Use your feminine wiles on him if you have to, whatever it takes, but get him to talk. I know you're new here, but if you come through on this, you'll have a bright future at the bank, very bright indeed. A golden apple has dropped in your lap, Miss Abruzzi. Do you understand what I'm saying?"

She understood all right. If she wanted to advance her career, the pig expected her to whore herself out. "It's perfectly clear, Mr. Bannan."

McGill held his briefcase in front of him so the other passengers in the hotel elevator would not notice that every cell in his body—every nerve cell, every bone cell, every red-blood cell and brain cell and skin cell and sperm cell—were all up on their feet like a crowd at a football game and chanting in unison, "We want Jenny! We want Jenny! We want Jenny!"

He waddled to his room, pulled a fistful of paper off the bathroom roll, flopped back on the bed, undid his belt, and envisioned the expressions on the face of the most beautiful woman on the planet as he sent her soaring over the highest peaks of ecstasy. She moaned for him and groaned for him and whimpered, "Oh, Artie, you're good, oh so *good!*" As he teased her closer to the ultimate crescendo the unspeakable pleasure of his mighty thrusts swept through her perfect body until she begged, "Don't stop, Artie, please don't stop, oh Artie, oh...oh my God, Artie, you're so good. *Too* good!" Higher and higher he took her until she convulsed in unfathomable ecstasy, crying, "Oh my God, Artie, oh Artie, Artie, oh, oh, oh Artie...*OOOOO!*"

———————

Chapter 29

Déjà Vu All Over Again

JENNY WAS BOILING WITH RAGE THE WHOLE BUS RIDE HOME. SHE TOOK A QUICK shower, put on a light sweater, slacks, and sneakers, and caught a bus back downtown to his hotel. She tried to calm down, remembering she was going to a baseball game. It wasn't the worst thing in the world to do for your job. She loved baseball, and as the bus chugged along she noticed her reflection in the window, triggering a memory of a *clackety-clack-clack* ride on the old electric trolley to the 1960 World Series and getting knocked out by a Mickey Mantle foul ball. Now *that* was a baseball game.

It was five to six when she called his room from the lobby.

"Can you come up?" he said. "I'm trying to make a call, and the line's busy, so I know somebody's there. Come on in if I'm on the phone."

She went up, saw the door ajar, and just as she went to knock she heard him say, "Hello, Mrs. Wright. It's Art McGill."

She knocked softly and peeked inside. He beckoned her in as he continued his conversation. She sat on the bed, next to a beautiful Guild guitar, a yellow legal pad, and a portable cassette tape recorder.

"I haven't been able to reach Vince, Mrs. Wright. Do you know where he is?…Santa Cruz. That's what I thought. When do you think you'll see him?…The Snake River? I'm jealous. Do you think you'll talk to him before you leave?…No? Well, if you do, would you have him call me at the Hilton Hotel, in Pittsburgh…No, the one in Pennsylvania….And tell him my brother Tommy is trying to reach him too…. That's right. Say hello to Mr. Wright for me, and good luck with those trout."

He hung up and looked at her. "Hello again, Miss Abruzzi."

"What a nice guitar, Mr. McGill. What kind of music do you play?"

"Oh, I do James Taylor, Simon and Garfunkel, some Beatles, Dylan, stuff like that. I'm more of a songwriter than a performer."

"Would you play me something?" she said.

"You mean…right now?"

"Why not? We have some time."

"Well, okay, but on one condition."

"Oh," she said, feeling cautious. "What's that?"

"I can't sing to a woman with no first name, so how about when we're not on the job you call me Art, and I call you Jenny. What do you say?"

It was a reasonable request. "All right…Art."

"That's great…Jenny. Now, what would you like to hear?"

"How about something we both know. Maybe a Beatles' song?"

"Sure," and he put the strap over his shoulder, sat next to her on the bed, tuned up, strummed a chord, and began finger-picking "I Will," the tender love song from *The White Album*.

His voice was scratchy, but pleasant, a bluesy baritone; his playing wasn't spectacular, but functional, kind of folky. He could probably hold his own in a band as a rhythm player. She was mildly impressed. He looked her in the eye and sang, "For if I ever find you/Your song will fill the air…" She felt uneasy, sensing a deep sincerity, as if he were trying to convey that Lennon and McCartney had written this wonderful song just for him to sing to her.

"You have a nice voice, Art," she said when he finished.

"People say it's okay. It's my playing that sucks."

"You're no Eric Clapton, but you do just fine. Play it again, and I'll find a harmony."

She had fun trying different parts. By the third try, she had it.

"Let's see how we sound together," he said, and turned on the tape recorder. They sang it through, and when he plucked the last chord they both fell into a satisfied fit of laughter. He rewound the tape and played it back. She was surprised at how well their voices blended.

"Jeez, Jen, we sound great together. We should start a band."

She was suddenly too comfortable, a little too at ease. "We should go."

Three Rivers Stadium was a short stroll from the hotel to the Sixth Street Bridge and across the Allegheny River. The ticket taker directed them to an elevator to the exclusive Allegheny Club, high atop the stadium. A maitre d' showed them to the best table in the house, behind a giant window undoubtedly manufactured by Pittsburgh Plate Glass. A waitress brought menus and asked, "Y'uns want sump'thun from the bar?"

"A whiskey sour," Jenny said.

"A whiskey sour for the lady," he said, "and a tall gin-and-tonic for me."

"The game starts at five after seven," the waitress said. "If y'uns order now it'll be out about the third inning."

The game was a nail-biter. Every time Roberto Clemente came up they joined the crowd in chanting his nickname—"Arriba! Arriba!"—Spanish for "hurry up" because he was always hustling. Two years earlier Clemente had nearly died in a plane crash while flying emergency relief supplies to victims of an earthquake in Nicaragua. Doctors predicted he'd never walk again, much less play baseball, but somehow he was back. He turned a double into a triple with daring base-running and threw a runner out at the plate with a javelin thrower's pinpoint strike from deep right field. In the bottom of the ninth, down seven to six with two outs, he beat out a slow-roller to first, giving slugger Willie Stargell another chance. Windmilling his bat to intimidate the pitcher like nobody else in baseball, Stargell fouled off pitch after pitch until he caught a hanging curve and blasted it into the upper deck for the game-winning homer. The stadium went wild, and McGill could have died and gone to heaven when Jenny screamed and gave him a spontaneous hug, and let him hug her back.

Returning to the hotel they stopped in the middle of the bridge and took in the view of the bejeweled city skyline and the lights of the flotilla of small boats and a paddlewheel tour boat cruising beneath them. They took the path along the river, and when the brightly lit fountain at The Point came into view he asked, "Have you been to the new park yet?"

"Once, but not at night. I've only been back a few weeks."

"What do you say we check it out?"

"Sure, why not?"

"So where have you been?" he asked.

"In Paris, at the Sorbonne."

"A grad course?"

"Yes. International legal procedures."

"Pittsburgh must be pretty boring after Paris. Why'd you come back?"

She hesitated, like she was guilty of something. "The dollar went down, and I ran out of money. It was time to be practical."

They went up to the fountain, close enough to feel the spray from the geyser spouting 150 feet into the night sky. They found an empty bench and sat under a silvery quarter moon.

"It's beautiful here at night," she said.

"This whole day has been beautiful," and he took a deep breath and put his arm around her shoulder.

"Uh, Art. Don't you think we should keep this strictly business?"

He summoned up every last iota of courage. "No, Jen, I don't."

He kissed pretty good, but before it went too far she broke it off. "I think we'd better stick to business."

He gave her a naughty, puppy-dog smile. "Bummer."

She glanced at her watch. "It's getting late. I should get a cab."

They walked through the park to the taxi stand at the hotel.

"Thank you for a wonderful evening, Art," she said as a cabbie opened the door. "I had a very nice time."

"So did I, Jen. Way better than nice. So what about tomorrow? Should I pick you up?"

"I suppose that's best. Say at eight o'clock. Two-sixty-four Oaklawn. It's off Penn Avenue, in Bloomfield."

He took a pen and notepad from his pocket. "Give me your phone number too."

He wrote everything down, then pulled her close and kissed her. She gently pushed him away and climbed into the taxi.

"Good-night, Art. And thank you again."

"I'm really looking forward to tomorrow, Jen," and he handed the driver a twenty and said, "Take good care of her."

As the cab pulled away she looked out the side window and watched him waving good-bye. She smiled and gave him a little wave, surprised to realize that she too was looking forward to tomorrow.

———————

McGill parked across the street from the address, a three-story, red-brick house with a covered front porch, a white wooden railing, and a bench swing. Like every other house on the block, it had a small front lawn he could have mown in about two minutes. As he approached, a family of squirrels chattered at him and scurried up the oak tree which anchored a corner of the lot. He straightened his tie, bounded up the steps two at a time, crossed his fingers, and rang the bell.

A very attractive, brown-haired woman about his Mom's age answered. If this was Jenny's mother, it was a good sign that twenty or thirty years down the road Jenny's looks would hold up.

"Hello. Is this the Abruzzi residence?"

"Yes. Won't you come in? Jenny's expecting you. I'm her mother."

"Pleased to meet you, Mrs. Abruzzi. I'm Art McGill."

Unlike yesterday's fumbling handshake with Jenny, he had no doubt what to do when meeting a woman of his parents' generation. He knew from the manners class his mom forced him to take at the Milltowne Country Club that *Emily Post's Blue Book of Etiquette* insisted it was not proper for a gentleman to offer to shake a lady's hand unless the lady offered hers first, which according to Emily Post, they seldom did.

Mrs. Abruzzi did not offer. "Nice to meet you too, Mr. McGill. Jenny's upstairs on the phone. I think it's her boss. Would you care for coffee?"

"Please don't go to any trouble."

"It's no trouble at all. I have a fresh pot. How do you take it?"

"Black."

"Would you like a donut? I have glazed or powdered."

"Glazed would be nice."

"I'll bring one of each, just in case."

He started to protest, but she was already through the swinging kitchen door. He looked around, eager to inspect the house where the woman of his dreams had grown up. He stuck his head into the dining room; a Catholic crucifix hung on a wall, flanked on one side by photographs of Franklin Roosevelt and Harry Truman, and on the other by Jack and Bobby Kennedy. He wandered into the living room, stopping at a collection of family photos. He recognized a teenage Jenny in several. Further into the room, behind the sofa, was a big family photograph, a formal, sit-down portrait of Mr. and Mrs. Abruzzi with three boys between about ten and fifteen, and a younger girl, maybe six or seven. Except for her hair and eyes, the girl was strikingly different from the teenage Jenny in the photos.

"Who are *you*?" a voice asked. He turned to see a boy of ten or eleven, with a rolled-up towel under his arm.

Just then Mrs. Abruzzi came from the kitchen with a serving tray and said, "Dominic, this is Mr. McGill. This is Jenny's nephew, Dominic. His father's in the Navy, and Dominic and his mother are staying with us this summer while he's at sea."

McGill said, "Hello there, Dominic."

The boy said, "Everybody but Gramma calls me Dom."

"Uh…then hello there, Dom."

Mrs. Abruzzi put the tray on a coffee table. "Here you are, Mr. McGill."

"Thank you, Ma'am." As he picked up the coffee and a glazed donut, he nodded his head toward the photograph. "Is that Jenny, Mrs. Abruzzi?"

She looked at it, uncomfortable about something, "Yes."

"How old was she?"

"She was seven when that was taken."

"She sure looks different than in the photos over there."

Dom blurted out, "That's before she got a nose job. My dad says they used to call her Honker."

Mrs. Abruzzi gasped. "Dominic Abruzzi, you—"

"I gotta go, Gramma. Can't be late for swim class," and the boy zoomed off, crashing open the screen door and dashing down the steps.

McGill felt a sense of unease creeping over him as Mrs. Abruzzi wrung her hands and cast a furtive glance up the stairs. "Please don't say anything, Mr. McGill. Jenny's very sensitive."

"Oh I won't, Ma'am. Scout's honor."

"They had terrible names for her when she was a girl."

"Children can be very mean."

"The boys were absolutely awful, and it got so bad we…" She paused, glanced up the stairs, and lowered her voice to a whisper, "we got her a rhinoplasty."

Just then a buzzer went off in the kitchen. "Oh, there's my rolls. Excuse me," and she disappeared through the swinging door.

Did it matter if the woman of his dreams wasn't naturally perfect? He had never given it any thought. He took a bite of donut and studied the family portrait. Her father and her brothers all had the nose. On the males it was kind of masculine, but on Jenny it was much more prominent. It was easy to see why they called her Honker.

He walked around the room, worrying about their daughters having huge honkers. He stopped at a bookcase filled with trophies, awards, ribbons, and photos of her brothers on football and baseball teams, and her father's bowling team. There were photos of Jenny in a swimsuit poised on a high-dive, and spinning in mid-air. He read the inscription on a large trophy with a bronze figure of a woman in a swan dive:

JENNIFER MARIE ABRUZZI
First Place
West Penn Y.W.C.A. Championships
1965

On top of everything, the woman of his dreams was a fearless high-diver. That settled it—her nose job didn't matter, and if their daughters had huge honkers, he'd get them all nose jobs, no matter what it cost. The boys too if they needed them.

On another shelf was a baseball on a display stand. He set his coffee cup on a table, and as he picked up the ball he felt an eerie tingling. The ball had two autographs—Vernon Law and, holy cow...*Mickey Mantle!* The stand had a small brass plaque. He bent down to read the caption:

Foul ball hit by
Mickey Mantle off Vernon Law
Game One, World Series
October 5, 1960
Pirates 6, Yankees 4

An overwhelming blast of déjà vu buckled him at his knees, and he had to brace himself against the wall to keep from falling. He had been at that game, with his dad and Grampa Art, and he had caught a Mickey Mantle foul ball. But his glove had hit a girl next to him and knocked her out. They'd stopped the game until she came to. Everybody said it wasn't his fault, but he had felt so bad that after the game he gave her the ball.

Next to the ball's stand was a picture in a frame, a Polaroid of the world's most famous crooner, Bing Crosby, with his mouth open and his finger under the teenage Jenny's chin, like he was singing to her. It almost looked like a movie promotion. He had met Bing Crosby and Bob Hope at the World Series that day, and Grampa Art had taken dozens of Polaroids. It all came spinning back like a Tilt-a-Whirl—the World Series, Bob Hope and Bing Crosby, the Mickey Mantle foul ball, and...the girl.

Mrs. Abruzzi came in, gasped, "Oh my!" and said in a worried tone, "Are you all right, Mr. McGill? You look very pale."

"I...I'm fine, thanks."

"Perhaps you should sit down? You really don't look well."

"No, I'm fine, honest." He must know more, much more, without revealing what he was after. "Mrs. Abruzzi, may I ask you something?"

"Certainly."

Where to start? "Can you...can you tell me about that picture?"

"The one of Bing and Jenny? Oh, that's my favorite." She picked it up and blew off a speck of dust. "We met him and Bob Hope at the World Series. Jenny was twelve, in seventh grade. She got hit in the face with that baseball you're holding not fifteen minutes after this was taken."

He stared at the ball. "She...she got hit with it?"

"Actually a boy caught it, and it was his glove that hit her. The doctor said she could have been killed if it had hit her straight on. We were scared to death for a few minutes. He had to give her smelling salts to wake her up. She had the worst black eye you've ever seen for a month."

McGill had a million questions. "If…if another kid caught it, how did you get it? And how did you get the autographs?"

"The boy gave it to her after the game. I think he felt guilty. And my husband played poker with the mayor, so that night he told him what happened, and the next day the mayor took the ball to the dugouts and asked Mr. Mantle and Mr. Law to sign it for her. They were very gracious."

Could it be that all those years ago he had saved the life of the girl who was now the woman of his dreams? It had to be her, but he must be absolutely certain.

He remembered some photographs in his mom's photo album that his grandfather had taken of him with the foul ball, and of the girl with the ice-towel up to her face. They would prove it, one way or the other.

If it was Jenny, and he was sure it was, he must be careful not to tell her before the time was right. He did not want to guilt-trip her into liking him. He wanted her to like him for who he was today, not because he might have accidentally saved her life when they were kids.

"Mrs. Abruzzi, do you believe in fate?"

"Oh my gracious, no, Mr. McGill. Fate is for Presbyterians. We Catholics believe in free will. Why do you ask?"

"Oh, no particular reason."

Chapter 30

The Rich Are Different

JENNY SLAMMED DOWN THE PHONE IN HER PARENTS' BEDROOM, MUTTERED, "Bastard," to herself, picked up her briefcase, and started down the hall. If she could learn what McGill was after without using her "feminine wiles," as Bannan had again suggested…fine. But she would not lead him on merely to get ahead in a job she loathed.

As she came down the stairs, she saw McGill talking with her mom at the far end of the living room. She stopped and studied him for a minute from a distance, his mannerisms, his body language. He was kind of cute in a gawky, Jimmy Stewart kind of way. And she did have fun with him at the game last night, and enjoyed singing with him. He even kissed okay. She sort of liked him, even if he were a Republican. But no matter what her bastard boss said she would not mislead him into thinking there could be anything between them. She would keep it strictly professional.

She entered the room and said, "What are you two gossiping about?"

He glanced up, like she'd caught him with his hand in the cookie jar. "Uh…your mom was just telling me about, uh…about this picture of you and Bing Crosby."

Why was he acting guilty? Her mom had a guilty look too. "That was a long time ago," she said. "We should go. Nobody keeps the Mellons waiting."

"Please drive carefully, Mr. McGill," her mom said.

"Don't you worry, Mrs. A," he said, "I'll take extra-good care of her."

As they walked to the car Jenny said, "How did you know my friends call my mother Mrs. A? I never told you that."

"I, uh…I didn't. It just seemed natural somehow."

He was quiet as he drove, as if his mind were a million miles away. If she could learn what he was up to without leading him on, she would; it was a lawyer's job. But she would not whore herself out. The important thing was to let him down easy. Men took rejection so personally, and this wasn't personal at all. She broached the subject at a red light. "Mr. McGill, about last night—"

"Oh, so now we're back to Mister, are we?"

Oh God no, he was overreacting, exactly what she hoped to avoid. She tried to be gentle. "I just think it would be better if we kept things on a professional level. Please, don't take it personally."

"Don't take it personally? If I didn't take it personally, I wouldn't have to take it at all!"

The light turned green, and the car peeled out in a smoky squeal of burning rubber that jerked her back in her seat.

"What do you think you're doing?" she yelled.

His face was red with embarrassment as he took his foot off the gas and slowed down. "It was an accident, I swear. It's a rental, it got away from me. It won't happen again, *Miss* Abruzzi. Nothing will ever happen again, *Miss* Abruzzi."

Please, God, don't let him break out crying. "Look," she said softly, "I think you're a nice guy, and under other circumstances, who knows. But I'm only here with you because it's my job."

They rode in awkward silence for a few blocks. He finally said, "So what did you tell your boss?"

"What do you mean?"

"You're reporting to him about me, aren't you? What did you tell him."

"I was objective." That was true enough.

"So the better you know me, the more objective you can be. Right?"

She was grateful to hear the sense of humor back in his voice. "You know it doesn't work like that."

"Who says? Is there some legal doctrine only Yalies know about?"

"Look...I don't want to argue."

"Why not? You're a lawyer. It's what we lawyers do for fun. We argue."

"Mr. McGill—"

"Are you a lawyer, or are you not? Come on—negotiate. So try this on for size. I promise I won't hit on you, or do anything unprofessional, and all you have to do is not call me Mr. McGill when we're by ourselves. I'm Art, or Stick, or just plain McGill. But cut the Mister stuff. And you're Jen, or Jenny, and maybe when I'm pissed off at you like I am right now, you're Jennifer Marie. Now that's a deal for you, counselor."

"You're really very strange. You know that, don't you?"

"So what? Everybody's strange. Do we have a deal?"

It was an easy compromise if he kept his part of the bargain. "We'll keep it strictly business?"

"Absolutely."

"And we won't discuss anything personal?"

"Scout's honor," and he held up three fingers like a Boy Scout. "But when I'm finished with this project, the deal's over. Then you can shoot me down in flames, and I'll crash and burn and slink out of town with my tail between my legs. But like you said, who knows? I mean, who would have ever dreamed John would break up the Beatles over Yoko? So, do we have a deal?" He put out his hand.

"Okay. Deal."

They shook, a solid shake of mutual agreement, a compact, if not quite a formal, mutually binding legal contract.

Sewickley Heights, on the bluffs above the Ohio River, was home to many palatial estates built by the titans of industry who had made Pittsburgh the premier manufacturing center of the Industrial Age. The guard at the gate confirmed their appointment, and they drove past stables and gardens and came to a stop in front of a giant fountain filled with frolicking naked cherubs that looked like it belonged at the palace at Versailles.

Her boss had briefed her on the many conflicts within the large Mellon family. Grudges had been passed down for generations over the inequities of inheritances, and grievances over slights between various ancestors had taken on mythic proportions among Mellon descendants and their acolytes. Now, a possible murder was roiling the family waters.

"Remember, Art, they've just had a tragedy," she reminded him as a red-suited valet approached the car. "And Bannan said don't expect too much, because neither Petey or Richie will be here."

"So this is the Mellon minor leagues?"

"It's the best he could do. Try to be diplomatic."

"Just call me Mr. Diplomacy."

A butler appeared and led them to a book-lined room thick with cigar smoke where a group of three men and four women were conversing over coffee. They seemed to be in their sixties or older, though it was hard to be sure as even the men had well-tanned, wrinkle-free, face-lifted skin.

After thanking them on Nixon's behalf, McGill set up a tape recorder and said, "We're interested in how Andrew Mellon picked his investments, how he chose which technologies and companies to back."

"Uncle Andy was quite a bit older than any of us, and he never asked us for business advice," one of the women said.

"She's right," said one of the men. "I don't think any of us knows much about that." The other Mellons nodded in agreement.

"Did he ever give you business advice?" McGill asked.

One of the men said, "He was always telling us that it wasn't money that counted, but capital."

"And he told us to never be ashamed of our money," a woman said. "He said we had it because God wanted us to have it."

Jenny realized that these were ordinary people who, had their ancestors been bakers of bread instead of bankers of money, would have lived among the petite bourgeoisie, selling insurance, teaching school, or running a corner grocery store. None of them had any talent she could perceive, nor even an appreciation of why they were rich, only that their riches were predestined by the grace of a Calvinist God who wanted them to have it. They were under no obligation to use it to benefit their fellow man, and their only God-given duty was to enjoy it.

Afterward, as they waited for the valet to bring the car, she asked, "Did you get what you were hoping for, Art?"

"No, they were dumb as goldfish."

As they drove away he pointed to the mansion. "Can you imagine what it's like growing up in a place like that?"

"I spent a month at Catherine's estate in Grosse Pointe one summer," she said, "and the whole time I kept thinking about the conversation Fitzgerald and Hemingway had about the rich."

"You mean when Fitzgerald said, 'The rich are different from you and me,' and Hemingway said, 'Yes, they have more money.'"

"That's the one," she said, and they both laughed.

The drive back to the city took them down the hill from the rarefied heights of the super-rich with their horse stables and servants to the industrial towns along the Ohio River, with their barber shops, car lots, railroad yards, corner stores and empty hulks of once-booming steel mills. Suddenly McGill twisted around, gaped at something on the other side of the road and said, "Mind if we make a quick stop, Jen?"

"For what?"

"I've got this, uh...personal project. It'll just take a minute."

"My boss said to help you any way I can. If you need to stop—stop."

He doubled back around the block, pulled into the parking lot of a Salvation Army Thrift Store, and parked under a *Leave Donations Here* sign. In the nearby alley a handful of men were smoking and drinking from a bottle in a brown paper bag.

McGill said, "I'll be right back."

"If you think I'm sitting here by myself, you're nuts."

She opened her own door and tagged along as he headed for the kitchenware section and the silverware bins. His face lit up like a searchlight when he found a big wooden crate of utensils marked *10¢ each.*

"There must be hundreds here," he said, beaming as he picked up a handful. "I've never seen this many in one place before."

"Whatever are you doing?" she asked as he started sorting through.

"Looking for a certain type of fork."

"But why?"

"It's a personal project. It has nothing at all to do with my job."

"What are you going to do with them?"

He paused, grinned, and said, "Turn them into gold."

"*What?*"

"I'm going to transmogrify these poor, orphaned forks into an estate in Sewickley Heights, or a yacht off Acapulco. Or both."

"Whatever do you mean?"

He smiled and said with an air of mystery, "I promise to tell you all about it on our first real date."

Her curiosity was piqued, but she pretended not to care, and tried to change the subject, yet keep it open. "Can I help?"

"Sure. What we're looking for are forks with long tines. Like this...."

He showed her the differences, and she took a handful and began to hunt for the long-tined dinner forks lurking among the various forks, knives, and spoons. Several hundred pieces later they came to the bottom of the crate. Her pile had twenty-two. "How are these?" she asked.

He looked them over. "These are all good." He added them to the ones he'd found. "Forty-eight all together. That's pretty good, Jen."

"You're the expert."

"You think this is pretty weird, don't you?"

"Oh no, not at all. People buy forks in thrift shops every day."

They stopped for hamburgers and fries at a White Castle, then went to the bank and spent the afternoon in the archives, working back to 1921, the year Mellon resigned from the bank to become Secretary of the Treasury, a post he would hold for the next eleven years.

At the end of the day they packed up their briefcases and walked to the elevator. "Like a ride home?" he asked.

"Thank you, but I'm meeting somebody."

"Your boyfriend?"

"No personal questions, remember?"

————————————

McGill was consumed with jealously as he drove to his parents' house. Who was she seeing? What was he up against? Money? Muscles? He had to be absolutely sure Jenny was the girl from the World Series.

His mom was surprised to see him. "What are you doing home, Arthur? We didn't expect you until the weekend."

"I forgot something, Mom. I'm heading right back."

"We've already had dinner, but there's some meatloaf in the refrigerator. Why don't you make yourself a sandwich?"

"Thanks, I will. Is Tommy around?"

"He went to see his new girlfriend."

"Do you know if he talked to my friend from California?"

"He hasn't said anything about it."

He made a sandwich, snuck into the den, and took the family albums out of the cabinet. He came to a section of photos from the World Series. There was the one they always showed off, of his Dad shaking hands with Bob Hope, whom he had known in World War II, and another of Hope and Bing Crosby with McGill, his dad, and Grampa Art. There was one of him smiling at the camera, and sitting next to him, with a pair of binoculars in her lap, was the teenage Jenny. There was one of him showing off the ball, and one of Jenny holding a towel up to her face trying to smile.

He put them in his briefcase, went to Tommy's room, and put the forks under the pillow where he couldn't miss them. He kissed his Mom good-bye, bought a six-pack at a bar, and on the way back to Pittsburgh had an idea for a song and began singing and trying out lyrics as he drove.

He spread the photos on the hotel bed next to his tape recorder and notepad, rolled a joint, cracked a beer, and began working out the song on the guitar. He didn't go to bed until he had a good first draft.

He arrived a few minutes before eight hoping for another chat with Jenny's mom. It couldn't hurt to be on Mrs. A's good side. He was disappointed when Dom, holding a transistor radio, answered the door. "Hi, Dom, remember me?"

"Aunt Jenny's in the bathroom."

"Will you tell her I'm here?"

"Are you trying to be her boyfriend?"

He wasn't expecting that. He tried to be honest with the kid, yet not admit anything. "We're working on a project together."

"I like her other boyfriend better."

The kid now had his full attention. "Why is that, Dom?"

"Because he's a deejay and brings me records."

Just then Jenny's honeysuckle voice called down the stairs, "I'll be right there, Art."

"She's coming," said the boy.

"Thanks. Say, Dom, who's this deejay who brings you records?"

"Rusty Limbergh. He's the best."

"Well, I might not be a deejay, but I play the guitar. Does that help?"

Dom eyed him warily. "Your hair's too short for you to be any good."

Jenny came down, and as they drove away he switched on the radio, punched the button for WDTO, and after a commercial the deejay said, "This is Rusty Limbergh, the Duke of Pittsburgh....'"

"So, Jen, what's it like dating royalty?"

"What do you mean?"

He pointed to the radio. "Aren't you dating the Duke?"

"Who told you that?"

"Dom let me know in no uncertain terms that the Duke is a far, far better boyfriend for you than I could ever hope to be."

"I'll kill him."

"Oh, he's just a kid. So is he?"

"Is who what?"

"Is the Duke your boyfriend?"

"It's none of your business," and with that she switched off the radio.

"Sorry, my fault. Let's change the subject. Do you know a good photo lab? I've got some old pictures I want to have enlarged."

She thought for a moment. "The bank uses Fort Pitt Photo. It's on the way if you want to stop. What kind of pictures are they?"

"Just some shots from when I was a kid."

"Can I see?"

"Can't get personal, remember? But if you're extra nice, maybe I'll show them to you after a few dates."

"I wouldn't count on it if I were you."

"Oh, but I am. You'll like them. I guarantee it."

Chapter 31

Hired Help

GULF OIL CORPORATION, ONE OF THE FABLED "SEVEN SISTERS" OF THE OIL industry, was ranked by *Fortune Magazine* as the seventh richest corporation in America in terms of assets, close behind Ford, and IBM. The Mellon family still controlled an estimated twenty-five percent of Gulf Oil's stock, the largest block of family-owned stock in any publicly traded corporation in the world.

Jenny and McGill took the elevator to the corporate boardroom in the forty-four story Gulf Oil Building. Completed in 1930, for forty years the Gulf Building had been Pittsburgh's signature landmark. Crowned by a four-story stepped-pyramid of neon lights, it was the city's barometer-in-the-sky, glowing Gulf orange, for fair weather, or Gulf blue, for wet weather. Until the sixty-four story U.S. Steel Building went up around the corner in 1970, it was the tallest structure between New York and Chicago.

"I'm winging it," McGill told her. "If there's anything you can think of to ask that I'm forgetting, jump in."

Executives in suits introduced themselves; a stenographer waited nearby; a secretary offered coffee and pastries. The Vice-President of Public Relations handed him a small folder, saying, "I had our people see what they could find, and I'm afraid we have very little. Andrew and Richard Mellon weren't oil men. It was their nephew, William Mellon, who ran things around here."

McGill frowned as he opened the skimpy folder. "This is it?"

"I'm afraid so. Perhaps you'd like to talk to the fellow who maintains our museum? If anyone knows the company's history, it's him."

The veep escorted them to the museum, where a tall, rail-thin black man with snow-white hair was dusting shelves. He wore a blue baseball cap and an attendant's uniform with the bright orange Gulf logo on the hat and above the breast pocket. He looked like he was ready to fill your tank and clean your windshield.

"This is Samuel," the veep said. "He's retired now, but we can't keep him out of the place. He's the museum's custodian."

"No, I ain't no custodian," Samuel insisted. "I's the *curator*."

"Of course," said the embarrassed veep, "the curator. How long did you work for us, Samuel?"

"From 1920, when I got back from the war, till 1966, when they made me take a gold watch. I wasn't ready to be retired. I still ain't."

"I'll leave you in Samuel's hands," the veep said. "If there's anything else we can do for you, please let me know."

The room was filled with oil-industry artifacts and scale models of supertankers, cracking plants, pipelines, geological formations—all sorts of petroleum industry bric-a-brac. Jenny was surprised that an exhibit titled *World's First Drive-in Service Station* had a local address. She asked, "Was the first gas station really here in Pittsburgh?"

"Yes'm. Opened in 1913. Rockefeller was hoppin' mad the Mellons beat him to it."

The centerpiece of the museum was a huge framed photograph showing dozens of men, coated head-to-toe in oil, whooping it up under a spouting gusher. The caption read: *Spindletop, Texas, 1901: The Gusher That Changed The World.*

"Samuel," McGill said, "we're trying to find out what made the Mellons tick, how they did their deals, that sort of thing."

"I only heard about the deals after they was done."

"Can you remember any in particular?" McGill asked.

"There was the time Andrew Mellon got us Kooowait. Esso and Shell and Texaco and them said it was cheatin' for him to be ambassador to England and be makin' deals for Gulf, but he done it anyway."

"Kuwait?" McGill said, and leafed through the folder. "They told me this was everything they had, but I don't see anything about Kuwait."

"That don't surprise me," Samuel said. "It wouldn't have looked good to put his name on it. But he did the deal all right."

As McGill's questioning continued, Jenny could tell he wasn't getting what he wanted. Finally, McGill said, "Can you think of any place we might look or anybody who might be able to help?"

Samuel didn't hesitate. "I'd go see Miss Hattie...Hattie Watters. She was Andrew Mellon's number-one maid for years and years. If there's anyone who knows what the Mellons was up to, it's Miss Hattie. She's gettin' on now. Got a place out in Mount Lebanon with her roses."

Samuel looked in the phone book and wrote out an address and a phone number on a Gulf Oil scratch pad. "If you see her, be sure to pay my respects. Tell her Samuel Calhoun sends his best, and that me and the Mrs. is doin' fine."

The address was in a tree-lined neighborhood with large, well-tended lawns. McGill parked on the street, and they walked up the long driveway. A very old black woman in a wide-brimmed straw hat was watering rose bushes surrounding a handsome, three-story, sandstone house.

"Hello, Ma'am," McGill said. "We're looking for Hattie Watters."

"I'm Hattie Watters."

"Hello, Miss Watters, I'm—"

"That's *Mrs.* Watters, young man," the woman said in a no-nonsense tone that belied her frail appearance.

McGill was taken aback. "I'm, uh, sorry. I meant no disrespect, Mrs. Watters. We were told to ask for Miss Hattie, so I assumed—"

"That's quite all right, young man. You may call me Miss Hattie, but never Miss Watters. I was a properly married woman. Now, how may I help you?"

"We'd like to ask you some questions about Andrew Mellon. Samuel Calhoun said there isn't anyone who knows more about him than you. He asked us to pay his respects, and to tell you he and his wife are doing fine."

"Young Samuel? He's my friend June's boy, rest her soul. Why, after he came back from fighting the Kaiser, I got Mr. Andrew to get Mr. William to hire him on at Gulf. Mr. William was always good to colored folks who were willin' to work. I'm pleased to hear he's well. But nobody's asked me about Mr. Andrew in years and years. Why are you interested?"

"I'm doing research for President Nixon," McGill said as he handed her Nixon's letter.

She adjusted her glasses and read. "I'd be pleased to help if I can. Let's go inside where it's cooler. I'll have Nelson fix us some iced tea." She yelled toward the house in a sing-song voice, "Nel-*son!* Nel-*son!*"

The front door opened, and a butler straight from central casting came out and said in a refined British accent, "You called, Mrs. Watters?"

"We have company, Nelson. From the White House. We'll take iced tea in the parlor, and make sure the mint's fresh. Pick it your ownself."

"Of course, Mrs. Watters."

"Nelson's a fine butler," Miss Hattie said as they made their way inside. "He's from England. They teach 'em good over there."

Jenny had been surprised to see a butler employed by a former maid, and was even more surprised at the expensive decor. There were Chinese vases, Chippendale furniture, and modern art, a score of paintings, not prints, but real paint on real canvas. She recognized the styles of Picasso,

Matisse, Klimt, Braque, Klee, and Chagall. Could they all be real?

McGill set up his tape recorder, and after the butler served iced tea, he asked, "Can you tell us a little about Andrew Mellon, Miss Hattie? What was he like?"

"Mr. Andrew, oh, he was a quiet type…but you better not cross him. He had an iron will made out o' carbon steel. He was always workin', goin' over numbers, and he always had one of those thin stogie cigars. And he was real shy around the ladies, didn't marry Miz Nora till his forties. Her family owned that big brewery, Guinness. Then the divorce tore him up. My, what a scandal, her cheatin' with that gigolo and people laughin' at Mr. Andrew for bein' a cuckold. He had detectives hide listenin' boxes all over the house to hear what she was up to, and he had to pay everybody in Harrisburg to fix the divorce laws so she couldn't steal too much."

McGill had told her to jump in if she thought of something he didn't, so she did, asking, "You mean he *bugged* her?"

"They call it that now, Missy, but in 1910, nobody'd ever heard of such a thing. He was the first. After the divorce, he was about the saddest man you ever saw. All he cared about for the rest o' his life besides money was raisin' Miss Ailsa and Master Paul up right."

"How long did you work for him?" McGill asked.

"My mammy worked for his pappy, Judge Thomas, and she got me on in Mr. Andrew's laundry room in 1899, when I was fifteen. When Mr. Andrew and Miz Nora got hitched, in '01, he made me a downstairs maid 'cause I could read. After the divorce, he fired Miz Nora's favorites and made me number one 'cause Miss Ailsa liked me best. She passed on a few years back, poor thing, but Master Paul sends me a card every Christmas."

"So you must have known Mellon pretty well?" McGill said.

"I expect I saw more of Mr. Andrew than anyone except his brother, Mr. Richard. But nobody really knew him."

Jenny was fascinated by the old woman's story. "You must have met a lot of famous people working for him, Miss Hattie."

"I was a maid, Missy, hired help. Maids don't meet people…maids *serve* people. Mr. Andrew never introduced me to his guests, not a one. But I served 'em all, presidents and tycoons and the kings and queens of England, the Kaiser, the Czar. Even Mussolini. Twice."

"It must have been exciting just being around so many important people," McGill said.

"One thing you learn servin' rich folks, young man, is to never feel underneath 'em. All your big shots put their pants on one leg at a time, same as you. The only difference is they have a butler to help 'em do it. And they need 'em, too, especially those born to it. They're the worst."

"Miss Hattie," McGill said, "we're interested in how Mellon made his investment decisions. Can you tell us anything about that?"

"How do you mean?"

"How did he pick the winners?"

"Well, Mr. Andrew and Mr. Richard, they were a team. Mr. Andrew was the inside man, good with numbers and such, and Mr. Richard was the handshake man, always goin' to New York and Chicago and San Francisco. If Mr. Richard heard about somethin' new that might be good, he'd bring the man doin' it around to meet Mr. Andrew. If Mr. Andrew liked the idea, and they both liked the man, thought he could be what they called a 'Mellon man,' they'd lend out enough to make it work, at a good interest. But their secret was takin' back stock as part of the deal, like with Alcoa. They owned over half of Alcoa, you know. Nowadays they'd call 'em venture capitalists, but back then people just called 'em real smart."

"You must have seen some big transactions," McGill said.

"Oh my, yes," Miss Hattie said. "And I got in on a few. If a deal was good enough for Mr. Andrew's friends down at the Duquesne Club, it was good enough for me. Nothin' big, mind you, a share here, a few shares there, but it added up."

"Really?" McGill said. "Mellon let you in on his deals?"

"Oh my, no. He'd have fired me lickety-split if he knew. I just kept my ears open, and when he told his friends about somethin' that sounded good, I'd take a peek at his paperwork when he was out. And I went to the library all the time and read up on cash-flow and capitalization and so on until I understood it. And I bought a doctor's stethoscope so I could hear through doors better, and I sewed little pockets in my petticoats to keep it handy. When Mr. Andrew bought, I bought, and when he sold, I sold. Who'd have thought a colored maid whose mammy was the personal property o' ol' Henry Clay himself would end up with an English butler?"

"Miss Hattie," McGill said, "may I ask how, uh—"

"You want to know what I'm worth, don't you?"

"Yes, Ma'am," McGill admitted. "I do."

"I don't mind. I'm not like those born to it who's too ashamed how they got it to talk about it. I made mine. My last statement said my stocks and bonds are two-million-three. And that doesn't count real estate or jewelry. And I have forty-two paintings the dealers say would fetch more than the rest together if I put 'em up for auction. The Carnegie Museum wants me to donate 'em, but I've got my grandkids to think about. I want to leave enough to let 'em do what they want, but not so much they get snooty, like some kind of uppity black DuPonts."

Jenny asked, "You mean all these paintings are real, Miss Hattie?"

"No, the insurance makes me copies and keeps the originals in a vault. They only let me have two real ones here at a time, and I'm not supposed to tell which ones they are, but I always do. This month that Matisse," Miss Hattie said as she pointed to a painting on the wall. "That one's real. He's my favorite 'cause he's so colorful. And that Picasso over there, from his blue period, that's real too."

Jenny walked over and studied the Matisse. "How did you get so many fine pieces, Miss Hattie?"

"Mr. Andrew collected old masters, Rembrandts and Vermeers and such, like the ones he gave to the National Gallery. Every time he went over to do some buyin', he took some of us with him. The dealers always wanted him to go for painters just comin' up. Mr. Andrew would give 'em a look, but he usually let 'em go. I couldn't afford old masters on a maid's wages, so I'd listen to what the dealers were sayin' about who was up and comin', and in my free time I'd go around lookin' for deals. I brought a few back, every trip. Some turned out real big."

"Miss Hattie," McGill said, "I've read Mellon was the richest man in the world. Do you think it was true?"

"It depends when you count it up. After Carnegie sold out to J.P. Morgan for six hundred million, he was the richest, cash wise. But Carnegie started giving it away, and Mr. Andrew and Rockefeller kept on goin'. A lot of people said Rockefeller was number one and Mr. Andrew number two. But Rockefeller wasn't smart like Mr. Andrew...just mean. He had the most oil, but Mr. Andrew, he was diversified. He had the bank and coal mines and big pieces of Gulf and Alcoa and Carborundum and Koppers and Pullman and Westinghouse and a hundred more. And don't forget Mr. Richard. He was almost as rich as Mr. Andrew. And Mr. William made Gulf what it was, so he wasn't no slouch. You put 'em together, and the Mellons had Rockefeller beat by a country mile."

McGill said, "Miss Hattie, when he was Treasury Secretary, he appointed a friend to head the Bureau of Narcotics, Harry Anslinger—"

The old woman's face scrinched up in a scowl. "Ooohh, just hearin' that name gets my blood to boilin.'" She grabbed a hand-bell from a table and rang it furiously, like a fire alarm—*clang-clang-clang*—"Nel-*son!*"—*clang-clang-clang*—"Nel-*son!*"

The butler rushed in. "Are you all right, Mrs. Watters?"

"No, I ain't. Fetch me my bottle. And three glasses."

The butler cocked his head and frowned. "Mrs. Watters, you know what the doctor—"

"You back-talkin' me, Nelson?"

"No, Mrs. Watters, but—"

"Then you go fetch it—you hear?"

"Yes, Mrs. Watters."

The butler returned with a serving tray with three shot glasses and a bottle of Old Overholt Straight Rye Whiskey. He filled the glasses and proffered her the tray. Jenny picked up a glass and stared into the shimmering brown liquid, dreading the thought of drinking it.

McGill and Miss Hattie each took a glass. Miss Hattie held hers high, said, "Bottoms up," and downed it in a gulp. "Ah, that's better."

McGill said, "Bottoms up," downed his, and convulsed in a shiver.

"Go ahead, Missy," Miss Hattie said. "Do it quick. It won't bite too bad if you don't give it time."

She took a deep breath, as if she were on the ten-meter springboard going for a triple back-flip. "Bottoms up," and she threw the awful liquid down her throat. She coughed and gagged and choked, out of control.

"Hee-hee," Miss Hattie laughed. "You got spunk, Missy. Now, where were we?"

"You were going to tell us about Harry Anslinger," McGill said.

"Oh, you mean Mr. *Pain*slinger?" Miss Hattie said, spitting out the epithet. "That's what I call him. *Pain*slinger. What do you want to know about Mr. *Pain*slinger?"

"I take it you don't like him?" McGill said.

"You take that right, young man. I do my best to be a good Christian of the Baptist persuasion, so I know I should trust to the Lord to give him his comeuppance. But that man ain't nothin' but pure meanness and hatred, with a head o' stone and a heart o' ice."

"What don't you like about him?" McGill asked.

"He was always lyin' to white folks, making speeches sayin' drugs made black men crazy to rape white women. One time he sent a note to his men to watch out for a boy he called a 'ginger-colored nigger.' Well, somebody snuck it to the newspapers, and it stirred up colored folks like a hornets' nest. People in the government weren't supposed to be usin' nigger in the open, and Painslinger did it in writin'. Roosevelt should have fired him, but he never did. After Roosevelt died, word got around Painslinger was goin' to arrest jazz musicians like Louis Armstrong and Count Basie, round 'em up all at once and put 'em in jail. Harry Truman had to stop him that time."

McGill asked, "What's he like in person, Miss Hattie?"

"Oh, he's smooth around his betters, I'll give him that. He's real good at keepin' his nose up their behinds."

"Do you know how he got to be Commissioner?" McGill asked.

"Mr. Andrew ran the Treasury, so he was in charge of Prohibition. Not that he cared for Prohibition, mind you. He owned Old Overholt—that's why I drink it. Whiskey's a tradition in these parts, you know. When Prohibition came along, a lot of drys said Mr. Andrew owned a distillery so his heart couldn't be in stoppin' drinkin'. And they were right."

"How do you mean?" McGill asked.

"All the Mellons were dry on the outside and wet on the inside. And some were *real* wet."

"But why did he pick Anslinger?" McGill said.

"He'd worked in the Prohibition Department, so Mr. Andrew knew him a bit from that. Then he got engaged to Miss Ailsa's best friend, Miss Martha. Miss Ailsa was the hostess at all o' Mr. Andrew's parties—she was the queen of Washington in the Twenties—and Miss Martha brought him around a lot. Mr. Andrew got to know him, said he had the makin's of a Mellon Man, and moved him up."

"Is it true Mellon said the Depression was a good thing," McGill said.

"People got all riled up at him after he said the Depression wasn't so bad 'cause it'd clear out all the dead wood. After the Democrats took Congress, they started tryin' to blame the Depression all on him, so Hoover made him ambassador to England to get him out of the country."

"Miss Hattie," McGill said, "can you tell us anything about Mellon's dealings with the DuPonts? Were they close?"

"If the DuPonts were doin' a deal, you can bet the Mellons had a piece. Like when they took over General Motors, Mr. Andrew smoothed things out. About the only time he shied away from a DuPont deal was when they tried to throw Roosevelt out. He was too smart to get into that one."

"What are you talking about, Miss Hattie?" McGill asked.

"After Roosevelt started the New Deal, the DuPonts wanted to kick him out and take over, like Mussolini and Hitler had done. Rich folks hated Roosevelt, called him a traitor to his class who wanted to turn the country over to the Reds. The DuPont brothers got together with Wall Streeters from J.P. Morgan and some big shots from General Motors, Goodyear, and the American Legion. But they didn't count on General Butler. He pretended to go along, then he cut 'em short and blew the whistle before they made their move. The newspapers called him crazy in the head, but Congress held a hearin', and some Wall Streeters got caught lyin', but Roosevelt never went after 'em. They hushed it up after that, but my friend Etta Lee was Irénée DuPont's number-two maid, and she told me what the general was sayin' was as true as the sky is blue."

"Do you think we could talk with her about it?" McGill said.

"You'd need a crystal ball. She passed on, in '54."

"You don't like the DuPonts much, do you, Miss Hattie?" Jenny asked.

"Silver-spoon stuck-ups like that, no, hell no. But as an investment, that's different. When the Depression came, there wasn't any stock better than DuPont, dividend-wise. They always paid ten percent, no matter how many people they had to fire. Mr. Andrew used to joke DuPont was always sure to pay a dividend 'cause so many DuPonts were livin' off it. I don't cotton to the DuPonts as people, but I still keeps the stock in my portfolio."

McGill asked, "What made the stock so good?"

"They made hundreds of millions selling gunpowder in the war and used it to take over General Motors. People called 'em merchants of death, but they didn't care. Then Mr. Andrew fixed it so DuPont got the German patents in war reparations. And he fixed it so the official report said lead in gasoline was good. Later on, Painslinger put the fix in for DuPont's paper patents with his tax law."

"We're interested in the tax law part, Miss Hattie," McGill said. "How did they do it?"

"Oh, they were real sneaky. I think I have an old report that talks a bit about it. You have to read between the lines, but it's there all right."

"Can we see it?" McGill said.

"Come along to my office, and I'll see if I can find it."

Miss Hattie led them to a room down the hall. A stock-ticker under a glass dome clattered away in a corner, and the walls were covered with framed stock certificates. Above the fireplace hung a photograph of Andrew Mellon with a much younger Miss Hattie and a score of other servants—butlers, maids, valets, chefs, chauffeurs—all in uniforms. Jenny asked, "What was the occasion, Miss Hattie?"

"That's the staff at the embassy to the Court of St. James, on Armistice Day, 1932. It was just after Roosevelt beat Hoover. Mr. Andrew called us out and said he wanted a picture while he was still ambassador. He signed it, there, in the corner."

Jenny read the inscription: *To Miss Hattie, My number-one maid for over twenty years. Warmest regards, Andrew W. Mellon, Nov. 11, 1932.*

McGill was admiring the stock certificates. "What are you buying these days, Miss Hattie?"

"Jap car stocks. They're real up-and-comers. Detroit don't know how to make nothin' but gas hogs."

"Speaking of Detroit, what about Henry Ford?" McGill said. "Did Mellon work with him much?"

"With Ford? Oh my, no. He always sided with DuPont and General Motors against Ford. He said people with money should stick together, and Ford was always goin' the other way, like when he gave workers five dollars a day. And he fought Ford to put lead into gasoline because General Motors had the patent. Irénée DuPont signed the deal for DuPont to make it, and his brother, Pierre, signed for General Motors to get the royalty. Pretty soon some DuPont workers started goin' crazy and dyin' from what they called 'looney gas.' There was a big scare, with doctors sayin' lead was bad, but General Motors and DuPont kept sayin' it was safe. Some government scientists took a look, and Mr. Andrew fixed it so they gave it the okay. But Ford kept sayin' it was bad, so Mr. Andrew got Congress to make it a crime to badmouth it in advertising. After that, every time you put gas in your car, you were payin' General Motors and DuPont a few pennies for the lead. They made over three-hundred million on it till just a couple years back when it came out they'd been lyin' the whole time."

McGill asked, "How about the things he didn't invest in, Miss Hattie, the ones he turned down?"

"Oh, that's harder. There were so many."

"Do you recall if he ever considered a machine called a 'decorticator?'"

Miss Hattie's eyes brightened. "Oh my, the decorticator. I remember the decorticator, all right. But he didn't invest in it. He killed it."

McGill sprang up from his chair like he'd sat on a tack. "*Killed it!* What year was that? 1935? 1936?"

"Oh, no," Miss Hattie said. "It was 1917, right after we got into the war."

McGill seemed puzzled. "1917? We know about one in 1938, but—"

"No, not that one. Painslinger killed that one with his tax law. I'm talkin' about the *first* decorticator."

McGill stared in disbelief. "Please, Miss Hattie, tell us all about it."

"Excuse me," Jenny said, "but what is it?"

McGill waved her to be quiet. "I'll tell you later. Please, Miss Hattie, tell us anything you remember about it."

"Let me see. The Mellons did a lot of business with Mr. Timkin, from Canton, over in Ohio. His pappy invented the roller-bearings used in railroad cars, and the Mellons were big in railroad cars and electric streetcars. Well, Mr. Timkin started a steel company, Latrobe Steel, to make a special kind. It was close by Ligonier, where the Mellons had their country houses and Mr. Richard was building the Rolling Rock Club. Mr. Timkin would come around from time to time and they made him loans for one thing or another. Mr. Andrew said he ran good, solid companies.

"So one day he brings along Mr. Scripps, the newspaper man. Well, I was servin' lunch when they put out some photographs and were sayin' how much they'd need to make the new machine go. They said the man who invented it wanted to use it to make clothes, real cheap. But they didn't care about that. They were kickin' up their heels like a couple o' billy goats about makin' paper for Mr. Scripps' newspapers out of a byproduct they'd just be throwin' away.

"Now, the Mellons were always for new things, but only when it didn't hurt their loans and investments. So Mr. Andrew told 'em no and said they had to drop it 'cause it'd make too big a mess for everybody if the hemp problem came back."

"*The hemp problem!*" McGill said, almost shouting. "Are you sure?"

"There's nothin' wrong with my memory, young man."

"Yes, ma'am, I can see that. But how would the Mellons have known about hemp?"

"Oh, their grandpappy grew it on his farm out in Hempfield Township. It was big when Mr. Andrew and Mr. Richard were growin' up."

"How did you know about it, Miss Hattie?" McGill asked.

"Me? Why, my mammy was a slave girl down in Kentucky, on Henry Clay's biggest hemp plantation. She always grew a patch, every summer. Only new clothes we ever had came out o' Mammy's patch."

McGill asked, "Is it very hard to grow?"

"That's the easy part. It's bringin' it in takes the work. First, you cut it down and spread it on the ground for a few weeks to ret it, so it gets real loose. Then you had to scutch it. That's the real hard part...the scutchin.'"

"Scutchin'?" McGill said. "What's that?"

"You take a batch and beat it like crazy till the hurds fall out. They said the new machine would get rid o' both the rettin' and the scutchin'. If it worked like they said it did, it would have made growin' hemp real easy."

McGill asked, "What did Mellon mean by 'too much of a mess?'"

"The war was on, and things were goin' good. Bringin' it back to make paper and clothes in new ways would have upset too many apple carts."

"But Timkin and Scripps were both millionaires," McGill said. "Why didn't they just do it on their own?"

"Oh, they had a little money, but nothin' like Mr. Andrew and Mr. Richard. Little big shots like them were always borrowin' for this or for that. They'd have had to been plum crazy to buck the Mellons after they told 'em to drop it. They'd never get another loan from them or J.P. Morgan ever again if they'd gone against 'em."

"Did the Mellons really have that much power?" Jenny asked.

"Have you heard o' the 'smoke-filled room,' Missy?" Miss Hattie said, her eyes twinkling.

"Yes. It's a room where political deals are made," Jenny said. "Why?"

"Know where it comes from?" Miss Hattie said.

"No, I haven't the slightest idea," she said.

"Me neither," McGill said.

"It's from the 1920 Republican Convention in Chicago," Miss Hattie said. "Nobody had enough votes, so the big shots went to Senator Lodge's room at the Blackstone Hotel to drink whiskey, smoke cigars, and work out a deal. The reporters were all out in the hall when the door opened and big clouds o' smoke came pourin' out and they told everybody that Senator Harding from Ohio was gonna be the next President."

"And when Harding won," McGill said, "he made Mellon Secretary of the Treasury."

"That was part o' the deal," Miss Hattie said. "I was surprised when he took it. He was sixty-five and had all the money in the world. But he was lonely and wanted to try somethin' new. And runnin' the Treasury was a real good investment." She paused, as if she'd lost her train of thought. "I'm bein' forgetful. Why'd we come in here, anyhow?"

"Something about Anslinger and a report," McGill said.

"*Pains*linger," she said with a sneer, then stood up and went to a shelf and began to search. "Oh…here it is. *The DuPont Corporation Annual Report, 1937.* He'd brown-nosed in tight with Democrats by then, but he was still a Mellon Man, kind of like a secret agent inside the New Deal."

She found the page and gave it to McGill. "There. That's it."

He read it aloud: "*The revenue-raising power of government can be converted into an instrument for forcing acceptance of sudden new ideas of industrial and social reorganization.*"

McGill seemed puzzled. "I…don't understand."

"That revenue raisin' power it's talkin' about is Painslinger's marijuana tax," Miss Hattie said. "It worked, too…got rid of the hemp problem."

Just then there was a knock, and the butler called through the door, "It's time for your medications and your nap, Mrs. Watters."

"Thank you, Nelson. I'll be along in a minute."

"What does marijuana have to do with it?" Jenny asked.

"I'll tell you later, Jen," McGill said, then held up the report and asked, "Miss Hattie, may I make a copy of this?"

"You can keep it. I won't be needin' it."

"You have President Nixon's gratitude," McGill said.

"I'm pleased to help out, though I don't see what good it'll do."

Miss Hattie escorted them to the vestibule, and when the butler opened the door, it was pouring rain outside.

"I'll pull the car up so you don't get wet," McGill said. He hoisted his suitcoat over his head, hugged his briefcase close to his chest, said, "Thank you again, Miss Hattie," and dashed down the driveway.

As they watched him sprint through the downpour, Miss Hattie said, "He's a fine young man, Missy. You two make a nice couple, real nice."

Jenny could hardly believe it. "We're not a couple, Miss Hattie. We just met two days ago."

"Well, any fool can see he's got the eye for you. Now, it's none o' my business, but don't let him get away till you try him out. I have a knack for seein' how young folks'd hitch up, and you'd hitch up good, real good. He's a bit on the skinny side, though, so you'll want to fatten him up some before you start to havin' his babies. How's your cookin'?"

She and McGill waved good-bye as they drove down the driveway. When they got to the street, she asked, "So what is this decorticator thing? And what does it have to do with marijuana?"

"Uh…it's a kind of threshing machine."

"For hemp?"

"Right."

"Isn't hemp what they use for rope?"

"It can be used for a lot of things."

"So what's marijuana have to do with it?"

"Hemp and marijuana are different species of the same plant, like breeds of dogs. Chihuahuas and Great Danes are as different as night and day, right, but they're both still dogs."

"So does this thing harvest marijuana too?"

"No. It's grown a whole different way."

"So what's it have to do with Mellon's decisions at Treasury?"

"I...don't know."

"But that's why you said you're here."

"Uh...."

"So what are you really after?"

"I told you. I'm researching economic policies."

He was lying. "Then you won't mind if I tell my boss how interested you are in hemp and marijuana and decorticators and Anslinger?"

"No, Jen, you can't!"

"I can't? Why not?"

"I can't tell you, Jen. National security."

"That's Nixon's excuse for everything. Well it doesn't wash. I'm going to tell my boss and let him figure it out."

"Please, Jen. You *can't*!"

"So you want me to lie to him based on what...your say-so?"

"You don't have to lie exactly, just don't tell him about hemp or the decorticator or Anslinger or Miss Hattie. It's not lying if you don't tell him everything. America's national security is at stake."

"You make it sound like the country's future depends on what I tell him."

"It might. If it gets out, the whole thing could blow up before Nixon has a chance to get it off the ground."

"Get *what* off the ground?"

"Jen, you have to trust me."

"I don't trust anyone who won't tell the truth. I swear, Art McGill, if you don't tell me what this is all about—the truth the whole truth and nothing but the truth, right now—I'm going to Bannan this afternoon."

"If you won't do it for me, do it for your friend DeWolfe."

"I'm not one for blind faith, even for my friends." She folded her arms and sat back. The ball was in his court.

Neither spoke until he pointed to a Park 'n' Dine coming up in the next block. "How about lunch? We can eat in the car and talk."

"Sure."

A carhop in a rain slicker and a mini-skirt roller-skated over with menus. When she'd taken their orders and left, McGill said, "Jen, if I tell you, you have to promise not to tell your boss or anybody else. Deal?"

"I promise to consider it. That's all."

He slumped against the door. Minutes went by. Neither spoke.

The car-hop skated over and hooked trays to the outsides of their windows. McGill paid, and when the carhop left he let out a sigh and said, "I guess I'll have to trust you'll do the right thing."

She sipped her chocolate shake and said, "I'm waiting."

"Have you heard about Nixon's Project Independence?"

"Of course. It's all over the news."

"Well, what you don't know is that Nixon has a secret plan to win the energy war over oil...."

She listened as he related a scheme to convert the American economy from one running on oil to an economy running on energy made from farm crops, and the only crop that could do the job was hemp. It was a fascinating proposition.

"Why keep it secret?" she said. "It sounds like a great idea."

"Because if millions of farmers were growing it, the supply of raw materials would be democratized, not only for energy, but for half the economy. Paper and textiles and plastics, fertilizers, anything that can be made from oil could be replaced. It can even replace steel for things like car bodies and refrigerators. If millions of farmers were growing hemp, corporations would lose their grip over natural resources. If Nixon can pull this off, it will change everything, Jen. *Everything.* But he's up against the biggest corporations in the world. He's got to catch them with their pants down to have a chance."

"Why doesn't he just come out and call for a national campaign to grow it?"

"It's all confused by his war on drugs. My job is to find evidence of a conspiracy to ban hemp, and Miss Hattie just gave it to me. They used drugs as an excuse to kill the competition."

"No, she didn't, Art. It was just the recollections and speculations of an old woman. It would never hold up in a court of law."

"It's the court of public opinion that counts, Jen. And now that she's told us where to look, we just might find a smoking gun that will hold up in court. But we have to keep it secret. So…can I count on you? Can your country count on you?"

"Don't get hokey on me. I need to think about it."

He stopped at the South Hills Mall to buy a second tape deck so he could make a duplicate of the interview. On the drive downtown he suddenly got excited, checked his mirror, said, "Hold on, Jen," and spun the car in a screeching U-turn.

"What is it?"

"A Goodwill."

She threw her hands up in amazement. "You are one strange cookie, Art McGill. One minute you're saving the country, the next you're preoccupied with old forks."

"You're absolutely right," he said with a grin as he parked. "Want to come help me get rich?"

"It beats sitting out here in the rain."

He opened her door and held his coat over her head to keep her dry. He certainly was well-mannered, she had to give him that. As much as she believed in total and complete equality of the sexes, she did not want to give up being treated like a lady. She knew it was not a logically consistent position, but she couldn't help how she felt, logic or no logic.

"So how do you turn these into gold?" she asked as they sorted through the silverware bins.

"I promise to tell you on our first date."

They found nineteen that met his requirements, and as they waited to check out, he spread them on the counter. "Which one's your favorite?"

"I don't have a favorite."

"Oh, come on. Pretend your best friend is getting married and you're at Kaufman's helping her pick out a silverware pattern."

There was one with a nice filigree, with *Oneida* and *Sterling* engraved on the back of the handle. "If I had to choose, maybe this one. Why?"

"I'm curious about what you like. I learned at lunch you like chocolate over vanilla. I guess we can't agree on everything."

"You really are a strange bird."

He grinned. "There's more truth to that than you know."

He was being deliberately obtuse again; she wouldn't respond. "So what will we be doing tomorrow? I have to tell my boss something."

"So you won't tell him about Miss Hattie and the rest of it?"

"I'll give you the benefit of the doubt for now. Just don't push your luck. So what about tomorrow?"

"I need to tell my office all about Miss Hattie. My guess is they'll want me to go to Ohio and check out Timkin. Why don't you come along?"

"How will I explain that to Bannan?"

"Yeah, you're right," he said with a sigh. "Dumb idea."

"Well, I have to tell him something in about twenty minutes."

"Tell him I was called away, but that I'm coming back next week. Will that work?"

"I can make him buy it."

"So what do you say we get that first date out of the way tomorrow night? I can be back by nine or so if I haul ass on the turnpike."

"There's a birthday dinner for my grandmother."

"Then how about Saturday?"

"I have a commitment."

"With Limbergh?"

"You're beginning to tick me off."

"Yeah, okay, sorry. Then how about Sunday?"

"I'm busy all day Sunday, too."

He pulled over in front of the bank to drop her off, looking for all the world like a sad-eyed puppy whimpering for a table scrap. "Then how about Sunday night? A movie, a drink, a chocolate sundae, something…?"

Miss Hattie's comment about wanting to fatten him up before having his babies unexpectedly popped into her mind, probably because he mentioned chocolate. She chuckled to herself and gave him a peck on the cheek. "Call me Sunday evening, around seven, and we'll talk."

———————

Chapter 32

My God's Better

THE WEEKS HAD FLOWN BY. MULLIGAN HAD NEVER FELT SO ALIVE, WORKING for the President to save the country by day and making love to a magnificent Earth-goddess every night.

His idea for small-scale methanol cracking plants moving around on trains and barges, like migrant workers following the harvests, was totally feasible. By adapting the high-tech, space-saving technologies used in nuclear submarines to Henry Ford's 1930's experiments, he could improve Ford's results by at least fifty percent. Minimum. If he could convince Nixon to get behind it, there was no way Project Independence could fail.

He glanced at his watch: 18:32. Catherine would be preparing dinner, and Leary would be checking gauges in the Lab tent. Leary had been invaluable, ever-ready with a willing pair of hands or a word of encouragement. After weeks of working next to him and listening to ball games with him, Mulligan had come to trust Leary implicitly. If they could smuggle him into Canada, he was convinced he would not betray them.

He was using his slide rule on some pyrolysis calculations when he heard Catherine's husky voice call, "Miiiike. Tiiiim. Diiiinner."

When they first arrived she couldn't fry an egg, but she had vowed that if she were to be stuck on a mountain with no servants or restaurants, she would learn to cook. He requisitioned her a supply of spices and a shelf of cookbooks, from *The Joy of Cooking* to *Mysteries of the Wok*, and now all her meals were gourmet treats. She really was officer material.

As the three of them lounged at the picnic table over freshly-baked cherry pie, the walkie-talkie squawked: "Sentry Three to Farmboy. Over. Sentry Three to Farmboy. Over."

He picked it up. "Farmboy here. Over."

"The C-I-C just passed your gate. Over."

They all froze.

"Is he walking King Timahoe again?" Mulligan said. "Over."

"Negative. He's in a Secret Service vehicle. Over."

"Roger, Sentry three. Farmboy out." He switched it off. "Tim, get out of sight. He'll be here any second."

Leary slid off the bench, crouched low and scrambled toward the trailer, while he and Catherine frantically policed the area of anything that might indicate the presence of a third person.

Two black Fords emerged from the woods. The second stopped at the far end of the meadow. Three men got out and watched through binoculars as the lead car continued on. As it came up the lane, he could see it was Nixon himself behind the wheel. He brought the car to a jerky stop and fumbled with the gearshift before finally turning it off. He stuck his head out the window. "I haven't been behind the wheel of a car in years. Always have some damned chauffeur."

"Would you like some cherry pie, Mr. President?" Catherine asked. "I made it myself."

"No time. My helicopter's warming up right now."

"How about some fresh-squeezed lemonade?"

Nixon's eyes brightened. "I'll try some lemonade if it's fresh-squeezed." He got out of the car, and she filled a paper cup from the pitcher.

Nixon took a sip. "Oh my, that's good. Reminds me of my mother's. We had a citrus grove when I was a boy, and if there's one thing I know, it's lemonade, and this is excellent, Ms. DeWolfe."

"Thank you, Mr. President," Catherine said. "Where is it you're going?"

"Some rubber-chicken fund-raiser somewhere," Nixon said. "Lieutenant, you drive. We'll talk on the way. Oh, and Ms. DeWolfe, the Lieutenant assures me you've done as much as you can up here for now, so I'll arrange for a car to take you home. Rose Mary will send the couriers to your house, so you can keep editing *The Hemp Papers* from there while you take care of your affairs. You're doing a crackerjack job on those, and I don't want anything to change on that. But don't contact anybody from your team, and if you run into them, clam up. No leaks. Understand?"

"Oh yes. Mr. President. No leaks. I promise. And thank you."

Mulligan drove Nixon to the helicopter landing zone, and when he returned half an hour later he told them, "Nixon bought it. He's arranging for engineers at the Air Force Institute of Technology to help me on a prototype. The C.I.A is delivering a truck so I can haul the trailer out there. I'll work there until it's time for the harvest. That's when we'll bring the others up to help. If Washington and Jefferson's journals are right, it should be about a month."

"But what about me?" Leary said.

He smiled, said, "Follow me," led them to the big map in the Drafting tent, and used a pencil as a pointer. "Camp David is here, Washington is here, Wright-Patterson Air Base is here, Niagara Falls is here, and the Pittsburgh airport is here. When the truck gets delivered tomorrow, we'll load the trailer, and Catherine will go to Washington. On Wednesday morning, I'll haul the trailer out the gate, with you in the compartment in your disguise. Meanwhile, Catherine will fly ahead to Pittsburgh, rent a car, and double back on the turnpike. We'll rendezvous about noon at a truck stop *here*," and he tapped the map and drew a circle, "at the Somerset exit. You'll switch vehicles. I'll go to Wright-Pat, and you'll go with Catherine to Niagara Falls. It's about three hundred miles, so your E-T-A should be around 16:00. She'll buy two tickets for the *Maid of the Mist*, and when they let the tourists off to see the Canadian Falls, you keep on going and she'll fly back from Buffalo."

Leary hollered, "Yahoo," and danced an Irish jig around the tent.

"Let's make sure your disguise works," Catherine said, and she took Leary to her tent to help him with his make-up. An hour later Leary pranced into the tent. He looked every bit the dowdy German Hausfrau as he minced around, talking in a perfect German-accented falsetto, "Guten Abend, Herr Leutnant. Ich bin Helga Kaulbeck, aus Frankfurt. So pleased to meet you I am."

Nixon was in a sour mood the next morning as he entered the Oval Office. Haldeman, Ehrlichman, Kissinger and Bullcannon greeted him with their usual out-of-sync, "Good morning, Mr. President."

"What's so fucking good about it?" Nixon growled as he slumped into his chair and scanned the front page of *The New York Times*:

RECESSION DEEPENS
Layoffs Surge, Dollar Hits Record Low
Gas Lines Growing Longer
Arabs Vow No Oil
Chinese Repulsed in Battle for Hanoi

"Shit!" Nixon yelled as he ripped the page off the paper, crumpled it into a ball, and hurled it against the wall. "Commies killing commies blows the whole damned domino theory right out of the fucking water. You know how many elections that bullshit theory's won for us? And those assholes in the Middle-fucking-East and their my-god's-better-than-your-god crap. One's as bad as the other. The Arabs have the oil and the Jews have the media and between 'em they have me squeezed into a rat hole. Nothing but gas lines day after fucking day. I want some good news for a change. Henry, what's the latest out of camel-land?"

Kissinger peered over his glasses and spoke in his gravelly German accent, "Mr. President, the Arabs vant—"

Nixon thumped his fist on the desk. "I don't give a shit what the rag-heads want, Henry—I want a fucking deal!"

"I'm vorking on it, Mr. President."

"So what's the problem? There's what, three million Israelis and two hundred million Arabs...right?"

Kissinger adjusted his glasses. "Approximately, but—"

"And maybe a billion Muslims all together...right?"

"Approximately, but—"

"Jeezel peezel, Henry, do the math. They've got the numbers and they've got the oil, so get 'em to buy out the Jews lock, stock and barrel. You end the bullshit tomorrow—kaput, it's over, Henry, fucking over!—and you get that Nobel Prize you're always slobbering after."

Kissinger smiled, dimpling his cheeks, and said, very playfully, "You have been dreaming again, haven't you, Mr. President?"

"Of course I've been dreaming, Henry. I'm always dreaming. Anything worth doing starts with a goddamn dream. So play along with me on this. Why the hell can't you just get one side to buy out the other? The Jews buy out the Arabs, the Arabs buy out the Jews—I don't give a rat's ass which way it goes as long as you get it done."

"If it ver possible, Mr. President, the Israelis vould have to be the vuns to move, logistically speaking. But vhere vould they go?"

"Hell, bring 'em over here. We've got what...two hundred and twenty million? What's another three? Chump change, Henry. Chump fucking change. And throw in the Christians in Lebanon to sweeten the deal. Let the rag-heads have the whole damned desert. Who gives a shit?"

"But five million all at vunce vould be very disruptive, and—"

"Hells bells, Henry, taking in refugees is the American way. You've heard of the Statue of Liberty, haven't you? And it's got to be better for me politically than sending American boys off to die in camel-land. And for what? There's nothing there but a few olive trees and some stray fucking sheep."

Kissinger shuffled uncomfortably in his chair. "But, Mr. President, there are strategic considerations. The Soviets vill—"

"Dammit Henry, this is Nixon you're talking to, not some twit reporter from *Newsweek*. We both know the argument that it's strategic is a crock of shit. It's a thousand times more trouble than it's worth."

Bullcannon was fidgeting, unhappy at the direction of the discussion. "But, Mr. President, we don't need any more foreigners in this country. There's too damned many here already."

Nixon glanced at his flame-throwing speechwriter. "Bart, sometimes you get your head stuck up the crack of your ass even worse than Henry, and that's saying something. This country's built on the backs of foreigners. Hell, we get that many wetbacks over the Rio Grande every year."

"Exactly my point, Mr. President," Bullcannon argued. "They're diluting our bloodlines and polluting what it means to be a real American. Besides, where would we put them?"

"Oh, come on," Nixon said with a dismissive wave of his hand. "We've got wide open spaces out the ass. How about Utah? The Salt Lake's a lot like the Dead Sea, so they'll feel right at home. And they'll balance out the Mormons, so everybody wins. Ha...it's perfect. Perfect!"

"I vish it ver dat easy, Mr. President," Kissinger said. "But the Orthodox Jews believe that vhen Solomon's Temple is rebuilt, the Biblical prophecy vill be fulfilled, the Messiah vill come and—"

"So then turn it around on 'em," Nixon said. "Get the Jews around the world to chip in and buy out the Muslims. Think big, Henry, think big!"

"They vould if they could, Mr. President," Kissinger said, "but the Muslims believe dat Mohammed ascended into heaven from vhere the Dome of the Rock mosque now stands, which is the exact same spot vhere the Jews believe they must rebuild the Temple. So to fulfill the prophecy, the mosque vould have to be torn down, and dat vould start a holy var."

"And don't forget the Christians, Mr. President," Bullcannon chimed in. "The Church of the Holy Sepulcher is sacred to Catholics, and it's right next to the Dome, so it would have to come down too. The Pope would be pissed, but it fits nicely with your Southern Strategy. There's millions of fundamentalists down there dying to help the Jews rebuild the Temple so the prophecy can be fulfilled."

"What's supposed to happen after it gets built?" Ehrlichman asked.

"They believe it signals the Second Coming of Christ," Bullcannon said, "and any Jews who don't convert will be slaughtered."

"Let me get this straight," Haldeman said. "They want us to help the Jews rebuild the Temple, but once they get it up, then all the Jews die?"

"If they don't convert, that's about the size of it," Bullcannon said.

Nixon shook his head. "What a pain in the ass that place is. The Jews say it's holy. The Muslims say it's holy. The Christians say it's holy. Next thing you know the goddamned commies will be saying it's holy. It's a chunk of fucking rock, for crying out loud. If I had my way, I'd fix their wagons good and turn the damned thing into a nuclear waste dump so nobody could go near it for a hundred thousand years. Maybe by then they'd be over their my-god's-better-than-your-god crap. And that's what it is, dogmatic fucking crap!"

Just then Nixon felt a surge of inspiration. It was as if the gods of ancient Greece, gazing down on the Oval Office from atop Mount Olympus, had taken pity on him. To ease his troubled mind, they dispatched three Muses—Calliope, Clio, and Euterpe—Epic Poetry, History, and Music, who alighted invisibly behind his chair. Singing in three-part harmony in a range only Nixon could hear, they sounded exactly like his all-time favorite trio, the Andrews Sisters, and infused America's Commander-in-Chief with a heavy dose of divine inspiration. Surprising everyone in the room, Nixon burst into song, spontaneously singing new lyrics to the tune of "My Dog's Better Than Your Dog," the Ken-L-Ration dog-food jingle:

> "My god's better than your god
> My god's better than yours
> My god's better way goddamn better
> My god's better than yours."

His aides gaped as Nixon chuckled, pleased with himself. It wasn't every day he could say he wrote a song. "I can't wait to try it out on the piano. We need a piano in here. Bob, make a note to get one. A nice upright."

"Where would you like it?" Haldeman asked.

"Oh, I don't care," Nixon said. "In a corner somewhere."

"This is the Oval Office, sir," Haldeman said. "There are no corners."

Rose Mary's voice came over the intercom: "Mr. Duberman is here, Mr. President. He says he has good news."

"I can use some," Nixon said. "When Henry leaves, send him in."

"Yes, Mr. President."

"So, Henry, I have a domestic matter to deal with. Doesn't concern you at all. I want you to get your diplomatic ass in gear and shuttle off to Cairo or Baghdad or Timbuktu or wherever the hell it is you go on those secret missions of yours and make us a goddamned deal to end this embargo."

Kissinger pushed his glasses high up the ridge of his nose and snapped his briefcase shut. "As you vish, Mr. President."

As Kissinger sulked toward the door, Nixon called out, "Remember, Henry, think *big*! Think fucking *BIG*!"

"I vill certainly try, Mr. President."

Moments later Duberman came in. "I hear you have good news," Nixon said.

"Yes, sir," Duberman said. "We found a witness to the hemp conspiracy. McGill's got an interview on tape."

"A witness...who?"

"Andrew Mellon's maid. McGill says the conspiracy goes back two decades earlier than we thought."

Duberman recounted the story and asked, "Mr. President, do you want him to follow up that lead in Ohio?"

"Hmmm... You say there's a tape?"

"Yes, Mr. President."

"Tell the boy to hold off for now. I want to hear it before we make another move. For the White House to be looking into the history of a former Secretary of the Treasury is one thing, but to be looking into the affairs of a private citizen who's been dead for decades just isn't plausible. We don't want to tip anybody off."

"Mr. President," Bullcannon said, "even if the story is true, it was forty or fifty years ago. Everybody involved is long since dead."

"Yes," Nixon said, "but dollars to donuts their families are still raking it in. That's why they're Republicans. But if they've hurt national security as much as I think they have, Nixon can turn it around so it bites 'em in the ass. But we have to keep our cards close to the vest. No leaks until I'm ready, because when Nixon goes on television and tells the world how we've been gouged on gasoline and toilet paper for fifty years to line the pockets of blue-blooded billionaires, the American people will be so pissed off nobody will dare to stand in Nixon's way—*nobody*!"

Chapter 33

Let's Get Rich

MCGILL GLANCED AT HIS WATCH—NINE-FIFTEEN. HIS SUITCASE WAS PACKED, an Ohio roadmap lay spread out on the bed. He should have been on the road two hours ago. Why didn't Duberman call? He looked out at the rush-hour traffic below. There was a lot of activity in the new park across the street as workers set up rows of tents for the weekend fair.

He played his guitar and practiced the song he wrote for Jenny, wondering what she was doing. He heard a knock. Probably an over-eager maid. He opened the door and was shocked to see Tommy beaming at him. "Hey Big Bro, look what the cat drug in."

"Shit, McGill, you look like a narc with that haircut."

"*Vince*? What the hell are you doing here?" he said, totally astonished as Vince's big arms wrapped him up in a California hug.

"You hooked me up with Tommy, and he had an idea to sell Birds at some kind of hippie fair you're having back here."

Tommy was popping with excitement. "They'd just had a cancellation when I called. Only two hundred for a double-size booth."

"And flying's cheap because of the recession," Vince said. "So I told him to grab it, boxed up all the Birds we'd made and parts for a thousand more, and hopped a redeye."

"So why didn't you tell me?" McGill said.

"We only figured it out last night," Tommy said. "I borrowed two torches and the portable workbench from the shop, and I got your old mic and amp. We have everything we need to put on a show."

McGill was confused. "A show? What do you mean put on a show?"

"We'll make Birds right on the spot," Tommy said, "like a carnival act."

Tommy and Vince seemed to have hit it off like gin and tonic. If they could work as a team, maybe he could keep his White House job and reap profits off the Bird while they did all the work. It's how a true capitalist would do it. Andrew Mellon would be proud.

"Your brother came up with a good one," Vince said. "How come you didn't think of it?"

Why hadn't he thought of it? The fair would draw thousands of people in the exact counter-culture demographic of their target market.

"I figure we'll set up the booth and bust ass making Birds all day today and sell like crazy all weekend," Tommy said. "My new girlfriend's coming down tomorrow to help."

"What did you tell Mom and Dad?" McGill said.

"They think I went camping up in Cook's Forest."

The plan made sense, except he was hoping to bring back Jenny to his room Sunday evening and get laid. "When are you going back, Vince?"

"I got a flight Sunday night around six."

"Good, because I have a hot date. Company's the last thing I need."

"Who is she?" Tommy asked.

"A chick from the bank. She looks like Mrs. Peel on *The Avengers*, only better."

"So you gonna help, McGill?" Vince said. "We got Birds to make."

The phone rang, and McGill said, "I'll know more after this. Hello."

"McGill, it's Duberman. The President is very excited about what you turned up."

"I knew he would be. So should I go to Ohio and check out Timkin?"

"No. He wants to hear the tape first. We have a meeting Monday at eleven to play it for him, so come on back. I want to hear it today."

"I have, uh, commitments here. Look, I already dubbed a copy. I'll go to the airport and send it air-freight. You'll have it this afternoon, and I can answer any questions over the phone. I'll catch an early flight Monday and be there in plenty of time to see Nixon."

"Yeah, I guess it's okay," Duberman said.

"Any word from the drug czar on that interview with Anslinger?"

"No, but he promised he'd let me know soon."

When he hung up he said, "I have to run out to the airport and send off a package, then I'm free till a meeting with Nixon on Monday. Can you believe Nixon scheduled a meeting just for me?"

"Fuck that lowlife asshole," Vince said. "Let's get *rich!*"

McGill considered calling Jenny, but she had made it clear she had plans, and he didn't want to blow it by coming on too strong. There was only one way to put her out of his mind. "What the hell...*let's get rich!*"

At two o'clock Saturday afternoon the doorbell rang, and her mom's voice came wafting up the stairs, "Jenny, dear, Rusty's here."

"I'll be right down." She put the finishing touches on her make-up, tied her hair in a ponytail, and turned off the fan on her dresser. The radio said it would be hot and humid, so she wore shorts, sneakers, and a summer blouse, and carried a light sweater for when it cooled off in the evening. She brought her big straw bag for anything she might buy.

She heard a gang of boys come rumbling up the stairs and race down the hall. Dom burst in and thrust a 45 record into her hands. "Aunt Jenny, look what Rusty gave me! The Doors joined the Allman Brothers!"

She gasped when she saw the title: "Go! Susannah." The record jacket showed the two bands with the Eiffel Tower in the background. Morrison, cocky as ever in a beret and skin-tight leather pants, was proffering a bouquet of roses. Next to him, a grinning Duane Allman, in jeans and a cowboy hat, straddled a motorcycle. On a nearby park bench, Jimi Hendrix and Janis Joplin were casually blowing soap bubbles. She couldn't help chuckle at the band's name: "Les AllmaDoors & Amis."

"Let's go!" Dom shouted, snatched the record from her, and he and his friends went thundering up the third-floor stairs.

She was breathless, unable to move, remembering the raunchy lyrics they'd sung as she twirled tassels in the go-go cage. The first bars of the famous melody drifted down the stairs on Allman's honey-sweet slide-guitar. She raced into the hall to hear better just as the two bands kicked in full-blast and Morrison growled:

> "Well I laughed so hard
> The day you left
> My tears would not go dry
> Your love's so hot
> I froze to death
> Susannah make me cry."

Her heart was pounding as they joined in singing on the chorus:

> "Singin' go, Susannah,
> Go-go-go for me
> 'Cause I came from Alabama
> Just to love you in Paree."
> Singin' go, Susannah,
> Go-go-go for me
> But you tripped off to California
> With Timothy Leary."

She knew a hit song when she heard one, and this had number-one-with-a-bullet tattooed all over it: the most famous melody in American history, rocked out with first-rate musicianship and an extra-heavy dose of star power. They even cleaned up the "With a hard-on to Paree" line for the radio. This song was *good*.

"Dominic!" her mom shouted up from the bottom of the stairs, "Turn down that awful racket this very instant!"

The volume went way down. Jenny strained to hear, but it was too low to make out the words. Damn. She took some deep breaths, telling herself calm down, Jennifer, be practical, calm down, be practical. Think, Jennifer, think. What did it mean? What are the consequences?

She knew Oskar would keep her secret, and that no one would ever know from him about her double-life or her fling with Morrison or helping Leary escape. But when this hit the charts, the celebrity press was sure to go snooping around to find out who Susannah was. Her arms prickled with goosebumps at the thought of being discovered. Why-oh-why did Morrison make a record about her?

"Jenny, Rusty's waiting," her mom called. "What's taking you?"

She must not let anyone see she was upset. "I'll be right down."

Limbergh wore tan Bermuda shorts and a forest-green polo shirt, like he was off for a round of golf. He had grown up down the block, and she had known him since third grade. He was cute in a cherubic way, not quite pudgy—stout, without being muscular—like Porky Pig. He was about five-ten and parted his straight brown hair on the side in a "Princeton," like McGill and half the Republican men she knew. They had never been romantic, but she liked him, and accepted his invitation for the fair today and water skiing tomorrow to see whether there could be anything between them.

When they got to the fair, he used a press pass to park in the VIP area and brought along a tape recorder, the same model McGill used.

"What do you plan to record, Rusty?"

"With all the long-haired, maggot-infested hippies running around, there's got to be some laughs I can use on the show."

His attitude unsettled her. "Rusty, how can you be a deejay if you don't respect your audience?"

"I don't have to respect 'em, just entertain 'em."

The fair was like an Oriental bazaar, acres of booths under rows of colorful, open-faced tents. A rock band was playing on the central stage, and the air was fragrant with exotic aromas from the food stands mixing with incense, patchouli oil, and an occasional whiff of pot.

Assorted practitioners of astrology, tarot, numerology, and palmistry mixed in among booths hawking everything from leather sandals to bongs and roach clips. There were also political groups passing out flyers and signing up members, including Greenpeace and N.O.R.M.L. She insisted on stopping at the N.O.W. booth to sign the petition demanding passage of the Equal Rights Amendment, and after some cajoling, she convinced Limbergh to sign it too.

As they browsed the aisles he played the role of the roving deejay with his tape recorder. "Hi, you're talking to Rusty Limbergh, the Duke of Pittsburgh, your drive-time dittohead deejay on the tri-state's number one station, WDTO, 1440 on your AM dial. And what brings *you* here today?"

They ran into a WDTO-TV camera crew and Limbergh asked the reporter, "Getting anything good?"

"Nothing worth a damn," the reporter said. "We're going back to edit for the early news. See ya, Limbergh."

When the TV crew left, Limbergh said, "It just frosts me they let that idiot on and don't give me a shot. If I had a crew to work with, I'd damned sure find something newsworthy even if I had to make it up myself."

A crowd was gathered around a booth at the corner of the aisle. From inside came an amplified announcement: "Step on up and see the world's greatest roach clip made right before your very eyes. Next show starts in five minutes. Five minutes to showtime."

"C'mon, Jennifer," Limbergh said. "This could be a story."

"You go ahead. I'll browse around."

"Don't go far." He pushed into the crowd, saying, "I'm with the press. Make way for the press."

The large booth was at the end of an aisle, so people could watch from two directions. A tall college-age boy in a Penn State T-shirt said into a microphone, "Next show's in four minutes."

At a side table, a girl in a Slippery Rock T-shirt was making change out of a cigar box brimming with cash. She picked a flyer off the ground, smiled at the cartoon drawing of something called "The Bird," and chuckled at *Made By Genuine Hippies*. She overheard somebody say, "Do they really make them out of forks?"

"Forks?" Jenny said to herself, tingling all over. She wedged her way forward and looked closely at the side table, which was filled with metallic statuettes. She reached between two people and picked one up. It had once been a fork all right. Could McGill be involved? She turned it over and saw *U.S. Government* stamped under the tail. She looked at the other statuettes on the table. One with a *Not For Sale* tag caught her eye. She picked it up; "Oneida" and "Sterling" were engraved under the tail. Ka-*thump*.

She asked the girl, "How much for this one?"

"I'm sorry, it's not for sale. See the tag?"

"Why not?"

"The boss made it special for someone."

Jenny gestured towards the college boy. "Is he the boss?"

"Oh no, he's my new boyfriend. The boss is his big brother."

Big brother? She studied the boy's face; it bore a strong resemblance to McGill's. "Is the boss here?"

"He's on a break."

"Come one, come all," the boy was saying into the mic. "Check out the Bird, the world's greatest clip. It's easy to pass, it stands on it's own, it won't fly away, and it's legal in all fifty states and the District of Columbia. The show starts in two minutes."

She put the Oneida Bird down and saw another with a fancy filigree. She picked it up and said, "How much for this one?"

"That's real silver," said the girl. "Twenty dollars."

"Twenty's way too much."

"The stainless steel ones are only ten."

"But I like this one."

"Tommy," the girl called, "you want to talk to this customer?"

The boy came over. "That's a good one, lady. I made it myself."

"It's very expensive," Jenny said.

"You know how hard it is to find a fork like that? Tell you what. Because you're so cute, I'll throw in a regular Bird for free."

Jenny pointed to the Oneida Bird. "That's the one I really want."

"Sorry, lady," said the boy, "no can do. My brother made it for some chick he's got the hots for. He thinks it's going to get him laid. He'd kill me if I sold it."

She felt a surge of embarrassment and knew she must be blushing. At least if he noticed he could never have guessed why.

"Tell you what," said the boy. "Fifteen for the one you got, and you take your pick of any stainless steel Bird for free. I can't do better than that."

"Okay," she said. "It's a deal."

She paid and put the Birds in her bag. Rusty was at the far end of the crowded booth by the demonstration area and hadn't seen her make the purchase. She went into the aisle, saw McGill coming, and ducked into the next booth so he couldn't see her. He wore cut-off jeans, Topsiders with no socks, and a Grateful Dead T-shirt. With him was a muscular guy with shoulder-length blonde hair wearing sandals, cut-offs, a green Oakland A's baseball cap and a silver and black Oakland Raiders T-shirt.

She ducked out of McGill's line of sight, watching as he took the microphone from his brother. "Ladies and gentlemen, gather round and watch an ordinary fork transformed into a functional piece of New Age art by the metal master himself, Mr. Vince Wright, who is with us today all the way from Beserkley, California. Let's give him a hearty Steel City round of applause."

The crowd applauded politely as Vince smiled and waved, turned his cap backwards, like a catcher, put on a pair of goggles, picked up the torch, turned the valves on the tanks, and clicked a flint striker. A flame leaped out in a yellow plume, spewing black smoke. He adjusted the valves until it burned low, like a candle, and set it in a holder on a workbench.

"Ladies and gentlemen...."

McGill worked to the crowd like a carnival barker, describing the process as it progressed—from cutting the fork in two with metal shears, to heating the tines just enough to curl them into wings, to brazing the pieces together, to dousing the hot metal in a bucket of water, to polishing off the burrs with a stiff wire brush. It took about five minutes, and as Vince held the finished Bird up high McGill said, "Right before your very eyes, a Bird is born. How about a round of applause for Mr. Vince Wright, metal sculptor extraordinaire."

Vince removed his cap with a flourish and took a bow, and McGill launched into a sales pitch. "Don't go home without your very own Bird. They make the perfect gift for all your friends, your lovers, even your mothers. The Bird will help you fly...."

As people lined up at the side table to buy, she heard Limbergh shout, "Hey, Birdman! Birdman!"

"Yes, sir," McGill said.

"Will you answer a question?"

She felt a rush of apprehension as McGill walked over to Limbergh and said, "This gentleman has a question. What is your name, sir?" McGill stuck his mic out to him, but Limbergh pulled out his own mic and said,

"You're talking to Rusty Limbergh, the Duke of Pittsburgh, WDTO, 1440 on your AM dial. And my question is this: Tell us, Birdman, how do you sleep at night knowing you're sending America's youth down the road to hell?"

The color drained from McGill's face like dishwater from a sink. Limbergh stuck his mic up closer and shouted, "I said, how do you sleep knowing you're sending kids down the road to hell?"

McGill's eyes flared in anger. He backed away and said into his own mic, "Ladies and gentlemen, the Douche of Pittsburgh does not appreciate the artistry and craftsmanship that go into each and every Bird. Nor does he appreciate the Bird's superior functionality."

Limbergh went nuts, shouting, "Answer the question, Birdman! How do you sleep knowing you're sending America's youth down the road to hell!"

"Sorry, Mr. Douche, but I sleep quite well knowing we make the world's greatest clip. And now, it's break time. Next show's in fifteen minutes, so step up to the table and take home your very own Bird."

McGill hopped up on a chair, scanning the crowd, probably looking for her. He had already guessed she had a date with Limbergh today. She backed into a booth across the aisle and peeked around the tent flap.

She watched Limbergh buy some Birds from the girl before heading off in the other direction and calling, "Jennifer. Jennifer."

She went to the next aisle and raced to greet him when he turned the far corner. "Oh, Rusty, there you are."

"Did you see me?" he said.

"See you what?"

"Take on Birdman. I got it all on tape for the police."

She gulped. "The *police*? Why the police?"

"They're making roach clips...right in the open."

"But a lot of people here are selling that kind of thing. It's perfectly legal."

"I don't care. I'm going to nail 'em. Look at this." He flipped a Bird over and pointed to the *U.S. Government* inscription.

"So?"

"Don't you understand? If using government property to make money off drugs isn't against the law, it damn well should be." He checked his watch. "Come on. I need to get to the station and show these damned things to the news director. When he sees what they're doing, I know he'll give me a camera crew tomorrow. This could be my big break."

"But we have dinner reservations."

"We can eat any time. If I'm going to bust these assholes, I need to get my ducks in a row."

"Rusty, I don't want to spend my day off watching you work."

"But you're my date. I'm responsible for you."

"That's totally sexist. This is the Seventies."

"No-no-no. I believe in the equal pay for equal work. I signed that stupid petition, didn't I? But on a date I'm responsible."

"You can't just go changing things in the middle and expect me to go along. You go ahead. I'll stay and see the rest of the fair."

"But...but how will you get home?"

"Rusty, I take the bus every day."

"Yeah, okay. But we're still on for tomorrow, aren't we? I'll pick you up at noon, like we planned, and you can be there when I bust 'em."

"I thought we were going water skiing."

"This is more important, Jennifer. They're using government property to promote drugs. I tell you; this could take me national. *Sixty Minutes* will beg for it. I figure we'll hit 'em about two-thirty, when the crowds are heaviest. Maybe I'll do a citizen's arrest on camera. What do you think? Citizen's arrests are legal, aren't they?"

"If you see a crime in progress, yes, but there's nothing to arrest them for. They could sue you for slander and defamation of character and who knows what else."

"The station has insurance for that kind of crap. But you're right, I need to be careful. Wait a minute...a friend of mine from broadcasting school's a big shot in the War on Drugs down in Washington. He'll know how to handle it. Come on."

"No, Rusty. You go do what you have to do. I'll be fine."

"Okay, but we're still on for tomorrow. I'll pick you up at noon."

She wanted to say no, but if he were going to harass McGill she wanted to know his plans. "Call first," she said, and the instant he left she made a beeline for the Bird booth.

Chapter 34

Love and Money

ANOTHER BIRD-MAKING DEMONSTRATION WAS UNDERWAY, THIS TIME WITH McGill's brother doing the talking. McGill was nowhere to be seen. She asked the girl, "Where's the guy who did the announcing the last time?"

"He won't be back until tomorrow."

She looked across the park to his room on the top floor of the Hilton. Ten-to-one he was in it.

When she got off the elevator, a room-service waiter was backing out his door with a fistful of cash. "Thank you, sir, thank you *very* much."

She knocked. He opened the door, lighting up when he saw her. All he had on was a pair of cut-offs, like he was at the beach. He had no hair on his chest, and while he was skinny, he was athletic-looking, sinewy, like a tennis player, or a lanky long-distance runner. He looked up and down the hall. "You didn't bring your douchebag boyfriend, did you?"

"No…and he's not my boyfriend."

He showed her in and closed the door. "Like a beer?"

"Sure."

The room was steamy from a recent shower. His guitar was on the bed next to several piles of carefully-stacked currency. An ice-bucket full of green-and-white Rolling Rock beers and a large envelope from Fort Pitt Photo Lab were on the dresser. He used the opener on a Swiss Army knife and handed her a bottle.

"Are those the pictures you dropped at the lab?" she asked, pointing to the envelope.

"Uh, yeah."

"Can I see?"

"Maybe on our third date."

"Our third date? We haven't had a first date."

"Don't worry. It's in the stars."

She took a sip and changed the subject. "So how was Ohio?"

"Nixon didn't want me to go. I thought about calling you, but you had your grandmother's party and a date with the Douche."

"You never mentioned anything about the fair," she said.

"It came up out of the blue. I was waiting to hear about Ohio when my kid brother showed up with my partner from California and told me they got a booth. So I guess you know all about the forks, huh?"

"I saw a demonstration. You're a good emcee."

He pointed to the stacks of money on the bed. "You didn't believe I could turn forks into gold, did you?"

"No, that's for sure."

He was brimming with enthusiasm. "We made over seven grand, Jen, and the day's not over. And the crowds will be even bigger tomorrow."

"Art, there's something I need to tell you—"

"Whoa," he said, holding his hands up in a T, the football time-out signal. "Me first. I wanted to surprise you, but since you know."

He opened his briefcase and took out the Oneida Bird, removed the Not-For-Sale tag, and handed it to her. "This is for you, Jen."

She felt herself blushing as she remembered his brother saying, "He thinks it's going to get him laid." She must pretend to be surprised. "It's made from the one I picked as my favorite, isn't it?"

He smiled sheepishly. "Yeah."

"That was very sweet of you, Artie. Thank you."

"So what do you think? Is it cool, or what?"

"I have to admit, it's ingenious. Is it your idea?"

"No. Nobody knows who made the first one. I came up with the name and got the company started."

"So what does it have to do with national security?"

He seemed surprised. "Why...nothing."

"Do you expect me to believe you're working for Nixon to expose a hemp conspiracy while you stand to make a fortune selling roach clips if he legalizes it?"

"Do you think I'm lying?"

"Why didn't you tell me what you were doing with the forks?"

"You're the one who insisted we couldn't get personal. So, do you want to hear now?"

"Sure."

"Well, I'd been hoping to land a job in Nixon's administration...."

He told her a story so off-the-wall it was almost plausible.

"...and when my buddy Mulligan offered me the White House job, I jumped at it. And that's the truth, Jen. Cross my heart and hope to die."

"So does Nixon know you make roach clips?"

"Do you think I'm crazy?"

"Absolutely."

"Yeah, maybe. But I don't give a damn what your boyfriend thinks. The Douche of Pittsburgh can kiss my ass."

"He's not my boyfriend. Please quit calling him that."

"He's not?"

"No. We're friends, that's all. I've known him since third grade."

"Super!" He caught her off guard with a spontaneous kiss, but broke it right off and guided her to the edge of the bed. "Here, sit down. I want to try a song out on you."

Boy, was he ever strange.

He picked up his guitar, slung the strap over his shoulder, tuned up, strummed a G chord, sat next to her and said, "Here goes nothing.

> I've been concealing this feeling
> And hiding my fears
> Afraid of striking out
> After so many years
> But now I'm coming to bat
> Gonna win the whole thing
> 'Cause you can't get a hit
> If you don't take a swing.

>> I want to be your guy
>> I want you to be my woman
>> I want to be your guy
>> And your best friend
>> I want some kids
>> I want you to be their mother
>> And in the night
>> I want to be your man
>> Yeah in the night
>> I want to be your man.

> I want to be on your side
> Share the same dream
> Make love every day
> Procreate our own team
> And if you give me the chance
> To play ball with you

We'll win it all
When we say I do."

It was a tender but totally corny love song, with a nice melody and a baseball theme. When he finished the final chorus she clapped and said, "I don't think I've ever heard it before. Who does it?"

He gave her the most sincere look she had ever seen on a guy. "I do it, Jen."

"I know that," she said with a laugh. "But I mean who wrote it? Except for the schmaltzy lyrics, it almost sounds like a James Taylor song."

His face wrenched in agony, as if she had skewered him with a shish kabob spear. "*I* wrote it, Jen, after we went to the Pirate game."

She felt tiny, small, guilty, awful. How could she be so utterly stupid? "Oh, Artie, I…I…."

He stood the guitar against the wall and hung his head. "I guess I was hoping it would get me to first base."

"I am so sorry, Artie. I…I don't know what to say."

He was still for a few moments, staring at the floor, then suddenly bolted upright and looked at her with an undaunted defiance. "Maybe shmaltzy's not so bad. The shmaltziest songs are the biggest hits, right? And like the song says, you can't get a hit if you don't take a swing," and with that he pulled her close and kissed her.

She did not consider herself prudish when it came to sex. Neither did she think of herself as promiscuous. She had not gone "all the way" until her junior year in college, and she had been very selective, one boyfriend at a time, with long stretches in between. She did not think she became what men called "horny" if she did without. Her fling with Morrison had been an aberration, the exception that proved the rule. So why did kissing this guy feel so good? Was it the song? Why was she liking this guy?

After a few minutes, he gently took her beer out of her hand, set it on the table, and laid her back on the bed, accidentally spilling a money-pile on the floor. He picked up a handful of bills and threw them high in the air, grinning like a madman as greenbacks fluttered down around them like autumn leaves. She picked up a stack and playfully threw them in his face, and instantly they were ten-year-olds in an October leaf pile, laughing and hurling fistfuls of greenbacks at each other as fast as they could grab them.

They fell back on the bed, laughing amid the scattered bills. He drew close and kissed her. Soon, she felt his hand slip under her blouse and move softly, up her side, over her bra. He squeezed gently, and she did not resist when he stole second base—fondling, petting, gratefully sucking, back and forth, one to the other. After a while he pulled her tight, torso-to-torso, warm and sensuous. He gently nibbled an ear lobe and sent shivers through her as he kissed the nape of her neck. Then, like every man she had ever dated, his hands began to roam too far.

"No, Artie, please."

He retreated to her breasts, circling her rosettes, playfully nipping the tips of her nipples, but when she shifted ever-so-slightly underneath him, he howled, "Ow!" and pushed off, his face wrenched in pain.

"What's the matter?"

"Have you ever had a hard-on inside a pair of jeans?"

She laughed. "No."

"Well, if you ever do, don't get yourself in the wrong position, because it hurts like hell."

He reached down and undid the button, but when he started to pull down his zipper she said, "No, Artie, please. I hardly know you."

"Just the jeans, Jen. Honest. If my underwear comes off, it will be because you're the one who takes it off. Scout's honor," and he held up three fingers like a Boy Scout.

"Artie, that's the oldest line in the book."

"That doesn't mean it isn't true."

She did not say yes, but neither did she say no. He fixed his eye on hers, and she was careful not to look as he slipped out of his cut-offs and kicked them to the floor. He pulled her close, and she could feel the bulge beneath his jockey-style underwear. He kissed around her eyes, down her neck, around each breast, down her stomach, circling her navel, and back up to her breasts.

She felt him take her wrist, and as he sucked her breast, his hand guided her hand down and placed her palm over the bulge in his underwear. He kept gently sucking and fondling, and when she finally closed her fingers around him of her own free will, he moaned a rapturous "Aahh." She didn't stop him when his hands began to roam again, unbuttoning her shorts and slipping them off. He went to his knees, kissing up and down her thighs. She let him slip her panties off, and she spread her legs wide as he kissed up, down, around, inside-out and everywhere in between. He was keeping his promise, and when she couldn't stand it one more instant, she grabbed the elastic band on his underwear, pulled them down, and guided him in….

The soft orange rays of the setting sun shot horizontally through the window, sparkling the beads of perspiration that covered her perfect body like a thousand tiny diamonds. She was on her back, breathing heavily. McGill propped himself up on an elbow, mesmerized by the afterglow radiating from her glistening body. He wanted to swing through the hotel lobby on a vine doing Tarzan yells to let the world know that it was he, Art McGill, who had brought such contentment to this most wondrous of faces. "Jen, do you have any idea how beautiful you are?"

She opened her eyes.

"Why, look at you," he said. "You're blushing."

"I am not."

He gently stroked her forehead. "You know Jen, I'd have gone for you even if you'd never had a nose job."

Her eyes flashed red as she bolted upright. "*What!*"

Oh shit, big mistake. "I didn't mean it like that, Jen. Honest. I'd think you were gorgeous no matter what."

She shoved him away, got out of the bed, and furiously began to gather her clothes. "Oh, you, you…how did you know?"

"There's a picture in your living room, and Dom said—"

Just then they heard a key in the lock and some giggly laughter. The door swung open, and Tommy yelled, "Hey Artie—let's party!"

Jenny jumped back in bed and scrambled under the covers, hiding her face in a pillow as Tommy and his girlfriend blundered in.

"Don't you know how to knock?" McGill shouted.

"Oops, sorry, I had no idea," Tommy said as he looked at the money strewn everywhere. "What the hell happened? You going kinky on me?"

"Don't ask," McGill said. "Where's Vince?"

"Some chicks took him to a party. He said he'd be back in the morning. Chicks really dig him."

"He's got the blonde surfer thing going for him," McGill said. "They're not used to that back here. So how'd we do after I left?"

Tommy passed the cigar box. "Almost three grand. I pinched a hundred to party on. So did Vince. We'll really clean up tomorrow."

Jenny mumbled something, but it was muffled by the pillow.

"What was that?" McGill asked her.

She rolled over and sat halfway up, holding the covers up to her neck. "I don't think you'll be cleaning up tomorrow."

"Hey," Tommy said, "I remember you."

"Be quiet, please," Jenny insisted. "This is important. I tried to tell you before, Artie. It's why I came to see you. Rusty's going to call a drug agent friend of his and try to get you arrested tomorrow. And even if he can't arrest you, he wants a confrontation on camera."

"*Arrested?*" Tommy said. "But Art, you said the Bird was legit."

"It *is* legit," McGill assured him. "It's totally legal."

"Rusty doesn't care if it's legal or not," Jenny said. "He says having 'U.S. Government' on them makes it a hot story. He thinks it could make *Sixty Minutes.*"

"Wow, that's great!" Tommy said. "We couldn't buy that kind of publicity in a million years."

"No, it's *not* great," McGill said. "If it gets out I'm involved, it could screw up everything."

"Screw what up?" Tommy asked.

"I can't talk about it," McGill said. "National security."

"But we made ten grand today," Tommy said. "Everybody says we'll do even better tomorrow. Do you want to just blow it off because of some dirt-bag with a TV camera?"

"You'll have more than that in legal fees if you do get arrested," Jenny said. "Even if you win."

McGill sat up, stuck a pillow against the headboard, and leaned back. "Let's slow down and think about this."

He put his arm around Jenny and pulled her to him, breathing a sigh of relief when she didn't resist. It was as if she'd forgotten how angry she'd been with him a minute ago. He asked, "What time's he coming, Jen?"

"He mentioned two-thirty. He said it will be a better story if there's a lot of people around."

Tommy laughed. "Can you imagine if Mom saw us on TV selling roach clips?"

"Yeah," McGill said, "Dad might be okay with it after he saw the money, but not Mom."

"My parents would kill me," Becky said.

"Tommy, who filled out the paperwork for the booth?" McGill asked.

"Vince did when he went to pay. Why?"

"Is there anything with your name on it? Did he give them your phone number, anything like that?"

"I don't think so."

"So as far as they know, Vince just flew in from California?"

Tommy shrugged. "I guess. Why?"

"Because nobody knows him here, so it won't matter if he's on TV."

Jenny broke in, "Don't be stupid, Art. You've already made a lot of money. Just clear out."

"We can't just walk away from ten grand," Tommy said.

"Say, Art," Becky asked, "if some reporter found out you work at the White House and make roach clips, wouldn't it be kind of, you know...controversial?"

"I don't even want to think about it," McGill said.

———————————

Chapter 35

A Bird in the Hand

A S THEY GATHERED UP THE MONEY, COUNTING AND RUBBER-BANDING IT INTO thousand-dollar bundles, Jenny couldn't help wondering what she would be doing right this very instant had it not been for McGill and his stupid forks. Probably bored stiff listening to Limbergh brag how great he was. One thing about McGill—he was definitely *not* boring.

McGill went to the closet, took out a bright-red *Milltowne Tornados* gym bag, and put in the bundles. "Can you believe it…nine thousand, six hundred and seventy-five green American dollars!"

"What about tomorrow?" Tommy said.

"If you're smart," Jenny said, "you'll clear out."

"We can't just pull the plug, Jen," McGill said. "We're talking ten grand, at least, and Vince came all the way from California. Let's sleep on it and figure it out when he's here in the morning."

After Tommy and Becky left for their own room, McGill picked up her Bird and said, "Let's break it in."

She had long preferred the mild buzz of pot to the stupor of alcohol, and people didn't get crazy on it like when they drank too much. When the joint burned low he clipped it in the Bird and passed it, tail first. "You do the honors, Jen."

The Bird really was a better mousetrap and could easily be the next Hula Hoop or Frisbee, the brass ring on the merry-go-round of the get-rich-quick American dream. She had no doubt the world would beat a path to the door of the makers of this whimsical piece of practical folk art.

"So will you stay the night?" McGill asked when the joint was done.

"No, I better not. My mother's a worrier."

"Call her and say you met some friends, and you're going to a party."

"So now you want me to lie to my mother too?"

"Doesn't everybody? And what about tomorrow?"

"Rusty was supposed to pick me up at noon to go water-skiing, but after he started talking about harassing you, I told him to call first."

"What an asshole."

"He's not really a bad person, Art, he's just a conservative Republican."

"But Jenny, *I'm* a Republican."

"But you're no conservative, not making roach clips."

McGill smiled. "Point taken. So are you really going to see him?"

"If I'm going to have any chance of helping you, I need to know what he's up to. Maybe I can talk him out of it."

"Jen, you're the greatest. So what about tonight? I really want to wake up next to you in the morning."

She didn't answer but excused herself, took her purse, shut the bathroom door, looked in the mirror, and asked, "What do *you* want, Jennifer?"

She took out her birth control dispenser and washed down tomorrow's pill with a gulp of water. She liked McGill, but she wasn't ready to have his baby. She used her traveling toothbrush, and when she came out she sat on the edge of the bed, picked up the phone, and called home.

"Hi, Mom, Rusty had something come up with work, and—"

"You're not with Rusty?" her mother asked in her worried tone.

"No, he had to leave, but I ran into some old friends, and I'm going to a party and didn't want you to worry. Rusty's supposed to call in the morning. If I'm not back, tell him not to come before noon."

"You know your father and I don't approve of you staying out all night, young lady."

"Mom, I'm twenty-five years old. I'll see you in the morning."

She hung up, and McGill yelled, "Yahoo!"

They both got under the covers and snuggled up.

"So Jen, what made you decide to stay?"

"I like you, Artie, and I don't know why."

He smiled an impish grin. "Maybe it was the schmaltzy song?"

"I considered that, but I liked you before you sang it."

"Maybe it's the Bird?"

That gave her a giggle. "No, I'm absolutely certain that's not it."

"Then it must be the power thing. Has to be."

"What power thing?"

"Don't you know? Power is the ultimate aphrodisiac."

"That's nonsense. Who says?"

"Henry Kissinger."

"You mean...Nixon's national security advisor?"

"Yeah. The guy looks like a ferret, but he gets dynamite chicks out the wazoo. If he's right, you like me because I work for the White House."

"That's absurd. I despise Nixon."

"Then maybe it's because I can't keep my hands off you. I mean, what good is being as beautiful as you are if you don't let some schmaltzy schmuck like me take you over the moon every once in a while?"

"That doesn't make any sense."

"Sure it does," he said as his hand slid up her side and caressed her breast. "Let me show you...."

Later, McGill ordered filet mignon and champagne from room service, and they sang songs while he played guitar. It was eerie how good they sounded together, how well their voices blended. At eleven, he turned on the TV to catch the news and ball scores. Once again, the lead story was gas lines.

"Jen, you need to get up to speed with the rest of us." He opened his suitcase and handed her a three-ring binder. TOP SECRET screamed off the cover in red letters. "We call this *The Hemp Papers*. We do the research, and DeWolfe edits and types it up for Nixon. Read this, and you'll know everything Nixon knows."

She leafed through. "What would happen if the press got hold of this?"

"If it's before Nixon makes his move, the shit hits the fan. After that, it's proof positive he's right."

"And what about the Bird?"

"You saw how people go nuts over it. If you think what we did today was something, when the *Rolling Stone* ad hits—look out."

"I didn't mean that. I mean what happens when it comes out that you work for Nixon?"

"There's no reason it has to."

"Artie, be realistic. Even if Rusty doesn't bring the cops or a TV crew tomorrow, he knows what you look like, he has your voice on tape, and he has the flyers with your address. I know him, he's relentless. If he really thinks this could be his big break, he'll track you down. And if the Bird sells like you think it will, it's going to be a big story anyway, so somebody is bound to find out, even if it isn't him. If you ask me, your days at the White House are numbered."

She turned on the light by her side of the bed and opened the binder while he watched a late movie. Soon he was asleep, but she kept reading, getting angrier and angrier at how the one plant which could have already saved the country from the oil industry, OPEC, deforestation, and untold pollution, had been criminalized and the truth about its history and its uses suppressed. This was big. It really could change the world. She vowed to put aside her antipathy toward Nixon and do whatever she could—lie to her boss, distract Limbergh—anything she could do, she would do it.

It was four-thirty when she turned off the light. Next thing she knew, there was a *rap-rap-rapping* on the door. The clock read seven-thirty.

"Hey McGill, it's me." *Rap-rap-rap.* "Come on, man, open up."

"Cool your jets," McGill called as he got out of bed. He locked *The Hemp Papers* in his suitcase, put on his cut-offs, and opened the door.

Vince came in, bags under his eyes. "Man, those chicks wore me out. Hey, who's your friend?"

"Vince, I'd like to introduce Jenny. Jenny, this is my partner, Vince."

"Hello there," Vince said. "You're right, McGill, she does kind of look like that chick on *The Avengers*."

McGill said, "We've got a problem…."

She showered while McGill filled Vince in. Room service brought three breakfasts, and they discussed alternatives. The old plan had been to work the booth till late afternoon, and for McGill to take Vince to the airport while Tommy and Becky closed up.

"You should just clear out, Artie," she told them. "You've made a lot of money. A bird in the hand is worth two in the bush. No pun intended."

He gave her a half-smile. "Ten grand is a lot of money to walk away from because the Douche of Pittsburgh has a bug up his butt."

"And I'm not about to chicken out because some asshole has a TV camera," Vince said.

"But what if he brings the police to arrest you?" she said.

"But what if he doesn't?" McGill said. "Besides, they've got nothing."

"Artie, they don't need anything."

When it was time for her to go, they had still reached no conclusion. McGill took her downstairs, and as the cabbie held the door, he put his hands on her shoulders and whispered, "In case you haven't noticed, Jennifer Marie Abruzzi, I'm crazy about you."

"I like you too, Artie. Whatever happens, be careful."

———————————

"So do you think we should bail?" Vince asked when McGill came back.

"No. We know he's not coming till after twelve, and probably not till after two. So I say we cut our prices in half, sell everything we can, and clear out early. We'll still do okay money-wise, and we'll avoid any problems."

"I don't get it," Vince said. "All this time you been telling me the Bird's legit, and now we got the cops on our case."

"It is legit. But it's not worth dealing with cops. Even if we win, we lose."

"Let's roll one and think about it," Vince said. "Where's your stash?"

"Top drawer. I'm going to take a shower."

When he came out of the bathroom, Vince had a joint ready to burn and was looking at the photos from the Fort Pitt envelope.

"What the hell you think you're doing?" McGill said. "Nobody said you could look in my stuff."

Vince was stunned. "Sorry man, too late now. This one's cool. Is that you with Bob Hope and Bing Crosby at a baseball game?"

"Yeah, the 1960 Series, when we beat the Yankees. That's my dad and my grandfather. My dad knew Hope in the war and ran into him."

"Man, were you ever a dork. How old were you?"

"Seventh grade."

Vince held up a photo of him with the baseball. "You catch a foul ball?"

"Yeah. Mickey Mantle hit it."

"Wow, Mickey Mantle. Is that cool, or *what*?" He shuffled the photos to the next shot. "What's with the girl with the towel?"

"It's full of ice. The ball I caught knocked her out."

"You knocked her out?"

"No. She didn't duck, and the ball carried my glove into her face. If I hadn't been there, it would have hit her dead on."

"Far out. It must be worth a lot."

"I don't have it."

"You sell it?"

"No. I gave it to her after the game."

"You caught a Mickey Mantle foul ball at the World Series…and fucking gave it away? Are you crazy?"

"It seemed like the right thing to do at the time."

Vince held up a photo of him sitting beside Jenny and her binoculars. "Is that the same girl with the towel?"

"Yeah. Right before she got hit."

Vince looked closely. "She looks a little like that chick you had here this morning."

McGill was dying to tell somebody. "It is her."

"But…didn't you say you just met?"

"Yeah. Her boss assigned her to work with me."

"I don't get it. You knew her, but you didn't know her?"

"I went to her house and saw a ball on a stand with Mantle's autograph and a plaque saying it was from the World Series. Right next to it was a picture of her with Bing Crosby. I about shit, so I asked her mother. She said if it hadn't been for the kid next to her catching the ball, she could have been killed."

"Man, what great karma. No wonder you got laid."

"That had nothing to do with it."

"You mean…she doesn't know?"

"No. And don't you dare say anything. Promise?"

"Okay, I guess. But why?"

"I don't want it to influence how she feels about me."

"Are you nuts? You've got to tell her. You owe it to her."

"I want her to like me for who I am today, not for something that happened when we were kids."

"Man, you are *warped*. You got a fancy law degree, and you think you're oh-so-cool because you work at the White House, but when it comes to chicks you are one dumb mother. Now listen up, McGill, and listen up good—you can't think like *you* think with chicks, you gotta think like *they* think. I'm tellin' you, if you don't tell her, and tell her soon, you'll blow the whole thing."

Chapter 36

Best Laid Plans

HER MOM AND DOM WERE ON THE FRONT PORCH SWING, STILL WEARING their Sunday best. Her mom was drilling him on his catechism like she had her when she was Dom's age, a long, tedious hour every Sunday after mass.

"Hi, Aunt Jenny," Dom said as she came up the steps.

"Hi, Dom. My, don't you look handsome in a suit and tie."

"I guess," he said without enthusiasm. Her mom scowled at her. "Father Zyhowski asked about you this morning, Jennifer. You haven't been to mass or confession even once since you've been home. No doubt you have a lot to confess from last night alone."

"Mom, I don't have to account to you for what I do any more."

Her mom muttered something about accounting to God as Dom watched with a puzzled expression.

"Say, Dom," Jenny said, "do you think I could borrow that record Rusty gave you yesterday?"

"Sure!" and he zoomed inside, eager for an excuse to get away.

She attached the 45-rpm spindle to her record player and put on "Go! Susannah" with the volume low. Allman's soulful slide-guitar interpretation of Stephen Foster's spirited melody was destined to become a rock classic. But Morrison's lyrics told the tale of Leary's escape and Susannah's disappearance, and she had a deep foreboding her life was about to change. How long would it be before some *Rolling Stone* reporter tracked down rock's new mystery girl?

She set the changer-arm to replay the record, lay down on her bed, and listened to it a few times, thinking how strange it was to have not just one, but two songs written for her—Morrison's so edgy, so hip, so cool; McGill's, so earnest, so sincere, so…schmaltzy.

Next thing she knew her mom was shaking her by the shoulder. "Jenny, dear, wake up. Jennifer. How can you sleep with that awful noise going?"

"Oh my. What time is it, Mom?"

"It's almost twelve-thirty."

"Oh no! Rusty will be here any minute," and she got right up.

"No, he phoned to say he won't be here until after one."

"Why didn't you tell me? I needed to talk to him."

"I called up the stairs, and when you didn't answer, I told him you must be in the bathroom. He said to tell you he's going to pick up somebody at the airport, and that everything is a go. What did he mean by that?"

A shot of fear tingled up her spine—was he picking up his drug agent friend? "Oh, Mom, you know Rusty. It could be anything."

She went to her parents' room to use the upstairs phone to call McGill. There was no answer, and she guessed he had ignored her advice and was in the booth selling Birds. "I'd like to leave a message," she told the clerk. "Please write: Big brother is definitely coming. And underline *definitely*."

Outside, it was clouding up. With luck it would rain and wash out the fair. She switched on her radio, but the forecast said the rain would not move in until tonight. At one-fifteen she heard a screech of tires and looked out to see a WDTO News van. The side door rolled open and Limbergh hopped out. She called from her window, "Be right down, Rusty."

"Hurry," he shouted. "We're meeting the police in twenty minutes."

"The police!" called her mom's worried voice from the porch below.

"Actually, they're federal agents from the D.E.A.," Limbergh said.

"Oh, Rusty, I don't like the sound of that," said her mom. "You're not taking Jenny anywhere dangerous, are you?"

"We call it a 'ride along' in the news business, Mrs. A," Limbergh said. "It's perfectly safe."

Jenny rushed to the phone and tried McGill one more time. No luck. She asked the clerk if he had picked up her first message. No.

When she came out, Limbergh was next to the van talking with a man with a bushy mustache, wearing a suit and a fedora hat. As she approached, the man removed his hat, revealing a completely bald cranium that made him look for all the world like a mustachioed cue ball. The bald head, the mustache...where had she seen him before?

Limbergh did the introductions. "Jennifer Abruzzi, Grayson Gridley."

Oh my God...it was the man who led the raid on the chateau! Could he recognize her as Susannah? Oh God.

They climbed into the van and sat in the rear bench seat, her by the window, Limbergh in the middle, and Gridley on the end. Limbergh introduced the soundman, who was driving, and the cameraman, who was riding shotgun.

Gridley was eyeing her as they drove away. "Have we met before,

Miss Abruzzi? You look very familiar."

She was shuddering, scared. "I'm sure I'd remember if we had."

The soundman looked in his rearview mirror and asked, "Say, aren't you the same guy who's after Timothy Leary?"

Oh God no, please, don't let them talk about Leary. Not now.

"I've been on his case since 1963," Gridley said.

"What was he doing way back then?" the soundman asked.

"He was up to no good," Gridley said.

Before she knew it, the dumbest thing she ever said in her life popped out of her mouth. "I didn't know being up to no good was a violation of the penal code, Mr. Gridley." She must be crazy.

Gridley laughed. "I like this girl, Rusty. You're coming up in the world." He stared at her again. "Are you sure we haven't met?"

Limbergh put his arm around her shoulder. "Everybody says Jenny looks familiar. I think it's because she looks so much like Natalie Wood."

Gridley studied her face even harder. "No, I'd say she's closer to Audrey Hepburn."

She felt herself blushing, a combination of fear and embarrassment.

The cameraman asked, "So, Mr. Gridley, what are you going to arrest these people for?"

Gridley took a Bird from a pocket. "For this," and he turned it over and pointed to the U.S. Government engraving under the tail. "They're turning equipment made for America's fighting forces into dope paraphernalia." He pinched the Bird's beak open and closed a few times and looked at the stamp on the bottom. "Made by genuine hippies my ass."

"But roach clips are legal, aren't they?" said the soundman.

"Not for long," Gridley said with a sneer. "I've got legislation in the hopper to put a stop to it."

"But if it's not illegal yet," the cameraman said, "what will you arrest them for?"

"I've got a federal John Doe right here," Gridley said as he tapped his inside suit-coat pocket, "for theft of government property."

Theft? What was he talking about? Most of the Birds they sold yesterday had been stamped U.S. Government, but she hadn't thought to ask McGill where he got them. She asked, "What makes you think they're stolen, Mr. Gridley?"

"The fact they have so many is probable enough cause for me."

"But what if they bought them legally?" she said. "At an Army-Navy store, or a Goodwill?"

"So what? All that matters is I've convinced a judge to issue a warrant. If we don't get 'em on that, we'll get 'em on something else. Rusty's right about this thing," he said as he held up the Bird. "We've got a national story on our hands if we play it right. It's a god-send in the war on drugs."

The soundman asked, "You with the F.B.I.?"

"No. I'm director of the O.N.O."

"Never heard of it," said the cameraman.

"Stands for Office of Narcotics Operations," Gridley said. "We strategize policy for the F.B.I., the D.E.A., the I.N.S., Customs, all of 'em."

"What is the D.E.A., anyway?" the cameraman said. "I'd never heard of it before either, and now it's all over the news."

"It's the Drug Enforcement Administration," Gridley said. "I convinced Nixon to merge the Narcotics Bureau and some other agencies under a single roof. We're taking a whole new legal approach under the Controlled Substances Act."

"What's different about it?" the cameraman asked.

"It used to be to ban a drug we'd have to get Congress to pass a tax on it to get around the crap in the Constitution," Gridley said. "It didn't make a drug illegal, just taxed the hell out of it. Worked fine until Leary got the Supreme Court to declare it unconstitutional. He won that round, but he forced us to come up with a whole new approach with the Controlled Substances Act. Now when we put a drug on Schedule One, that's that...it's over. In the long run, Leary did us a favor."

"So if Leary won," said the cameraman, "why is he on the run?"

"From a different conviction," Gridley said.

"Did he really get thirty years for two roaches?" the cameraman asked.

"He got off easy," Gridley said.

"Was the evidence really planted?" the soundman asked.

Gridley chuckled, gave Limbergh a wink, and said, "I wasn't in on that one, but cops never plant evidence."

"What exactly is Schedule One?" asked the cameraman.

"The highest prohibited level," Gridley said. "A drug on Schedule One has no medical or scientific value."

"Who decides what gets on it?" the cameraman asked.

Gridley smirked. "The D.E.A. takes care of everything, so no pansy-assed science boys can come along with their bullshit, like shrinks pretending LSD works in therapy, or quacks who claim pot helps cancer patients. With this new system, we'll win the war on drugs in no time."

"Are you saying science doesn't matter, Mr. Gridley?" Jenny asked.

"When it comes to drugs, Miss Abruzzi, if the D.E.A. says the sun rises in the west, as a legal matter, the sun rises in the west. There is no appeal."

"So why," said the soundman, "would a big-shot like you come all the way from Washington to make a small-time arrest?"

"Publicity," Gridley said. "When Rusty told me this piece of shit had U.S. Government on it, I knew we had a winner. And I was coming up here for a conference next week, anyway, so the timing's perfect."

They parked in the VIP lot. Five men in suits were smoking cigarettes near the entrance. At a convention of insurance agents they would have blended in, but at a New Age fair they stood out like cops on horseback.

"Who's in charge?" Gridley said.

"Ashkopf, Assistant Regional Director," one said. He was about her age, with a close-cropped crew-cut and a rectangular face that looked like it had never once broken into a smile.

"This is Rusty Limbergh and his crew, and this is his girlfriend," Gridley said. "He tipped us, so he gets the exclusive."

She winced at being described as anybody's girlfriend, but kept quiet.

"What's the target?" Ashkopf asked.

Gridley passed around a Bird and a flyer. "This is what the perps are up to. Check the engraving under the tail."

"Would you look at this piece of shit."

"They're asking for it."

"What's the charge?"

"The warrant says theft of government property," Gridley said, "but that's just for starters. We're going to make this a high-profile case, so no rough stuff on-camera unless we can get them to start it. Save it for the ride to the lock-up. And no visible marks."

As the agents huddled, Limbergh moved close to her and wrapped his arm around her waist. "Isn't this exciting, Jennifer?"

She removed his arm and stepped away. "I'm not thrilled, Rusty. You're harassing these people and maybe ruining their lives just to get publicity. You have no evidence the forks are stolen."

His eyes widened in disbelief. "But Jennifer, look what they're doing."

"So what? It's not illegal."

"Hey, Rusty," Gridley said, beckoning them over to view a map of the fair's layout. "We'll station men here and here in case they make a run for it. Give us a five-minute head start, then you go in with your camera and piss them off as bad as you can. If you can get 'em worked up enough, maybe they'll resist arrest when we make our move."

The agents prowled off like a pack of wolves. Limbergh checked his watch, lit a cigarette, tucked in his shirt, and adjusted his tie. "How do I look, Jennifer?"

All she could bring herself to say was, "Very professional, Rusty."

When five minutes was up, Limbergh took a last heavy drag, ground out his butt with his shoe, and said, "Let's go bust some druggies."

As they trekked through the crowd, it felt as though someone were inside her stomach trying to saw his way out with a rough-toothed pruning saw. When they were two aisles from the booth, Gridley came charging around the corner. "Have you seen them?"

"No," Limbergh said. "Why?"

"They're gone. The booth is empty."

Limbergh was crestfallen. "Gone?"

"Could they have been tipped off?" Gridley said.

Uh, oh...would they suspect her?

"No way," Limbergh said. "Nobody but us knew."

Gridley questioned vendors in the adjacent booths, who said the Bird people had cut their prices, sold out their inventory, and left an hour ago.

Jenny smothered a grateful sigh as Limbergh screamed, "Sold out!" and stomped around like a kid in a tantrum. "God fucking dammit!"

"It's not over yet," Gridley said. They followed him to the administration tent, where he burst in and flashed his badge at a woman behind a desk. "I want answers—now! What do you have on the people in the booths?"

The woman's face turned white as milk. "You mean...the vendors?"

Gridley practically accused her of criminal complicity. "Who the hell else would I mean?"

"All we have is a standard contract," the woman said, and with shaky hands she pulled a brown accordion file from a cabinet.

Gridley ripped the papers out of the "B" slot. "Here it is. BirdCo, Inc. Vincent Wright, President. Same PO box as the flyer. No phone. Ashkopf, call the Oakland office and tell them to get on it. And get the locals here to check hotels and flights for anybody named Wright. The perps are still here...I can smell 'em."

Ashkopf picked up a phone as Gridley threatened the woman. "If you know what's good for you, you'll tell me all about them."

The frightened creature couldn't spit it out fast enough. "Somebody called about a booth, and I said we just had a cancellation, and he said he'd take it and came by Friday to pay, and I swear that's all I know."

"What did they look like? What were they wearing?"

"I only saw one man. He was tall, very tan, and had long blonde hair. Oh, and he had a green-and-yellow baseball cap."

"That's the dirt bag with the welding torch," Limbergh said.

Outside a loudspeaker announced: "And here they are, the Steel City's own good-time rock-and-rollers…Tommy James and the Shondells."

Limbergh had a worried look on his face. "Grayson, is it okay if we go check out the band? If I don't get some kind of story, my producer will nail me to the wall."

Gridley looked at his watch. "Go ahead. It'll take a while to turn up any leads. And if you see 'em, come get me right away."

They cut through the vendor parking area and passed a red pick-up with a tarp over the bed and a sign on the door: *McGill Motors.*

She let out a gasp, stumbled, and nearly fell to the ground.

Limbergh grabbed her arm and said, "Are you okay, Jennifer?"

"I just tripped. I'm fine, thanks."

But fine she wasn't. Her insides felt like a chunk of mozzarella being grated up for pizza topping. Why hadn't they cleared out? How could McGill be so stupid?

Several thousand people were on the grass in a semi-circle around the stage, and the sweet fragrance of pot filled the air. Limbergh tapped the cameraman's shoulder and pointed to a guy using a Bird to pass a roach. "Anytime you see some asshole using one of those things, shoot 'em, but don't let 'em know. We'll make a story out of this yet."

There was safety in numbers, and no one in the crowd seemed the least bit concerned about the police, who were nowhere to be seen.

Half an hour later Gridley came looking for them. "The perp's got a seven o'clock flight to San Francisco. We'll nail them at the airport."

Limbergh checked his watch and told his crew, "Saddle up, boys."

She had to warn McGill. As they started to leave, she pulled Limbergh aside and said, "Rusty, I don't feel well. It must be the heat. And I've had enough cops and robbers for one day. I'll just stay here and listen to the music and take a bus home."

"But this could be my big break. It could mean *Sixty Minutes.*"

"Rusty, I don't want to spend my day off at the airport."

Limbergh pleaded, begged, cajoled, but she held firm. Finally, he gave up and said, "I'll call you later."

"No, please don't. If I'm not there, you'll just make my mom worry. We'll talk tomorrow."

She made a point of not wishing him luck, and when she was sure they'd gone she hurried to McGill's room at the hotel.

Vince opened the door and greeted her with an angry, "Do you know how much we lost thanks to your douchebag friend? Five grand. At least!"

"You're lucky you got out or you'd be on your way to jail," she told them. "There were six federal agents ready to haul you away, and Rusty had a camera crew to put it on TV. And they got your name from the contract you signed," she said, looking at Vince. "They know the flight you're on and went to the airport to arrest you when you try to board."

Vince gaped, open-mouthed.

"Why do they want us so bad?" Tommy said. "We're not hurting anybody."

"Because you're making roach clips," she said.

"But it's legal," McGill insisted. "How can they arrest us?"

"They have a federal warrant for theft of government property. They say you stole forks from the military."

"But that's nuts!" McGill yelled as he waved his hands in the air like a wild man. "I bought them from government surplus. We have receipts and everything."

McGill did not have a clue what he was up against. "Artie, if it wasn't this they'd have trumped up some other charge, corrupting minors or something. Rusty and the agent think having U.S. Government on the Bird makes it a national story. The agent wants to use it to publicize a law he's pushing to make selling paraphernalia a felony. They think they can turn the Bird into a kind of poster child for the war on drugs."

"Boy," Tommy said with a grin, "I bet they'd really shit their pants if they knew about that *Rolling Stone* ad you have coming out."

Vince bleated like a pregnant goat as he threw himself in a heap on a chair. "Somebody roll a fattie and gimme a beer. Fucking narcs!"

"Gee, it's almost like the Bird is too cool for your own good," Becky said as she reached into the ice bucket and handed Vince a beer. "I guess this means you won't be getting rich quick after all, huh?"

A pall of deflation filled the room, and the future seemed as foreboding as the flashing black thunderhead on the horizon which was pushing up the Ohio valley. Fairgoers in the park below began streaming out ahead of the approaching storm.

"We should get our stuff out to the truck and under the tarp if we don't want to get soaked," Tommy said as he looked out the window.

McGill opened the gym bag and dumped the rubber-banded money on the bed: sixteen bundles of a thousand dollars each. He divided them up: $6,000 to him; $6,000 to Vince; $2,000 to Tommy; $1,000 to Becky.

Becky was thrilled. "A thousand dollars! This is more than I'll make all summer making milkshakes at the Dairy Shack."

"So…McGill, you're the idea man," Vince said as he stuffed his money in his backpack. "What do we do about the fucking narcs?"

McGill forced a smile. "We'll go to Plan B."

"Yeah, B for bullshit," Vince said, radiating gloom and doom.

"Look on the bright side, man," McGill said. "We've got plenty of cash to work with, and the Bird's not illegal yet. We just need time to think. First thing we do is change your reservation to a later flight. If they really want us, they'll hang at the airport expecting you to show, so at least we won't have to worry about them until tomorrow."

"Pin 'em down," Vince said, brightening as he reached for the phone. "Yeah, that's good, McGill."

"Don't call from here," McGill said. "We'll find a pay phone. Now, let's think this through. They'll get your home address from the airline, so I figure they'll be knocking on your mom and dad's door early tomorrow."

"We caught a break there," Vince said. "They're camping up in Idaho. But what about you? Your name's on the incorporation papers, the country license, and the trademark application."

"All they've got is the PO box," McGill said. "And the phone at bungalow isn't listed. They'll need a subpoena to get it, and it'll take them a while to check out every Arthur McGill in Northern California. Besides, if they go knocking at my door, there won't be anybody there."

"Susie could be," Vince said. "She's been staying with me."

McGill said, "You mean she's there now?"

"Maybe. She's supposed to pick me up at the airport tonight."

"We have to get hold of her and tell her to get out," McGill said. "Tell her we'll pay for a motel. Where are the forks I shipped you?"

"In Dad's shop."

"And when does the Rolling Stone ad hit?" McGill asked.

"Two weeks from tomorrow," Vince said.

"That means we'll be getting orders in about three weeks," McGill said. "Okay, first things first. Jen, you know the city. We need a place with a pay phone where we can talk in private. Somewhere where lawyers do deals."

"Gilson's Steak House, on Market Square," she said.

Tommy and Becky took their things to the truck while she, McGill and Vince made the ten-minute walk to the newly-renovated historic square and took a booth with high-backed oak benches. McGill ordered a pitcher of Rolling Rock and a triple-order of nachos. Jenny waited for Tommy and Becky while McGill and Vince used the phones in the back.

Vince was all smiles when they returned. "Everything's covered. Susie'll take McGill's van, pick up the forks at the shop, and hang out in Santa Cruz until I get back."

"And we changed Vince's flight to ten-fifteen," McGill said with a chuckle in his voice. "I'd love to see their faces when he doesn't show."

Despite the money bulging in their pockets, there was no celebration. Jenny was impressed at how McGill was able to bolster their spirits. "We need to keep our cool," he told them. "We have problems, sure, but we haven't done anything illegal. They haven't held hearings on a change in the law, and they don't know about the ad. By the time they get the law changed, we'll have a bank account in the Bahamas and have Birds made in Hong Kong. The thing now is to lay low until the checks start rolling in. We have three weeks, plenty of cash, and a big advantage."

"Advantage?" Vince said. "What kind of advantage?"

"They don't know we know they're after us."

"So what do we do while we're laying low?" Vince asked. "And how am I gonna get back? And what do I do when I get there? I won't be able to use Dad's shop if they're watching it."

A quirky smile came over McGill's face. "Why not drive back?"

"To California?" Vince said, confused.

"Sure. We'll buy you a truck and make it a portable shop. You can take your time, see the country, make Birds and sell them at flea markets along the way. Tommy can go with you."

Tommy lit up like a Christmas tree. "You want me to go to California?"

"Vince is going to need a lot of help, and you're great with a torch. We'll have to come up with an excuse for Mom and Dad, though. Does Dad have anything on the used-car lot like my camper van?"

"A GMC with a camper-shell came in last month. It's got a stove and a fridge and a double-bunk. I think it runs pretty good."

"What about forks?" Vince said. "We used up all the ones I brought."

"Scrounge at Goodwills on the way," McGill said.

"But what about the bases?" Vince said. "We can't scrounge those."

"This is steel country," Tommy said. "We'll find a scrap pile of slugs in about two minutes."

Plan B evolved over dinner. Vince would go to Milltowne with Tommy, who would talk their father into selling his "friend from college" a camper at a good price and concoct a reason for riding out to California with him. They would scrounge forks, make Birds and sell at flea markets around Chicago and Denver. By the time they got to California, McGill would have figured out a way to deal with the narcs.

All things considered, she thought McGill had devised a pretty good, seat-of-his-pants Plan B. After dinner they said good-bye to the others, McGill put the umbrella up, and they walked arm-in-arm through the warm and rainy summer evening to the hotel.

"So will you stay the night, Jen?" he asked. "I have the meeting with Nixon in the morning, and I don't know when I'll be back."

"I can't, Artie. Tomorrow's a workday, and all my things are at home."

He checked at the desk for messages, and the clerk handed him a Western Union telegram. He read it over and showed it to her:

NIXON INSPECTING MIDWEST FLOODS. STOP.
MEETING POSTPONED. STOP.
WAIT FOR INSTRUCTIONS. STOP.
                                  DUBERMAN

"Does this mean you're not leaving in the morning?" she said.

"I don't know. I have no idea what Mr. Dubious has in mind."

"Mr. Dubious?"

He tapped his finger to the name on the telegram. "Rudy Duberman, my other boss. DeWolfe hung it on him after he grabbed her ass one time. She took him to his knees in a judo hold and twisted his ear like in a Three Stooges movie. Funniest thing you ever saw."

They agreed to meet for an early breakfast in the coffee shop. Before taking a taxi home, she went to his room, where they smoked a joint and sang a few songs. She asked him to sing the schmaltzy song he wrote for her, and when he finished he put down the guitar and pulled her close....

Chapter 37

Into the Fire

THE SHINY BLACK MACK TRUCK THE C.I.A. AGENTS DELIVERED TO THE meadow early Monday morning had *Potomac Freightways* in fancy gold script on the doors and a chrome bulldog ornament on the hood. Catherine had often heard the expression *like getting run over by a Mack truck*, but this Mack was extra special. Besides a sleeping rack, mini-fridge, and stove, it had bullet-proof windows and tires, a titanium alloy grill and bumper for ramming barricades, and its cab and fuel tanks were made of quarter-inch steel that would repel anything short of a bazooka shell. The cab was outfitted with a military-band radio, and secret compartments in the doors came stocked with an arsenal of weapons and spy goodies, including infrared night-vision binoculars, a knockout drug in both aerosol and powdered forms, miniature walkie-talkies, and a variety of bugging and tracking devices. Listening as the agents explained how to use it all was like being in a James Bond movie, when 007 is briefed on the nifty new gadgets he'll have on his mission.

The agents gave them paperwork for their new identities. They were still the Benningtons, Jim and Peggy, but instead of a commodities broker from Chicago and his spendthrift wife, they were now a long-haul husband-and-wife trucking team from Baltimore. Their covers included Maryland drivers licenses and Orioles warm-up jackets and baseball caps. When the agents left they got in, and he started it up to show her how everything worked. "How do you know so much about trucks, Mike?"

"My Uncle Danny has a rig. When I was in high school, I used to ride with him sometimes and spell him at the wheel."

After a passionate good-bye in her tent, they went to the compound gate, where a Secret Service sedan was waiting. It felt awful to leave her Honey Bear, but she had to be sure if she were pregnant.

It was late afternoon when the sedan dropped her on the sidewalk in front of her Georgetown home. She opened the wrought-iron gate and admired her classic red-brick townhouse and its white lattice shutters. What an odd feeling of pride, she thought, having your very own house. The lilac blooms were long gone, but the variety of roses compensated wonderfully. The White House gardeners had done a fine job. She sniffed every variety of rose and picked one of each.

A mailman in postal shorts and a white pith helmet came along. He rummaged in his leather sack and handed her some letters, junk except for a J.C. DeWolfe Trust Fund check. The trustee's letter bragged that this month's twelve-percent increase—to $11,347.83—was the result of his deft insider trading in oil futures made possible by the embargo. Included with the check was her invitation to the Heirs Committee meeting. She was already worried sick about what Mulligan would say when she told him he might be a father, and she hated the notion that her decision about whether to have his baby could be clouded by considerations about the Heirs Committee and the baby's legitimacy. It just wasn't fair.

She and Leary would need cash, so she called her bank and told them to have $1,000 ready in twenties and $10,000 in hundreds. She phoned the local N.O.W. chapter for a referral to a gynecologist and made an appointment at a women's clinic for "Mrs. Smith" that very evening.

She mulled over the plan, which had changed a little since Mulligan first proposed it. Now she was to fly to Pittsburgh Wednesday morning, rent a car, drive to the Somerset turnpike exit and register at the Cloverleaf Motel next to the Pitt Stop Truck Plaza. Mulligan would arrive around noon with Leary in the secret compartment. They would sneak Leary into the motel, and Mulligan would continue on to the Air Force Base by himself in the truck. But rather than her driving Leary all the way to Niagara Falls that same afternoon, they decided it would be better to arrive earlier in the day in case they encountered problems. The new plan was for her and Leary to stay in the motel and get a good night's sleep, and at the crack of dawn Peggy Bennington would drive Helga Kaulbeck to Niagara Falls for a one-way ride to freedom on the *Maid of the Mist*.

How odd, she thought, to be flying to, of all places, Pittsburgh— Jenny's home town. Would Jenny be there? She was dying to tell her all about Mulligan and to find out how she was doing after Paris. But how much could either of them say about that? Would Jenny lie to her about being Susannah, or knowing Oskar, or Morrison, or Leary? Would she lie to Jenny? It could be very awkward. Maybe she would just play dumb and only talk about Mulligan and the baby? Yes, of course. Why not fly up a day early and surprise her? She could say she was just passing by on her way to Michigan, and spend time talking with her best friend about becoming a mother.

When she left for work Monday morning, Jenny had pushed the swinging door half-open and called into the kitchen, "Bye Mom, I have an early meeting."

It had rained all night, and the gutters were filled with leaves and twigs swirling in the rushing water. On the bus ride downtown she concluded, very logically, that it was too early to consider what she was feeling as "love," but when she walked into the coffee shop and saw McGill waving to her from a corner table, an unexpected *pang* scrambled her logic.

He pulled out a chair for her and shook her hand as they pretended to be merely colleagues at a breakfast meeting.

"Did you talk to your office?" she asked.

"I called, but Duberman's not in yet. I told the clerk at the desk to page me in here if he calls. So what are you going to do today?"

"If you don't need me, I guess I'll just go to work as usual."

"I definitely need you," and he gently cupped his hands on top of hers.

"I didn't mean like *that*," she said, and quickly withdrew her hands, hoping no one had seen. He could be so corny sometimes.

A waitress took their orders, and moments later a voice directly beside her said, "Why, if it isn't Miss Abruzzi. What a pleasant surprise."

She looked up, saw the bald head and bushy eyebrows, and shivered all over. *Be calm, Jennifer, be calm.* "Oh, Mr. Gridley, you gave me a start. You shouldn't sneak up on people like that."

"Sorry. It's the C.I.A. training. Old habits die hard. So how are you feeling? Rusty said you took ill from the heat yesterday."

"Much better, thank you. But what are you doing here?"

"I'm looking for Mr. McGill," and he extended his hand to him. "Grayson Gridley, of the O.N.O. We met a few weeks ago, at Pachyderm's."

They *knew* each other? Holy cow! She had told McGill that Limbergh's friend was a drug agent, but his name hadn't seemed important.

McGill's face registered panic as he stammered, "Uh, uh....of course. But why are you looking for...*me*?"

"We'll be working together for a few days. Hasn't Duberman told you?"

"All I got was a telegram telling me to wait for instructions."

"Well, consider them delivered. So how do you know Miss Abruzzi?"

"Uh...her boss lent her to me."

Gridley raised an eyebrow. "*Lent* her to you?"

"I'm assisting Mr. McGill in his research," she said.

"I had her jumping through hoops all last week," McGill said, and pointing back-and-forth between her and Gridley, asked, "So…how do you two know each other?"

"We have a mutual friend," Jenny said, conveying in a glance that yes indeed, this is the same agent who tried to arrest you yesterday.

"Sure is a small world sometimes," Gridley said as he pulled up a chair, grabbed a coffee cup from the next table and waved it high in the air, yelling, "Can I get some service over here?"

"Did you catch who you were after, Mr. Gridley?" she asked sweetly.

Gridley's face soured. "Nah. The perp changed flights, then never showed. Wasted a whole damned day for nothing."

She tried her best to appear concerned. "I hope Rusty wasn't too disappointed he didn't get a story."

"He says he has enough footage to do something if his producer gives the okay," Gridley said. "It just won't be as exciting as a live bust."

"So Gridley, what is it we'll be doing?" McGill asked.

"You know that Duberman's been bugging me to arrange an interview with Commissioner Anslinger, right?"

"Yes, but I hadn't heard anything on it," McGill said.

"When opportunity knocks, open the door," Gridley said. "The commissioner and I are speaking at a conference near here this week, and when I found myself up here early, I called to see how he was doing. His housekeeper said he was at the Mayo Clinic and wasn't flying in until today. So I called him there to see if he wanted me to pick him up at the airport, and asked if he'd mind being interviewed on the way. He was all for it. He hasn't had a request from the White House since Ike was President. So I called Duberman and told him to get one of your people on the next flight, and he said you were already here. You can ride along and ask him whatever you want."

"Want me to drive?" McGill asked. "I've got a rental, and Pittsburgh's a tough town if you don't know it. There's an old joke it was laid out by a mountain goat."

"Fine with me," Gridley said.

"So where is it we're going?" McGill asked.

"The Rolling Rock Club," Gridley said. "We'll be staying at the Seven Springs ski resort down the road. Duberman's booked you a room."

"Wow…*Rolling Rock*," McGill said. "What's the conference about?"

"The Mellons got a bug up their butts to pump a hundred million into think-tanks and magazines to bury liberals once and for all. When billionaires like that snap their fingers, they expect people to jump, and God bless 'em, people do. The biggest money-men in the country will be there, along with everybody who's anybody in the movement—Goldwater, Reagan, Buckley, Agnew, Thurmond, Will, Graham—even Nixon. This could be a watershed that changes American politics for generations."

"Nixon's coming *here*?" McGill said.

"He's the keynote speaker," Gridley said. "How about you, Miss Abruzzi? Will you be joining us?"

"*Me*?" she said, shuddering at the thought of spending another second around Gridley.

McGill exploded in enthusiasm. "But of *course* you are! You work for Mellon Bank, right? And this is put on by the Mellons, right? And your boss lent you to me for as long as I need you, right?"

"You'll be a witness to history, Miss Abruzzi," Gridley said.

"I really need you to be there," McGill said. "I'll get Duberman to reserve you a room."

Gridley looked at his watch. "Well, I've got things to do. The commissioner's flight gets in about one. How about if we meet at noon, in front of the hotel. I hope you can make it, Miss Abruzzi."

While Jenny took a taxi home to pack, McGill went to his room, opened his gym bag, took out a $1,000 bundle of twenties and stuffed them in his wallet. He emptied his nearly-empty baggie of Panama Red on to a magazine, rolled the last of it into a fattie, and put it in his inside jacket pocket. He put the Fort Pitt Photo envelope, his sample Birds, *The Hemp Papers*, and the twin tape decks in the gym bag. He went to the car in the parking garage, got in the back, and threaded a microphone cord through the springs under the seat, wedging the mic in tight where it could not be seen. He put in a tape and tested it: "Four score and seven years ago..." He played it back; it was fuzzy, but it was audible. He hid the deck under the driver's seat where he could work the buttons.

Shortly after he returned to his room, the phone rang. "Hello."

"McGill, it's Duberman. Did the drug czar find you?"

"Yes, I saw him at breakfast. He's set me up to interview Anslinger on the way to some conference."

"You're lucky you get to go. If we weren't shorthanded, I'd be up there myself."

"Gridley made it sound like a big deal. And he said Nixon's coming."

"I know. I already asked Haldeman to set up a meeting with him so you can answer his questions, but it's not firmed up."

"So what did Nixon think about Mellon's maid?"

"He left before I could play it for him, so I gave a copy to Bullcannon. He's meeting *Air Force One* in St. Louis and will give it to Nixon there."

"So what did you think about it?" McGill said.

"It's interesting, but it's not the smoking gun he wants."

Duberman didn't get how significant it was, but there was no point in arguing. Nixon would get it. "Any word from Mulligan?"

"No, but Ehrlichman said we're to have a suitcase by the door and be ready to go on a moment's notice. And to pack for outdoor labor."

"Outdoor labor? What's that about?"

"Damned if I know."

He went to the gift shop, bought four packs of batteries and traded two $20 bills for quarters. He set up the second cassette deck in a phone booth in the lobby and called Mulligan's number; a machine picked up.

"You gotta hear this Mulligan and I'm pressed for time. I'm going with Gridley to the Rolling Rock Club to interview Anslinger, and I'll be staying at the hotel at Seven Springs. Hope this works, here goes."

He sat for an hour feeding quarters into the phone while Miss Hattie's interview played into the receiver, then went to his room. At twenty-to-twelve Jenny knocked. She was tense, anxious, wringing her hands.

"Artie, it's really not a good idea for me to be going with you."

He enveloped her in his arms. "It'll be all right, Jen. Gridley has no idea I have anything to do with the Bird. And even if he finds out, he thinks we're just acquaintances."

"Artie, it's not that...you...you don't understand."

"Just keep calling me Mr. McGill around him so he doesn't get suspicious, and everything will be fine."

Jenny was waiting with McGill next to his car under the hotel canopy when Gridley came out, followed by a bellhop with a suitcase and a set of golf clubs. McGill opened the trunk as Gridley said, "I'm meeting somebody. Should be here any time."

A white Plymouth with a whip antenna pulled up. Ashkopf got out of the passenger door, took out a spiral notepad, and said to Gridley,

"Oakland ID'd a Vincent Raymond Wright, twenty-two, six-three, blonde hair, blue eyes, two hundred pounds, ex-Army sergeant, honorable discharge. Works as a carpenter, surfs, lives with his parents. The neighbors say the parents are on a fishing trip in Idaho, and nobody knows where the son is. They want to know if you want the house staked out."

"Affirmative," Gridley said, "but don't make a move without my say-so. What about the others?"

"Nothing yet," Ashkopf said.

Jenny felt the frozen points of a hundred icicles stabbing up from under her skin while McGill listened, seemingly unaffected. When Ashkopf left they got into McGill's car. Gridley sat in back, lit a cigarette, and began spouting off about how hippies were worse than commies and liberal courts were screwing up the country and the Pill was ruining American womanhood and unions caused the recession and nobody had the right to tell God-fearing whites to integrate the races and on and on.

Twenty minutes later they pulled to the ARRIVALS curb at the airport. Gridley flashed his badge at a security guard and said, "Official business. Keep an eye on the car."

They went to the gate, and as the passengers streamed out Gridley said, "Remember, he likes to be called Mr. Commissioner. That's him now."

A hunched figure, propped up by a cane, emerged from the tunnel; at one time he must have stood over six feet tall.

"Mr. Commissioner, it's good to see you again, sir," Gridley said, shaking the old man's hand. "You're looking well."

Anslinger tilted his head as though he were blind in one eye and said in a gruff voice, "You lie as well as you ever did, Grayson. Who are your friends?"

"This is Miss Abruzzi, with Mellon Bank."

"It's an honor, Mr. Commissioner," she said as she held out her hand.

Anslinger removed his hat, revealing a baldpate with a faint trace of gray hair, like a bathtub ring, just above his large, protruding ears, almost like Dumbo, the flying elephant. He took her hand. "My pleasure, Miss."

"And this is Mr. McGill, from the White House," Gridley said. "He wants to interview you about the early days of the Bureau."

"I've heard a lot about you, Mr. Commissioner," McGill said.

The old man had a wary look in his good eye. "I'll just bet you have."

McGill put Anslinger's luggage in the trunk. Jenny rode shotgun, and the drug czars sat in back. As McGill put the key in the ignition, she saw him reach under his seat with his left hand for something. *A tape deck*! He started the engine, simultaneously pressing the RECORD button.

"Mr. Commissioner, sir," McGill said. "Do you want us to drive you to your place in Holidaysburg first, and then back to Rolling Rock?"

"No, I have everything I need. But we have to make a stop downtown at the Keystone Pharmacy, on Smithfield Street. I'm getting low on my morphine. Only take a minute. The clinic already phoned it in."

Gridley was startled. "Morphine, Mr. Commissioner?"

"You get to be my age, Grayson, and things start to fall apart. These days I need it just to get around. But imagine the headlines if my enemies knew: *Narcotics Commissioner on morphine*. But it's like I've always said, opium is the finger of God. It smites, and it heals. It is the gift of heaven when it stills the agonies of death."

"Mr. Commissioner," McGill said, "I've heard rumors Joe McCarthy was addicted to morphine. Do you know anything about that?"

"Some quacks got him hooked when they tried it to cure his drinking. Joe was a boozer, and that's what finally killed him."

"They use morphine to treat alcoholics?" Gridley asked.

"It didn't work on Joe," Anslinger said. "If you ask me, doctors don't know what the hell they're doing. Watch out for do-good doctors in your job, Grayson. They fought me for years. In my book, addicts are criminals, pure and simple, but the damned doctors kept trying to say addiction is a disease, not a crime. Go easy, they'd say. Rehabilitate, they'd say. *Bullshit*, that's what I said. You do drugs to get high, you're a felon and deserve no pity, no mercy. That's what the laws in this county say, and I ought to know, because I wrote them. I showed the damned doctors, for thirty-two years I damn-well showed them. In one year alone I prosecuted three thousand of the bastards for giving drugs to addicts. What they called 'treatment centers' were nothing but morphine cattle troughs. When I started sending their asses to prison, the whole damned A.M.A. shut the hell up and got with my program. I damn sure showed *them*."

She remembered Miss Hattie's description of "Painslinger" as having "a head o' stone and a heart o' ice." She asked him, "Mr. Commissioner, if all addicts are felons, then what was McCarthy?"

"Joe McCarthy was a great man, a true patriot," Anslinger said with admiration. "If it ever got out he was shooting up every day, the commies could have blackmailed him, so I had to supply him myself."

She and McGill grew quiet as the drug czars bantered in the back seat, filling the car with clouds of tobacco smoke and laughing uproariously at how mandatory minimums would lock druggies away forever.

"Mr. Commissioner," Gridley said, "I'd like you to come down to Washington and testify for a new law I want to put through. You carry a lot of weight on The Hill."

"Not like in the old days, Grayson. I can't get anybody to do anything about the damned hippies. Hippies are the biggest threat this country faces, and it's all because of permissive parents, college administrators, pusillanimous judiciary officials, do-gooders, bleeding hearts and new-breed sociologists with fluid notions of morality."

"I couldn't agree more, Mr. Commissioner," Gridley said.

"So what's this new law of yours about, Grayson?" Anslinger asked.

"It'll make it a felony to make, sell, or possess paraphernalia," Gridley said. "I call it the Drug Implements Extermination Act...the DIE Act."

Anslinger laughed. "I like it, Grayson, I really like it."

"Take a look at what these bastards are doing," Gridley said as he pulled a Bird out of his pocket and handed it to Anslinger, pointing to the engraving under the tail. "They're using military forks for smoking dope."

Anslinger glared at The Bird and snarled. "Criminalize 'em, that's the way to go, all right. Turn 'em into felons and throw away the key. That's how I did it. Fear, Grayson, *fear*! Put the fear of God into the bastards. Especially the niggers and Mexicans. Chinks and Japs too. And now there's these white-trash hippies everywhere you look. And if that damned jazz wasn't bad enough, this rock and roll crap is ten times worse."

"Mr. Commissioner," McGill said, "I've read smoking marijuana changes a jazz player's sense of time and lets them slip an extra beat into a measure. Is it true? Is that really how they do it?"

"It's not a theory," Anslinger said as he handed the Bird back to Gridley, "it's a fact. Anybody with half an ear for music can hear it."

McGill was watching in the rearview mirror and asked Gridley, "Mind if I take a look at that thing?"

"Be my guest," Gridley said, and passed the Bird forward.

"Interesting," McGill said as he casually pinched the clip open and shut a few times. "What's it for?"

Chapter 38

Pinocchios

JENNY WAITED WITH MCGILL IN THE CAR WHILE THE TWO DRUG CZARS WENT into the pharmacy. As soon as the door closed, McGill said, "Let's see if it worked." He pulled the cassette deck from under the seat, rewound a bit, and hit PLAY. The voices were muffled, but she could hear everything.

"Not bad," he said. "I'm going to try to get Anslinger to talk without them suspecting what I'm after."

"How will you do that?"

"I haven't the slightest idea. But play along with whatever I do."

She saw the pharmacy door open and said, "Here they come."

"Grayson," Anslinger said as McGill pulled the car into traffic, "I like the way you're going after Leary. Reminds me of me when I was your age."

"I couldn't have done it if you hadn't got the Mellons to pressure their brats to kick him out of that rich-man's playpen."

"Every family has rotten apples, Grayson. Even Mellons. Setting him up like a hippie prince was bad enough, but bankrolling that LSD ring was a criminal enterprise. The Brotherhood of Eternal Love my ass. It's nothing but a hippie mafia."

McGill asked, "Can I ask about your relationship with Andrew Mellon, Mr. Commissioner? Did you know him before he appointed you?"

"I met A.W. when I worked in the Prohibition Bureau and he was Treasury Secretary, but I really got to know him when I started courting my wife, Martha, rest her soul. Her father owned coal and steel companies around Altoona, and he and A.W. were friends from way back. Belonged to all the same clubs. Martha used to play with his daughter, Ailsa, when they were children. She even called him 'Uncle Andy.' Not many could do that. Ailsa was the toast of Washington in the Twenties, and she was always inviting us to their parties."

"Have you been to the Rolling Rock Club before?" McGill asked.

"It's practically my second home. A.W. gave me a lifetime membership when I married Martha. Nothing's as exhilarating as hounds and horses chasing a fox all over hell and gone. I'm too old for that sort of thing now, but I go to the Gold Cup steeplechase every year. Wouldn't miss it."

At the turnpike on-ramp McGill took the ticket from the dispenser, looked at the list of interchanges, and asked, "What's the best exit, Mr. Commissioner? Donegal or Somerset?"

"Donegal's the one," Anslinger said. "Say, do you think we could stop at the Howard Johnson's rest stop for lunch? It's about halfway, and I just love their ice cream. Did you know they have twenty-seven flavors?"

"Anything you want, Mr. Commissioner," Gridley said.

McGill pointed to the gas gauge. "I need to fill up anyway."

"So, Grayson," said the Commissioner, "when are the hearings on this new bill of yours?"

"Right after summer recess," Gridley said as he took the Bird out of his pocket and scowled at it. "And I'm going to use this damned thing to publicize it. We know where one of the perps lives, and when we nab him I'll call a press conference, show this to the world, and get the ball rolling."

"What are you charging them with?" Anslinger said.

"Theft of government property."

"Good, Grayson, good. I like your approach. The government angle plays into your hands. It will keep it in the public eye. That's the way to get this law of yours passed. Publicity, and lots of it. Not like it was for me. I had to sneak mine through."

"Sneak what through, Mr. Commissioner?" McGill asked.

"The Marijuana Tax Act," Anslinger said. "Nobody challenged it for thirty years until that bastard Leary came along. I think it still holds the record for the shortest hearings ever held on a piece of major legislation."

"Sounds exciting, Mr. Commissioner," McGill said. "Can you tell us how you did it?"

"This is off the record, isn't it?" Anslinger asked.

"Oh, yes sir, Mr. Commissioner," McGill assured him. "Abso*lutely.*"

"Well, when A.W. split narcotics off from the Prohibition Bureau and made me commissioner, I only had about three hundred agents, not like that bastard Edgar over at the F.B.I. He had thousands. My job was to enforce the laws against heroin and cocaine and so forth, but with the Depression Congress wanted to cut my budget, so I had to find something new to go after. So I went around giving speeches, doing interviews, and testifying before state legislatures about how it turned the lower races into rapists and killers, and made white women easy prey for niggers. I did everything I could to scare the shit out of people over it. Fear's the key to your job, Grayson. *Fear.* It's fear that gets the job done."

"I agree completely," Gridley said. "But I'm curious. What do you mean about sneaking it through? And how did you do it?"

"Well, everybody in law enforcement had been looking for a way to keep Tommy guns out of the hands of the mobs. Al Capone, Dutch Schultz, Machine Gun Kelly, Saint Valentine's Day Massacre and all that. So Congress put a whopping tax on machine guns, and anybody who didn't pay went to the slammer. It was a whole new way to use the tax powers, but nobody knew if the Supreme Court would let it stand. But if it did, I knew it would open up the same approach to go after druggies. So I worked up a bill, and when the Court said the tax was Constitutional, I had our friends introduce it in the House two weeks later."

"It sounds like something out of a spy novel," McGill said.

"In a way it was," Anslinger said. "A law like that should have been considered by the Judiciary Committee, but they knew too much about criminal laws, and I didn't want them asking questions and rewriting it. Since on its face it was a tax law, and the chairman of Ways and Means was a friend of ours, I had him hold the hearings. I testified it was the most dangerous drug known to man, showed my gore file from the Hearst papers I'd been collecting, and gave them the best lines from my speeches."

"What kind of lines?" McGill asked. "Can you give us an example?"

Anslinger heaved a wistful sigh and smiled. "Oh, I used to be so good at this." He made a fist, punctuating his oratory like he was at a podium: "*If the hideous monster Frankenstein ever came face to face with the monster of marijuana, he would drop dead of fright.* They ate it up. Every time."

"Did you present any scientific evidence?" Jenny asked.

"Yes, of course," Anslinger said. "A pharmacologist friend of mine from Temple University, Dr. Munch, testified he'd injected the active ingredient into the brains of three hundred dogs, and two of them died."

"Ouch!" McGill said with a grin as he thumped the side of his head with the heel of his hand, "that had to hurt," but his joke fell flat.

She tried to help. "So why did he use dogs instead of something else, monkeys...or rats?"

Anslinger chuckled. "Somebody on the committee asked him if he used dogs because their minds worked like humans, but Munch said he wasn't a dog psychologist. He got a good laugh out of that one."

Everyone chuckled, and Jenny asked, "So how did injecting the dogs make him an expert?"

"You have to understand, Miss, he was all the science I had. I didn't know the active ingredient wouldn't even be identified until years later."

"So what did he give to the dogs?" McGill asked.

"I have no idea," Anslinger said.

"But what about doctors?" Jenny said. "Wouldn't they have known about the medical effects?"

"Their lobbyist came in at the last minute bitching and moaning they'd only learned about the hearing two days before. I can still hear him whining, 'The American Medical Association knows of no evidence that marijuana is a dangerous drug.' He went on and on about how the word marijuana was what he called a 'mongrel' word, and how the medical profession had all sorts of uses for what they called 'cannabis.' One of my friends on the committee put him in his place: 'Doctor, if you can't say something good about what we are trying to do, why don't you go home?' Then another told him: 'Doctor, if you haven't got something better to say than that, we are sick of hearing you.'"

"Ha ha!" Gridley laughed.

"It was beautiful, Grayson," Anslinger said. "You'd have loved it."

"But why were they so rude to a doctor?" Jenny asked.

"Because doctors are Republicans, and by that time Congress was run by New Deal Democrats. He was their Washington mouthpiece and was always testifying against New Deal bills. They really were sick of him."

"Who else testified, Mr. Commissioner?" McGill asked.

"I had people come in from the rope, paint, and birdseed industries. The rope people said they could use Manila hemp from the Philippines, so they didn't care if we banned it. And the paint people said they didn't care any more because DuPont had a new synthetic drying agent. Only the birdseed people had a problem. Some damn thing in the seeds makes birds sing and keeps their feathers shiny, so I gave them an exemption if they denatured the seeds so they couldn't germinate."

"Mr. Commissioner," McGill asked, "why did you ask those industries to testify, but not the doctors?"

"Because they said it had been in the *U.S. Pharmacopoeia* since 1860 and was the most widely-prescribed medicine of the last century. I said bullshit to that, and in 1942 I made them take it out. Oh, here it comes," Anslinger said as he peered out his window. "Don't forget to stop."

They all looked out and read the green and white turnpike sign:

HEMPFIELD SERVICE PLAZA
2 MILES

"We played Hempfield for the West Penn championship my senior year," McGill said. "Milltowne 21, Hempfield 17. My buddy Mulligan caught the winning touchdown on the last play of the game. You met him, Mr. Gridley, that time in Pachyderm's. He was the guy in the Navy uniform."

They drove into the plaza with its handsome gray fieldstone building, which like all the others on the nation's first super-highway was in the classic style of early-American roadside inns. McGill pointed to the long line of cars waiting to gas up. "Why don't you go in and get a table while I fill up? Order me a hamburger, fries and a lemonade, will you, Miss Abruzzi?"

He dropped them at the door and drove toward the pumps. She assumed he would use the opportunity to check his recorder and maybe put in a new tape. Fifteen minutes later he joined them as lunch was being served. When the waitress returned for the dessert order, McGill asked her, "Ma'am, I'm curious. How come this rest-area is called Hempfield?"

"I guess because it's in Hempfield Township."

"Is there a big field of hemp around here somewhere?"

"Why, I don't even know what it is," the waitress said. "I think it was big back in pioneer days or something."

On Anslinger's recommendation they ordered double-scoop ice cream cones to go. She got bing-cherry and her favorite, chocolate fudge ripple. McGill brought the car around and picked them up in front of the door, and just before they pulled away, he pointed to the blue HEMPFIELD lettering above the entrance and asked, "Mr. Commissioner, is it true hemp and marijuana are just different names for the same thing?"

Anslinger frowned, obviously annoyed. "Forget about hemp, young man. It just confuses people, gets them all bollixed up. You know when I got the Bureau started there were some exhibits at the Smithsonian that talked about hemp being used for rope, and for Betsy Ross' flag, and canvas for clipper ships and Conestoga wagons, and for printing the Constitution, and for this and for that. They even claimed Washington and Jefferson grew it. Well, I got that crap the hell out of there in a hurry, you bet your sweet ass I did. Every last bit of it. Today, there is not one shred of evidence in the Smithsonian that hemp ever existed in America. Not a *shred*. And I got it the hell out of Mount Vernon and Monticello too."

"Mr. Commissioner," McGill said, "were you aware of a movement back in the Thirties to make paper from hemp by-products?"

"Oh yes," Anslinger said. "A.W. talked about the hemp problem all the time. The Mellons and DuPonts had been keeping an eye on it since before the First World War. They got worried about a machine coming out that could make an old paper-making process economical. They said if I played my cards right, I could get rid of the hemp problem once and for all and get my bureau a budget increase to boot. Amazing how things fell into place. If that machine had come out six months earlier, and farmers had started growing it for paper before the Court made my tax law possible, we'd have never gotten rid of it."

"What kind of machine was it?" Jenny asked.

"Some kind of harvester," Anslinger said. "Had a funny name—decorpulator, something like that. Doesn't matter now. It's gone."

"Who had this machine?" Jenny asked.

"Some small-time operators out in Illinois. They were trying to raise capital to get an assembly line going and convince farmers to grow hemp so they could process it."

"What happened?" McGill asked.

A broad smile crossed Anslinger's face. "I inspected them to death."

McGill said, "I don't understand, Mr. Commissioner."

"You see, the Tax Act banned the leaves and flowers, but not the stalks, which is what they used for rope and so forth, so I couldn't just ban the whole damned plant like I wanted. But anybody growing it or processing it had to get a special tax stamp from me, and I made sure when I wrote the law that it left it up to me to write the regulations. I told my boys make sure every last bit of leaf was stripped off every plant. We strangled them in red tape until they folded up and blew away."

"Mr. Commissioner, is it true that Henry Ford was experimenting with hemp as a fuel source back then?" McGill asked.

"The asshole thought he could make an end-run around the oil companies," Anslinger said. "Wanted to use it for methanol, called it 'wood gas.' And he had a cockamamie notion about growing cars from the soil. Ford was the biggest reason I had to sneak the law through Congress. If he'd known what we were doing, he could have raised a big enough stink to stop us. But he only heard about it after I sent my boys around to shut down his experiments. He squawked like a plucked chicken, but I rolled him like an empty barrel."

"It's just fascinating that you had to keep a great law like that such a secret to get it passed," Gridley said.

"Oh yes, Grayson. Only a few of us knew what it was really all about.

You won't find the word 'hemp' anywhere in the bill. Today they'd call it 'under the radar.' And I made sure it came up for a vote late on a Friday afternoon. It was the middle of summer, before air-conditioning, and Washington's a hellhole that time of year. I got Sam Rayburn to bring it to the floor just as they were trying to adjourn for the weekend. A Republican from New York got up and asked, 'Mr. Speaker, what is this bill about?' So Rayburn tells him, 'I don't know. It has something to do with a thing called marijuana. I think it's a narcotic of some kind.' Then the Republican asked if doctors supported it, so one of our friends, Fred Vinson, stood up and said he was on the Ways and Means committee that held the hearings, and that a doctor from the A.M.A. came in and supported the law one hundred percent."

"But Mr. Commissioner," Jenny said, "didn't you just tell us that the A.M.A. doctor had testified *against* the bill?"

"That's right, Miss, he did."

"Is that the same Vinson who became Chief Justice?" McGill asked.

"One and the same," Anslinger said. "After the war, Truman kicked out Morganthau and put Fred in at Treasury, so he was my boss for a while. Then in '47 Truman bumped him up to Chief Justice."

Jenny could hardly believe it. "Are you saying that a future Chief Justice stood up on the floor of the House and lied to his fellow Congressmen about testimony before his own committee?"

Anslinger seemed surprised at the question. "You can say anything you want to on the floors of the House or the Senate, Miss, and nobody can do a thing about it. It's called Congressional immunity, and it's right there in the Constitution. I was in the gallery, and by my watch the debate took one minute and thirty-seven seconds. When it went over to the Senate they held one day of hearings, sent it to the floor, and it sailed through without a single word of debate. Not one word. Roosevelt signed without a whimper, and that's how I criminalized marijuana and ended the hemp problem once and for all."

Gridley was in awe of his mentor. "That's beautiful, Mr. Commissioner. What a great story."

"Yes," Anslinger agreed, "it is a good one if I say so myself. And I do."

"Mr. Commissioner," McGill said, "can I ask you a personal question?"

"I suppose, as long as you don't make me lie too much."

"Well, you were appointed by Hoover, a Republican. So how did you keep your job under Roosevelt and Truman?"

"Let's just say I know how to work both sides of the fence."

McGill said, "I'm confused about something. Didn't you testify that marijuana was the most violence-producing drug known to man?"

"Hell, yes. You know the word 'assassin' comes from 'hashish,' don't you? They'd get all hopped up and then go out and fight the Crusaders."

"But after the war, didn't you testify it turned people into pacifists?"

"The commies were taking over everything, sapping our will to fight, so I told them it leads to pacifism and leaves our boys susceptible to brainwashing."

"I guess that's why I'm confused," McGill said. "I mean, how could it make somebody both violent *and* passive simultaneously?"

"We had a Cold War to win, young man," Anslinger said. "Besides, it was ten years later. There was a whole new crop of dolts in Congress. Nobody remembered what the hell I said the first time around."

McGill seemed baffled how to respond. They rode in silence for a few awkward moments until she posed a legal question. "Mr. Commissioner, after you testified it made people insane, didn't that open the door for lawyers to use it as an insanity defense in criminal cases?"

Anslinger laughed and slapped his knee. "Did it *ever*! Now, that's a story and a half. Have I told you that one, Grayson?"

"No, I don't think so, Mr. Commissioner."

Anslinger leaned forward, like a counselor at a campfire. "After I pushed the Tax Act through, I called a scientific conference. I was looking for experts to represent us at symposiums and so forth, so I invited everybody I could think of who might have some expertise. But one after the other they got up and said they didn't know why they were at a conference on marijuana because they didn't know anything about it. The only people who claimed to know anything at all were the idiot doctor from the A.M.A. and my old friend, Dr. Munch."

"The pharmacologist who injected the dogs?" Jenny said.

"Yes. Now, I couldn't very well appoint a doctor who was out there calling me a liar and contradicting everything I'm saying as our official expert, so that left Munch. And like you said, Miss, right off the bat some shysters tried to use my testimony to get perps off. The next year five murder trials came up where perps pleaded not guilty because of marijuana insanity."

"That makes sense," Jenny said. "You opened the door."

"It was supposed to be just for the idiots in Congress," Anslinger said. "I never dreamed the courts would take it seriously. And it would have been fine if Munch hadn't gone into the expert-witness business on the side. The first case to come up was in Newark. Two women robbed and murdered a bus driver. Very sensational. Every newspaper in New Jersey had reporters there. The defense called Munch to testify, and the lawyer asked him what he knew about the drug. So Munch tells them about the dogs, and some articles he'd written, and about his testimony to Congress. Then he showed them my certificate to prove he was the Narcotics Bureau's official expert. Then he goes and tells them he's smoked it himself."

"What?" Jenny said. "He admitted smoking it...himself?"

Anslinger was grinning. "It gets much better. When the lawyer asked what happened, Munch told the jury he took two puffs, turned into a bat, and flew around the room for fifteen minutes and crashed at the bottom of a two-hundred-foot ink well."

"Turned into a bat?" Gridley said as everybody broke out laughing. "Oh, Mr. Commissioner, you've got to be kidding."

"No, it's true, Grayson, I swear," Anslinger said with a jolly smile. "You can check the *Newark Star Ledger*, October 12, 1938. The headline reads: 'Killer Drug Turns Doctor to Bat!'"

McGill smiled and joked, "Sounds more like a bummer acid trip."

Neither Gridley nor Anslinger laughed.

"How did the trial turn out?" Gridley asked.

"Well, the next day one of the perps gets up on the stand and the lawyer asks her to tell the jury what happened the night of the murder. She said after they smoked it her incisor teeth grew six inches and dripped with blood. And the jury bought it. And they weren't the only ones Munch got off. In a case in New York, a perp went on a rampage, killing dogs and cats and two cops. The lawyer said the perp hadn't even smoked any, but that a bag of it in his room had been giving off homicidal vibrations that sent him on a killing spree. Then the lawyer brings in Munch, and he tells his bat story, and the jury let the perp live."

"Wow," McGill said, "I mean, talk about bad vibes."

"It wasn't funny," Anslinger said. "How do you think it made me feel? I'm down there in Washington watching murderers escaping the electric chair because my expert is running around telling juries marijuana turned him into a bat. So I hauled him in and told him I'd revoke his official status if he didn't get out of the defense-witness business. He promised to quit, and he did, and no perp has gotten off using the marijuana insanity defense since."

Jenny was incredulous. "You kept him even *after* the bats?"

"You have to understand, Miss, he was the only scientist I had. Whenever we needed an expert for an international conference, or to testify to Congress, Dr. Jimmy Munch was our man, right up to 1962 when Kennedy forced me out. Oh, here it comes," and he pointed out the window to the exit sign. "This is where we get off for Rolling Rock. Better get to the right."

Chapter 39

Horses & Hounds

ARMY ONE SETTLED IN FOR A LANDING ON THE TARMAC OF THE ST. LOUIS airport. Its passengers included the governors of Illinois and Missouri, who were returning with Nixon after a tour of the massive flooding. Nixon had seen enough. "Rose Mary, take this down."

Rose Mary Woods pulled a yellow legal pad out of the chopper's fold-up desk, and Nixon dictated the Federal Declaration of Disaster. She typed it on White House stationery, and Nixon signed it then and there.

After bidding the governors good-bye in front of the cameras, Nixon, Haldeman and Ehrlichman boarded *Air Force One*, where Bullcannon was waiting. "Hello, Mr. President. I have that tape you wanted."

They went with Nixon to his private quarters at the back of the plane. Ehrlichman put it in a deck, and they listened as Andrew Mellon's maid told her story. Nixon was ecstatic. "I *knew* it. I was right all along. But when I told the boys to follow the money, I had no idea it would lead to two of the richest families in America."

"I'm surprised it goes back twenty years earlier than we thought," Haldeman said.

"They were slick all right," Ehrlichman said, "but it doesn't prove anything. It's all hearsay."

Bullcannon piped up, "Mr. President, the public doesn't give a damn what the hell happened in 1917, or 1937, or even 1967. I just don't see how you can use it without alienating the party's two biggest supporters."

"I wouldn't be so sure about people not caring," Nixon said. "Not after Nixon tells them how they've been paying out the ass for toilet paper and gasoline for the last fifty years just to fill the pockets of blue-blooded billionaires. And as for alienating contributors, let me just say this about that—there's more than one way to skin a fat cat."

Gridley was gazing absent-mindedly out the window as the flunky McGill drove them along the winding country road, though he barely noticed the scenic white-fenced horse country nestled between the green ridges of the bucolic Ligonier Valley. It could have been a traffic jam on the Beltway for all he cared. The rain had stopped, and the sun was peeking through when the Dago Babe asked, "Do you think we could open the windows and get some fresh air?"

"Of course, Miss Abruzzi," said the Commissioner.

Gridley rolled down his window, thinking how women are such a pain in the ass. He took a last drag and flicked the butt out the window. Soon, they came upon a sign:

CAUTION

HORSES & HOUNDS

PLEASE DRIVE SLOWLY

At the top of the sign was a graphic of the face of a fox and the letters RRH. The Dago Babe asked, "What do the initials stand for, Mr. Commissioner?"

"Rolling Rock Hunt," Anslinger said, then leaned forward and tapped the flunky on the back of the shoulder. "We're almost there, young man. When you see the big red *DO NOT ENTER* sign don't pay any attention to it, just drive right in and go up the hill to the top."

They passed the sign and started up the steep hill. After half a mile the road leveled out a bit as they drove among the greens and fairways of a perfectly manicured golf course. As they approached the crest, the Commissioner said, "That's the clubhouse, Grayson. Has about thirty rooms for the members. For the steeplechase and fox hunting events, the Mellons' guests stay at the estates up the valley, and the hoi polloi stay at the ski resorts or the inns in Ligonier."

The stately clubhouse was built of very dark red bricks; it reminded Gridley of an English country estate befitting a duke or a prince. There was even a circular stone turret with a pointed slate roof, like a watchtower. A huge green-and-white striped tent—the Mellons' colors, Anslinger had informed them—was set up on the lawn, with streamers fluttering from atop the tent poles. Power. This was power. God, how he loved it.

The flunky dropped them at the clubhouse door and went to park. A concierge in a bright green sport coat greeted them. "Nice to see you again, Mr. Commissioner. We have your favorite room made up the way you like it. You and your party can get badges and schedules at the office at the end of the hall. There are cocktails and hors'-d'oeuvres in the bar, and a buffet in the dining room at six-thirty. If any in your party intend to play golf, I suggest they reserve tee times right away. It's early, but the slots will fill up fast."

The flunky joined them at the registration desk. A sign on an easel read:

WELCOME
Conservative Activists Coordinating Alliance
First Annual Conference

Gridley signed up for tee-off times, and a secretary gave them CACA Conference name badges and a schedule. He was to lead a seminar right after lunch the day after tomorrow: "The War on Drugs—a Killer Conservative Issue." As part of his presentation, Gridley planned to have the Commissioner say a few words about the old days, and now he had the Bird as an example of everything wrong with hippies. He could hardly believe his luck. The Bird was the perfect media vehicle to help pass his Drug Implements Extermination Act. He could already hear the applause for pushing it through. It could make him a Senator.

Anslinger stopped at the elevator. "Well, Grayson, thank you for the ride. It's always a pleasure, but it's time for my nap, and I'm having dinner at Richie's with some of the family, so I won't see you until tomorrow."

After the elevator closed Gridley said, "Let's have a drink in the bar."

"Fine with me," said the flunky. "It's not every day you get to hang out at the most exclusive club in America."

"I'm going to the ladies' room," said the Dago Babe.

The flunky had been drooling over her all day, and as they watched her walk away Gridley told him, "Your Dago Babe is a real looker, but I wouldn't get my pecker too hard if I were you. She's out of your league. So what do you know about her?"

"About Miss Abruzzi?"

This guy was a doofus on top of being a wise-ass. "No, asshole, about the fucking tooth fairy."

"Uh...not much," the flunky said. "I've only known her a few days."

"I can't help feeling I've seen her before. What's her background?"

"We...we haven't gotten too personal. I know she grew up in Pittsburgh and went to Bryn Mawr, and Yale Law, and she's done graduate work at the Sorbonne, and—"

Something clicked, a light switched on. What was it? He leaned in a little closer to the flunky. "The Sorbonne, in Paris?"

"She just got back. She's only had her job at the bank a few weeks."

Jenny saw McGill at a cocktail table, near one of the TVs hanging from the wall. There were fifty or sixty men in the bar wearing CACA Conference badges. Except for cocktail waitresses, she saw no other women. She sat down and said, "Where's Gridley?"

"He went to make a call," he said, then leaned forward, whispering in excitement, "I think I got it all, Jen, everything Anslinger said. It's the smoking gun Nixon needs to blow the conspiracy out of the water. I'm going to dupe a copy for you. If something happens to me, you've got to get it to Nixon. Promise?"

She was about to say it was a bad idea to give her anything when Gridley returned and sat down. Then a tall woman in her forties, with sandy hair and a gaudy diamond broach, walked up to her and said, "Excuse me, are you Jennifer Abruzzi?"

"Yes."

"I asked at the desk if there were any other unescorted ladies here, and they said so far there was only you. So I thought I'd say hello. We girls have to stick together at these things. I'm Phylamena Sharpley."

The very name gave Jenny a shiver: Phylamena Sharpley, foundress of the Anti-Liberal Forum, dogged opponent of the Equal Rights Amendment, fanatical enemy of Women's Liberation, iconess of the far right. "Nice to meet you," Jenny said as they shook hands, lady-to-lady.

Gridley and McGill both stood up like gentlemen and Gridley said, "I'm Grayson Gridley, Mrs. Sharply, and this is Mr., uh...McGill. I'm a big admirer of yours. The Anti-Liberal Forum is doing great things."

"*You're* Grayson Gridley?" Sharpley said. "Oh, I've heard so much about you. Please, call me Phyl."

"And you must call me Grayson. Will you join us for a drink, Phyl?"

McGill pulled out a chair for her as she said, "Isn't it nice here? So woodsy." Turning to her, Sharpley said, "You know, Jennifer, I saw Nancy and Ronnie at the airport. Nancy's looking mahvelous, absolutely mahvelous. So what is your connection to the conservative movement, my dear?"

"I'm with Mellon Bank, but—"

"Oh, I just *adore* the Mellons," Sharpley said. "Petey's such a sweetie, and Richie's just the tops. And their idea for a network of think-tanks and magazines to shape public opinion to our way of thinking is brilliant, just brilliant. Don't you agree? And it's all tax-free because it's supposed to be for social research. Why, they tell me this entire event is a tax deduction.

Isn't that rich? I knew there were brain cells up there somewhere. With Mellon money behind us, we conservatives will be back in charge before you know it. But how are they holding up after that dreadful murder scandal?"

"I've never—"

"And there was that business with their cousins, and that awful Timothy Leary person, and a special kind of that LSD…something about oranges."

"They called it 'orange sunshine,' Phyl," Gridley said. "From the bright orange pills they were using. They made ten million doses we know about. Pop one of those babies, and it'll take you to the moon."

Jenny and McGill kept quiet as Gridley and Sharpley got to know each other, exchanging opinions about the state of the culture and how America was going to hell on a runaway liberal freight train when somebody called out, "Hey bartender, can you turn on the news."

A moment later the TV above them blinked on in the middle of a jingle: "Winston tastes good, like a—CLAP-CLAP—cigarette should," followed by an announcer's voice: "And now, the WDTO Tri-State Report."

The camera cut to the news desk, where the anchorman ran through film clips from the upcoming stories. "At city hall, the mayor and the city council are still at odds over the budget. In New Castle, a three-alarm fire takes the life of an elderly shut-in. In Ligonier, the rich and famous arrive for a conference at the Rolling Rock Club. In sports, the Pirates extend their lead in the National League East, and in weather, the rains are gone, but the Tri-state's in for a heat wave. But first, a WDTO special report by Rusty Limbergh on the rampant drug use at the Golden Triangle Music and Art festival last weekend. Tell us what you found, Rusty."

Her stomach knotted up; McGill gulped his drink and went into a choking spasm; Gridley yelled, "Hey everybody! Watch this!"

The room quieted, and the camera panned to Limbergh, who was seated at the news desk. "Well Jim, I was astonished at the brazen flouting of America's drug laws in a public park. Take a look at this."

The TV cut to a scene from the concert, zeroing in on people using Birds to smoke joints and pass roaches.

"What's that thing they're using, Rusty," asked the anchorman.

"It's called a roach clip, Jim, and they were selling them right out in the open." The camera cut to the studio and Limbergh held up a Bird. "This one's particularly bad because it's pretending to be sanctioned by the government. If we could get a close-up."

The camera zoomed in on US Government on the back of the Bird, and the anchorman asked, "So where were the police when all this was going on, Rusty?"

"That's what a lot of people are asking, Jim."

"Isn't there a law against that sort of thing?"

"No, Jim, not yet," Limbergh said. "But a bill called the Drug Implements Extermination Act will soon be introduced in Congress that will put a stop to this kind of thing forever. I'll be interviewing E. Grayson Gridley, the director of the Office of Narcotic Operations, about it later this week."

Gridley leaped to his feet yelling, "That's me, and I've got one of those things right here." He took a Bird out of his pocket and held it high. "I'll bring it around so you can all see just how brazen the bastards are."

As Gridley went from table to table showing off the Bird, Sharpley asked her, "Are you coming to the Conservative Ladies' Council at Fallingwater tomorrow, Jennifer?"

"I don't know anything about it," Jenny said.

"Oh, there's a champagne breakfast and a fashion show, then after lunch I'm leading a seminar on 'Feminism: Scourge of Femininity.' Nancy and Jean Kilpatrick are on the panel, and some girls about your age, Fannie Colder and Peggy Nooner. Why don't you ride with Nancy and me in the morning. It's going to be such fun."

Chapter 40

Cradle and All

THE GYNECOLOGIST AGREED CATHERINE HAD ALL THE SYMPTOMS, BUT THERE was no way to be sure until the results of the rabbit test were known. "Call tomorrow after three, Mrs. Smith," he had told her. "They're usually back by then."

She decided to fly up a day early and try to see Jenny. On Tuesday morning she packed and put on jeans, cowgirl boots, and a frilly red-and-white western blouse with mother-of-pearl buttons. She took a taxi to National Airport and hopped a thirty-seat, twin-engine turboprop for the short flight to Pittsburgh. She rented a car and followed the map Mulligan had plotted out with a yellow highlighter, heading east to the turnpike, exiting at Somerset, and registering at the Cloverleaf Motel as Peggy Bennington, just another truckin' gal comin' to meet her man.

She went next door to the Pitt Stop Truck Plaza and used a pay phone in the restaurant to call Jenny's house. A woman answered, "Hello."

"Hello, is this Mrs. Abruzzi?"

"Yes."

"This is Catherine DeWolfe, Mrs. Abruzzi, Jenny's friend from law school."

"Yes, Catherine, of course. How nice to hear from you again. How are you?"

"Very well, thank you. I was just driving by on the turnpike on my way to Michigan, and I thought I might get lucky and catch Jenny at home. Is she back from Paris yet?"

"Yes, she came home not long after you called the last time. Ran out of money, poor thing. She took a job at Mellon Bank, but I'm afraid they've sent her to a conference of some kind for a few days."

Her heart sank. "Oh no, bad timing."

"Maybe not. You say you're on the turnpike, dear?"

"Just off it, at a truck stop."

"Which exit are you at?"

"I think it's called Somerset. Why?"

"Then she's not too far from you. Her conference is at the Rolling Rock Club, and she's staying at the hotel at Seven Springs, the ski resort, room

319. Why don't you try her there? You might get lucky."

Catherine thanked her, hung up, and looked at her watch: 14:15 hours. No. Here in the real world she must not think in Mulligan's military time. It was two-fifteen, a quarter after two. She called the hotel and asked for Jennifer Abruzzi's room. No answer. Should she call the conference and have her paged? No, she would probably be in a meeting on foreclosures or interest rates or some such. She decided to call the women's clinic for the results of her rabbit test first, then drive over to the hotel and try to catch Jenny before dinner. Forty-five minutes to kill.

She went to the Pitt Stop's lunch counter, ordered a roast-beef-on-rye sandwich and a strawberry shake, and asked the waitress to show her where Seven Springs was on the map. Not far at all, less than half an hour. "What about the Rolling Rock Club? Where's that?"

"It's along this road here," the waitress said, "but the only signs you'll see say to keep out. They like to keep it real private."

She had been to Rolling Rock several times as a girl, part of the DeWolfe family contingent to watch her uncle's champion horse, Green Gold, compete in America's most prestigious steeplechase competition, the King of Spain Gold Cup. She remembered one year, she must have been twelve or thirteen, when many of the 15,000 in the gallery, even men in top hats and tuxedos, had the new Made in Japan transistor radios up to their ears listening to a World Series game. They hardly seemed to care about the steeplechase at all, and a cheer had gone up when the local team won. Wait, that would have been the Pittsburgh team, right? *Mike's team!* She felt closer to him than ever.

She sat at the Formica-topped lunch counter drinking weak coffee as the juke box played "Okie from Muskogee" and "Me and Bobby Magee" over and over. She smiled appreciatively at the come-ons from the truckers and flashed her C.I.A. wedding ring to fend them off. She couldn't help worrying how she would tell Mike, and wondering how she and the baby would live if he spurned her, and her father and the Heirs Committee disinherited her. Maybe instead of practicing law, she would start a business of her own, a café maybe, so she could raise the baby in a back room. She would serve real coffee, like in Europe. Could Americans ever go for real coffee? Could truckers?

She unfolded the map and studied the route yet again. If they left at dawn, they should be at Niagara Falls between noon and one, plenty of time for a tour on the *Maid of the Mist*. The route took them within twenty miles of Milltowne, where Mulligan grew up. Would there be time for a detour to see his house or catch a glimpse of his family? A couple hours couldn't matter much, could it?

Time crept along like a lazy caterpillar; she hated it when she got all goosebumpy like this. At 14:55 hours, no, at five-to-three, she went to a phone booth, shut the door extra-tight, and dumped all her change on the metal counter. The instant the second-hand of her watch touched the twelve, she put a dime in the slot and dialed. The operator announced, "That will be a dollar sixty-five for the first three minutes."

A woman answered, "Columbia Women's Clinic."

"Hello. The doctor said my results should be back by now."

"The lab just sent everything over. What's your name, and I'll check."

"Mrs. Margaret Smith."

Her heart was hammering like a roofing crew setting shingles. After an eternity the woman said, "Congratulations, Mrs. Smith. You're going to be a mother."

Before she left yesterday, Catherine had given him a regulation Navy haircut, and he had shaved off his beard. He would be in his Navy uniform at the Air Force base, no phony names or disguises, and he found himself irritated that he would again be required to shave.

He and Leary spent the afternoon working in the seed patch, pulling up every male with the telltale furry balls so the pollinated females could spread out and grow heavy with seed. The crop would be on its own for a few weeks as Mother Nature worked her magic. Before turning in for the night, they had outfitted Leary's compartment with enough food and water to last a week, just in case.

At 07:00, two young Marines, a private and a corporal, arrived in a deuce-and-a-half military truck with a load of packing and crating materials. They helped crate up the prototypes and load the trailer, and after they left, Leary emerged from his compartment. At about 13:00, he sent Leary to the office tent for something. A few minutes later Leary called out, "Hey, Mike, the phone machine's blinking."

Shit. The office had been Catherine's domain, and he forgot to check for messages. Cursing his incompetence, he ran to the tent and hit PLAY: "You have one message, recorded yesterday at ten-thirty-two, A.M...."

"Damn it, Mulligan, I wish you were there," said McGill's voice. "I'm gonna play this interview I did with Andrew Mellon's maid and hope your machine gets it all. I was supposed to play it for Nixon this morning, but he flew off to a flood somewhere. If you see him before I do, make sure he hears this. Duberman's too dense to get how important it is.

"And remember the chrome-dome narc we met at Pachyderm's, Gridley? He finally set up an interview with Anslinger. I'm driving him and a woman from Mellon Bank out to the airport to pick Anslinger up, then we're all going to a conference at the Rolling Rock Club. Pretty swanky, huh? Nixon's coming in a day or two, and Dubious is trying to schedule me time with him there. I have no idea what's going on at this thing, but Dubious booked us rooms at Seven Springs, so try me there if you need me. Here goes...."

There was a mechanical click, a quiet whirr of tape machine, and McGill's voice began asking questions. The replies came from an old woman with an African-American accent. After a minute, a second woman asked a question. Leary jerked straight up and said, "Who is that, Mike?"

"The woman working with McGill, I guess. Why?"

"Her voice sounds very familiar."

When the interview ended McGill's voice said, "That's it. Hope your machine got it. And Mulligan, that chick I'm working with is so out of sight you won't believe it. Her name's Jenny Abruzzi, and she looks like Mrs. Peel on *The Avengers*, only better. And get this: she knows DeWolfe and Thompkins from law school, and—"

"*That's Susannah!*" Leary cried. "Catherine's friend, the one who helped me escape!"

Mulligan hit the PAUSE button. "You're joking?"

"I wish I were. I thought I recognized the voice, and he said they know each other. Play it back so we can be sure."

"Let's hear the rest first."

He pushed PLAY, and McGill's voice said, "But this is even more far out. Remember in seventh grade when I went to the World Series and you and Dombrowski ragged me for years for giving away a Mickey Mantle foul ball to a chick I'd never met? Well, it's her, Mulligan, and I've got the photos to prove it. Is that cosmic, or what? But don't say a thing to DeWolfe or I'll string you up by your short hairs. Jenny doesn't know yet, and I'm waiting for the timing to be right. This could be it, Mulligan. Fate, love, destiny—know what I mean? Wish me luck, 'cause I'm going to need it.

"Oh, and speaking of luck, the other kind, there's been a new uh…development. Now don't go getting pissed, but it's about the Bird. You remember the Bird, right? I won't go into details, but if you see Nixon before I do, tell him if I don't talk to him soon the whole operation could blow up in our faces. Catch you later." Click.

"Goddamnit!" Mulligan shouted at the machine. "I told him I'd fire his ass if he didn't forget the goddamned Bird! *Shit!*"

"What is it?" Leary said.

"A roach clip made out of a fork that looks like a fucking bird. I'm going to kill him."

"But how did he get involved with Catherine's friend?"

"I don't know. He said she works for Mellon Bank. Maybe it's not who you think it is?"

"No, it's the woman I knew as Susannah," Leary said. "You've seen her picture—like Mrs. Peel, only better. And I knew she was from Pittsburgh the first time she opened her mouth. The accent is very distinctive. My guess is after Oskar got her out of France she went home, took a job, and your friend stumbled across her. Like he said, this whole thing is pretty cosmic. There's serious karma coming down, Mike—you, me, Catherine, Nixon, Susannah or Jennifer, whoever she is, your friend, Oskar, and now, Gridley. It's very Jungian if you think about it. There are no coincidences, if you know what I mean."

Mulligan had only the vaguest notion what Jungian psychology was about and had learned to tune Leary out when he started spouting New Age crapola. "It just sounds like big trouble to me."

"So how does Gridley fit in with your friend?" Leary asked.

"He was supposed to arrange an interview for us with Anslinger. Sounds like he's done it."

"Hmmm. Your friend left this yesterday, and if Gridley has recognized Susannah, he'll have learned she went to Yale, realized she knows Catherine, added two and two, and know who it was that tipped me off. They might already be watching her. We have to try to warn her."

Mulligan called Catherine's house, got her machine, and left a briefest of messages so they couldn't trace the call. "Call me from a pay phone as soon as you hear this. And be careful. Somebody may be following you."

He called the Seven Springs hotel. "I'm looking for Mr. McGill. What room is he in?"

"Mr. McGill is in room 315. I'll try it, but most of the guests who are here for the conference are out at the Rolling Rock Club."

There was no answer, so he left a terse message. "We need to talk. Call me as soon as you hear this."

"I have a bad feeling about this, Mike," Leary said. "Try Catherine at the motel where we're supposed to meet tomorrow."

"But she's not leaving until morning."

"Mike...just try."

He called the Cloverleaf and asked for Peggy Bennington, and was stunned when the clerk said, "She's in room seventy-four. I'll ring it."

No answer; he left a message: "Just what in the hell do you think you're doing? Don't go anywhere, and don't call your friend or try to see anybody. Anybody at all. And that's an *order*." He slammed down the receiver. "I can't believe she'd endanger the mission like this."

"Mike, she's a spoiled rich girl who knows nothing about military discipline. She doesn't expect us until tomorrow, and she hasn't had another woman to talk to in weeks. The temptation of going to her friend's home town was too much. She probably thinks she can talk to her about you and the baby while lying about me and Oskar and everything else. In a way, it's all my fault. I should have seen it coming."

Mulligan felt a chasm open in his gut. "What...what baby?"

Leary sighed and put a comforting hand on his shoulder. "I'm sure she'd prefer to tell you herself, but I think Catherine's pregnant. That's why she wanted to get away so badly, so she could see a doctor and be sure."

Mulligan leaned on the desk to steady himself. "Has...has she told you?"

"No, but I've worked with hundreds of women in therapy, and I've noticed a definite change in her mood. Women know it's true, though it's hard to get them to admit it. Do you know what morning sickness is?"

"Uh...kind of."

"Early morning nausea. It's one of the surest signs of pregnancy. I'm a light sleeper, and twice last week I heard her throwing up in the woods by the outhouse."

"But she's on the pill."

"Nothing's foolproof, Mike," Leary said with a wry smile. "My guess is she's missed her period and has been wrestling with what to tell you. It's only natural she would feel the need to talk it over with a friend."

"Get into your disguise, Tim. We're out of here, right now."

Gridley had insisted on hanging out at the Rolling Rock bar, and it wasn't until one-thirty that they arrived at the Seven Springs hotel. Their rooms were in a row, Gridley's between his and Jenny's, too risky for a visit, so they just went to bed.

In the morning Sharpley whisked Jenny off for an anti-feminist seminar at Fallingwater, so McGill ate breakfast alone, then drove Gridley to Rolling Rock for his eight-thirty tee-off time. At least on the golf course Gridley wouldn't be getting updates about the BirdCo gang. If he could talk to Nixon, come clean about the Bird and get him to call Gridley off, he might yet skate out of this mess in one piece, though he was now resigned to losing his White House job.

Uniformed Pinkerton guards with guns and badges were stopping traffic at the turnoff to the club. McGill held up his name tag and the guard waved them through. He dropped Gridley at the pro shop, then parked and went to the clubhouse.

The lobby was crowded with well-scrubbed young conservatives schmoozing over coffee and donuts. He used a pay phone to call the office before the seminars started. Duberman answered.

"Rudy, McGill here. I'm at that conference, and I taped a smoking gun interview with Anslinger. Did you get me time with Nixon?"

"Maybe. Haldeman's secretary said to check with him as soon as they get there."

"When are they coming?"

"They aren't scheduled until tomorrow, but she said Nixon's bored with floods so they may show up late this afternoon or this evening."

He had the day to kill, and there was a smorgasbord of seminars to choose from on the theme: "Winning the Culture Wars." For the morning session he picked "Nurturing a Conservative Punditry," and for the afternoon "Controlling the Grammar of Politics."

The first seminar almost put him to sleep, but at the second a fire-breathing history professor about his own age named Kingrich made a lot of sense advocating a strategy of attacking liberals and their motives at every opportunity.

"The goal is to control the very language itself," Kingrich told them. "By framing the arguments in terms we choose, we win the debate."

Among his many suggestions was one that every true-blue movement-conservative immediately stop using the term "Democratic Party."

"The word 'democratic' has far too many positive connotations to let

Democrats have it to themselves," Kingrich insisted. "The answer is for us to always say and write Demo*crat* Party, and when you can, say it with a sneer, like you're cussing them out...Demo*CRAT*! Party. You can't do it with 'democratic' because the unaccented '*ick*' sound gets in the way. And even if we could, we wouldn't want to because people might think we were disparaging the very idea of democracy itself, and that's not something conservatives want to publicize. But if we sneer out '*crat*' some people will subconsciously hear '*rat*' and associate Democrats with rodents and vermin, while others will hear '*crap*' and see a steaming pile of dog shit.

"Okay, now why don't you all give it a try? Trip it off your tongue with utter contempt, like in the movies...'you dirty *RAT*!' Really spit it out...Demo*CRAT*! Party. See what I mean? Pretend the person next to you is a liberal, and you want to insult the son-of-a-bitch. Go ahead, don't be shy...Demo*CRAT*! Party."

A cacophonous *ROAR* went up as sixty eager activists began Demo*CRAT*ing each other as insultingly as possible—Demo*CRAT*! Party, Demo*CRAP*! Party, Demofucking*CRAT*! Party.

McGill and the guy beside him, whose badge read "Tom DeKaye," Demo*CRAT*ed back and forth, nastier and nastier until Kingrich said into the microphone, "Didn't take long to get the hang of it, did it?"

Everyone laughed, and the room quieted down.

"So how did it feel?" Kingrich asked with a puckish smile. "Bet it felt *g-o-o-o-d*, didn't it?"

The consensus was that it had indeed felt good. Very, *very* good.

"So when you leave here, go out and spread the word," Kingrich said. "Whenever you hear somebody on our side say Democratic Party, take them off into a corner and tell them about our language-control program. Make sure they understand how important it is for all conservatives to be on the same page. If we all pretend it's as common as butter on bread, we can sneak it into usage before the damned Democrats know what hit 'em. Now, are there any questions?"

McGill raised his hand. "But professor, isn't that usage just flat out wrong? I mean, 'democrat' is a noun, right? And 'democratic' is an adjective. I'd have gotten big red check marks from every teacher I ever had if I'd used it like that. Conservatives don't want to sound illiterate, do we?"

"Don't give it a second thought," Kingrich assured them. "Language evolves with usage, which means it can be manipulated, and liberals haven't figured that out yet. Now I agree that good grammar has its place, but it's a quaint notion we can quietly toss into the dumpster when we need to, and believe me, hardly anyone will notice. And if we use it often enough, some day even *Websters* will be forced to accept it. In the long run, my friend, divorcing Democrats from the word democratic in the public's mind is worth breaking a few petty rules, wouldn't you say? And who's going to punish us if we're caught...the grammar police?"

Laughter filled the room as McGill raised his hand for a follow-up. "But do we really want to be deliberately insulting? Democratic Party is their legal name, part of their heritage, and refusing to use somebody's name is a slap in the face, a slur, like calling somebody 'boy' or telling them your mama wears combat boots. And it's historically wrong. Do we really want to be seen violating the ideals of civility and respect for tradition conservatives are supposed to stand for? Aren't we opening ourselves up to charges of hypocrisy?"

Kingrich's moon-face beamed with confidence, like a TV actor in a deodorant commercial. "Voters don't know the first thing about history, my friend, and nobody has ever gone to jail for hypocrisy. And as for it being a slap in the face, that's exactly right. Every time we use it we get a free backhanded slap at their ugly liberal faces and they can't slap us back. What the hell can they do...start calling us 'Republic Party?' Ha! A lot of good that'll do the bastards. Next question...."

Catherine had been crazy to talk to her best friend after learning she was pregnant—about having a baby, about being in love, about everything. She drove straight to the hotel at Seven Springs and knocked on Jenny's door. No answer. It was only four, so she asked at the desk, "I'm here for a conference at the Rolling Rock Club. Can you tell me how to get there?"

The clerk gave her a program with a map and a schedule. The next event was cocktail hour, followed by an informal buffet at seven. Ten-to-one Jenny would not return to her room for several hours. She decided to go to the club and bluff her way in. What could be easier?

Mike and Leary wouldn't arrive at the Cloverleaf until noon tomorrow, so it made sense to stay at Seven Springs tonight. She requested a room near her friend, Ms. Abruzzi; the clerk gave her 323, two doors down.

The truckin' gal outfit she was wearing for the eighteen-wheel crowd at the Pitt Stop wouldn't do at all for a bankers' soirée at Rolling Rock. She whirlwinded through the resort's boutiques, bought a pair of dressy Gucci low-heels and a practical Coco Channel power-suit ensemble, showered, and followed the map to the big red *DO NOT ENTER* sign where the directions said go up the hill.

A Pinkerton Security Services car and a WDTO-TV news van were parked at the corner. Two guards were stopping traffic and talking to drivers while a news crew filmed the vehicles waiting in line—a dozen cars, several limousines, and a catering truck emblazoned with fluorescent orange Day-Glo signage:

SUNSHINE CATERING

"Serving High Society"

A Pinkerton with a .38 pistol came over. She powered down the window and acted as if she belonged. "This is the right place, isn't it, officer?"

"Just go up the hill and follow the signs to the parking lot, Ma'am."

After the seminars, McGill wandered around reading names on badges, a *Who's Who* of Biddles, DuPonts, Vanderbilts, Whitneys, Pews, Posts, Coors, Rockefellers, and up from Texas in their ten-gallon hats, Hunts and Bass's. How many billions upon billions in unearned, hereditary fortunes had heeded the Mellons' call-to-arms to eradicate liberals from the face of the Earth? He saw 'Edward DeWolfe' on a badge and wondered if he was their DeWolfe's father? Jenny would know. Where the hell was she?

Rubbing elbows with hereditary aristocrats who had done nothing to earn their privileged positions in society was interesting, but he was far more impressed at being in the same room with the brightest stars of the conservative firmament—Senators Goldwater, Thurmond, and Helms; Reverends Moon and Graham; governors Wallace and Reagan; pundits Bunckley, Blovak, Spinfire and Chill; Hollywood heroes Wayne and Heston—la creme-de-la-conservative-creme—all yukking it up like good ol' boys over a jug of moonshine down at the country store.

He docked on a corner barstool and was on his second gin-and-tonic when he saw Gridley enter. He had been considering letting him in on the

Bird problem before it got out of control, thinking if Gridley was loyal to Nixon he would do what was in Nixon's best interest and drop it. It made sense, but his gut told him E. Grayson Gridley was loyal only to himself. Better to cross his fingers, be cool, and hope to talk to Nixon first.

Gridley walked over. "Come with me. Now."

They went out into the muggy heat. The white Plymouth narcmobile with a whip antenna was in a NO PARKING area with the windows up and the engine running. Two men were inside, keeping cool in the air conditioning. As they approached, the men got out. He recognized one from yesterday—Ashkopf. He expected them to break out handcuffs, read him his rights, and haul him away on a charge of stealing government forks. Instead, Gridley got in the drivers side and said, "Get in."

Ashkopf and the other narc went for a walk as he got in the passenger seat. Gridley took an envelope from the back. "Go ahead, open it."

It contained a batch of 8"x10" black-and-white photos of a party by a swimming pool. Whatever this was, it wasn't about the Bird. Whew.

"Recognize anybody?" Gridley said.

"*Hey*—John Lennon and Yoko Ono?"

"Keep going."

"Holy *shit*—Jimi Hendrix and Jerry Garcia—*jamming*! That must have been one hell of a party."

Gridley snorted in disgust. "Just keep going."

McGill flipped to the next photo—three women sitting on the edge of the pool, legs dangling in the water. "That's Yoko on the left, and—wow, Janis Joplin in the middle, and—*Miss Abruzzi*!"

"It's your Dago Babe all right. Check out the next one."

There was Jenny again, next to a diving board with a guy draped all over her. "Is that—"

"The biggest asshole of them all…Jim fucking Morrison. I knew she looked familiar the first time I saw her, but she was with a friend of mine, so I didn't make the connection until you said she'd been in France."

McGill leafed through the photos, turning neon-green with jealousy at one of Jenny snuggled up on an air mattress next to Morrison.

"She was over there all right," Gridley said, "screwing that asshole and working at a strip joint and calling herself Susannah, La Cowgirl Américaine. And that's not the half of it. Know who that is?"

McGill was dizzy, almost nauseous, but he forced himself to study the grainy blow-up of a man on a balcony. "No."

"That's the guru of LSD himself, Timothy Leary, and it was your Dago Babe who helped him escape. I've had a Federal Jane Doe for aiding and abetting a fugitive out with Interpol on the bitch for months. She'll get five to ten on that count alone."

This was nuts. Jenny working in a strip joint, helping the world's most wanted fugitive elude an Interpol dragnet, and screwing, no—*fucking*—Jim Morrison? Is that what he was up against, not some local douchebag deejay, but a mega-famous rock star? And if she went to jail, it would be *his fault*! He had to throw Gridley off and give himself time to think. "Are you saying you're going to arrest Miss Abruzzi?"

"You bet your rosy-red ass we are, as soon as she shows up. I'm only telling you because I don't want you to make a stink when we haul her away. And you know what?" Gridley said, not finished with surprises, "I think your Miss Moneybags is in on it too."

"*Ms. DeWolfe*? I…I don't understand."

"Right before I went over to nab Leary I stopped by your office to see Duberman. She was the only one there, and I showed her some of these photos. After you told me about the Dago Babe being in Paris yesterday, I had my office courier these up here, and when I knew I was right I called my friend Rusty and had him tell me all about her. Know where she went to law school—*Yale*. Know where Moneybags went?"

"Uh…

"Fucking Yale. So I called New Haven and told the boys up there to nose around. And guess what…they graduated the same day, even lived for two whole years in the same feminazi rooming house. So I think after I showed her these photos she tipped off the Dago Babe, and that's the only reason Leary's still on the loose. Where's Moneybags been, anyway? I haven't seen her since."

"Nobody knows. Haldeman told us she's on a special assignment for Nixon, but he wouldn't say what it's about. But why would she want to help Leary?"

"She went to orgies at his druggie playpen when she was in college. I arrested her there once, locked up her and some of her friends to put a real scare into them. When I saw her working in the White House, I figured she was over it…youthful indiscretions and all. But I was wrong. Something big is going on, and I intend to get to the bottom of it, and when I do, I'm going to send Leary and Moneybags and the Dago Babe and anybody who's helped them up the river until their teeth fall out."

Just then they heard the sound of an approaching helicopter. "Here's Nixon now," Gridley said as he powered down his window to watch.

What to do? All eyes were on the chopper as it circled the clubhouse, then hovered before descending on the lawn near the big green-and-white striped tent. Think, McGill, think. What would Nixon do? What? What?...Yes, *of course!*

"Look, Gridley, I don't know anything about this Leary business, but I'm warning you, keep your hands off Miss Abruzzi. National security is at stake in this. Understand? *National fucking security!*"

Gridley's eyes bugged out. "*What?*"

McGill shifted into bullshitting overdrive, hit the gas, popped the clutch, and peeled out in a smoky-blue cloud of burning bullshit rubber. "If you arrest her, you'll blow our operation sky high and Nixon will have your ass in a fucking *sling*. Don't you *dare* make a move against her without the okay from Nixon himself."

He had to get to Nixon first. He opened his door, but as he went to get out he couldn't help reaching over and grabbing Gridley's tie just below the knot and giving it a forceful tug. "And if I ever hear you call her Dago Babe again I'll beat your chrome-domed ass to pulp. *Understand?*"

He shoved Gridley back, jumped out, slammed the door, and dashed to his car thinking that was really dumb, McGill. Gridley's a cop who can kick your ass from here to Tuesday. He grabbed his gym bag from the trunk, and raced to where *Army One* had landed, praying he'd bought enough time to figure out how to save Jenny.

It had been a short haul from Camp David to the Pitt Stop, barely 140 miles. Mulligan pulled the Mack off the turnpike and parked at the far end of the lot between a GMC and a Peterbilt. He got out, made sure no one was around, and told Leary in the secret compartment, "Wait for me. I'm going to try to find her."

He didn't want to show himself to the Cloverleaf's desk clerk, so he went to the Pitt Stop's restaurant and used the pay phone and asked for room seventy-four. No answer. He told the clerk, "This is Mr. Bennington. I'm trying to track down my wife. Any idea where she might be?"

"I saw her in the coffee shop a few hours ago."

"Do you know what she's driving?"

"I have the registration card right here. It says it's a 1974 blue

Oldsmobile Cutlass."

He asked for the license number. On his way to the room he surveyed the parking lot, but there was no blue Olds. He knocked, but there was no answer, so he picked the lock and slipped in. No Catherine, no luggage, no note, no nothing. He went outside to the truck, gave Leary the okay to slip out, and they went back to the room to figure out what to do.

Leary turned on the TV; the Six O'clock News was starting as Mulligan picked up the phone and said, "If McGill's checked his messages he knows he's supposed to be there at six. Cross your fingers."

"Wouldn't it be safer to use a pay phone?" Leary asked.

"It's local, so there won't be a record. Turn down the TV so I can hear."

He dialed Seven Springs and asked for McGill's room. No luck. He asked for Miss Abruzzi's room, wondering what he would say to this woman he'd never met if she answered, but she didn't. On a hunch he asked for Catherine DeWolfe's room. Not registered. He asked for Peggy Bennington's.

"I'll ring it," said the clerk. His guess was right—she had registered at both places. After six rings the clerk said, "Sorry, sir, there's no answer."

He asked if there was a schedule of events for the conference, wrote everything down, and thanked the clerk for his help.

"Well!" Leary said, anxious for an answer.

"She registered there too. We should go try to find her."

Leary shook his head. "You know Gridley, right?"

"We met once…in a bar. Why?"

"He'll remember, and if he sees you it'll just make it worse. Your chances of finding Catherine without running into him are slim. The clubhouse isn't that big."

Leary seemed to know the place. "You've been there?" Mulligan asked.

"Yes, several times. During the war I was stationed at the Army hospital over in Butler, and I always came down for the fox hunts and steeplechases. It was the best place to meet rich, beautiful women you could imagine. I've ridden the Rolling Rock trails, played billiards in the club room, and made love on the golf course. It's been thirty years, but I doubt that it's changed much."

"Can we take the truck in?"

"Hay trucks and horse trailers used to go up there all the time, but I'm sure they'll have guards at the gate for an event like this."

"Is there a back way in, maybe a horse trail?"

"Mike, you're in love and talking crazy. Get a grip, my friend. If you show up it'll just make it worse. And we can't risk waiting for her here. If Gridley arrests her and finds a room key or a receipt, we're all dead. And he'll find the map and *Maid of the Mist* departure times, so that's out."

Leary was right—he was talking crazy. Catherine would have to get out of this on her own. "Okay. I say we head west and rent a boat on Lake St. Clair and get you over the border where it's narrow."

"Mike!" Leary said, pointing to the TV, an aerial shot of what looked like an English country estate with a huge green-and-white striped tent on the lawn.

"...live from the Rolling Rock Club near Ligonier. What's going on out there, Rusty?"

The camera cut to a newsman in front of a patio where waiters were setting tables. "This looks to be the biggest gathering of conservatives in modern American history, Jim," the newsman said. "President Nixon came a day early, arriving half an hour ago and surprising everybody."

"Holy *shit!*" Leary shouted, pointing at the TV.

"What?"

"That waiter. I think it's a Prankster!" and he crouched down on his haunches in front of the screen, peering hard. "That short guy with the wiry hair is Lovenuts from the Merry Pranksters. I'd know him anywhere. And son of a bitch—*Brother Jupiter!*"

"*Who?*"

"Jupiter, of the Brotherhood of Eternal Love. And *there!*" Leary shouted, tapping his finger on the screen. "Pushing that cart. That's Dartain, of the Weathermen. Mike, the Pranksters have teamed up with the Brotherhood *and* the Weathermen! It's an acid test. It has to be. They're going to spike Nixon's Kool-Aid!"

"They're going to *what?*"

"Like in *The Electric Kool-Aid Acid Test,* they're going to spike the punch or the champagne or the water and send Nixon and everybody else in that place off on a major acid trip, whether they want to go or not."

"You mean without telling them?"

Leary shook his head, amazed. "Damn you can be dense—*YES!*"

"But how can you be sure it's them?"

"That's Lovenuts looking exactly like he did in the photo spread they ran of them in *Life.*"

"But how would they get in there?"

"It isn't the Pentagon or the White House, Mike, it's just a club. And my Mellon friends who lent us Millbrook and financed the Brotherhood's orange sunshine operation have been going to Rolling Rock with their horsey friends all their lives. All it would take was somebody on the inside to set it up—an assistant manager, somebody like that. It wouldn't take much to fix a catering contract or hire some ringers. It only takes one person to spike a punch bowl."

"But *why*? What's their game?"

Leary sat on a corner of the bed. "I don't know, but let's try to think like them. They get everybody tripped out and then...what?"

Mulligan felt things about to spin out of control, as if Klingons had taken over the *Enterprise* and beamed him into a sailboat in a hurricane.

"I don't know, Mike," Leary said. "My guess is the Pranksters are doing it for laughs—tripping out the establishment—ha–ha–ha. But the Brotherhood doesn't move unless there's money, and for the Weathermen, it's all about bringing down the system. But their karmas are light years apart. I can't imagine the three of them agreeing on a plan."

"Maybe one of them's double-crossing the others, telling them what they want to hear?"

"Or it's a three-sided triple cross," Leary said with a sigh as he put his elbows on his knees, slumped forward, and rested his chin in his hands.

"You know, Tim," Mulligan said, "ever since Catherine got mugged I've been worried about somebody grabbing her for ransom. If Getty's grandson's ear can bring a million, what could a convention of the richest Republicans in the country and the President bring?"

"Billions, but it would take a small army to control hundreds of freaked-out Republicans. And if there was a ransom, how would they get out of there?"

"Whatever they're planning, they'd have to neutralize the security guards," Mulligan said. "And Nixon has the Secret Service."

"That wouldn't be too hard," Leary said. "There's a drug called DMSO, dimethyl sulfoxide, that penetrates directly through the skin and gets into the bloodstream in seconds. It can piggyback other molecules along with it, so if they mix up a batch laced with LSD into an oil or a cream, all they have to do is smear it on door knobs or toilet seats or urinal handles, and forty minutes later anyone who touched it is off and tripping with their senses, judgement, reflexes, everything out of kilter. It would be easy to overpower anybody on a trip."

"Do they have the balls for something like that?"

"The Pranksters may be crazy, but they're not criminal. To them it's a prank—spike the drinks and get out of there, laughing all the way. Violence isn't the Brotherhood's game either. They're just surfers from Laguna Beach out for a good time. The Weathermen, on the other hand...."

"But what if Nixon isn't part of their plans?" Mulligan asked.

"I don't get you."

"The report said he came in early. What if that's screwing them up?"

"I guess it's possible. Or maybe they're not making their move until tomorrow? Or it could be a C.I.A. operation."

"What the hell does the C.I.A. have to do with LSD?"

"If it weren't for the C.I.A. you'd never have even heard of LSD. They handed out tens of thousands of doses to researchers at universities like Michigan and Harvard and Stanford for tests on human guinea pigs, including Allen Ginsberg and Ken Kesey. When the C.I.A. asked Sandoz Labs to make a few kilos—enough for a hundred million doses—Sandoz said no. So they got Eli Lily to violate the patent laws and supply them in the name of national security. The first illegal acid was made under contract for the C.I.A., and now they're trying to stuff the genie back in the bottle."

"What were they testing for?"

"The Holy Grail of espionage, Mike...mind-control. They believe they're on a noble, patriotic quest for the drug that will make friend and foe alike do anything they want."

"You mean brainwashing, like in *The Manchurian Candidate*?"

"Exactly."

"But it doesn't make sense the C.I.A. would be working with these groups. Especially the Weathermen."

"Not working with, Mike...*using*. The C.I.A. wouldn't hesitate to double-cross anyone. What if they've infiltrated the Pranksters, or the Brotherhood, or the Weathermen—or all three—and suckered them into this to set them up for a fall to discredit the counter-culture? That's how they like to work. Then again, they may not even be involved."

"Okay, Tim, you've convinced me. We have to warn Nixon."

"Warn Nixon? Are you crazy?"

"We need to get going if we're going to stop them."

"You are crazy. What are you going to say...Timothy Leary says don't drink the electric Kool-Aid? Do that and you and me and Catherine and her friend all go to jail—me for thirty years. No thanks. Besides, like you said, he may not even be the target."

"We can't take that chance, Tim. Don't worry, I'll keep you out of it."

"Oh, bullshit. There's no way you can guarantee that and you know it, and I'm not going to risk spending the rest of my life in prison for a bunch of plutocrats who'd just as soon see me dead. Let's just get the hell out of here and keep going to Canada."

"We have to warn the President. It's our duty."

"*Duty*? After what that prick's done to me you want me to risk everything to keep him from an acid trip? Hell, it's exactly what the son-of-a-bitch needs to get his head out of his ass."

"But what if it's more than a prank? What if they are planning to kidnap him, or hold him hostage? Would you risk it then?"

"It's fucking Nixon, Mike. I'd have to think about it."

"Well think about this—is there anybody besides you who might have seen that news report who could recognize those people and realize that the President of the United States might be in danger?"

Leary gave him a wary look. "What are you trying to say?"

"You're the one always yammering about good-karma this and bad-karma that. Well, if that wasn't Timothy Leary's karma that just came down on that news report, then who in the hell's was it?"

After the flunky choked him Gridley jumped out of the car and started to chase him down to beat the shit out of him, but he pulled up after a few steps. What if the Dago Babe did work for Nixon? It would be just like Nixon. The flunky could wait. He'd be talking to Nixon soon, and if the flunky was lying he'd bore him a new asshole with a power drill.

"We're not going to arrest her," Gridley told his agents. "Not yet, anyway. We're just going to have an informal interview. I'm going to see if they have a place we can use."

He went into the clubhouse and flashed his badge at the concierge. "I need a room with a telephone where I can conduct meetings without anyone knowing."

The concierge checked his watch. "I suppose you could use the office in the maintenance building. They've gone for the day. It's just down the hill a bit, if that's suitable?"

"Perfect."

"I'll have my assistant meet you there with a key."

As he went to inform the others, he was astonished to see none other than Miss Moneybags at the far end of the parking lot. What the hell was she doing here? This was too good to be true.

He ducked behind a parked limousine and scurried in a crouch along the rows of cars until he was just ahead of her. When she walked by he stood up, catching her by surprise. "So, Miss DeWolfe, we meet again."

She gasped, jumping back. "Mr. Gridley!"

He had scared her shitless—good. He walked up to her, hating the fact that she was taller than him. "Let's take a walk and have ourselves a chat."

"But, but...I'm...I'm meeting somebody."

"Yes, Miss Abruzzi. What a coincidence. I'm waiting for her too. I'll have one of my men escort her over as soon as she arrives, and we can all play a little game of who-do-you-know. Won't that be fun?"

"I'm...I'm sorry, but I can't."

She turned to leave, so he grabbed her wrist. "Oh, but I insist."

"What are you doing? Take your hands off me!"

She certainly was a spirited bitch. He dug his fingertips into her arm to show her who was boss. "I said we're going for a walk."

To his astonishment he suddenly found himself—*AIRBORNE*—flipping like a flapjack and thumping to the ground with a *WHUMP* that knocked the wind out of him.

"Don't you ever *dare* put your hands on me again!" she yelled as she pushed his face into the blacktop with one hand and judoed his wrist into a pretzel with the other. "*Understand!*"

He was barely able to utter a feeble, "Yes," when he heard Ashkopf yell, "Get off him!"

They pulled her away and he scrambled to his knees and grabbed her by an ankle, holding on with all his might while the others scuffled her to the ground and wrestled her into handcuffs.

Chapter 41

Smoking Guns

FALLINGWATER, THE WONDER-HOUSE DESIGNED BY ARCHITECT FRANK LLOYD Wright, straddles a rippling waterfall on a little creek called Bear Run. Built during the Great Depression for department-store magnate Edgar Kaufman as a retreat from the smoke and soot of industrial Pittsburgh, it had been donated to a nonprofit conservancy for conservation. Wright had been the model for Howard Roark, Ayn Rand's ultra-conservative protagonist in *The Fountainhead*, making it the perfect location for a Conservative Ladies' Council's fashion show and seminar on the calamities certain to befall women if the Equal Rights Amendment ever passed.

Jenny had kept a low profile among the elite of anti-feminist America, fibbing about everything except her name and occupation. She had been glad, though, to be away from Gridley, and for the chance to visit Fallingwater for the first time. She was entranced with how the natural stone architecture blended so effortlessly with Mother Nature. Who wouldn't be happy in such a home?

It was after six when the caravan of limos departed for the ride to the clubhouse. At the crest of Rolling Rock hill they saw a military helicopter parked on the lawn and Nancy Reagan exulted, "Nixon's here!"

People were milling about outside, cocktails in hand; a tuxedoed jazz combo in the gazebo was playing "Chattanooga Choo Choo." She was hoping McGill would be waiting, but to her dismay Ashkopf, his left arm in a makeshift sling, walked up and said, "Please come with me."

"What happened to you?"

"Just follow me," he said with a snarl.

She complied, a silent hurry-up hike around the back of the clubhouse. They went down a sloping driveway and came to an ivy-covered stone building tucked back in the woods, its four industrial garage doors shut tight. Nearby was a big-rig with *Rolling Rock Farms* on the door, its trailer stacked with bales of hay. A white Plymouth with a whip antenna was parked beside a set of wooden steps going up to a second story.

Another of Gridley's agents came out on the landing and glared down at her. Ashkopf motioned for her to go up. When she hesitated, he gave her a shove. "After you, Miss Cowgirl."

They knew! She held tightly to the railing, taking one slow step at a time, like she was climbing a gallows.

The agent on the landing held the screen door, and as she went in she noticed his lip was cut and swollen.

Gridley was on the phone. "That's right, sergeant. The Cloverleaf Motel, room seventy-four, and Seven Springs, room 323. How long?… Good. Get back to me here as soon as you know anything."

He hung up and turned to her; he had a large red abrasion on his forehead, as though he'd skinned it falling off a bicycle. "Well, Miss Abruzzi, or should I say Mademoiselle Susannah?" He grinned a wicked *gotcha*.

She was trembling all over, but kept silent.

"You're a lawyer," he said. "Take a peek at the evidence." He pointed to photographs spread across the desk. "I knew you looked familiar, but you were with Rusty, so I didn't make the connection. Then your flunky friend said you'd been living in Paris, and it clicked."

She was stunned to see a photo of herself snuggled up with Morrison on an air mattress, and others of her partying with Janis, Jimi, Duane, John, and Yoko. This was bad.

Gridley was leering, triumphant. "That *is* you, isn't it?"

It was her all right, but she kept quiet.

"Cat got your tongue?" He picked up one of the photos, leaned across the desk, and stuck it in her face. "That's Timothy Leary on the balcony of the same room where you were fucking Morrison. It's Leary I want, not you. Turn him over and I'll see to it that you and your rich-bitch friend who tipped you off don't do too much time."

He wasn't making sense. Was he talking about Catherine? Was he saying it was Catherine who warned them about the raid? Impossible.

"So what will it be?" Gridley said. "Will you cooperate, or do I throw the book at you both for aiding and abetting a fugitive and revealing government secrets and a dozen other charges I haven't thought of yet?"

Maybe it wasn't so impossible? Catherine had been to events at Millbrook when she was at Vassar, and would have tried to help Leary if she could. And she had been working for Nixon, so she might have known about the raid. One thing for sure, Catherine was the only person she knew who had the wherewithal to just snap her fingers and make people jump through hoops of fire. Now that she thought about it, who else *but* Catherine could have helped them?

"I'm waiting, Miss Abruzzi," Gridley said as he took a blood-stained handkerchief from his pocket and gingerly patted his wounded forehead.

For some reason she thought of McGill and wished she could have been truthful with him. She wondered what he would do in her shoes, and nearly laughed out loud when it hit her. She had nothing to lose. "I'm sorry, Mr. Gridley, but for reasons of national security, I am not permitted to answer your questions."

Hundreds of ecstatic Republicans had poured out of the Rolling Rock clubhouse and swarmed across the lawn to greet the surprise arrival of *Army One* and the President of the United States. Nixon acknowledged the applause from the helicopter's door with his double-fisted V-for-Victory signs, then walked down the short flight of steps and into the crowd, glad-handing and back-slapping and sweating like a ditch-digger in the heat. Finally, Haldeman got him into a limousine that ferried him to a guest house less than two minutes away. At a larger house just down the way the travelling White House staff was setting up operations.

The guest house was comfortable—oriental carpets, stone fireplace, French doors leading to a patio with picturesque views of the valley on one side and a fairway on the other, a Steinway grand piano in the main room, and artworks of steeplechases and fox hunts everywhere. He took a shower and shaved his heavy five-o'clock shadow while Manolo prepared a martini with three olives, shined his black wing-tip shoes, and laid out a summer-weight blue suit for the rubber-chicken dinner coming up. Nixon could use a night off, but this would not be it.

The new schedule was for Haldeman, Ehrlichman, and Bullcannon to fly to Washington tonight in the backup helicopter, leaving him with a skeleton staff. In the morning he was to play golf in a foursome with Billy Graham, local golf legend Arnold Palmer, and the CACA Conference sponsor, Richie Mellon. The afternoon was for schmoozing and wheedling contributions out of the fattest cats in the country for the Committee to Re-Elect the President—CREEP. Pat and the girls were to fly to Washington from California in the morning, where they would join Haldeman, Ehrlichman, Bullcannon and their wives, and helicopter up together for the big banquet tomorrow night.

Nixon took a call from the minority leader of the U.S. Senate, Everett Dirksen of Illinois. "Yes Ev, I know, I know, a billion here, a billion there, pretty soon we're talking real money....Yes, the tobacco states are

Democratic, but not for long, Ev, not for long. Our Southern Strategy is working exactly like I said it would. Letting Democrats take the blame for giving equal rights to blacks is turning all the bubbas into Republicans. Just tell the tobacco boys we'll take care of them if they cough up what we need now…What? *Me*…make a joke?…Tobacco coughing it up? Why, I guess I did…That bad, huh?…Well send me to the punitentiary! Ha!…You too, Ev. Let me know when you get 'em all signed up."

As Nixon put down the receiver Haldeman said, "That boy who made the maid tape is here, and he claims he has something better."

McGill ignored the Secret Service agent stationed outside Nixon's door and kept a firm grip on his gym bag as he paced the second-floor hallway, wondering if his bluff had kept Gridley from arresting Jenny and wishing he had a cigarette. Man, did he ever need a cigarette.

After forty minutes Nixon's Filipino valet came out carrying an armful of clothes, followed by Haldeman, who beckoned him to come in. Nixon, in slacks and a white shirt, was bent over in a chair, tying his shoes. McGill took a deep breath. "Hello, Mr. President."

Nixon glanced up. "Hello to you too. What's your name again?"

"Art McGill, Mr. President."

"We listened to your interview with the maid, Mr. McGill. Seems you've traced the conspiracy back another twenty years. Good job, son."

"Thank you, sir, but you have to hear this new tape I made of Commissioner Anslinger right away. He admits everything, even brags about it. I'm certain it's the smoking gun you've been looking for."

"Very well," Nixon said as he stood up and went to the mirror to tie his tie. "Bob, better get John in here for this."

"Yes sir. What about Bullcannon?"

"No, not this time," Nixon said. "He's not getting behind the project like I hoped he would."

Haldeman opened the door and yelled down the hall; McGill took one of the tape decks from his gym bag and set it up on a coffee table; Ehrlichman arrived and closed the door.

"I made this yesterday when I was driving Commissioner Anslinger here from the airport," McGill said as they drew chairs in close. "It's a little fuzzy because I had to hide the microphone under the seat."

Nixon arched an eyebrow. "You mean you bugged him?"

SMOKING GUNS | 373

"I thought he might open up if he didn't know."

"Ha," Nixon laughed. "A man after my own heart. Go ahead, son."

"Yes sir," McGill said and hit PLAY. "I'm driving, the woman from the bank who's been helping me, Miss Abruzzi, is riding shotgun, and Anslinger and Gridley are in the back."

He turned up the volume, pausing the tape from time to time to answer questions. When they got to Anslinger's story of the scientific expert turning into a bat, they all roared in laughter.

When it ended Nixon said, "A fine job, young man, a fine job. This is exactly what I need to convince people they've been gouged on gasoline and toilet paper for forty years by a conspiracy of billionaires."

"Thank you, sir."

"Does Gridley know about the tape?" Ehrlichman asked.

"No, sir, I didn't think it wise to inform him."

"How about the woman?" Haldeman asked.

"Yes, sir. I had to take her into my confidence. It's like she's a member of the team. I couldn't have done it without her."

Nixon frowned, his eyes darting back and forth between Haldeman and Ehrlichman.

"Can she be trusted?" Ehrlichman asked.

"Absolutely," McGill said. "She went to law school with Ms. DeWolfe. But there are some new problems."

"Problems?" Ehrlichman said. "What kind of problems?"

"Mr. President, I need to speak with you about it alone, if that's okay."

"*What?*" Nixon said.

"Please, sir, I can't tell anybody but you."

"You are nothing if not audacious, young man," Nixon said.

"I don't have any choice, Mr. President. Please, sir, it could make all the difference in whether Project Independence succeeds or fails."

Nixon sighed and said, "Very well, you've earned it."

After the others left McGill said, "Mr. President, I had no idea my actions could ever lead to this kind of situation."

"Just what kind of situation are we talking about, son?"

"Well, sir, just before Mulligan offered me this job, a friend and I had started a business."

"Nothing illegal I hope."

"Oh no, sir. It was perfectly legal, and it still is, but, uh...."

"Then what's the problem?"

"Well sir, we make a certain item," and McGill reached into his gym bag, pulled out a Bird, and handed it to Nixon.

Nixon pinched the alligator clip open and closed a few times. "Looks like some kind of a bird. A stork or something."

"That's what we call it—*The Bird*. Take a look at the bottom. We've even applied for a trademark."

Nixon flipped it over, chuckling as he read MADE BY GENUINE HIPPIES. "Are you a genuine hippie, Mr. McGill?"

"More like a semi-hippie, Mr. President."

"So you were getting it off the ground when you came to work for me? Is that right?"

"Yes, sir."

"So what's the problem, son?"

Was Nixon putting him on? "Well, sir, you see...it's a roach clip."

Nixon wrinkled his brow as he turned the Bird every which way. "I don't see how it could catch any bugs."

"No, sir. 'Roach' is slang for the end of a joint."

Nixon was perplexed at his explanation. "A joint? I don't understand."

"'Joint' is a slang term for a marijuana cigarette, same as a 'doobie,' and a 'roach' is the end when it burns down, like a cigarette butt. It comes from the cockroach song you sang us, remember?" and McGill sang out:

> "La Cucaracha, la cucaracha
> Ya no puedo caminar
> Por que no tiene, por que no tiene
> Marijuana que fumar."

Nixon put his hand to his mouth and let out a little *burrrp*, like he had indigestion.

"You see, Mr. President, because pot's illegal it's expensive, so you want to smoke a roach all the way down, so nothing goes to waste. But roaches are hard to pass, and you're always burning your fingers and your lips. The Bird makes them easy to pass and easy to smoke. It solves problems, it's inexpensive, and it's cool because it's made out of an old fork. It's the world's best roach clip, Mr. President. Everybody says it's worth millions. Just last weekend we had a booth at a fair up here," and he reached into his gym bag and pulled out several thousand-dollar bundles of bills. Nixon's eyes popped.

"We took in more than twice this much, Mr. President. We can't make them fast enough. And we've got an ad coming out in *Rolling Stone* in a couple of weeks." He pulled out his copy of the ad and handed it to Nixon. "It's like the old saying about a better mousetrap. People are going to beat a path to our door."

Nixon leaned back to read, the ad in one hand, the Bird in the other.

"I'm really sorry, sir, but I didn't think selling them up here could be a problem. But a reporter saw a story in it, and he knows Gridley, and he has a law he wants to get passed that would make things like the Bird illegal, so he got a warrant to arrest us to stir up publicity for it."

"Is this the thing Gridley and Anslinger talked about on your tape?"

"Yes, sir."

"Hmmm…What's the charge, exactly?"

"Theft of government property. He's saying we stole the forks, but I bought them at Navy surplus down in Newport News, and have receipts and everything. But he doesn't care if it sticks. He just wants to hold the Bird up at a press conference as an example of how bad hippies are."

Nixon studied the Bird more closely. "I can see what he's thinking. This thing may be a better mousetrap, but it's for helping people break the law, and it says U.S. Government on it, like it's officially sanctioned, and I don't like that, son," Nixon said sternly. "Not one bit."

"But sir, you know the law only passed because of a conspiracy of lies, and if it weren't on the books, we could have been growing our own fuel since the 1930's. And now that you can prove who did it, you'll be able to fix it. It's your *duty*, Mr. President."

Nixon was silent for a few moments. "But I have a problem with the drug aspect, son. Everybody knows people drink to have fun. They use drugs just to get high."

"Mr. President, with all due respect, that's totally out to lunch. Your own commission said it was harmless compared to alcohol and tobacco…remember? Those drugs kill hundreds of thousands every year, and no one in all of history has ever died from pot. Even if it had nothing to do with hemp and energy and paper and national security and all the rest of it, it's still an evil law, Mr. President."

Nixon snorted an irritated *humph*, and sensing it was now or never, McGill reached into his pocket, took out the fattie, and offered it to Nixon. "Mr. President, you need to try this. You owe it to America."

"What is it?"

"Most people call it a 'joint' or a 'doobie,' Mr. President. Joints like this are 'fatties,' because they're so thick. Smoke it with a few friends, and you'll see for yourself it's more fun than alcohol. And there's no hangover."

Nixon put the ad on the table and took the joint from him, his jowly face puckering up as if he were sucking on a lemon. After glaring at it for a few seconds, Nixon flashed a tiny, frustrated smile, picked up the Bird, pinched open the clip, and to McGill's total astonishment, snipped in the fattie and said, "Is this how it works?"

"Yes sir, Mr. President, that's the idea."

"So if I smoke this thing, will I fly around the room like a bat and land at the bottom of an inkwell?"

"No, sir, that's more like what happens on a bad acid trip. But if you do it with some friends, you'll probably all laugh your asses off."

"Ha! Will it let me slip in an extra beat on the piano, like Harry says the jazzbos do? Will it make Nixon a jazzbo?"

"No, sir. But it might inspire you when you're jamming."

"Jamming? You mean improvising?"

"Yes, sir. If you'd like to give it a try, I saw a piano downstairs, and I have my guitar out in the car."

"Are you suggesting that you and I smoke this thing and play music together?"

"Uh…only if you're in the mood, Mr. President. And it's Panama Red, so you don't need much. We can do a few tokes, and you can save the roach for later."

Nixon rolled his eyes as he gave his head a shake, then looked at him with the sincerity of a pastor discussing the afterlife. "Son, let's get back to the business at hand."

"Yes, sir."

"I'm confused. If Gridley has a warrant, why hasn't he arrested you?"

"It's a John Doe, and he doesn't know it's me he's after. But he has agents tracking us down, and my name's on the incorporation papers, so he's bound to find out pretty soon. And if he calls a news conference, and it comes out I work for you…."

"Yes, I see what you mean. The operation could go up in smoke. Ha!"

McGill couldn't even fake a laugh. "I can't tell you how sorry I am, Mr. President."

"You certainly are full of surprises, young man."

"And that's not the worst of it, sir. You have to call Gridley off Miss Abruzzi before he arrests her too."

"Call him off *who*?"

"The woman who's been helping me. I tried to bluff him out of it, but I don't know if it worked. I couldn't have done any of this without her. You've got to help her, Mr. President, you've just *got* to!"

"Bluff him off?" Nixon said. "I don't understand."

"An hour ago Gridley showed me some photos of her at a party with some rock stars and Timothy Leary—"

"*Timothy Leary!*"

"Yes, sir. He said he was going to arrest her for helping him escape, so I told him she was working undercover for you, and if he laid a finger on her he'd ruin our operation and you'd have his ass in a sling."

Nixon was incredulous. "You told Gridley that someone who's helping Timothy Leary is working for *me*?"

"It was all I could think of, and it's halfway true. Without her, we wouldn't have any proof about the conspiracy."

Nixon frowned, set the Bird on the table, leaned back, and started drumming his fingertips on the leather chair…drumming…drumming. "I thought he was looking for an American stripper over in France?"

"He thinks it's Miss Abruzzi. She was there at the time, studying at the Sorbonne. She's only had her job at the bank for a few weeks."

"And how exactly did you get involved with this woman, son?"

"She was just there in the room when I went to the bank to research Mellon, and they assigned her to help me."

"Hmmm…that's quite a coincidence, wouldn't you say?"

"That's nothing, Mr. President. If you want to talk about a coincidence that's totally cosmic, take a look at these!"

He pulled the Fort Pitt Photo envelope from the gym bag and handed Nixon the enlargements. "My grandfather took a lot of Polaroids at the World Series the year the Pirates beat the Yankees. I've just had these blown up. That's my dad, that's me, and that's Miss Abruzzi next to me."

"So your families went to the game together?"

"No, sir, they were just sitting next to us. We'd never met them."

"How old were you?"

"Seventh grade."

Nixon flipped to the next enlargement. "Is that you with Bob Hope and Bing Crosby?"

"Yes, sir. My dad knew Hope from the war, and we ran into them at the game. I'm pretty sure it was Miss Abruzzi's father who took that one for us with my grandfather's Polaroid."

Nixon flipped to the next photo and asked, "Why's she holding a towel to her face?"

McGill recounted the story of the Mickey Mantle foul ball. "But I haven't told her any of this yet, Mr. President. I want her to like me for who I am today, not for something that happened when we were kids."

Nixon gazed at him in bemused bewilderment. "So years ago you might have saved her life at a baseball game, you hadn't seen her since, she doesn't remember you from back then, and now you think you're in love with her? Is that it, son?"

"*Exactly*, Mr. President! It's fate, or predestination, or karma, or in the stars—whatever you want to call it—we're soul mates."

Nixon huffed a heavy sigh, leaned forward, put his hand on McGill's knee, and looked him in the eye. "I don't have any boys of my own, so I don't often give romantic advice, man-to-man. But I have to say that keeping something like this from a woman isn't in your best interest, son. You've got to think strategically with women—like with China, and Russia. Do you understand?"

"Uh…not exactly, Mr. President."

"What I mean is these pictures will tilt her in your favor, son. Women live and die for this sort of thing. You do want to win her hand, don't you?"

"Oh *yes*, Mr. President, more than anything. But now I'm worried that because of me Gridley will arrest her, and she'll go to prison and never talk to me again."

Nixon removed his hand from McGill's knee and leaned back, his face tightening as his voice turned from soothing to somber. "If she helped Leary get away, that's aiding and abetting a fugitive, a serious charge, son, very serious."

"Yes, sir, I know. But even if she did it, it's only because she believes in justice and everybody knows Leary was framed by crooked cops. You'll give her a pardon, won't you, sir? You owe it to her, and if we become self-sufficient in energy because the tapes expose the conspiracy, the whole country will owe her too."

Nixon handed him back the photos, picked up the Bird, the fattie still clipped in the beak, and stared at it. "I must say this is one of the most unusual situations I've ever been involved in, and I've been in some doozies. I'll have a talk with Gridley and try to sort it out. You say he's here, and the woman too?"

"Yes sir."

"Good. For now, do what you young people say—'Float with the current.'"

"Uh…I think you mean 'go with the flow,' Mr. President."

"Just what the hell is that supposed to mean, anyway?"

"It's about how to deal with an acid trip if it starts turning into a bummer. It means don't try to fight it, because fighting only makes you freak out even worse."

They heard a *knock-knock-knock*. Nixon pinched open the clip to take out the fattie, but it dropped to the rug and rolled under his chair. "*Shit!*" He bent over and picked it up barely in time to stick it and the Bird in his jacket pocket as Haldeman peeked around the door. "Mr. President?"

"Yes, Bob," Nixon said, expertly feigning innocence. "What is it?"

"Sir, they want to know if you'll be coming for dinner."

"Damn. They weren't expecting me until tomorrow, were they?"

Haldeman seemed surprised. "No, but you said—"

"Well, I've changed my mind. Fuck the rubber chicken."

"They'll be disappointed, Mr. President."

"Of course they will, but I need to relax, take a night off, maybe play a little piano. I haven't had a night to myself in weeks. Tell them I need my beauty sleep, or I'm saving the planet from World War III."

"Would you like them to send something over?" Haldeman asked.

"Maybe just a tray of cold cuts and some potato salad, that's all I want. Are cold cuts all right with you, son, or do you prefer the rubber chicken?"

McGill was flabbergasted—had he just been invited to dine with Nixon? "Cold cuts are fine, Mr. President."

"Well, you never know," Nixon said. "Bob, have them send over both, enough for everybody."

"Everybody?" Haldeman said.

"Since you and John are leaving, Mr. McGill and the woman who's been helping him will be using your rooms. I want to keep them out of trouble until we sort this out. What's her name again, son?"

"Miss Jennifer Abruzzi," McGill said.

"She's here somewhere," Nixon said. "Have her come over right away. And tell Gridley that I said to lay off if he is giving her a hard time."

"He'll want to see you, sir," Haldeman said.

"No, not now. I want to hear the tape again and sleep on it before I see him. After breakfast will be soon enough."

"Yes, Mr. President."

"Oh, and Bob, see if they'll make up some fresh-squeezed lemonade. It'll go good with vodka on a hot night like this."

Gridley's men had left Catherine handcuffed, roped to a chair, and her mouth gagged. Her screams came out as inaudible grunts, but she could hear every word through the paper-thin walls as Gridley badgered Jenny to answer questions about Leary. And what was all the talk about McGill? It sounded as if Jenny were working with him? How could it be that they knew each other? And was Nixon here too? Whatever this was, it was more than a bankers' conference. Mulligan would be furious at how she'd screwed up. Worse, he and Leary were about to walk into a trap, and if they ended up in prison, it would be all her fault.

Gridley had gone through her purse and found two wallets. "What's with the phony ID, Miss DeWolfe? Or is it Mrs. Bennington? Got something to hide, do we?" He found the motel and hotel room keys and alerted the Pennsylvania State Police, who dispatched units to the Cloverleaf and Seven Springs. His men searched her car and found the maps with the route to Niagara Falls, and upon finding the receipt from the women's clinic, Gridley said with a knowing smirk, "So we're a little bit preggers, are we? Is Dr. Leary the daddy?" He called his Washington office and ordered them to get subpoenas to search her house, phone records, and bank accounts.

The phone rang. "Gridley here....Yes, sergeant....Nothing?...You sure?...Shit. Stake them both out....Don't worry about overtime, the White House will cover it...Good. Page me at the clubhouse if you miss me here...No, don't arrest them unless you're sure it's Leary and only if he's about to escape. He's honey to flies. We don't want to scare the others away....Yes. Trace all calls, take photographs, and keep them under surveillance until I get there....Thanks."

She heard the phone hang up and Gridley say, "Ready to talk yet, Miss Abruzzi? Or perhaps you prefer Susannah?"

"I told you," she heard Jenny say, "I am not permitted to answer for reasons of national security. Now may I please leave?"

"I've got a little surprise that might change your mind," Gridley said. "Ashkopf, introduce her to our other guest."

The door swung open, and her eyes met Jenny's.

"*Catherine?*" Jenny said.

"Yes," Gridley said, "it's your old law school chum and current partner in crime."

The phone rang, and Gridley pounced on it. "Yes sergeant, what have you got?....Oh, hi Bob, I wasn't expecting you....You're looking for *who?*...Yes, she's here. Why do you want her?...No, I'm not giving her a hard time....Of course not, but...but...yes, of course." His eyes burned with anger as he stuck the receiver out to Jenny and said, "It's for you."

Jenny took it. "Hello?...Yes, I'm working with Mr. McGill....Meet the President?...I'd be happy to....Yes, may I bring my friend Catherine DeWolfe along? She's working with Mr. McGill too....Yes, she's right here....I'll hold...."

Nixon noodled on the Steinway, playing the warm-up exercises his piano teacher had taught him decades ago. His young aide ran to fetch a guitar, and Haldeman was on the phone tracking down the woman. Nixon wasn't sure what to think about Gridley and roach clips and Leary. All he knew for sure was his aide had found a smoking gun, and he intended to use it.

McGill returned with his guitar, dripping with perspiration from jogging in the heat. "Let me tune to you, Mr. President," he said as he took it out of the case. "Give me A below Middle C."

Nixon hit the note, holding the key down for sustain as McGill cocked his ear, tuned a couple of pegs, strummed a chord and said, "Got it."

"Where do we start," Nixon asked. "I haven't played in ages."

"When you're jamming with anybody new, starting with a familiar tune is a good way to loosen up and get in a groove. How about 'La Cucaracha,' or 'Happy Days Are Here Again?' What's your singing key?"

"Okay," Nixon said. "'Happy Days,' in G."

He pounded out chords on the piano and sang while his aide accompanied on guitar. This was fun. If things went well, maybe after Haldeman, Ehrlichman, and Bullcannon flew off he'd try a bit of the fattie, just to see what all the hullabaloo was about, and pray he didn't fly around the room like a bat and crash at the bottom of an inkwell.

They took a breather, and Manolo refilled their drinks just as Haldeman came down the staircase and announced, "We located the woman. She's in a maintenance building with Gridley. He says he isn't giving her a hard time, but I don't believe him."

"So is she coming?" Nixon asked.

"I have her on hold. She says Ms. DeWolfe is with her, and wants her to come along too, so I thought I'd better ask you first."

Catherine watched as Gridley's face glowed a translucent red, like a cherry lollipop, waiting in furious silence while Jenny held the phone to her ear.

"Yes, Mr. Haldeman," Jenny said. "A golf cart?...Thank you. We'll start walking up right away to meet it....Yes, here he is."

Jenny put her hand over the mouthpiece as she passed it to Gridley. "If you want to keep your job, you better let her go, right now."

Gridley snatched it out of her hands. "Bob, I've got to see the President, right away....Tomorrow? But Bob...but...yes, of course. Good-bye." He slammed down the receiver. "Turn the bitch fucking loose!"

Ashkopf unlocked the cuffs, untied the rope, and removed the gag.

She took her first deep breath in an hour and tried to stand up, but a leg buckled and dumped her back on the chair.

Jenny rushed in and took her by the shoulders. "Are you all right?"

"My leg's asleep, that's all."

Jenny helped her to her feet, and they embraced in a warm hug.

"This doesn't end here," Gridley said. "I don't know how you bamboozled Nixon, but before this is over I'll have enough evidence to send you both up the river till your pussies dry up."

"We have to be going," Jenny said calmly. "The President is waiting."

Catherine strove to be just as cool and collected as her friend. "Please return my things, Mr. Gridley. Right now."

Gridley was fuming as he picked up her wallet, keys, IDs, maps and receipts, jammed everything in her purse, and threw it to her like it was a medicine ball and he was trying to knock her off her feet.

She side-stepped and caught it like an infielder. "Thank you, Mr. Gridley. And you should have that little owwie on your forehead looked at before it gets infected and they have to amputate."

As they hurried down Jenny said, "What are you doing here?"

"I want to ask you the same thing. Are you really working with McGill?"

"For about a week."

"But how?"

"It's a long story. Did you really help Tim and me escape? Is he safe?

How did you do it?"

"If you don't know, they can't accuse you of lying."

"You're right. Thank you for whatever you did."

"Don't mention it. So where is McGill?"

"I haven't seen him since this morning, but he was hoping to meet with Nixon. He secretly taped an interview we had with Anslinger, and he thinks it's the smoking gun Nixon wants."

"So you know about the project?" Catherine said.

"Artie told me all about it, and I've read the reports."

"Artie? Oh…you mean McGill. Did you tell him about Tim?"

"I never said a word to anyone about Tim. How did you ever get a job working for Nixon?"

"That's a long story too."

There was so much to catch up on, but a golf cart driven by a man in a coat-and-tie and mirrored sunglasses rounded a curve and stopped in front of them. "Abruzzi and DeWolfe?"

They rode in silence, stifling their questions in front of a Secret Service agent. They came to a house, and another agent in mirrored sunglasses escorted them up the walk.

Jenny whispered, "What are we going to say about Tim?"

"Play dumb and deny everything, to both Nixon and McGill."

As Mulligan drove Leary, had been in the sleeping berth behind the driver's seat, peering out from behind the curtain and filling him in on what to expect if they encountered anyone voyaging through the netherworlds of neurospace on a surprise acid trip. He learned about "set and setting"—the mind-set of the person taking the trip, and the physical setting in which the trip took place, supposedly made all the difference in whether an LSD experience was one of euphoric, life-changing enlightenment or, if the setting was unpleasant or the tripper had psychological insecurities, it turned into a house-of-horrors roller-coaster through the brimstone fires of hell. He also learned more than he ever wanted to know about the stages of an LSD trip, and how to coach a freaked-out tripper through a bummer.

"The biggest problem," Mulligan said, "will be explaining how I think I know what they're planning to do."

"Maybe not," Leary said. "*Life Magazine* did a big photo spread on the

Pranksters a few years ago. Lovenuts was all over it. Just tell them you stopped at the truck stop and saw him on the news."

"You want me to say I recognized him from an old magazine?"

"You can say you saw the article doing your research. Don't mention that you recognized the others, though, just him."

"And what if Gridley's found Catherine, and the maps?"

"In that case, you tell them you're eloping, and taking a traditional American honeymoon at Niagara Falls. She's pregnant, so they'll buy it."

They got off the turnpike at the Donegal exit, a lonely rural tollbooth without even a gas station. At the intersection was a billboard with a skier pointing to Seven Springs Resort to the left and a sign with an arrow for Fallingwater to the right. He followed Leary's directions, and after a few miles came to an imposing *DO NOT ENTER* sign and a gate.

"Hasn't changed since the last time I was here in 1945," Leary said as they drove by and cased the entrance. "You'll be able to turn around at one of the estates up ahead."

The plan was for Leary to hide in the compartment while Mulligan talked his way onto the grounds, changed into a suit, found the waiters and strong-armed the one Leary said was the most vulnerable, Lovenuts, into revealing their plans. He would simultaneously try to avoid Gridley and find Catherine and McGill to help with whatever had to be done.

Included in the Mack's cornucopia of spy goodies was a pair of hand-held walkie-talkies small enough to fit inside a jacket pocket. He told Leary, "I'll try to keep you posted, but don't call me unless it's an emergency."

They agreed Leary would take his chances hitchhiking if things got crazy. Mulligan pulled the Mack into the driveway for Mellontree Stables and stopped. No people in sight, just horses. They shook hands, Leary got into his compartment, and he drove back to the club's entrance.

A Pinkerton with a pistol on his hip and a clipboard in his hand came to the cab's door, looked up and said, "Where do you think you're going?"

He flashed his White House ID card. "I need a place to park this thing while Nixon's here, somewhere out of the way."

The guard glanced at the card and consulted his clipboard. "Doesn't say anything here about a truck."

"Nixon changed plans on us. Try tomorrow's list."

"Only got today's. What's in the trailer?"

"Emergency radio equipment. Wherever the President goes, we go."

The guard bought it and pointed up the hill. "When you get to the top, follow the sign to the service area and keep going out the back till you come to a big garage. Plenty of room there."

As he came to the crest of the hill he saw *Army One* sitting next to a huge green-and-white striped tent at the far end of the lawn. He followed the guard's directions down the hill and parked beside another big-rig, changed into a suit and tie, put on his holster, checked the chamber on his Smith-and-Wesson, and attached the silencer. He got out, knocked softly on the trailer wall and told Leary, "I'm heading out."

"Don't keep me in the dark too long, Mike, or I'm gone."

"You're safer in there than anywhere and you know it. Now, stay put."

"Bullshit. If something happens to you and they find that radio they'll know you've got an accomplice and tear this trailer apart."

"Just trust me and stay put."

He walked up the hill and around the outside to the party on the patio, where a jazz group was playing "Girl From Ipanema." He went to a portable bar where he could get a good look at the waiters coming and going and told the bartender, "I just got in. So Nixon's here already?"

"Yeah, came in early and left."

"You mean he's gone?"

"He's down at a guest house. They're saying he won't be back up here until tomorrow. What can I get you?"

"Just a beer. No glass."

He watched as the bartender pulled a green-and-white Rolling Rock out of a tub of ice and used a hand-held church-key to open it. Leary had warned that if it was an acid test, and he didn't want to end up over the psychedelic rainbow himself, not to drink anything that didn't come from a sealed container. Leary also said if the acid wasn't in the drinks, it would be in something easy to mix, like whipped cream on a pie, icing on a cake, or salad dressing. When an hors'-d'oeuvres waiter proffered a tray of shrimp he declined, thinking it could be in the cocktail sauce. He asked the bartender, "All you bartenders and waiters work for the club?"

"I do, but for big events like this they bring in caterers to help."

He studied the food-service crew—waiters, caterers, Pranksters, Weathermen, C.I.A.—whoever the hell they were, none were the faces they'd seen on TV. Could they have spiked the drinks and left?

A loudspeaker announced: "Telephone for Mr. Gridley. Mr. Gridley, telephone at the front desk."

He spotted Gridley getting up and hurried into the clubhouse ahead of him, grabbed a *Wall Street Journal* off a coffee table, and sat in a plush leather chair where he could observe from behind the newspaper. Gridley came in, a gauze bandage on his forehead. He talked for a minute on the phone, then cradled the receiver with his shoulder, grabbed the scratch pad on the counter and a pencil from a dispenser, wrote furiously, said something, and hung up, smiling as he tore off the top sheet from the pad and went outside. Mulligan followed, stopping at the desk to pick up the pad and pencil Gridley had just used. When he was sure no one was looking, he lightly shaded the top sheet with the pencil, like he'd seen on dozens of cop shows. To his surprise, it worked, and out popped "BIRDCO—VINCENT R WRIGHT, PRES, ARTHUR B MCGILL, VP" with a heavy underline beneath <u>MCGILL</u>."

So Gridley was on to McGill and his stupid Bird. Fuck. If they ever got out of this he would wring McGill's skinny neck with his bare hands.

Gridley was taking his seat at a table with a bald old man he assumed was Anslinger, a vaguely familiar middle-aged woman, and the reporter they'd seen on the news. He scanned the tables for Catherine or McGill. No luck. He went in through the men's locker room, walking between the rows of lockers and looking at every face. He went through the kitchen, striding around like he owned it, but nobody matched up.

He was heading to the dining room when a chef in a tall white toque stopped him and asked, "Can I help you?"

"It's a nice operation you have here. Very professional."

He casually walked through the dining room, the bar, the ballroom and billiard, club, and card rooms—nothing. Where the hell were they?

Frustrated, he went to use a men's room and was contemplating his next move when a man with reddish hair tinged with gray and almost as tall as he was stepped into the next stall. Why did he look so familiar?

He couldn't read the man's badge while taking a leak without appearing to be some kind of pervert, so he went to the sinks and slowly washed up. When the man finished and came over Mulligan casually glanced over and read: Edward DeWolfe—*Catherine's father!*

He tossed his towel in the trash and was out the door in a flash, his heart racing at the astonishing encounter. What might he have said? Hello, Mr. DeWolfe, it's a pleasure to meet you. I'm Mike Mulligan, and Timothy Leary says there's a good chance I've knocked-up your daughter. May I have your permission to ask for her hand in marriage?

Chapter 42

Nixon in the Sky with Diamonds

NIXON GOT UP FROM THE PIANO AND WENT OUTSIDE TO BID GOOD-BYE TO Haldeman and the others as they left for the landing zone in chauffeured golf carts. He hurried back in, tossed his suit-coat on a couch, rolled up his sleeves, and loosened his tie. "I'm all warmed up now," he told McGill. "Do you know 'Accentuate the Positive?' It was a big hit when I was in the Navy."

"I think so. Bing Crosby and the Andrews Sister, right?

> Ac-cent—tchu-ate the positive
> Eee-lim—my-nate the negative—"

"That's it all right."

"I don't know all the lyrics. You sing and play and I'll follow your changes and come in on the chorus."

Three renditions of the uptempo tune later, Nixon was dripping with sweat. He hadn't had this kind of fun in years and years. As they took it from the top again he heard the doorbell ring, and soon Manolo escorted in Ms. DeWolfe and a lovely, dark-haired woman. They stood in front of the piano, smiling while he and McGill played through, ending with a smartly harmonized:

> "And don't mess with Mister In-Between."

The women applauded as Nixon pushed back the piano bench and stood up to greet them. "Thank you, thank you very much. I'm surprised to see you here, Ms. DeWolfe."

"I had no idea you'd be here either, Mr. President. I'd like you to meet my dearest friend, Jennifer Abruzzi."

The woman extended her hand and said in a kitteny voice that could have melted butter, "I'm honored, Mr. President, and what a treat to hear you sing. You sound just like Bing Crosby, but with a bluesy edge."

Nixon felt himself blushing with pride. It was easy to see why his young aide was so smitten with this woman.

"Miss Abruzzi is a great singer, Mr. President," McGill said as he took his guitar from his shoulder and asked DeWolfe, "Is Mulligan here too?"

388 | THE ENERGY CAPER

A worried look came over her face. "I'm not supposed to talk about that, am I, Mr. President?"

"Quite right," Nixon said. "National security. I gave the order myself. What I want to know is what's going on with these stories I'm hearing about you two and Timothy Leary and problems with Gridley."

The Abruzzi woman admitted having been at the party in France before Gridley raided it, but she said she had no knowledge of the raid or of Leary. Nixon was not happy to hear how much she knew about Operation Jackpot, everything except the hemp patches at Camp David. He would have to be very careful with her. He assumed she knew all about McGill's problem with Gridley, but he could just tell Gridley to back off. He tried to determine how the woman felt about his lovesick young aide, but it was easier reading the minds of Castro or Krushchev or Mao than the mind of any woman he had ever known.

DeWolfe explained that she was visiting old friends and family, had learned her friend was here, came looking for her, ran into Gridley in the parking lot, and used judo on him when he attacked her. She said she knew nothing of Leary, and had simply gone to Paris on a shopping trip before being asked by Bullcannon to work for Agnew. It was highly coincidental, but he would give them the benefit of the doubt until he heard Gridley's side in the morning. And he had to decide whether to tell Gridley about the smoking-gun tape. It was very complex.

As they talked, Nixon noticed his young aide's eyes were fixed on the Abruzzi woman as if he was a compass and she was magnetized. Maybe he could help him out in the romantic department? "Let's keep playing," he suggested. "Same song. We had almost nailed it." He sat back down at the piano and McGill picked up his guitar.

"Mr. McGill said you were a singer, Miss Abruzzi?" Nixon said.

"I've sung in choirs all my life, Mr. President."

"Good. How about you, Ms. DeWolfe?"

"Me? Oh, no. I can't carry a tune."

"Well, it's a sing-along, so give it a try no matter how bad you think you are. During the war when I was in New Caledonia I used to play in the officers club every night on a beat-up old upright, and everybody sang along. The more the merrier. Singing is great for morale."

The doorbell rang just as they began, and they kept singing as Manolo escorted in a Secret Service agent and three waiters pushing serving carts. The waiters set up the carts along the far wall, then Manolo showed them out. After they finished the song Nixon asked, "Did they make us some lemonade, Manolo?"

"Si, Señor Presidente."

"Bring me some and let me see if they did it right before we offer it to our guests. There's nothing worse than weak lemonade."

Manolo brought a glass and Nixon took a big sip. "Mmmm, almost as good as my mother used to make. Would you all like some? It goes great with vodka too."

"It's been a long day," DeWolfe said. "I could use a real drink."

"Me too," said Abruzzi.

"Me three," said McGill.

"And another for me, Manolo," Nixon said. "This time with vodka," and he guzzled down the rest of the glass.

Manolo went to make the drinks and McGill said, "What do you say we record one, Mr. President? I've got a tape deck in my gym bag."

"Sure, why not," Nixon said.

McGill set it up, and they took it from the top. When they finished Manolo served drinks as McGill rewound. As they listened Nixon said, "Holy smoke, we're hot!" He held up his glass and made a toast. "Here's to smoking music and smoking guns."

They all clinked their glasses and drank, then McGill said, "And here's to energy independence under your leadership, Mr. President," and they clinked and drank again.

After his surprise encounter with Catherine's father Mulligan walked through the halls of Rolling Rock's guest wings hoping to run into the waiters or McGill or Catherine. No luck. He needed help, so he went to the club's desk and flashed his ID. "I'm looking for Mr. McGill, with the White House staff. Do you know where I can find him?"

"If you don't see him here, he's probably with the other White House people at the guest houses."

"Where's that?"

"Half a mile down the hill, first driveway to the right. You can use one of the golf carts if you like."

The clerk gave him a key, and as he drove the cart away he took out his walkie-talkie and called Leary. "Come in. Over."

"I'm here. Over."

"I've been all over the clubhouse and didn't see your waiter friends or Catherine or McGill, just Gridley, but he didn't see me. I'm in a golf cart heading to where Nixon and the staff are staying. Over."

"Any sign it's an acid test? Over."

"No, so far everything seems normal. Over and out."

Twilight was falling, and as he was about to turn up the side driveway a meteor streaked across the sky, followed in quick succession by another, and another. He thought it must be the Perseid meteor shower, which always comes in mid-August. As he had done since early childhood whenever he saw a shooting star, he made wishes, one for each. "Let everything be all right, let everything be all right, let everything be all right."

As he neared the houses two Secret Service agents appeared. He knew one of them from pick-up basketball games in the EOB gym. He pulled the cart to a stop. "Jensen, how you doing?"

"Mulligan. Haven't seen you around in a while."

"I've been on assignment. I'm looking for a guy from my office, McGill, and our secretary. Know where I can find them?"

"They're in there with Nixon right now, singing."

"Singing?"

"Yeah. Nixon's playing piano. Can you believe it?"

"Is anybody else with them?"

"A woman who came with your secretary."

"Anybody else?"

"Nixon's valet is all."

"That's it? Nobody else in the house?"

"There's us Secret Service guys outside, and a maid's on-call in the servant's quarters. Why?"

"Has anybody else been here in the last hour or so?"

"Some waiters in a catering van came and went. Why?"

"Was one of them short, with wiry black hair?"

"Yeah, you could say that. What aren't you telling me, Mulligan?"

"I can't talk about it. Would you let them know I'm here."

"You'll have to ask Haldeman's deputy. I think he's up at the party."

"This can't wait."

"Sorry, Nixon gave orders not to interrupt."

"How about if I write a note and you give it to the valet and have him give it to McGill?"

"No can do."

"Look, Jensen, you know me, and you know those are my people in there. Nixon's going to want to see me, and I guarantee if you don't let them know I'm here right now you'll find your ass in Iceland or Bolivia or wherever it is they send Secret Service hardheads when you step on your dicks."

———————————

Nixon had led them through half a dozen of his favorite old songs, and after a full-throated rendition of "Get Happy" Manolo came over and handed McGill a note.

"What is it, son?" Nixon asked.

"It's Mulligan, Mr. President. He's outside and says he needs to speak with you."

"The Lieutenant is here?" Nixon said.

"Yes, sir."

"Show him in, Manolo," Nixon said. "And fix us another round."

The Lieutenant was dressed like a stock broker. Gone was the beard and the lumberjack shirt. DeWolfe seemed astonished to see him.

After everybody said hello, Nixon said, "Well, Lieutenant, the surprises just keep coming. First, your friend here walks in with the smoking gun we've been looking for, then Ms. DeWolfe shows up out of the blue, and now you. I thought you were on that mission we talked about?"

"Aye, sir. I was on my way when something disturbing came up."

"If it has to do with Gridley, I've been getting an earful."

"No sir, this is something else."

"Then go ahead, Lieutenant, spit it out."

"Well, sir, how are you feeling?"

"How am I *feeling*?"

"Aye, sir. Anything unusual?"

"Unusual? What makes you ask?"

"I was at a truck stop just off the turnpike, and I was watching the news on TV. I was surprised to see you up here, and then I thought I recognized one of the waiters in the background."

"One of the waiters?" Nixon said.

"Aye, sir. He looked like somebody I saw in a photo spread in *Life Magazine* about those crazy hippies called the Merry Pranksters. Sir, I'm worried they may be planning an acid test."

"A *what*?" Nixon said.

"An acid test," the Lieutenant said. "The Pranksters go around throwing parties putting LSD in Kool Aid, punch bowls, things like that. I'm worried they may try to spike the drinks or the food at the conference."

"I went to an acid test at Winterland once to catch the Grateful Dead and the Jefferson Airplane," McGill said. "The posters had a slogan—Can *you* pass the acid test?"

"Crazy hippies indeed," Nixon said. "Where is this waiter now?"

"A Secret Service agent told me one of the waiters who was just here fit the description. Have you had anything to eat or drink?"

Just then Manolo came over carrying five tall vodka-and-lemonades on a cocktail tray, smiled and held it out, expecting them to each take one—but they all just stared.

"Are you trying to tell us it's electric lemonade?" McGill said.

"Maybe," the Lieutenant said. "Have you had any, Mr. President?"

"We've all had some," Nixon said. "Manolo, have you had any lemonade?"

"Si, Señor Presidente, but no vodka."

"I don't think it's wise to have any more until we're sure it hasn't been spiked," the Lieutenant said. "And if it has been, we need to decide what to do before it takes effect."

"How soon will we know?" Nixon asked.

"I've read it takes about half an hour to forty-five minutes for the effects to begin. How long has it been?"

"I don't know, maybe half an hour or so," Nixon said.

"But why?" McGill asked. "I don't get it. What's their motive?"

"Sending the President and hundreds of big-shots on an acid trip would make them counter-culture superstars," the Lieutenant said.

"But how would they get through security?" Nixon asked.

"The Mellon heirs who were distributing LSD have been coming to steeplechase and fox-hunting events here all their lives, so—"

"I see what you're getting at," Nixon said. "An inside job."

"Aye, sir. But if it were today people up at the conference would be showing symptoms, but I didn't notice anything unusual. The closing banquet is tomorrow, so maybe they're holding off for that? Or maybe your coming early made them change their plans? Or maybe I was wrong, and the waiter wasn't who I thought it was?"

Everyone was quiet for a moment, pondering the implications, until the Abruzzi woman said, "I...I think I'm starting to feel kind of...kind of funny."

McGill put a hand on her shoulder, "You're the lightest of any of us, Jen, so you'd be the first to feel it. Have you ever tripped before?"

"No, but I've been around it a few times."

"Now that you mention it, I'm feeling a little strange myself," Nixon said. "Something's not right."

Manolo, who had been patiently holding the cocktail tray, said, "Yo también, Señor Presidente," and shakily put the tray down on a table and tumbled into the nearest chair.

"I feel it coming on too," DeWolfe said. "It is *definitely* LSD, Mr. President…no question about it."

"My God!" Nixon said, "we've been *poisoned!*"

"No, Mr. President," McGill said. "If it's acid, there's nothing to be afraid of. Remember what we talked about earlier? A trip can be a life-changing experience if you go with the flow."

"I like my life just the way it is," Nixon said. "So there's no way to stop it? No antidote?"

"No, sir," McGill said, "but I've read they give Thorazine to people who are freaking out to knock them out until the bummer's over."

"No, I won't have it!" Nixon yelled. "If Nixon's going on one of these trip things, he won't have history say he freaked out on a bummer and slept through it. Not Nixon!"

The Lieutenant said, "Sir, if it is LSD, you're going to be tripping for hours. Your judgement will be severely impaired, and one of the main symptoms of an acid trip is an inability to make decisions."

"An inability to make decisions?" Nixon said in a worried tone.

"Aye, sir. Even simple things, like what kind of salad dressing to have, become next to impossible. Should we alert the Vice President?"

"No!" Nixon said. "Imagine what the Kennedys would say if it ever got out that I couldn't make decisions and passed off presidential authority to that asshole. And Johnny Carson would kill me, fucking *kill* me."

Nixon was feeling wobbly now, like nothing he had ever experienced before. He sat down and gripped the sides of the piano bench to steady himself. "Lieutenant, you haven't had any, is that right?"

"No, sir, I don't think so."

"It looks like you'll be in charge until this is over," Nixon said.

"Should I tell the Secret Service to arrest the caterers in case they're trying to spike the drinks at the clubhouse?"

"No, not until Nixon gets through this. National security is at stake,

Lieutenant. The commies have spies everywhere, and the public might panic if they knew the President couldn't make decisions. This is a direct order from your Commander-in-Chief—no matter what happens up there at that clubhouse, nobody outside this room is to know Nixon's on an acid trip. Do you understand, Lieutenant? *Nobody*."

"Aye, aye, Mr. President."

"Oh, shit, it's getting stronger," Nixon said. "Much stronger. What in the hell is happening?"

"You're rushing, Mr. President," McGill said. "Rushes come in waves. Try to ride them like you're a surfer."

"Ooooo…here it comes again. I think I'd better lie down."

Mulligan helped Nixon up from the piano bench and over to a couch, sat him down, untied his laces and removed his shoes. "Just lie back and relax, Mr. President. I'll make sure you get through it just fine."

Nixon put his legs up and lay down, and Mulligan set a throw-pillow under his head.

"Everything seems so bright," Nixon said.

"Aye sir, that's one of the symptoms. I'll turn down the lights."

"That lemonade was just like my mother's," Nixon said. "Oh, I didn't mean it, mother, I'm sorry. Yours is better. I'm really sorry."

"She's not here, Mr. President, but I'm sure she understands."

"Mother knows I always try to be good."

Nixon quieted down and stared at the ceiling, and Mulligan turned off the table lamp next to his couch and used the switch on the wall to dim the chandelier, then he ducked into the walk-in coat room in the foyer, closed the door and took out the walkie-talkie and said in a whisper, "Come in. Over."

"I'm here. What's happening? Over."

"I was too late. Your Prankster friends gave them electric lemonade, and now they're all tripping like it's fucking Woodstock. Over.

"Who all is there? Over."

"Nixon, Catherine, McGill, Jennifer, and Nixon's valet. Everybody but me is over the rainbow. Over."

"How long since they dropped? Over."

"They haven't. They're all still conscious. Over."

"No, 'drop' means 'take.' How long since they took it? Over."

"Maybe an hour. They said they had some about half an hour before I got here. They seemed okay at first, then they started feeling it, pretty much all at once, and now they're all zoned-out in their own never-never lands. And Nixon's had twice as much as the others. He was talking to his mother like she was there in the room. What the hell do I do now? Over."

"You're the babysitter. You have to help keep their minds quiet if they start obsessing. The effects will keep increasing for a couple of hours, then there will be an hour or so where they'll be peaking, and then a slow gradual come-down for six or eight or ten hours. That's when they'll be most in control. A lot depends on the dose. Watch for irrational fears. One of the most common negative reactions is paranoia, and Nixon's as paranoid a personality as I've ever seen. They may have hallucinations, and objects will seem to change size and shape. You need to constantly reassure them that everything is all right. If there's a stereo, put on something soothing, Mozart or Bach, or maybe a comedy album, something zany that can get them all laughing. Their senses are all hyper-sensitive, so don't turn it up too loud. And use candles if you can. And offer to let them be alone, in a room by themselves if they want to. Some people do better when they don't have to socialize. I've seen people lie down on a bed with a lighted candle and just watch the shadows dancing on the ceiling all night long. Others freak out if they're left alone, so make sure you don't go too far. And some people become totally disinhibited, saying things they would never say in a million years. That's one reason it was so useful for psychotherapy before the paranoid idiots in Congress outlawed it. Over."

"What about eating and drinking? Over."

"They probably won't want anything till after they've peaked. They'll be able to function a little better after that. You can let them have whatever they want, but try to keep it simple. Everything will be complicated for them, and they could get frustrated if they have to use utensils or do anything that requires manual dexterity. Milkshakes through a straw are good because they're simple and they satisfy the eating and drinking urges at the same time. And when they have to use the bathroom, help them to the door. They'll be able to go all right, though it may take them a while to figure things out. What else? They may develop macroscopic vision, and everything will appear in fascinating slow-motion detail. I once watched an ice cube melt, drip by drip, for hours. And after they've peaked, they may want to get up and move around. You might take them outside and have them lie down under the stars. Over."

"What about sleep? Over."

"They won't be able to sleep except toward the end, sometime towards dawn if they took it when you say. Then they'll probably feel like crashing all at once. Over."

"When will they be back to normal? Over."

"Tomorrow they'll be okay, but tired, like after pulling an all-nighter. See if you can get hold of some B-vitamins, they'll help with an acid hangover. But I'm not waiting around, Mike. I'm going to take my chances hitchhiking, and I'm not giving you a chance to talk me out of it. Good luck, Mike, thanks for everything, and say good-bye to Catherine and Jennifer or Susannah or whoever she is for me. I'm turning this off now. Over and out."

Mulligan was powerless to stop him. All he could do was cross his fingers and hope for all their sakes that he made it to Canada and that they gave him asylum.

The living room was quiet, nobody saying anything. He went to Manolo, who had an expression of pure tranquillity. "How are you doing, Manolo?"

He looked up, wide-eyed and serene. "Muy bueno, señor, muy bueno."

"Is there a stereo or a record player here somewhere?"

"Si señor," and he pointed to a wall with built in cabinets.

It was a first-class stereo system, and there was an extensive record collection of classical, jazz, folk songs, Broadway shows, comedy, even a shelf of rock 'n' roll albums. He followed Leary's advice and put on Mozart, turned down low, then went into the dining room and grabbed a candelabra from the big table and candlesticks from the credenza, lighting them as he positioned them around the room. He remembered Leary's advice about set and setting: "The most important factors are the mindset of the tripper and the setting in which the trip takes place. Make the setting non-threatening and accommodating and you're halfway home."

The doorbell rang, and Manolo instinctively stirred, but Mulligan put a hand on his shoulder and said, "You sit. I'll get it. Be quiet everybody, we want to keep what's happening a secret."

"National security!" Nixon shouted.

"That's right, sir," Mulligan said, and opened the door.

"Everything all right in there?" agent Jensen asked.

"Yes. Why? What makes you ask?"

"Because all the lights on the first floor went out and all I see is candles. What's going on in there?"

"The President is giving us a little party. Why?"

"Just seems strange. It's not like him."

"Don't worry about it. And we'll all be spending the night. How are things up at the clubhouse?"

Jensen cocked his head, suspicious. "Cars are leaving, so it's winding down. Why do you ask?"

"Just curious. Oh, and to give you a heads up, we may be going for a walk on the golf course later on."

"A walk?"

"Yeah, there's a meteor shower tonight, and the President wants to see it. See you later."

He went to Catherine, who was sitting quietly, staring at a candle. Her pupils were completely dilated, as if her eyes had no irises at all. He kneeled down in front of her on one knee, took both her hands in his, and gently squeezed. He spoke softly, so only she could hear. "How are you doing?"

"The walls are breathing, and the ceiling is melting, but how...how did you know I was here? And what about Tim? And there's something, something I just have to tell you. I...I...oh Mike, I, I'm...."

He squeezed her hands a little tighter. "Is it that you're going to have a baby?"

"*How*...how did you know?"

"Tim figured it out. I love you, Catherine. Will you marry me?"

She gasped, squealed, "Honey Bear!" and engulfed him in a hug.

Nixon, startled by the commotion, sat straight up and said, "What's happening?"

"It's all right, Mr. President," he said as he came up for air from the kiss. "I think Ms. DeWolfe just agreed to marry me."

"Hey, Mulligan Man!" McGill yelled.

Jennifer cried, "That's wonderful!"

"Maravilloso!" cried Manolo. "Felicitaciones."

"Ha!" Nixon yelled, clapped his hands—CLOP—and flopped back down on the couch.

"I'd better see to the others," Mulligan said, and gave her a kiss.

McGill and Jenny were side by side on another couch. He squatted down in front of them. Both had loopy grins on their faces.

"Congratulations, Mulligan Man," McGill said.

"Thanks, Stick. So how are you two doing?"

"This is great stuff," McGill said. "More of a head trip than a body trip."

Mulligan had no idea about the differences between a head trip and a body trip. "How about you, Jenny?"

"I think I'm all right. I'm so happy for you. She's a wonderful person."

"Thanks. She tells me you're pretty wonderful too."

"Don't worry about us," McGill said. "Just make sure the President doesn't freak out. He's had twice as much as we have."

"The photographs, son!" Nixon shouted as he bolted up and spun his feet to the floor. "Show her the photographs!"

Mulligan asked, "What do you mean, Mr. President?"

"No, not you. Your friend. Show her the photographs and she'll tilt in your favor. Go ahead, son, show her! Get some balls! That's an order!"

"Do what he says," Mulligan whispered. "Don't let him freak out."

McGill raised his arm and pointed to the red *Milltowne* gym bag next to the piano. "In there. An envelope."

Mulligan took the envelope from the bag and handed it to McGill.

"Show her!" Nixon shouted.

McGill slowly removed a handful of 8"x10" black-and-white photos. "I've been waiting for the right time, Jen, and—"

"This is it, son!" Nixon yelled as he pumped his fist in the air. "Go with the flow, son, go with the flow!"

McGill handed her the photos. They all watched her as she leafed through. Tears began trickling down her cheeks, and she looked over at McGill. "Is that really you?"

"It's him all right!" Nixon said. "You're soul mates. It's *cosmic*!"

McGill gave her a little nod, and she threw her arms around him and burst into sobs.

"Hoooo-*whee*!" Nixon said. "What a *rush*!"

At long last Nixon understood that all was one and one was all, and oh how wonderful it was to be at the center of Universal Being with sparkles of rainbow diamonds dancing on the candle tips. How could he have missed it for so long? It was as though he were four years old, at the beach for the very first time, with the waves of the blue Pacific sweeping him in and out, upside over and outside down, tumbling him in the surf with its warm caresses, going with the flow. His compatriots—the Lieutenant and Ms. DeWolfe and his lovesick young aide and his girlfriend and Manolo—ha!—Manolo!— oh how he loved being with them all, riding the waves together, at one with the universe and Mozart, every note a color morphing into eternity and back to the here and now and into the flow, always going with the flow. He could feel himself floating in and out, with them one moment, off into his boyhood on the kaleidoscopic candle the next.

The Lieutenant brought stacks of records and told them each to choose one. "You go first, Mr. President."

It wasn't easy, but he finally picked *The Best of Artie Shaw* with "Begin the Beguine," the first song he and Pat ever danced to, and Shaw's liquid clarinet shot surging bolts of energy through him as the Lieutenant replayed it for him over and over and over. And then young what's-his-name said, "Mr. President, as long as you're tripping, you should check out *Sergeant Pepper's Lonely Hearts Club Band*, and *Electric Ladyland*, especially a song called '1984.'"

"Who sings it?"

"Jimi Hendrix, but it's the guitar that makes it psychedelic."

They put the Hendrix song on first, and the strangely soothing sounds swept his body into another dimension, a dimension of feeling and sound that amplified the flow like nothing he could have ever imagined.

The Lieutenant went to the kitchen and made them all milkshakes—peppermint milk shakes!—and Ms. DeWolfe chose an album by some group called Firesign Theater, saying, "It's non-linear acid comedy, Mr. President." It was so funny they played it twice, and he even fell off the couch in a howling gale of laughter.

Then the Lieutenant said, "What do you say we all take a walk out on the golf course and watch the meteor shower."

"There's a meteor shower going on?" Nixon said.

"Aye, sir, the Perseids. I saw some when I came in."

"Let's *go!*" Nixon said.

The Lieutenant found them some golf jackets in the coat closet, grabbed blankets off the beds, and led them to the patio, down a path through the narrow woods and onto the fairway.

They all lay on blankets under the canopy of the Milky Way, and the symphony of crickets was better than Mozart!

"Mr. President," the Lieutenant said, "I've read that these next few hours after you've peaked can be the best part of a trip because you can control your mind and begin to understand the meaning of life and your place in the universe."

"Hey, man," said McGill, "that's *heavy.*"

They lay quietly in the balmy summer night, and it wasn't long before a shooting star streaked across the star-spangled sky.

"There's one!"

"Wow."

"Far out."

More meteors streaked along, one every couple of minutes. Then a burning fireball blazed across the heavens, lighting up the night and sending the President of the United States of Being tripping off in a blissed-out, kaleidoscopic rush with the cosmic flow of Universal Oneness.

Babysitting the trippers had not been as difficult as Mulligan expected. Playing records had kept them occupied for the first few hours, and they could function well enough to get to the bathroom when they needed to. He found a gallon of peppermint ice cream in the freezer and made milkshakes in a blender. He also found bottles of assorted vitamins in the kitchen and blended B-vitamins with the milkshakes. He found a plastic drinking cooler and poured the glass pitcher of electric lemonade and the glasses of electric vodka-lemonades into it. He didn't want anybody else tripping, but thought it wise to keep it, either for evidence or in case Nixon, who seemed to be enjoying himself, wanted to try it again.

His charges all started getting restless around midnight, just as Leary predicted. The Secret Service gave them three flashlights, and he guided them down a path to the golf course as the agents watched from a distance.

The meteor shower and the crickets made it easy. He cuddled up on a blanket with Catherine, McGill and Jennifer cuddled up on another, and Nixon and Manolo each had his own, everybody ooohing and aaahhing at Mother Nature's light show.

Nixon, more than the others, seemed to be in his own private universe, occasionally speaking out loud, like he was debating with himself. Once he sat up and spoke like he was at a podium giving a speech, punctuating his points with hand gestures: "What have men in our history who have called themselves conservative ever done for America except to hold it back? Ask yourselves who stood against the revolution in 1776? Men calling themselves conservative, that's who. And who championed the right of one race to enslave another? Men calling themselves conservative, that's who. And when the horror of slavery ended, who fought to deny the Negro basic human rights with Jim Crow segregation? Men calling themselves conservative, that's who. And who denied women the right to vote until just fifty years ago? Men calling themselves conservative, that's who. And who fought against the creation of our national parks? Men calling themselves conservative. And who kept America out of the League of Nations and let Hitler come to power? Men calling themselves conservative. And who to this day is fighting to deny workers fair wages and safe working conditions and keep Negroes and women out of public life and deny a woman the right to control her own body? Men calling themselves conservative, that's who. Those who have opposed Civil Rights and Equal Rights at every turn of American history have called themselves by the same name—conservative. I say to all of us who have so piously and self-righteously called ourselves conservative that our label is not a badge of honor, but a mark of shame, dishonor, and disgrace. Thank you, and God bless America."

After that everybody was quiet for a long time until, along with the chirping of the crickets, they heard a soft snoring.

"Sounds like Manolo's crashed," said McGill.

Mulligan looked at his watch: 03:58. They had been tripping for eight or nine hours, so the effects of the acid should be starting to wear off. "What do you say we head back up to the house before it gets light, Mr. President? They're going to be looking for you pretty soon."

"Well, they're going to find a Nixon they've never seen before. Today when the sun rises in the East, the world will see a new Nixon!"

Then Nixon stood up and walked to the nearest tree, undid his zipper, and called back, "I can't remember the last time I pissed on a tree. It's not something Presidents are allowed to do these days. I doubt any President since Teddy Roosevelt has pissed on a tree. Ha!"

He pulled up his zipper and said, "Come on, let's get a move on. We're getting out of here, right now. Who says you can't make decisions when you're tripping? Not Nixon!"

They woke Manolo, and as they gathered up the blankets Nixon asked, "So when are you two getting married, Lieutenant?"

Mulligan looked at Catherine, who put her hands on her abdomen and said, "As soon as possible, Mr. President."

"How about today?" Nixon said. "Strike while the iron is hot."

Mulligan was astonished. "But we have to get a marriage license, and blood tests, and there's a waiting period, and—"

"Nonsense," Nixon said. "We'll fly you out to a ship somewhere and have the captain do it. We'll call it Operation Wedding Bells. Ha!"

———————————

As Jenny looked out the helicopter window she could see the first rays of the sun peeking over the mountain, then the rotors revved up, and soon the ground began receding as *Army One* rose up from Rolling Rock, climbed above the gentle morning mists of the Ligonier Valley, and roared eastward into the dawn.

It had been a frenetic hour since leaving the golf course. When they got to the house Nixon had shouted orders to a Secret Service agent, "Get everybody over here, right now, and warm up the helicopter."

It was as if a bugler had played reveille, and a minute later a coterie of unshaven, disheveled aides wiping the sleep from their eyes came scrambling over from the house next door.

"Call Haldeman and have him set everything up for a major speech," he told his bleary-eyed aides. "I'll give it today on the South Lawn as soon as I arrive. Tell him I want live network coverage and a loyal crowd. But first we have another mission to accomplish. Lt. Mulligan here is in charge. Follow his orders to the letter."

Mulligan said to the astonished aides, "We need to know the position of every U.S. Navy ship within fifty nautical miles of the coast from New Jersey to Virginia."

Jenny hadn't tried to keep track of the whirlwind of activity which ensued, and now here she was, holding hands with McGill, sitting right behind Nixon in the presidential helicopter on the way to Catherine's wedding. She felt McGill's hand squeeze tighter. "You doing okay, Jen?"

Neither she or McGill had been in a helicopter before, and she wasn't sure which of the sensations were from the helicopter, and which from the lingering effects of the trip. "I'm a little tired, but I feel fine."

"Tired?" Nixon said, turning around in his seat. "Can't have anybody feeling tired, not today." He switched on the intercom. "Captain."

"Yes, sir, Mr. President," came the voice from the cockpit.

"Do you have any of those little white go-pills you pilots use?"

"Yes, sir, in the medical kit. They're standard issue."

"We'll take them off your hands. It's been a long night, and we've got a big day ahead of us and everybody needs to be on their toes. And bring us a map, so everybody can see just where the hell we're going."

A few moments later the cockpit door opened and out came a sergeant wearing a communications helmet and carrying an aeronautical map and a white metal case with a red cross on it.

Mulligan took the map and held it so they could see. "We stop at Willow Grove Naval Air Station to refuel, shower, and have breakfast. Then we'll rendezvous with the *Enterprise* here, thirty nautical miles off Cape May. The captain will have everything ready, and after the ceremony, we fly to the White House for the President's speech."

The sergeant opened the medical kit and gave Nixon a bottle of pills. Nixon checked the label and said, "How long do these last?"

"Depends how far you have to go and how tired you are, sir. We're supposed to take one every six hours if we're feeling groggy. But don't take them unless you're sure you need them, and never take them on an empty stomach, or you'll get really wired."

"You heard him," Nixon said as he passed the bottle around. "Wait until after breakfast, and don't take any unless you need them."

As the cockpit door closed Nixon grinned and said, "It's going to be one hell of day, I can feel it. What's the date, anyhow?"

"August Ninth, Mr. President," Mulligan said.

"Mark my words, this is going to be one for the history books," Nixon said. He went to put the pill bottle in his jacket pocket, said, "Oops, I forgot about this," and pulled out a Bird. Then he fished in the bottom of his pocket, and took out a fat joint.

"You better hang on to these for now, son," Nixon said as he passed them to McGill. "We'll deal with Gridley and the rest of it after my speech."

"What is it?" Catherine asked, pointing to the Bird. "Can I see?"

"It's the world's greatest roach clip," McGill said as he handed it to her. "We call it the Bird. It was supposed to make me rich."

"I'm going to throttle you when I get you alone, Stick," Mulligan said. "You promised me you'd dropped the whole damned thing."

"Oh, don't be too hard on him, Lieutenant," Nixon said. "He's just chasing the American Dream."

"I wondered why you were always pilfering forks," Catherine said with a smile. McGill opened his gym bag to put the Bird away, and when Catherine saw the photo envelope sticking out she said, "Can I see those photographs of you two again? My head's a lot clearer now."

"I want to see them again too," Nixon said as he put on his glasses.

Jenny felt uncomfortable as Catherine looked at the top photo and passed it to Nixon. He glanced at it, looked up at them and studied their faces, then back down at the photo. "You two are soul mates," Nixon said. "It's perfectly clear that it's totally cosmic."

She saw McGill flush red and felt herself doing the same, swelling with…what? Guilt? Pride? Hope? Fear?…Love? McGill turned to her and said, "What do you say we make this a double wedding? Jennifer Marie Abruzzi…will you marry me?"

She felt herself swooning, conscious of everyone staring at her.

"It'll be a hell of a story to tell your grandchildren," Nixon said. "If I were you, young lady, I'd go with the flow."

McGill was staring at her, so sincere, so tortured, so terrified. She took a deep breath and made the biggest decision of her life. "Yes."

McGill pulled her close and kissed her as the others cheered and applauded.

Nixon was grinning. "Wait till the American people hear how Nixon played Cupid for a double wedding. Ha! Let's see how the bastards in the liberal press deal with *that!*"

After landing at Willow Grove, they rode in Navy sedans to the P-X so his young aide could buy a wedding ring and everyone else could buy personal effects, from socks to underwear to toothpaste. While the women went to the ladies' department, Nixon, Manolo, and the Lieutenant accompanied McGill to the jewelry section to help him pick out a ring.

"Don't you need a ring too, Lieutenant?" Nixon asked as they looked over the meager selection.

"No, sir, Mr. President. We have the ones you gave us."

"*I* gave you?"

"Aye, sir. Remember…as part of our C.I.A. cover? We're kind of used to them. I hope it's okay if we keep them?"

"Yes, yes, of course."

Just then the women came over and examined the ring they had helped McGill pick out, immediately rejected it, and chose another. Nixon had to admit, he just didn't understand women.

They went to the Bachelor Officers' Quarters to shower and change, then to breakfast in the Officers Mess, where the sight of the Commander-in-Chief in the chow line caused a sensation.

Ninety minutes later, *Army One* was once again airborne and heading toward the Atlantic and a rendezvous with the aircraft carrier *Enterprise*.

"Mr. President, can I ask you a question?" Ms. DeWolfe asked.

"Certainly."

"Well, sir," she said, "you haven't told us what you thought about your trip. How was it for you?"

Nixon pondered for a long moment. "Well, you know, for a while last night, out there under the stars, I understood the meaning of life and the purpose of existence, but this morning...I seem to have forgotten what it was."

"Ha, you got *that* right, Mr. P," McGill said, and everybody laughed.

"But one thing I do know for certain," Nixon said. "This energy war is the biggest issue of my presidency, and it is now clear, perfectly clear, what I must do."

Everyone was silent, waiting, until McGill's fiance asked, "Just what is it you intend to do, Mr. President?"

"Every President needs a war if he wants to be great, young lady, and like it or not, this is Nixon's war. And now that I understand what's...how do you young people say it...what's going down...I'm going to go out there and give a rock 'em, sock 'em, humdinger of a speech like when I went after commies and pinkos back in the Red Scare, only now I'm going after oil mongers and billionaires. Ha! When Nixon takes the truth to the American people and tells them how they've been gouged on gasoline and toilet paper for the last fifty years to line the pockets of greedy billionaires when we could have been growing our own fuel all along, why, they'll line up behind Nixon two hundred percent. Screw big oil. Screw big paper. Screw the Arabs. Screw DuPont. Screw 'em all. With the American people behind me, I'll roll any bastard who tries to stand in the way, and I guarantee that by the time I leave office this country will be growing its own fuel, or my name isn't Richard Milhous Nixon."

The End

Epilogue

HISTORY RECORDS A HELICOPTER CARRYING PRESIDENT RICHARD NIXON touched down on the South Lawn of the White House at two minutes before noon on August 9, 1974. Moments later, the hatch opened, and a beaming Nixon stepped out into the noonday sun. Cheers erupted as he gave an exaggerated salute, as if he were waving to someone way in the back. He thrust his hands high in the air, smiling and flashing the two-fisted V-for-Victory signs so beloved by his followers. He skipped down the steps, and as the Marine Corps band struck up "Hail to the Chief," he strode across the red carpet rolled out over the grass to where dozens of TV cameras and photographers were assembled for an impromptu address to the nation. Not even his closest aides had any idea what to expect.

He astonished his wife, Pat, by embracing her in a full-body hug and twirling her around like a tango dancer. He lightly put her down, gave her an uncharacteristically emotional kiss, and stepped up to the podium, confident, determined. "Thank you...thank you...thank you all, very much. Thank you."

He held up his hands for silence, and when the audience quieted, he began the speech that would establish his place in history. "My fellow Americans," he intoned in his deepest, most stentorian baritone, "a war is being waged against America, a war as fraught with peril to the American way of life as any we have ever fought—an energy war. I come to you today to tell you that I've been working on a secret plan to win this war, and to reveal to the American people, and to friend and foe alike, the secret weapon with which America is going to win it.

"But I'd like to start by telling our foes what we will not do. Some have suggested we lower the speed limit, bring it down to fifty-five—to what truckers call the 'double-nickel.' They claim that by slowing down, we could save a little gasoline. My fellow Americans, the message our great nation sends to the world must be perfectly clear—*America will never slow down!*"

Historians have long agreed that Richard Nixon secured his place in history with his visionary Energy Independence Act, commonly known as the "Hemp Act." He worked tirelessly, using all the powers of the presidency, to win the energy war, taking whistlestop tours around rural

America to inspire farmers with his vision, living in a caboose for days at a time. Using slide-shows, short movies, and handing out free copies of *The Hemp Papers,* he told rural America, "This plant was once grown everywhere. In colonial times, it was used as currency. You could even pay your taxes with it. Why, it was so valuable to the community that farmers were required by law to grow it. Thomas Jefferson called it 'America's most valuable crop,' and George Washington counseled his neighbors to grow it instead of tobacco. He even wrote a letter to his farm manager at Mount Vernon with orders to 'sow it everywhere!'

"Back then, they grew it for rope, canvas, clothing, and lamp oil. Today, we're going to grow it for fuel. It produces three times more biomass per acre than corn, enough for us to farm our way to freedom. America's national security is at stake, and if we are to win the energy war, we need our patriotic farmers to follow the advice of the father of our country and *sow it everywhere.*"

Just four years after Nixon's call-to-arms on America's farms, the cultivation of hemp had reshaped the economy. At first it was grown for methanol to defeat the enemy, or, as Nixon called them, "those bastard oil mongers." It wasn't long before hemp was also being turned into charcoal as a cheaper replacement for coal to generate electricity, ending the "acid rain" phenomenon which had been killing forests and lakes, and stopping the desecration of the streams and mountaintops of Appalachia.

Nixon ordered a study of its value as a food, and when scientists confirmed that the protein content of its seed truly did make it "the world's best vegetable," he ordered the Peace Corps to teach farmers throughout the Third World how to grow it for food. Thanks to Nixon's initiative, in a few short years the images of starving children in Africa had been relegated to history.

Consumers discovered clothes made from hemp were warmer and longer-lasting than clothing made from cotton. In addition, new technologies used the fiber to make cheaper and better substitutes for plywood, sheet-rock, and sheet metal for products such as cars and refrigerators. And the former byproduct, the hurds, so rich in cellulose compared to wood, quickly became the raw material for paper and a thousand other products.

The dream of the scientists in the chemurgy movement of the 1930's who claimed "Anything that can be made from oil can be made from a carbohydrate" became a reality, as did Henry Ford's dream of "Growing cars from the soil." For the first time since the dawn of the Industrial Age, the production of a basic raw material for industry was democratized, taken out of the hands of corporations, and the wealth spread among millions of farmers rather than accumulating in the bank accounts and trust funds of a few lucky owners of mines and oil wells.

But it was only thirty years ago, with the discovery of interdimensional transposition, that our scientists and historians began to realize the true magnitude of Nixon's accomplishment. Since then, studies into the histories of hundreds of other dimensions have proven that the Hemp Act not only revitalized and empowered our America, but halted the build-up of greenhouse gasses in our atmosphere and saved Earth One from the man-made catastrophe called "global warming" which devastated so many other dimensions.

On August 9, 1994, the twentieth anniversary of his famous *Never slow down* speech, a concert to honor former President Nixon and the aides who helped him was held on the Capitol Mall. Headlining the event were President Frank Zappa and the Prime Minister of Great Britain, John Lennon, and for the grand finale, Nixon himself, frail but full of spunk, played piano and led the singing as they jammed to "Accentuate the Positive." Nixon got a big laugh at the end when he told the crowd that Zappa and Lennon should start a band called The Heads of State.

A few months later, Richard Nixon passed away in his sleep at the age of eighty-one. Millions of mourners filed past the casket as his body lay in state under the Capitol Rotunda. The day after the funeral, America gave her beloved leader the ultimate honor when Congress unanimously passed a bill to enshrine Nixon's image on Mount Rushmore, where to this day the wise and kindly visage of Richard Milhous Nixon counsels and inspires the entire Prime Dimension.

———————

Selected Bibliography

Those interested in exploring the historical themes or the scientific ideas presented in this novel will find these selections a good place to start. Whether or not there was a conspiracy to criminalize the cultivation of the plant considered by America's Founding Fathers to be the nation's most valuable crop is not relevant to the future. What is indisputably true is that it has always been possible for America to farm its way to energy independence, and by growing its own fuel, to create economic prosperity and guarantee national security.

Archer, J.: *The Plot to Seize the White House*. Hawthorn Books (1973). ASIN: B0006COVHA. The story of the conspiracy to overthrow President Franklin Roosevelt and kill the New Deal.

Cars on Alcohol: A sixteen part series in *Greencar.com* magazine on the recent history of alcohol fuels from 1992–1997 which details the science and cynical politics of methanol vs. ethanol. http://www.greencar.com/perspective/

Colby, G.: *DuPont: Behind the Nylon Curtain*. Prentice-Hall (1974). ISBN: 0132210770. Behind the veil of an American dynasty.

Conrad, C.: *Hemp: Lifeline to the Future*. Creative Xpressions (1994). ISBN: 0963975412. A concise presentation of hemp's many potential uses.

Crosby, A. W.: *America, Russia, Hemp, and Napoleon: American Trade with Russia and the Baltic, 1783-1812*. Ohio State University Press (1965). ASIN: B0007DF3XY. As oil is for us, hemp was for Napoleon: the key strategic commodity of his time and worth risking a war over.

Dovring, F: *Farming for Fuel: The Political Economy of Energy Sources in the United States*. Greenwood Publishing Group (1988). ISBN: 0275930084.

Dolan, G.: "Methanol Transportation Fuels: A Look Back and a Look Forward." The 2005 International Symposia on Alcohol Fuels. http://methanol.org/pdfFrame.cfm?pdf=MIPaperforISAF.pdf.

Dvorak, J.: *Hempology.org*. (2006). This website has a large trove of articles, historical documents, links, and photos. Many of the documents mentioned in the novel can be found here in their entirety. http://www.hempology.org

Gray, C.L. Jr., & Alson, J.A.: "The Case for Methanol." *Scientific American* (Nov., 1989). A technical presentation of the advantages of methanol.

Green, L.: "The Demonized Seed." *The Los Angeles Times* (Jan. 18, 2004). http://www.latimes.com/news/local/valley/la-tm-hemp03jan18,1,7758705.story

Haldeman, B.: *The Haldeman Diaries: Inside the Nixon White House*. Putnam (1994). ISBN: 0399139621. The ultimate insider's book on Nixon.

Herer, J.: *The Emperor Wears No Clothes: The Authoritative Historical Record of Cannabis and the Conspiracy Against Marijuana, 11th ed*. Ah Ha Publishing (2000). ISBN: 1878125028. This is the book that spawned the modern hemp movement. Chock-full of facts, photos, documents, and tidbits.

Hersh, B.: *The Mellon Family: A Fortune in History*. Morrow (1978). ISBN: 0688032974. The authoritative history of America's greatest fortune.

Kitman, J. L.: "The Secret History of Lead." *The Nation* (Mar. 20, 2000). How a highly-profitable poison was kept on the market for sixty years while "studies" were done. http://www.mindfully.org/Pesticide/Lead-History.htm.

Kovarik, B.: "Henry Ford, Charles F. Kettering, and the Fuel of the Future." *Automotive History Review* (Spring 1998). An overview of the history of industrial alcohol in America and how the oil industry crushed its competition. http://www.radford.edu/~wkovarik/papers/fuel.html.

Leary, T.: *Flashbacks: An Autobiography.* Houghton Mifflin (1983). ISBN: 0874771773. The guru of the counter-culture in his own words.

Lorant, S.: *Pittsburgh: The Story of an American City, 5th ed.* The Derrydale Press (1999). ISBN: 0967410304. The definitive history of "the Burgh."

McCormick, J. R.D.: *Dr. Methanol's Homepage* (2006). A Ph.D. in organic chemistry explains methanol. http://dr_methanol.home.att.net/#Politics.

McWilliams, J. C. : *The Protectors: Harry J. Anslinger and the Federal Bureau of Narcotics, 1930-1962.* University of Delaware Press (1990). ISBN: 0874133521. The biography of the man most responsible for America's drug laws.

McWilliams, P.: *Ain't Nobody's Business if You Do: The Absurdity of Consensual Crimes in a Free Society.* Mary Books (1996). ISBN: 192976717X. If you care about freedom, this book is guaranteed to make you angry.

National Commission on Marihuana and Drug Abuse (The Shafer Commission): *Marihuana: A Signal of Misunderstanding* (1972). Its unanimous recommendations are as valid today as they were in 1972. http://www.druglibrary.org/schaffer/Library/studies/nc/ncmenu.htm.

Olah, G. A., Goeppert, A., & Prakash, G.K.S.: *Beyond Oil and Gas: The Methanol Economy.* Wiley (2006). ISBN: 3527312757. The answer to the energy problem from a Nobel Prize-winning chemist and his scientific colleagues.

Robinson, R.: *The Great Book of Hemp.* Park Street Press (1996). ISBN: 0892815418. A terrific resource on all aspects of the subject.

Roulac, J.: *Industrial Hemp: Practical Products–Paper to Fabric to Cosmetics.* Hemptech (1996). ISBN: 188687400X. Industrial nitty-gritty.

West, D. P.: *Dr. Dave's Hemp Archives* (2006). The biology and history of hemp by a Ph.D. in plant genetics. http://www.gametec.com/hemp/archives.html.

Whitebread, C.: "The History of the Non-Medical Use of Drugs in the United States." A Speech to the California Judges Association 1995 Annual Conference (1995). A concise, humorous account of the historical and legal aspects of prohibition and why it has never worked. Includes the story of Anslinger's bat! http://www.druglibrary.org/schaffer/History/whiteb1.htm.

Wills, G.: *Nixon Agonistes: The Crisis of the Self-Made Man.* Norman S. Berg Publisher (1978). ISBN: 0910220883. One of the best of the Nixon books.

Wolfe, T.: *The Electric Kool-Aid Acid Test.* Farrar Straus and Giroux (1968). ASIN: B000EW4XRU. Essential for anyone hoping to understand the times.

Woodward, B., & Bernstein, C.: *All the President's Men, 25th Anniv. ed.* Simon & Schuster (1999). ISBN: 0684863553. The saga of the Nixon White House from the reporters who broke the story of Watergate.

Printed in the United States
116082LV00005B/124-129/P